Also by Jane Feather

JANE FEATHER

A HUSBAND'S WICKED WAYS

POCKET STAR BOOKS

New York   London   Toronto   Sydney

Pocket Star Books
A Division of Simon & Schuster, Inc.
1230 Avenue of the Americas
New York, NY 10020

This book is a work of fiction. Names, characters, places, and incidents are products of the author's imagination or are used fictitiously. Any resemblance to actual events or locales or persons, living or dead, is entirely coincidental.

First Pocket Star Books paperback edition April 2009

POCKET STAR BOOKS and colophon are registered trademarks of Simon & Schuster, Inc.

For information regarding special discounts for bulk purchases, please contact Simon & Schuster Special Sales at 1-800-456-6798 or business@simonandschuster.com.

The Simon & Schuster Speakers Bureau can bring authors to your live event. For more information or to book an event contact the Simon & Schuster Speakers Bureau at 866-248-3049 or visit our website at www.simonspeakers.com.

Cover design by Lisa Litwack. Front cover illustration by Aleta Rafton.

Manufactured in the United States of America

10 9 8 7 6 5 4 3 2

ISBN-13: 978-1-4165-2553-0
ISBN-10:   1-4165-2553-X

A
Husband's
Wicked
Ways

Prologue

CORUNNA, SPAIN, JANUARY 16, 1809

THE MAN KNOWN TO HIS enemies only as the *asp* stepped into the shadow of a doorway in the narrow village street, his saber drawn. The sounds of the battle were all around him, the screams of horses, the clash of steel on steel, the roar of cannon as the tattered remnants of Sir John Moore's army fought their last-ditch rearguard battle in the village and on the heights above Corunna. Below in the bay, one hundred British transports escorted by twelve ships of the line waited to evacuate what was left of the general's army after the devastating retreat through the winter-locked Cantabrian Mountains.

The *asp* waited as the pursuit came closer to his doorway. He wasn't sure how many men there were, but he must hold them off until the ensign carrying the document was safely aboard one of the British ships. Thirty minutes should be long enough for the man to attain safety, and if the *asp* prevailed here, he would have time to make his own way to the harbor. If he did not . . .

His expression hardened. He would at least have secured the safety of the document, duty done. He was a soldier and always had been. It was a hard truth that men who fought battles tended to die in them eventually. But losing colleagues in battle didn't become easier, and even less so when they were as close a friend and partner as Frederick had been. If he could avenge Frederick's death in these streets this evening, he would take pleasure in doing so.

The French were searching the street, soldiers banging on doors, shouting commands and questions. But the inhabitants of Corunna were staying tight behind their doors, waiting for the raging battle to cease. When the *asp* judged the moment right, he stepped out in the lane facing the two men as they slammed the hilts of their sabers against the door across the lane.

"Messieurs . . . are you looking for me?" he inquired gently.

They spun around, swords at the ready. The *asp* kept the doorway at his back as he took a further step towards the enemy. *Only two of them.* He had more than a chance . . . unless there were reinforcements on the way.

He could hear only the distant mayhem of the battle, however, and with a grim little smile, he lunged. They were no novice swordsmen these two, he reflected, as he parried thrust after thrust, striving always to keep the doorway at his back as he danced, pirouetting, beating back the seemingly indefatigable blades. He saw an opening. The man on his left faltered as his boot tip caught on an uneven cobblestone, leaving his side open. The *asp*'s blade slid into flesh, and his opponent's sword clattered to the cobbles, the man swaying for an instant before crumpling, his hand pressed to the pumping wound under his arm.

The *asp* turned his attention to his remaining assailant. He was tiring himself now, but the knowledge that he had only one man to defeat and a death to avenge brought him a renewed burst of energy. His opponent fell back, feinted, then lunged. The *asp*'s point slipped beneath his guard and drove deep between his ribs.

The *asp* stepped back, holding his sword, point down, as the other man slid to the ground with a grunt, his sword dropping useless beside him. The victor kicked both weapons away from their wounded owners and stood looking down at them for a moment with cold gray eyes. Then he shrugged with faint resignation. Vengeance was one thing, cold-blooded murder another. He leaned down to pull the kerchief from one of the men's necks. Fastidiously he wiped his sword.

"I am probably going to regret this," he observed almost amiably. "But I have always found the prospect of killing a disarmed and wounded opponent distasteful. So, gentlemen, this is your lucky day."

He sheathed his saber, dropped the stained kerchief to the ground beside its unconscious owner, and loped off down the lane towards the harbor, his part in the battle now done.

As long as he could avoid any further encounters with the French on his way to the ships, he would win free . . . for this time anyway.

Chapter One

LONDON, MARCH 1809

Aurelia Farnham instinctively quickened her pace as she turned onto Cavendish Square from Wigmore Street. The footsteps behind her speeded up as she did. Her heart began to beat faster. *Was he following her?* More to the point, *who was following her?*

She slowed deliberately, and the footsteps adapted. It was late afternoon, the sun sinking behind the city's roofs and chimney pots, but the evening was by no means drawing in, and plenty of people were still around. Or at least there were on the busy streets she had just left; the square was rather quiet, no sounds of playing children coming from behind the railings of the large central garden.

But Aurelia's apprehension was giving way to annoyance. This was her home ground, and if an individual couldn't feel safe a mere twenty yards from her own front door, then something was seriously rotten in the state of Denmark.

She stopped abruptly and spun around. The man behind her stopped. He swept off his high-crowned beaver hat and bowed.

"Lady Farnham?" he inquired, his tone slightly clipped.

Aurelia gave a faint nod of acknowledgment. "Do I know you, sir?" There was nothing in his appearance to alarm. He was dressed with impeccable respectability, carrying nothing more threatening than a slender, silver-knobbed cane.

"Unfortunately, ma'am, we have not been formally introduced," he said, replacing his hat. "I left my card at your house an hour past, but . . ." He paused with a slight frown. "Forgive me, but I had little confidence that it would reach your hands. The . . . uh . . . servant to whom I entrusted it seemed disinclined to take it and did so only with the greatest reluctance. I thought I would return and try my luck again."

"Ah, that would be Morecombe," Aurelia said with something approaching a sigh. "His manner may be a little off-putting, sir, but I can assure you he can be relied upon." She regarded him interrogatively. "Is there something I can do for you?"

He offered another little bow. "Colonel, Sir Greville Falconer at your service, ma'am. Forgive this unconventional introduction, but I was a friend of your husband's."

"Of Frederick's?" Aurelia looked astonished. Her husband, First Lieutenant, Lord Frederick Farnham, had died at the Battle of Trafalgar, over three years earlier.

He'd have been a much younger man than this colonel, she reflected. Sir Greville seemed to dwarf her, towering over her, his wide shoulders filling the well-cut coat as if he had been poured into it. What she had seen of his short, dark hair was flecked with gray at the temples, and he had the unmistakable air of mature self-assurance that comes with experience and authority.

"Yes, of Frederick's," he agreed. A gust of March wind caught his hat, and he grabbed it swiftly. He glanced rather quizzically around the blustery square.

Aurelia remembered the courtesies, although nothing obliged her to offer hospitality to a stranger who'd accosted her on the street. But if he had been a friend of Frederick's, then she owed him more than the street. "Would you care to accompany me into the house, sir?"

"Thank you, ma'am." He offered her his arm. She took it with a politely noncommittal smile, immediately returning her hands inside her swan's-down muff. They walked the last few yards and up the steps to the front door in a silence that Aurelia found awkward, but that she was convinced her companion did not. He radiated confidence and self-possession.

Aurelia slipped one gloved hand from the muff and extracted a key from her reticule. The house's owners, Prince and Princess Prokov, had decided on the line of least resistance when it came to dealings with the ancient Morecombe. He could not be relied upon to hear the door knocker, and even when he did, his progress was so slow many visitors had given up in despair long before the door was opened to them. A modern lock had now been installed, and if the elderly retainer was on duty at the door, rather than the extremely efficient Boris, the house's occupants took their own keys.

She opened the door and stepped inside, inviting her companion to follow her.

Morecombe shuffled in his carpet slippers from the kitchen regions, peering myopically at the pair in the hall. "Oh, 'tis you," he declared.

"Yes, Morecombe, and I have a visitor," Aurelia said patiently. "We shall go into the salon." She turned aside into a large and beautifully furnished drawing room. "You must forgive Morecombe's eccentricities, Sir Greville. He has been a retainer here for many, many years." She set down her muff and drew off her gloves.

"Won't you sit down, sir."

The colonel had removed his hat and was looking appreciatively around the handsome apartment, his gaze drawn to the portrait over the fireplace. A rather beautiful woman in full court dress looked out from the canvas, her startling blue eyes seeming to follow the room's occupants. "A relative?" he asked, absently brushing at his hat brim.

"Not of mine," she said. "A close relative of Prince Prokov's. The house belongs to him and his wife, a very old friend of mine. I am staying here while they're in the country with their staff for several months. The princess awaits her confinement."

"I did wonder how you came to be living here," he observed, turning his gaze on her. A dark and unreadable gaze.

Aurelia was suddenly uneasy. Why would he wonder anything about her at all? Who was he? He was somehow giving the impression that he knew things that he had no business knowing. She had the strangest feeling that, as he looked at her, he was assessing her, comparing her with something, some image, some perception. And abruptly she wanted him out of the house.

"Forgive me, Colonel .... it was pleasant to meet you, but I'm afraid I have another engagement in an hour and must change my dress," she said, moving towards the door with an ushering gesture in his direction.

"I understand, ma'am, and I won't keep you long, but I have not as yet discharged my business." He did not move from his place before the fire.

Aurelia's nostrils flared with a surge of annoyance that did nothing to dispel the unease. She turned back to the room, standing close to the door. "Indeed, sir?" Her brown eyes had lost their habitual warmth and her fair eyebrows rose.

He smiled, a flash of white in a lean, tanned countenance. His eyes were a dark gray beneath thick, straight eyebrows, and disconcertingly, he had the longest, lushest eyelashes that Aurelia had ever seen on a woman, let alone a man. But apart from that feature, there was nothing conventionally handsome about his appearance. His countenance had a rather battered air, as if it and its owner had been through a lot together. But it was strangely compelling nevertheless.

And even as she thought this, she realized that her moment of taking stock had given her visitor implicit control. She should have pressed on with his dismissal; instead, she had looked at him far too closely for a mere casual and uninterested observation.

He set his hat and cane down on a console table against the wall and drew off his gloves, regarding her with a slight frown in his eyes as he slapped the gloves rhythmically into the palm of one hand. "I expected to find you in the country, at Farnham Manor," he said, and Aurelia, to her increased annoyance, thought she could detect a note of irritation in the statement.

"Indeed?" she said again in a tone of haughty indifference. "I wish you would tell me, Sir Greville, why you would go to such trouble to find me. My husband's been dead for more than three years, it seems a little late for a visit of condolence."

"Would you sit down, Lady Farnham."

It was not a question, or a request, it had all the force of a command. Aurelia stared at him. He was presuming to give her orders in what for the present was to all intents and purposes her own house. "I *beg* your pardon?"

"Believe me, ma'am, it would be better if you were to sit down," he said, gesturing to a sofa.

"I have no intention of doing so," Aurelia snapped, laying a hand on the back of a chair as if to emphasize her upright posture. "Now, state your business, Colonel, if you must, then oblige me with your departure."

"Very well." He nodded slightly. "Your husband, First Lieutenant, Lord Frederick Farnham, was alive until January sixteenth of this year. He was killed at the battle of Corunna."

"You are mad," Aurelia said, her fingers curling tightly over the chair.

He shook his head. "I witnessed his death, Lady Farnham."

What kind of cruel practical joke was this? Aurelia's knees shook a little, and there was a tight band around her head. She took a step sideways and dropped onto the sofa, gazing up at her visitor in dazed incomprehension. She couldn't dismiss what he'd said. He was regarding her with both understanding and something akin to compassion, and she knew that he was telling the truth, however unbelievable it was. He had the unmistakable air of a man who knew exactly what was going to happen next and was calmly prepared to deal with it.

He turned away and strode to a sideboard. He filled a glass from the cognac decanter and brought it over to her. "Drink this."

Aurelia took the glass in numb fingers and gulped. The fiery liquid scorched her throat, made her cough and splutter, but it warmed her belly and brought her back to full awareness. "I don't understand," she stated.

"No," he agreed. "How should you?" He returned to the sideboard and poured himself a glass of port. He came back, moved a chair slightly so that he was facing her, and sat down. "I will explain as much as I can at this juncture. Drink the cognac."

Aurelia took a more cautious sip. A flickering resurgence of her customary self wanted to tell him that he had no right to help himself to port without an invitation, but she recognized the urge as merely an attempt to reestablish some kind of control over her surroundings, since she had no control over what was happening, or of what would happen next.

"Frederick Farnham worked for me," her visitor announced, swirling the liquid in his glass.

"He was a first lieutenant in the navy," she protested. "You said you're a colonel . . . they don't have colonels in the navy."

"True," he agreed calmly. "But there is some overlap between the services." He gave her his white smile again. "We do all serve King George."

Aurelia stared at the contents of her glass, her mind a violent swirl of incomprehension. Finally, she looked up and said as steadily as she could, articulating every syllable as if it would invest her words with truth, "I have the letter from the War Ministry . . . the letter regretfully informing me that my husband had been killed at the Battle of Trafalgar. There can be no mistake . . . why would the War Ministry lie to me? If it wasn't Frederick who was killed, then who was it?"

"Many died in that battle," her visitor said. "But your husband was not one of them. He was not at the battle, he was with me in Bavaria, at Ulm, where General Mack was negotiating an armistice with Napoléon."

Aurelia shook her head. "Why was Frederick *there*? He was in the navy."

"Your husband was only peripherally attached to the navy. In fact he was an agent of the secret service."

"A *spy*, you mean?" Aurelia struggled to attach such a label to the man she thought she knew . . . the man who'd been a childhood companion, and her husband. The man she'd shared a bed with for close to four years. That man had been open, generous, kind. Above all, honest and honorable. He had no time for deceit or lies, even of the most trivial. Such a monumental deception as this was impossible.

She shook her head again, more vigorously this time. "I don't believe a word you're saying."

Greville inclined his head in acknowledgment. "I don't really expect you to take my word for it. But I hope you will take Frederick's." He reached into his coat and withdrew a packet. He tapped it lightly against his knee, looking at her with that same slight frown in the gray eyes. "This is from your husband. It was sent to you at Farnham Manor. I went there in search of you . . . Frederick assumed that you would still be there. With your daughter . . . ?" He raised an interrogative eyebrow. "Frances, I believe is her name. Franny, Frederick called her . . . she must be about six now?"

Aurelia said nothing, just gazed at him with all the fascination of a mesmerized rabbit.

"Anyway," he continued, when it seemed clear she was saying nothing, "I went in search of you and was told I would find you both here, in Cavendish Square. This"—he gestured with the packet—"was delivered to you a few days ago . . . your staff were preparing to send it on here by the mail coach." He gave a tiny shrug. "I saved them the trouble."

"Do you seriously expect me to believe that my staff gave you mail addressed to me without so much as a murmur?" Aurelia demanded. It was insultingly laughable for him to expect her to swallow such a tale.

"I had impeccable credentials," he said quietly. He reached again into his coat. "They recognized this . . . as I'm sure you do." He held the object out to her on his flat palm.

She took it automatically and gazed at it in openmouthed incredulity. It was Frederick's signet ring, the seal of the Farnhams embedded in the gold. She looked up and stared at Greville. "How did you get this?"

"Frederick gave it to me. He thought you might need proof of my story." A mobile eyebrow lifted. "It seems that you do."

Aurelia looked at the ring again, holding it up to the shaft of fading light from the long windows. She knew it was her husband's, she could feel his presence somehow. Did that mean that this entire farrago of deceit and lunacy was not a tissue of lies?

"If that packet is indeed addressed to me, perhaps you should give it to me," she declared, her words laced with sarcasm. She held out her hand imperiously.

The colonel did not immediately hand over the packet. "There are two things inside. One is for you, a personal communication from Frederick, the other is for the War Ministry. I cannot permit you to see that, as I'm sure you'll understand."

"Assuming I believe this lunatic story, why would Frederick send me something destined for the War Ministry?" she inquired, the sarcasm still heavy.

"The situation was desperate. We were under attack, and there was considerable doubt as to whether we would make it through. It was vital that this document reached the right hands. Frederick had the idea to send it to you . . . a destination that would draw no attention." He leaned forward and dropped the packet in her lap. "I imagine the letter to you will explain all you need to know."

Aurelia turned the packet over between her hands. The writing was definitely Frederick's, although it was not in his usual beautiful and forceful script. The letters were untidy, the ink slightly smudged as if written in haste. As indeed he would have been if this story was true.

"You survived the attack," she stated without expression.

"Yes," he agreed simply.

"But Frederick did not," she said softly, trying to absorb anew the knowledge of her husband's violent death. She had grieved for his loss once, and now it seemed she must do so again.

"No," her visitor said, watching her closely. "He was killed in a skirmish with half a dozen French soldiers. But by then we had entrusted the packet to an ensign to take to one of the ships in the harbor that were waiting to evacuate the survivors of General Moore's army."

Aurelia rose from the sofa and walked slowly across the room to a small satinwood secretaire that stood between two of the long windows. She took up a paper knife and slit the wafer that sealed the packet. With slow deliberation she examined the two sealed papers that it contained. One was addressed to Aurelia Farnham. No honorific, just the plain name in Frederick's script, which, unlike the other, was clear and unhurried. He must have written the letter itself when he was not in desperate straits.

The second sealed paper had a simple inscription. *To be delivered unopened to the War Ministry, Horseguards Parade, London.*

She became aware of her visitor's tall, broad form standing at her shoulder. She hadn't heard his approach across the expanse of Turkey carpet . . . surprising with such a big man, she thought irrelevantly.

"May I?" Without waiting for permission, he twitched the second paper from her suddenly nerveless fingers and slipped it inside his coat. "There is now no need for you to deliver this, as I am here. I suggest you read your letter. It will go much further than I can to explain what I can understand must seem like an elaborate and fantastic hoax."

Aurelia turned to look at him, disliking that she had to look up to do so. "I must ask you to excuse me, Colonel." Her voice was cold and stiff. "I would prefer to read my husband's letter in private."

"Of course." He bowed. "I will return in the morning. There are things we must discuss."

"Oh, I doubt that, sir," she retorted. "You've had your say, and we can have nothing further to talk about. If I'm to believe you, the last three and a bit years of my life have been a lie. And I have you to thank for it, it seems. I have no wish to lay eyes upon you again."

He shook his head. "I hope, ma'am, that you will change your mind about that. Read your letter. I trust it will enable you to see things in a different light." He offered another bow, then turned to the door, gathering up his hat and cane. "I will return in the morning." He left, closing the door firmly at his back.

Aurelia stared at the closed door, uncertain whether she was on the verge of hysterical laughter or tears. A fit of hysteria anyway. She couldn't believe what he'd told her, and yet she knew without a shadow of doubt that it was true. The ring and the unopened letter in her hand shrieked the horrendous, unbelievable truth.

Frederick Farnham did not die on October 21 in the year of our Lord 1805, he died at Corunna on January 16, 1809.

But where did that leave Cornelia's husband, Stephen? Viscount Dagenham had set sail with Frederick from Plymouth harbor in the early spring of 1805 on a frigate that was to meet up with Admiral Nelson's fleet. She and Cornelia had waved after the departing frigate, they had seen their husbands aboard together. And they had received official notifications of their husbands' deaths within a few days of each other. And yet Colonel Falconer had said that Frederick had never been in the Battle of Trafalgar. At the time that naval battle was being fought, he had been in Bavaria. *Bavaria, of all places.*

She couldn't for the life of her remember what was going on at Ulm in October of 1805. Had the English been involved? And if they hadn't been, why were Colonel Falconer and Frederick Farnham there?

Of course the answer was obvious. If they were spies, then they were covertly collecting information.

Aurelia followed the progress of this seemingly interminable conflict with the voracious tyrant Napoléon as best she could. She read the dispatches that were regularly published in the *Gazette,* and she listened with interest to the conversations of those who had an inside knowledge of the details. Mostly such conversations occurred around the Bonhams' dinner table, when Harry and his friends and ministry colleagues were gathered. But information in general was scanty and sporadic, except for the great battles in which the English fought, such as Trafalgar, which were reported in detail. Reports of Moore's gallant and horrendous retreat and stand at Corunna were only just making it to the English newspapers. But if what the colonel had told her was true, her husband's presence there would have been covert and his death would not make it to the regularly published lists of the killed and missing.

Frederick. She looked down at the unopened letter in her hand. She had to open it, yet she dreaded doing so. She knew absolutely that its contents would turn her ordered existence on its head. She wanted to pretend that this afternoon had never happened, put it out of her mind completely, and simply resume her customary life with Franny, with her friends, with the conventional, gentle social round.

Aurelia stared unseeing at the paper in her hand. It was the life she and Frederick had accepted as their due. Quiet, comfortable, lacking for nothing, bringing with its serene pleasures the customary obligations of privilege. A life lived by everyone they knew, lived by rules and expectations that were bred into them from birth.

But Frederick had not lived that life. He had pretended to do so, but he had been someone else, someone she didn't know at all. And he had been prepared to sacrifice his marriage, fatherhood, the friendships of a lifetime. *His wife.* And for what? To live underground as a spy. Dead to everyone who knew him, who loved him. Had he given a thought to his wife and child when he'd made that decision? Had he intended to come back to her if he survived the war?

A surge of hurt-fueled rage washed over Aurelia at this monumental deception her husband had practiced upon her. All the while he had been plotting his dangerous and exciting life, she had been plodding along on the established tracks and expecting to do so until her death.

Her reluctance to open the letter vanished. It was sealed with wax imprinted with Frederick's signet ring, which she still held tucked into her palm. She slit the wax impatiently with a fingernail and opened the sheet. Her head swam and her eyes blurred as she gazed at the sheet crammed with line after line in that flowing familiar handwriting. Her mouth was suddenly dry, and she swallowed convulsively. It was as if Frederick was in the room with her. She could see his smiling green eyes, his full mouth, the long, gangly length of him. He never looked perfectly groomed, something was always slightly awry with his attire. And if she ever pointed it out to him, he would simply laugh. She could hear that laugh now, a light, cheerfully dismissive chuckle that told her he had more important things to consider than his appearance.

And she knew full well now what those important things were. Not estate matters, or hunting issues, or any of the trivial pursuits that occupied his fellow country gentlemen. No, they were dangerous secrets, secrets that had led to his death. And in her hand now were his words, finally truthful words coming from beyond the grave.

My dearest Ellie . . .

A childish treble in the hall made her jump, then hastily fold the letter, pushing it into the shallow pocket of her skirt. Franny was back from her schoolroom day with Stevie Dagenham at the Bonhams' house on Mount Street. Aurelia and Cornelia had decided it made good sense for the two children to share a governess until Stevie was sent away to school. He was seven, and Cornelia was fighting a battle with his grandfather the Earl of Markby to keep him at home at least until he was ten. She had Stevie's stepfather on her side, and Harry had made a point of ingratiating himself with the earl, so Cornelia was hopeful. The shared governess was an arrangement that suited the children and their mothers, keeping the two households in close touch.

"Morecombe . . . Morecombe . . . where's Mama, I have to show her something." Franny's insistent voice brought Aurelia back to the present reality. The letter would wait. She'd waited for an entire marriage and three years beyond it for the truth, another hour would make no difference. She gathered her composure, painted a smile on her lips, and went to the drawing-room door.

"I'm here, Franny. Have you had a pleasant day?"

"Oh, so many things happened, Mama. We went to see the lions at the Exchange, and they roared an' roared. I think Stevie was just a tiny bit frightened . . . but I wasn't . . . not one little bit." The little girl ran to her mother, the words tumbling from her lips. "I drew a picture of the lions . . . see . . . they had all this hair, Miss Alison said it's called a mane . . ."

Aurelia admired the picture, listened attentively to the minute-by-minute description of her daughter's day, murmured with due appreciation or astonishment at the right moments, and gently eased the child upstairs to the nursery quarters.

She stayed with Franny during her supper and sat by the fire as Daisy, the nurserymaid, gave her a bath, listening to the endless prattle. Not for the first time it occurred to her that Franny was an unstoppable voice and had been from her first birthday. Frederick had been astonished at his little daughter's grasp of language . . .

Frederick. The letter in her pocket crackled against her thigh as she made an involuntary move. Later . . . there would be time enough later.

"What story should we read tonight, love?" she asked cheerfully, receiving her towel-swaddled daughter into her lap.

Chapter Two

Greville Falconer left the house on Cavendish Square and strode rapidly in the direction of Horseguards Parade, where the War Ministry was situated. The document he had retrieved was securely tucked into an inside pocket of his coat. He had no need to read it since he knew what it contained, although he would be hard-pressed himself to reproduce the map. Frederick Farnham's skills at cartography far exceeded his own, and the map that comprised the major content of the document was far too detailed for Greville to reproduce from memory. Although Frederick would have been able to do it.

He was aware once again of the sharp stab of loss. Frederick had been his friend. First as his student, apt, quicker than most to grasp the finer details of espionage, a pupil who shared his master's intellectual pleasure in the covert world of manipulation and deceit, who embraced the inherent dangers with a leap of the heart.

And then as his colleague, one to whom Greville could trust his life.

He would always mourn Frederick's death, would always wonder if he could have saved him if he'd made a different thrust with his saber, if he'd chosen a different lane in their headlong race through the streets of Corunna down to the harbor. Intellectually he knew it would have made no difference. The enemy was in every street, and they had been ambushed, hopelessly outnumbered. Frederick had died quickly, one clean sword thrust to the heart, and the young ensign had taken the document to the harbor while Greville had drawn off the pursuit. Two of Frederick's assailants had paid the price, and the map and its vital information had been sent. Frederick had not died in vain. It was some compensation, Greville supposed.

He showed his credentials to the sentry at the gatehouse and entered the outer courtyard of the ministry. He made his way to a narrow, arched doorway at the right-hand corner of the courtyard and climbed the curving flight of stone steps. He emerged into a corridor lined with grimy mullioned windows that let in very little light.

"Falconer, isn't it?"

He spun around at a vaguely familiar voice. A man had just emerged from a door behind him. His green eyes looked tired, his neckcloth had lost its starch, he was coatless, and the top buttons of his shirt were undone.

"Bonham." Greville extended his hand. "Are you still beavering away at your hieroglyphics?"

"Still at it," Harry said, shaking the offered hand warmly. "I don't think I've seen the light of day for three days." His gaze was shrewd as he regarded the colonel. "So, you got out of Corunna?"

Greville nodded soberly. "One of the few."

Harry returned the nod of acceptance in silence. The two men were only slightly acquainted, and they knew little about each other's particular business, but they were both at home in these shabby, hidden corridors of the War Ministry. They shared the same relish for the dark underworld of war, the secret maneuverings, the devious plotting, the heady excitement of a triumph that could be acknowledged only among fellow toilers in the underworld.

"Are you on your way to see the chief?" Bonham asked casually. It was an unspoken rule in their world that no one inquired too closely into a colleague's business.

"Checking in," Greville responded. "I only returned to London this morning."

"I'll look for you on St. James's Street if you're staying in town for a while," Harry said. "Assuming I ever get out of here." He raised a hand in farewell and turned to walk down the corridor in the opposite direction.

Greville made his way to a door that led into a suite of offices at the end of the long, dim corridor reeking of dust and mice. The door was ajar, and he tapped lightly before pushing it fully open.

The man sitting at a massive oak table between the windows got to his feet when he saw his visitor. "Greville . . . I am glad to see you safe." He leaned across the table to clasp the colonel's hand in both of his. "What a criminal mess that was . . . but Moore did his best."

"Aye, and died a brave death," Greville returned. His gray eyes were suddenly shadowed. He laid his hat on the table, along with his cane, and drew off his gloves.

"And Farnham, too," Simon Grant, the head of the secret service, said swiftly. He was the only other person who knew the true identities of both the *asp* and his late partner. "I was sorry to hear of his death, Greville. I know how much you valued him. As did I."

"I valued him as a colleague, but also as a friend." The colonel reached into his coat and withdrew the document. His tone was now brisk and businesslike.

"This is Farnham's map of the key passes over the Pyrenees into Spain. The French have to hold them if they're to continue to control Spain and Portugal." Greville unfolded the parchment and laid it on the table, smoothing out the creases. "By the same token, if we can take them ourselves, we can prevent the French advance and ensure that no supplies get through to them."

Simon Grant bent over the map, reaching for a magnifying glass. "The army's ready for transport to the Peninsula under Wellesley. He's planning a landing at Lisbon, and a campaign straight up the Tagus River." Grant looked up with a small smile. "He'll send the French packing out of Portugal in no time, you mark my words, Greville."

"I don't doubt it, sir," the colonel said drily. "Farnham and I made contact with guerrilla groups across the Peninsula. Remarkably cooperative they were. Bonaparte's miscalculated the opposition this time. The last thing he'll be expecting will be sneak attacks from partisan groups, passionately fired by patriotism. They're preparing to gather along the Tagus to offer support to the general."

Greville leaned across the table and turned the map over. "On the back here you'll find the code names and passwords of the various groups. Wellesley's spies will be able to contact them with that information, and they can be sure of a friendly reception."

Simon Grant examined the list of names and numbers for a moment before saying, "Should Bonham take a look at these, just to make sure there are no nasty surprises embedded in the codes?"

"Certainly. I would stake my honor on their authenticity, but . . ." Greville shrugged. "I know better than to stake lives on assumptions."

"Precisely." Grant rang a handbell on the table beside him and it was promptly answered by a young ensign. "Take these to Lord Bonham, Beringer."

The ensign clicked his heels as he bowed and took the parchment. "Right away, sir." He disappeared at a near run.

Simon grimaced. "Harry won't thank me for more work, the poor devil's not left the building for three days. Fortunately, his wife appears to be an understanding woman." He looked sharply at the colonel. "So, are you prepared for a stint at home, Greville?"

"If that's where you need me."

"We suspect the Spanish are trying to establish a foothold in the heart of our intelligence community. And you know how we can't allow that," Simon added with a faintly derisive smile. "Bonaparte now rules Spain, the king's in exile, and the Spanish intelligence networks report directly to Fouche in Paris . . . at least that's where he was when last we had tabs on him." His smile grew harder. "The man's as slippery as he's ruthless."

Greville nodded his agreement with a grim smile of his own. "So, do we know what approach the Spaniards are going to make?"

Simon nodded. "We think they're coming in through the upper echelons of society . . . you know the kind of thing, an exiled grandee, a poverty-stricken nobleman persecuted by the French."

"And they're actually in the pay of the French?"

Simon nodded. "We're fairly certain of it. Our information thus far has been spotty, few facts but hints, odd pieces of correspondence we intercepted. Nothing definite, but we'd like you to retire the *asp* for the moment and work under your own identity. We need you to set yourself up in London for a while, mingle with the upper ten thousand, frequent the clubs of St. James's, attend court when you can . . ."

"I'm not sure I'm equipped for the dancing role,"

Greville said with a twist of his lips. "I have no time for society nonsense, Simon, you know that. I'm more at home in the back alleys and taverns in the company of guerrilla fighters and men with poison-tipped daggers."

Simon laughed. "I know . . . I know, my friend. But you can also play this part . . . you were bred to it, after all. And you certainly look the part. But, make no mistake, this is no sinecure. The Spanish are as devious and dangerous as any. All their agents could give lessons to the Inquisition. You'll need all your skills, Greville, to stay one step ahead of them, and I don't have to tell you what will happen if they suspect you."

Greville contented himself with a raised eyebrow that spoke volumes.

Simon continued, "If you don't have sufficient social contacts in town, then we'll get Harry Bonham to take you around. He has a foot in every social puddle, although I think the frippery nonsense makes him as impatient as it makes you. But he also has entrées into the political and diplomatic scene. Let him introduce you to the influential folk. The rest will be up to you."

Greville inclined his head in acceptance. "If that's what you want me to do, then, of course, I will do it."

"Good." Simon Grant moved around the table to shake hands once more. "Where are you staying?"

"My esteemed aunt Agatha on Brook Street. I always stay there when I'm passing through town, but if I'm to take up residence in London for an extended period, then I shall have to make other arrangements."

"Let me know when you're settled then, and I'll have a word with Bonham." Simon clasped Greville's hand tightly. "It's good to have you back . . . we lose too many these days."

"Yes," the other man agreed without expansion, returning the firm handshake. He picked up his hat, gloves, and cane and turned to the door. He paused, his hand on the latch. "The department owed Farnham a fair sum of back pay, did they not?"

"That is so," Simon agreed, regarding Greville quizzically. "And there's a widow, I believe. We'd pay it out gladly to her if there was a way of making sure she didn't know where it came from."

Greville made a vague gesture that could have meant anything. "I'll look into it." He offered a half salute and left the office.

On the now dark street, he hailed a passing hackney and directed it to Brook Street. His aunt Agatha, Lady Broughton, was his late mother's widowed sister. She was a lady of considerable means and very fond of her own way, but otherwise a kindly soul and always delighted to see her nephew, although always somewhat disconcerted at his lack of social activities on his rare visits to town. She would be delighted to host her nephew for an extended period during the delights of the season, he knew, but a bachelor needed his own establishment.

He entered the hall with a nod of thanks to the butler, who had opened the door, and went straight up to his own bedchamber, an imposing if somewhat old-fashioned apartment. A fire blazed in the grate, the lamps had been lit, and Greville could appreciate comforts that rarely came his way when he was working. He walked to the window and drew aside the curtain. The gas lamps had been lit on the street, and a private carriage bowled past, its owner presumably on his or her way to an evening of social gaiety, if not outright dissipation.

It was not his world, any more than it had been Frederick Farnham's. But Frederick's wife had given every indication of fitting neatly into it. Not wife, he reminded himself. *Widow.*

He frowned into the fizzing yellow light of the lamp below his window. Frederick had talked often of Aurelia . . . Ellie, he'd called her. One evening in particular . . . when they'd both been drinking deep of a flagon of hard cider in a barn in Brittany, listening to the sounds of pursuit, the baying dogs, the shouts of the enemy, finally fading into the night.

You know, Greville, I don't think Ellie really knows who she is, or what she's capable of. She has strengths she doesn't know she has because she's never had to use them.

Greville let the curtain drop again over the window. There had been more in that vein, the younger man's voice redolent with the knowledge that the chances of seeing his wife again were almost too remote to contemplate. They'd grown up together in the same small country village, their neighboring families closely entwined in the way of County families, who made up the aristocracy of the countryside. They had married as a matter of course, fulfilling the expectations of both their families. But Frederick Farnham had recognized something in his wife that no one else had seen. He had followed his country's call, knowing full well that he would probably never live a normal life again, knowing that he would never have the opportunity to tap those hidden depths in his wife. He hadn't said it in so many words, but it had been implied in every word he spoke that concerned her.

How would he have felt if in his absence another man did that?

It was a startling thought, and Greville knew that it had grown from the recesses of his mind where, without his conscious intent, plans and strategies for his new assignment were breeding. He needed a cover, a front for his present task.

If Aurelia did indeed have the hidden and unacknowledged depths her husband had believed in, then perhaps she would be willing to help him, if he presented it correctly . . . if he offered the right incentives. Of course, she had given the impression that afternoon of disliking him intensely, but that was hardly surprising. He'd just told her she'd been living a lie for more than three years, and the man she'd married was not at all the man she'd thought him. Killing the messenger was the natural response. But first impressions could be amended. And there were, as he'd just reflected, always incentives.

Greville knew that he was no courtier. He had none of the smooth skills of flattery and flirtation. Oh, he could dissemble and act any part he deemed necessary in the interests of his work and survival, but those skills had no place in this particular situation. Honesty . . . a direct appeal to her inner nature, hidden to herself as well as to others. An appeal reinforced by her husband's example, and the example of other aristocratic women who variously put their diplomatic and social skills, their houses even, at the service of their country. It was by no means an outlandish suggestion. And it might work.

Aurelia sat by the fire in her bedchamber, the open letter lying on her lap. Her eyes gazed unseeing into the flickering flames in the hearth. The house was quiet around her, Morecombe and his wife and sister-in-law retired to their own apartments, the rest of the household gone to their beds. Franny was asleep in the night nursery, Daisy in her own little chamber next door, the adjoining door left ajar in case the child awoke in the night.

Aurelia picked up the letter again. She had read it three times already, and while she began to think she knew it almost by heart, she still couldn't make sense of it. Oh, the words were easy enough to understand, but not the man who had written them. That Frederick Farnham was not the man whom she had married, the man whose child she had borne. She remembered how overjoyed he'd been at Franny's birth, how he'd paced the corridor outside the chamber while his wife had labored throughout that eternal night. She saw again how he'd held his baby, his eyes wet with tears as he'd gazed down at the bundle in his arms with such awe and wonder. Surely that man could not have given it all up, cast his wife and child aside, without a second thought.

My dearest Ellie,

If you're reading this, it will mean that I am dead. I wrote this letter many months ago, ever since it became clear to me that my chances of survival are remote, to say the least. It's hard for me to explain how I come to be doing what I'm doing. Even harder to say how sorry I am for the hurt I know I have caused you. Believe me, love, I ache with the knowledge of your pain, but I can do nothing to lessen it. I know you will be angry, too, and in that I can find some comfort. Your anger is easier to bear than your hurt. Please try to understand. Try to understand the patriotic imperatives that drive a man to fight for his country. Bonaparte must be stopped before he colonizes the entire Continent. And rest assured he won't be satisfied with that. He has already set his sights on India and the trade routes, and it seems now that only England can stand firm against him amidst the shifting alliances. As long as he cannot invade our island, we can fight him and defeat him.

Soon after I left with Stephen to join Admiral Nelson's fleet off the coast of France, I met Colonel, Sir Greville Falconer. He joined our frigate just off Gibraltar. That meeting changed my life. Greville has become my closest friend and colleague. He is, to put it plainly, a master spy and he recruited me. I can only say that I was looking for something, I knew not what, until he offered it to me. I wanted to get away from the stifling hierarchy, the rigidity of the navy. I wanted to fight battles with my wits. I wanted to dig in the dirt, defeat the enemy in his own trenches, not look for glory. My dearest love, I don't know how else to explain why I was so drawn to the work Greville offered me. I was drawn to him, certainly, and if you meet him, you will understand why. I hope that he will survive whatever event has caused my death, the event that means you are now reading this letter. I know that if he has, he will seek you out, as he promised me he would. He is the only one I trust to carry my secret to you. A secret, my love, that you must keep for me. You can tell no one of this letter, of this knowledge that you now have. Greville Falconer's true identity is known only to a handful of people, and if it became common knowledge, it would sign his death warrant, and that of others. I cannot stress this enough, my love.

Too many lives are at stake, lives of friends, colleagues, both past and present, if the truth of Greville's identity and my activities in the last three years becomes known. He will tell you so himself. Trust him, Ellie. Trust him with your life. He will protect you as I can no longer do. I've met many women in the last years who've fought side by side with their men, who've given their lives in the battle against Bonaparte, who've used their wits as ably as any man. Indeed, my life has been saved on more than one occasion by the quick thinking and daring courage of such women, women who have all put their trust in Greville Falconer, and not regretted it.

In closing, my dear, I cannot sufficiently express my sorrow for the deception I have perforce practiced upon you. I can pray only that you will one day understand the imperatives that drove me to act as I have done. And I ask that you speak kindly of me to Franny. My heart aches at the knowledge that I will not see her grow to womanhood. But I made my choice and live with its consequences. I hope that you will marry again if that is what you wish for, and find fulfillment in your life, as I have found in mine. I give my life freely in my country's service, although not gladly. There is still so much work to be done. But I must leave the work to others. To you, Ellie, I send my undying love. Think well of me when you are able.

FF.

Aurelia watched her tears drop to the paper, smudging the ink. For a moment, there was satisfaction in the thought that her tears could obliterate the words, make them vanish as thoroughly as her husband had vanished from her life. Frederick had shed no tears for her. He had done what he chose to do, accepted the consequences for himself, but totally without consideration for anyone else affected by his choice. And then abruptly she snatched the letter aside, laying it in safety on the small, round table at her side.

She stood up and paced around the softly lit chamber, holding her elbows, her tears flowing unrestrained, but they were tears of anger now. Patriotism was all very well, particularly in wartime. She had accepted Frederick's death in battle. But this . . . this was too hard to accept. What would have happened if he hadn't died? Would he have calmly come back to her at the end of the war? Shown up on her doorstep, all smiles, the prodigal husband returned, ready to take up his roles as husband and father . . . until he became bored . . . "stifled" was the word he'd used . . . and decided to go off adventuring again?

How could she possibly accept such a thing? What if she had followed Cornelia's example and married again? What part would Frederick have played then in her life?

Oh, it was too absurd, too utterly *insulting* to think she had been duped in that dastardly fashion.

What power could that man Greville Falconer have

held over Frederick that he could compel him to behave in such a fashion . . . so alien to his character, to the open, honest, honorable man she had known him to be? There had to be a reason for Frederick's going so meekly to the slaughter. Had this Falconer blackmailed him with some shameful truth? Bribed him with something . . . no, no, that was unthinkable.

She leaned a hand on the mantelpiece and stared down into the fire as if the answer would somehow become manifest in the dancing flames. And slowly she came to accept that Frederick had given the explanation, incredible though it was. Greville Falconer had sowed his seed in fertile ground. Presumably he had been trained to recognize such ground, and in Frederick he'd seen the potential. He had seen what no one else had seen . . . what Aurelia still couldn't glean from her knowledge and memories of the man who had been her husband. And presumably this Greville Falconer had persuasive talents that she herself had not discerned in their brief meeting that afternoon.

His face seemed to form itself in the blue-tinged, orange-red glow of the fire. She was transfixed again by the straight gaze from the dark gray eyes beneath thick, black eyebrows. Nothing ordinary about his countenance. Not easily forgotten. And then there was the sheer force of his personality. It was as powerful as his physical presence. She would not admit that he had intimidated her on her own ground, but she had certainly found herself following his script. Had Frederick felt the same thing when the colonel had recruited him?

Well, she would not seek Greville Falconer out in a hurry. Presumably his business with her was completed with the safe delivery of whatever he had taken away with him.

But then Aurelia remembered his last words. She had told him she never wished to see him again, and he had replied, *I hope, ma'am, that you will change your mind.*

Just what did *that* mean? He'd told her he would return in the morning. She could not be obliged, compelled, to meet anyone she didn't wish to. She could deny him entrance. It was her house . . . for the duration, at least. Her house, her castle, and she could pull up the drawbridge.

But if she were to do that, she would be denying herself all possibility of understanding Frederick . . . of what had caused him to make this extraordinary sacrifice.

Carefully Aurelia folded her husband's letter and locked it away in her jewel casket. She was convinced it contained secrets she had not yet discovered. She snuffed the candles on the mantelpiece and climbed into bed, propping herself up against the lace-edged pillows at her back. Leaning sideways she blew out the bedside candle and lay back watching the firelight flicker on the ceiling. She felt lonelier than she had ever felt . . . lonelier even than when she had first been informed of her husband's death at the Battle of Trafalgar. That had been a shared grief. She and Cornelia had faced and accepted that together. If she honored Frederick's request, she could not share any of this with her dearest friend. There was no one now with whom she could share this double grief: the renewed loss of her husband, but also the loss of her belief in him, and in the life they'd led together.

Chapter Three

At six o'clock the following morning Greville was riding alone in the park. Apart from a few gardeners moving in desultory fashion among the shrubs, it was deserted, and he gave his rented hack free rein along the tan, the wide strip of sandy soil that ran parallel to the paved carriageway around the circuit.

He'd spent the previous evening reviving his lapsed memberships of the clubs of St. James's. It hadn't proved particularly difficult to remind the voting members of White's and Watier's that he was back in town and to let it be known that he intended to be around for the foreseeable future. He'd been elected to the clubs as a youngster fresh down from Oxford with a cornetcy in the Guards in the wings. No one questioned his frequent absences from town life during the war years. The cornet had become a colonel, and as such he was as welcome at the social well now as he had been in his youth. It had been a long and expensive evening however. While he could play a fair hand at whist, he had never been interested in gambling, and his inexperience showed. He'd lost heavily last night, but having shown his face at the tables, he would in the future be able to avoid serious gambling without drawing too much attention.

Next he needed to establish himself in suitable lodgings and set up his stables in a modest fashion. He corrected a sideways lunge of his mount with an exasperated sigh. Hired hacks developed bad habits without a consistent rider, and he definitely needed a riding horse of his own. He would need a carriage, too. A curricle, probably, with a decent pair. They wouldn't have to be top drawer at Tattersalls, but they'd need to make a respectable showing on the park circuit. He had no aspirations to the sporting world of the Corinthians. His fighting skills were rather more underhand than straightforward boxing and fencing. But in combat, when it mattered, he would back himself anytime. His lip curled in derision. Of all the assignments Simon could have given him, this was the least acceptable.

After an hour, when the first riders, showing off their prowess after a night of dissolution, began to appear in the park, Greville rode his horse back to Brook Street. The livery stable's groom took charge of the hack, and Greville went into the house to be greeted by the butler, who wore an air of some urgency.

"Ah, Sir Greville, her ladyship awaits you in the morning room," he announced with some portentousness. "She's been waiting for half an hour or more," he added, disapproval evident.

"What ails her ladyship, Seymour? She doesn't usually stir from her room until noon," Greville observed, handing over his crop, removing his hat, and drawing off his gloves.

"Nothing ails Lady Broughton, sir," the butler declared, gathering up Greville's discarded possessions and passing them to an attendant footman. "I understand she is anxious to talk with you. Breakfast will be served immediately."

Greville contemplated saying that he would like to change his dress, but it was a mischievous impulse, designed only to discomfit the disapproving butler, and as such not worth pursuing. He nodded acceptance and strode to the back of the house.

"Greville, my dear nephew, have you had a pleasant ride?" Aunt Agatha beamed at him from the far side of the round table. Her beauty had been legendary in her youth, and while that beauty had faded somewhat, she was still a handsome woman. She was swathed in Indian silks, her hair concealed beneath an impressive turban, and she was engaged in dipping fingers of toast into a bowl of tea.

"Pleasantly quiet, ma'am," he said, pulling out a chair opposite. "This is an ungodly hour for you, is it not?" He smiled as he raised an interrogative eyebrow.

"I own I would prefer to be taking tea in bed, but I wish to talk with you, Greville, and I knew once I missed you today, I would never find the opportunity." She dabbed at her lips with a snowy napkin. "So energetic, you are. You're never still for a minute."

Greville laughed gently. "I am always at your service, Aunt Agatha. You have only to summon me."

She regarded him across the table with narrowed eyes. "If I believed that, Nephew, I'd be as blind as your poor mother . . . may she rest in peace," she added piously.

Greville was saved from an immediate response by the entrance of two footmen bearing chafing dishes and a tankard of ale.

"Deviled kidneys, sir, and fried trout," one of them announced, removing the lids from the dishes as the other set the tankard at Greville's elbow. "Cook says there's coddled eggs and lamb chops if you'd like."

"I would," Greville said with enthusiasm. "I'll help myself, thank you."

"I'll bring the eggs an' the chops then, sir."

The footmen disappeared, and Greville took a deep draft of his ale before going to the sideboard to help himself from the chafing dishes. He brought a laden plate to the table, sat down, shook out his napkin, and addressed his aunt. "So, ma'am, what is so urgent that it gets you from your bed betimes?" He forked a kidney into his mouth.

Before responding, Aunt Agatha dipped another finger of toast into her tea. "You said you would be staying in town for a while, and I have it in mind to give a small party in your honor . . . no, no, hear me out, dear boy." She raised her free hand imperatively, and Greville stilled his tongue.

"You have spent so little time in town over the years. It's why you have no wife . . . now, forgive me if this is a sensitive subject, but you do owe it to the family, dear boy. If your mother were alive, she would be telling you the same thing. You were little more than a child when your father died, and no one expected you to assume family responsibilities for some years. But, dear boy, you need a wife, and you need an heir. And I don't see how you're to acquire either gallivanting around Europe on the heels of that tyrant. But now you're to be settled for a while at least, I intend to go to work."

Greville waited until the returning footman had placed the fresh dishes on the sideboard before he spoke. "I appreciate your concern, Aunt Agatha, although I doubt I shall be in town long enough to settle down in any permanent fashion." A humorous smile accompanied his pleasant tone. "I don't intend to be a charge upon you, my dear ma'am. I have it in my mind to find suitable lodgings and set up my own establishment."

"What nonsense . . . whatever for?" the lady demanded, her plump features creasing ominously. "This house is a mausoleum, far too big for me alone. You can have an entire wing to yourself if you wish a separate establishment."

Greville's smile didn't waver. "You are too generous, ma'am, but I couldn't possibly impose upon you in such fashion." Deftly he filleted the trout on his plate as he spoke.

Lady Broughton's frown transformed her amiable countenance, drawing her carefully plucked eyebrows together, narrowing her pale blue eyes. Her mouth took a downturn, and she fixed him with a glare.

Greville ignored the glare. He knew his aunt of old. She had been spoiled by a fond and indulgent husband and detested being thwarted in the most minor matters. He savored a mouthful of trout and allowed the glowering silence full rein.

Her ladyship broke first, as he knew she would. A disgusted snort prefaced her statement. "Well, you must please yourself, I suppose, as you always do. Your poor mother never could see how you twisted her around your little finger, even in short coats."

Greville contented himself with a sardonic twitch of his eyebrows. To his certain knowledge he had never twisted his mother around any finger, little or otherwise. She had barely laid eyes on him during his childhood, spending her time shut away in a wing of the ancient, creaky house, leaving her only child to the sometimes haphazard care of a series of nursemaids, until he'd been packed off to school at the age of eight. His father had died when he was twelve, but had been a shadowy figure in his son's life at best. Only his aunt Agatha had shown any interest in her sister's son, and that had been, while generous, fairly infrequent.

He sipped his ale. "Of course, ma'am, if you are seriously minded to give a small party for me, I would be most grateful."

The sun emerged from the clouds, and Aunt Agatha smiled again. She adored entertaining. "I'll prepare a guest list this morning . . . a rout party, I think. I haven't given one since last season, and it would be most suitable for such a purpose. A little dancing, not a big orchestra, but a few strings, a piano . . . and pink champagne . . . I'm sure we have plenty in the cellar . . . I'll check with Seymour." She tapped her teeth with a fingernail, her earlier disappointment forgotten, her good humor restored.

Greville laughed and pushed back his chair. "I'm sure, as always, Aunt, that you'll know what is best. Let me know when to present myself, and I'll be there in fine fig."

"Yes . . . yes . . . well, I have a lot to do." She waved him away and reached for the little silver bell beside her. "I'll discuss matters with Seymour at once."

Greville bowed and left her happily contemplating her wide circle of acquaintances and the prospect of giving a party that would be the talk of the town. He was perfectly happy to be the guest of honor at such a gathering, it would give him a head start in the business of reintroducing himself to society. Once one invitation was issued, the rest would flood in, and he could begin to play Simon Grant's game. He went upstairs to change from riding dress into something more suitable for paying morning calls.

Would Aurelia receive him?

A good question, but he was hoping that Frederick's letter would have had a softening effect on the lady. He had no idea what Frederick had written, but he knew he would have spoken well of his comrade, if he'd mentioned him at all. But it was difficult to imagine a letter in such circumstances that failed to mention Colonel Falconer.

Critically, he examined his image in the long mirror. He'd been away from the social circuit, apart from flying visits to London, for close to fifteen years, and he suspected the tailoring of his present garments was somewhat outmoded. He rarely gave thought to his dress; most of the time he was either in uniform or dressed for some activity that bore no relation to morning calls, rout parties, or Almack's Assembly Rooms. He'd clearly have to update his wardrobe, but for the moment he could find little to object to in his dark gray coat and buckskin britches. They'd been made for a younger man, but good tailoring will always tell, and the coat still fitted him well across the shoulders. He had tied his linen cravat in a modest but perfectly acceptable knot, and his top boots, while not cleaned with champagne, had a respectable shimmer to them.

He took up his beaver hat and gloves and hefted the slender, silver-knobbed cane he always carried, weighing it in his hand, feeling the delicate balance. The stick was transformed at the touch of a spring into a wickedly sharp sword and had proved indispensable on many occasions. Not that he expected to need it on the streets of

London during a cool March-morning stroll. But one never knew in his business.

❦

"Mama . . . mama . . . why are you taking me to Stevie's?" Franny tugged at her mother's arm. "Why isn't Daisy taking me?"

Aurelia looked down at her prancing daughter with a slightly distracted smile. "In a minute, Franny. I'm talking to Morecombe."

"Yes, but *why*?" the little girl demanded, but with less urgency in her tone; it was more a matter of form.

"Prince Prokov's wine merchant usually calls on the third Thursday of the month, Morecombe. When he comes today, if I'm not back, could you make sure he understands that this month's delivery is to be shipped to the country?" Aurelia drew on her gloves as she spoke. "And the prince is most insistent that two cases of the vintage champagne be included in the delivery."

"Oh, aye," Morecombe said. "That'll be for Lady Livia's confinement, I daresay."

"Yes . . . well, perhaps not the confinement itself but its results," Aurelia said with a smile. "Only another three weeks to go."

"Aye, well, we wishes her all the best fer a safe delivery," the old man declared. "Our Mavis an' our Ada 'ave been knittin' away for months now. There's bootees, an' caps, and whatnot all over the 'ouse."

Aurelia laughed. "They'll be well appreciated, More-combe. . . . All right, Franny. We're going now."

"I'll be late," Franny announced with a note of satis-faction. "And Miss Alison will be cross."

"No, she won't," her mother returned. "You won't be late anyway, it's barely a quarter to nine." She took her daughter's hand and hurried her out of the house.

"But why are you taking me an' not Daisy?" Franny repeated her unanswered question.

"Oh, I wanted to see Aunt Nell about something," Aurelia said vaguely. In truth, even though she knew she must honor Frederick's request that she say nothing about the extraordinary situation, she was driven to seek her friend's company this morning because she needed its familiarity, a return to a sense of normality that she hoped the easy comfort of Nell's presence would give her.

Franny was prattling in her inconsequential fashion as they walked briskly along the quiet streets. It was a chilly morning, a fresh March wind gusting around the corners, and they swung hands to keep themselves warm. Aurelia offered an occasional comment, an encouraging murmur now and again, and it seemed all that Franny needed to keep up her monologue. They reached Mount Street and the Bonhams' establishment just as Harry de-scended from a hackney carriage at the door.

"Good morning, Harry." Aurelia greeted his dishev-eled and weary appearance without surprise. "You don't look as if you've been home in a day or two."

"And so I haven't," he said with tired sigh. "Good

morning, Franny." He dropped a kiss on the child's up-turned brow as she launched into a minute description of a goldfish she and Stevie were keeping in a bowl in the schoolroom.

He accompanied them into the house, producing all the right sounds of astonishment and appreciation at the antics of the goldfish.

"Run along upstairs, Franny," Aurelia said, mercifully interrupting the flow. "Stevie and Miss Alison will be waiting for you." She bent to kiss her, unbuttoning the child's coat as she did so. "I'll see you this afternoon."

Franny scampered off and Aurelia shook her head with a resigned smile. "She never stops talking."

"She's a bright little thing," Harry responded with a chuckle, turning to his butler, who stood waiting to be noticed. "Hector, is Lady Bonham down yet?"

"Yes, of course I am." Cornelia's light tones sounded on the stairs. She descended with a quick step, both hands extended to her husband. "Oh, you poor dear. You look exhausted. Have you slept at all since you left three days ago?"

"I don't think so," he said, taking her hands in his and kissing her mouth. "You look as fresh as a daisy, wife of mine, and I am rank and as prickly as a cactus." He passed a hand over his stubbly chin. "I'm going to make myself presentable and leave you to enjoy Aurelia's company." He stepped aside to reveal Aurelia, who'd been standing quietly behind him, waiting for the couple to complete their greeting.

"Ellie, how lovely!" Cornelia exclaimed. "What brings you here so early?"

"I thought I'd bring Franny myself this morning . . . I felt like an early walk," Aurelia said. "But I've no need to stay. I don't want to intrude."

"As if you ever could," Cornelia scoffed. "Harry is going upstairs to repair himself and he'll probably sleep until this afternoon. So let's go and have coffee in the morning room. Have you had breakfast?" She linked arms with Aurelia and urged her towards the morning room.

Aurelia went willingly enough, but she was beginning to question the wisdom of this impulsive visit so soon after yesterday's revelations. The urge to pour out to her friend what was uppermost in her mind threatened to become irresistible, and she *must* resist it. She could think of little else and was afraid that Cornelia would sense her distraction immediately.

But fortunately Cornelia had her own preoccupations that morning. She poured coffee for them both before sinking gracefully onto a chaise. "What do you think of a black-and-white theme, Ellie?"

Aurelia blinked at this seeming non sequitur. "For what?"

"The ball, of course." Cornelia looked astonished that anyone could have forgotten this issue that occupied most of her waking hours at present.

"Oh, of course." Aurelia sipped her coffee and tried to give the question her full attention. "You mean the decor, or must the guests comply with the color code, too?"

"I thought it might make it a little more interesting. Everyone gets so tired of the endless round of balls and galas, something a little different might be appreciated."

"Absolutely," Aurelia agreed. "And after the success of your gala last April, you've a lot to live up to." She regarded her friend with a gleam in her eyes. "I believe you intend to stun the ton with a *squeeze* every year, Nell."

A faint pink blossomed on her friend's fashionably pale cheeks as she laughingly confessed, "I may have had some such idea. And it makes it all the more necessary to do something different this time, Ellie, otherwise everyone will say I've lost my touch."

"More power to you, love," Aurelia said warmly. "When's the date to be exactly?"

"I wanted to discuss that with you, too." Cornelia reached for the coffeepot and refilled their cups. "It would be lovely if Liv could make it. The baby's due in about three weeks, the beginning of April. I'd thought to give the ball in April, but she won't be able to travel so soon. Should I leave it until mid-May?"

"You know Livia, she'll come if it's humanly possible. But it depends on her confinement. If all goes smoothly, then six weeks should be long enough, but . . . ." Aurelia shrugged expressively.

Cornelia nodded. They'd both endured the rigors of childbirth, and while they and the infants had survived, they also knew that they had been lucky. "Liv's strong," she offered. "And determined."

"True enough. But Alex isn't going to let her take any risks, and you know how persuasive he can be."

Cornelia nodded again. Alexander Prokov had a way of ensuring things went according to his wishes. Livia, independent-minded though she was, was no proof against her husband's determination if he was really set upon something. And he would make absolutely certain his adored wife took no risks. It was a safe bet that he would set the bar for those risks high.

"Well, perhaps I'll make it the end of May," Cornelia said after a moment's thought. "Towards the end of the season. And we can open the conservatory and the garden. Black and white lanterns, or, no . . ." She held up a hand. "Not black and white at all, *silver* and black. How would that be, Ellie?"

"Pure magic," Aurelia said, setting aside her coffee cup. "I foresee a critical success, my dear. And now I must be on my way. Thank you for the coffee." She kissed her friend, who had risen from the chaise as Aurelia stood up. "I'll send Daisy for Franny this afternoon. Will I see you at Cecily Langton's luncheon?"

"Yes, I said I'd be there." Cornelia accompanied Aurelia to the front door. "What are we raising money for this time?"

"A new infirmary at Chelsea Hospital, I believe. But she also mentioned that she's sponsoring a newcomer to London . . . to the country, actually. A Spanish lady, recently married to the Earl of Lessingham. Have you come across her?"

"Oh, I think Harry may have mentioned her . . . or rather the marriage," Cornelia said vaguely. "I gather Lessingham's a lot older than she is, but totally devoted to her."

"Well, he's been a widower for ten years, let's hope she's as devoted to him," Aurelia said with a wicked chuckle.

Cornelia grinned. "If Cecily's taken her up, she'll have plenty of opportunity to spread her wings."

"Indeed. Cecily's always reliable when it comes to good causes, whether it's a foundling hospital, an infirmary for disabled soldiers, or a newcomer to society."

"Unlike Letitia Oglethorpe," Cornelia observed.

They both laughed, wrinkling their noses at the thought of their bête noire. Aurelia waved a hand in farewell and stepped out into a morning that had brightened in the time she'd spent with Cornelia. She strolled back towards Cavendish Square, reflecting that if Livia and Alex returned to London at the end of May, she'd have to give some thought to her own lodging. She couldn't expect to stay as a semipermanent guest under their roof, and neither could she stay with Cornelia and Harry. For close to a year she and Franny had moved between the two households, and when Livia and Alex had gone into the country to await Livia's confinement, they had left her in charge at Cavendish Square. The arrangement suited everyone, but she didn't think she could revert to being a peripatetic guest.

Which rather left her with the choice of either returning to the country and her widow's rustic existence, or somehow finding the funds to set up her own modest establishment in town. Her efforts to find such funds had so far fallen upon stony ground. It wasn't that she didn't have funds, more than sufficient for such a purpose, but her inheritance was held in trust by her late husband's relatives, a group controlled by the Earl of Markby, Cornelia's ex-father-in-law and a distant relative of her own. Markby was notoriously difficult to persuade when it came to disbursing funds from the trusts, and he had thus far resisted all such requests from Aurelia.

Maybe she should go down to Hampshire in person and try a face-to-face appeal. She had managed to avoid the ordeal until now, but if she wanted to remain in London, it was going to have to be done.

Her swift pace slowed as she saw someone coming down the steps of the house, back to the street. It was Colonel, Sir Greville Falconer. And the sight of him had the strangest effect on her. Her stomach seemed to turn to water, her thighs to jelly. It was as if she were terrified. Then her heart began to beat, her skin to prickle, and she was prompted by an urge to turn and run.

She held herself still, chiding herself for being so ridiculous. The man could do nothing more to her. He'd sprung his surprise, there was nothing more to be frightened of. He couldn't hurt her anymore. So she told herself, but the reassurance did nothing to steady her erratic heartbeat . . . or explain it.

She walked forward slowly, taking deep breaths. He

had seen her now and was waiting on the pavement at the bottom of the steps, one gloved hand resting on the iron railing to the steps, the other on the silver hilt of his cane.

He bowed as she came close. "Lady Farnham, I just called and your butler said you were not at home."

"He would appear to have been correct, Sir Greville," she said, amazed at the even tenor of her voice. She had even managed a lightly ironic lilt to her tone.

"So it would appear, ma'am." He smiled that flashing white smile in the bronzed complexion. "I confess I was afraid your servant had been instructed to deny me."

"I see no reason to do that, sir," Aurelia said, proud of the careless shrug that accompanied the statement. She might be terrified, or whatever it was she was feeling, but she seemed able to conceal it.

"No, neither do I," he agreed amiably. "May I?" He went ahead of her to the door and banged the brass knocker with a vigor that indicated he had learned the necessity for a loud and imperative knock.

Aurelia came up beside him, a key in her hand. "It's easier this way," she said, fitting the key to the lock. The door swung open just as Morecombe, puffing and grumbling, reached the door.

"Can't think why ye 'ave to be a bangin' an' a thumpin' like that," he complained. "Only jest got t' the kitchen an' it starts up again . . . an' you've a key," he accused, blinking rheumy eyes at her.

"I know, forgive me, Morecombe. It was Sir Greville

who knocked. He was unaware that I had a key," Aurelia explained apologetically as she stepped into the hall. "Don't let us disturb you further. We'll be in the salon and I'll see Sir Greville out myself."

"Right y'are then." Morecombe sniffed and shuffled away.

"Extraordinary servant," Greville observed, as so many had done before him. "Fancy having to apologize to him for expecting him to do his job."

Aurelia turned an icy glare upon him. "I hardly think it's your place, sir, to criticize the management of my household."

"No," he agreed, with that disconcertingly charming smile. "I ask your pardon. I was somewhat taken aback."

Aurelia hesitated, but there was something truly infectious about the colonel's smile and she couldn't help a slight, answering chuckle. "You are not alone in that, Sir Greville. Most people on first meeting Morecombe have such a response. He is more family than servant." She led the way into the drawing room. "If you'd like coffee, I can fetch some immediately."

He glanced towards the bell rope by the fireplace but wisely refrained from comment. "No, I thank you."

"Very well." She unbuttoned her pelisse, letting it drop from her shoulders over the back of a chair, before unpinning her hat. "So, to what do I owe the pleasure, Sir Greville?"

She wasn't going to make it easy for him, Greville

reflected. But then why should she? "Two things, really. First, I wanted to be absolutely certain that you understood the need for complete secrecy. You can tell no one of what you know."

"I understand," she said flatly. "Frederick made it very clear that your life would be in danger if your identity was discovered."

"That is so . . . and not just mine. Believe me, if Frederick hadn't believed you could be trusted with the truth, I would not have permitted him to write that letter."

Aurelia looked at him in surprise. "You believe you could have prevented him?"

"Yes, ma'am, I could." It was a flat declaration. "But now you know so much, I wonder if you have anything further you wish to ask me. I don't know exactly what Frederick's letter contained, but it seems a fair assumption that it contained matters that could benefit from further explanation."

Aurelia sat down, gesturing that he should do the same. At some point in the last few minutes she had regained her composure. Her heart rate had slowed and her mind was once again clear. She *did* have questions, and maybe he could answer them. "You recruited Frederick at sea just off the coast of Gibraltar. *Why*?" She clasped her hands lightly in her lap and regarded him, her head slightly to one side.

Like an inquisitive bird, he thought. She was small-boned, fine-featured, her hair the color of corn silk clustered in artfully arranged ringlets. Her dark brown eyes were warm and glowing like rich velvet.

The description surprised him. He was not accustomed to assessing the purely physical charms of society women, at least not since he'd joined the service. As a young man-about-town, he'd had his share of dalliances, including a heady liaison with the wife of a most distinguished politician.

Now why in the world had he started to remember Dorothea? She hadn't popped into his head for close to twelve years. Was there a resemblance between the two women? Perhaps, he thought. Just a little. He gave himself a mental shake and sat down on the sofa opposite her. "It's part of my job," he said simply. "To look for likely recruits to my particular branch of service."

"Why Frederick?" She leaned forward a little, intent on the answer, certain it would give her insight into the man she thought she had known and now knew that she had not.

Greville had decided earlier that the best way to win this woman's confidence was the direct and honest route. He wasn't sure as yet whether she was right for what he wanted, but he would proceed as if she were. "I had recently lost some men," he stated baldly. "I boarded the ships anchored off Gibraltar looking for replacements. The men and women who do our particular brand of war work have to be of a certain caliber. They have to have particular character traits, and while they don't need the necessary skills to be recruited, they do need the ability and willingness to learn them. Frederick Farnham was such a man."

"Were there others?"

He shook his head. "I spent two weeks with the fleet, a day or two on each vessel. I identified several men, officers and sailors alike, who could be used in other ways, but only Frederick was capable of partnering me." He regarded her with a slight smile. "I only ever work with one partner anyway, so my recruiting mission was entirely successful."

"You haven't told me what those particular traits are," she pressed. "I need to know what Frederick had . . . was . . . that through all the years of my knowing him escaped me, and not you in a few short days."

"A readiness to be tested, to break barriers, cross boundaries, to face danger with relish. Oh, a healthy fear is necessary, too, make no mistake, but to do this work one must have the courage to overcome fear."

Aurelia leaned back in her chair, letting her head fall back, her eyes closing for a moment. Frederick *had* been a reckless huntsman, always first over the fences. He'd played every sport at school and university with a fierce competitiveness that usually brought him out on top. He'd joined the navy without hesitation at the start of the war and had fretted about the lack of action. And yet she hadn't thought him any different from any of his peers. Greville Falconer had seen something different, and with Frederick's own words playing in her head she had to acknowledge that he had seen what was there, even if she and his friends and family had not fully understood it.

"Any further questions?"

The quiet voice broke into her reverie and she sat up abruptly. Her body was reacting strangely again, hot and cold, heart beating fast. But this time she knew the cause. A confused knowledge certainly, but it had everything to do with the man sitting opposite her and the almost palpable currents of danger, mystery, intrigue, that seemed to swirl around him.

"What are you going to be doing in London?" Her voice had the tiniest quaver, but she didn't think he would notice. Then she knew that he had of course noticed it. This man was trained to notice everything.

"A little work," he said casually, careful not to appear to be watching her too closely. She reminded him again of a bird, one that sensed the approach of a possible hunter but was still unsure. Ready to flee at a moment's notice, yet hovering. Something in what he'd said had caught her attention.

"Perhaps you could help me," he said, watching her start of shock and surprise.

"Help you? How?" Aurelia was fully upright now. She looked straight at him.

"I need lodgings," he said with a deprecating smile. "I am staying with my aunt on Brook Street at present, but if I'm to make an extended stay in town, as I intend, then I must set up my own establishment. Perhaps you know of somewhere suitable."

The request was a welcome cold shower. "I am not in the landlord business, Sir Greville." Her voice was cool and dispassionate.

"I didn't imagine you were, ma'am. I merely thought that since you've been in town for some time, you might have heard of something . . . a tenant giving up some rooms, perhaps. It's not a wildly unreasonable assumption." He rose to his feet. "But I won't keep you any longer."

Aurelia stood up. "No, not an unreasonable assumption, I suppose. If I hear of anything, I'll let you know if you'll give me an address where I can reach you." She extended her hand in farewell.

"I am staying with my aunt, Lady Broughton, on Brook Street," he said, taking the hand with a meticulous bow. "But I trust I may call upon you again soon, ma'am."

Was there more to that than the surface platitude? Why did she have the absolute sense that this man never did or said anything without a specific purpose? And how should he have any purpose that concerned her? Once he'd reclaimed the package for the ministry, she should be of no further interest to him.

"Please do," she heard herself respond politely. "I'll see you out."

Chapter Four

Aurelia CLOSED THE DOOR on her departed guest and went up to her bedchamber. She took Frederick's letter from the jewel casket and sat down to read it again, but this time with dispassionate knowledge of its contents. Now she could tease out meanings, read between the lines, try to understand properly what had driven her husband to abandon everything that she believed he had held dear. And she did believe that he had loved her and their child. So how had he been able in good conscience to sacrifice not just himself but his wife, leaving her to a life of widowhood, at first a pretense and now a reality?

She was not happy in her widowhood. In motherhood, yes, but there was a barrenness to her present existence. Maybe she was selfish to complain, maybe she should be satisfied with motherhood, but Aurelia found it difficult to accept that that was all there was to her life from now on. In her heart of hearts she knew that she envied her friends who had found love. A second chance for Nell. She would welcome her own second chance, there was no point pretending otherwise.

Once again she was flooded by that strange pulse of energy, the feeling that was a combination of excitement and fear. She had no idea what prompted it, but she could feel her cheeks flush, a slight mist of perspiration on her brow, and her heart was fluttering as frantically as a wild bird in a cage. Was it the appeal of a double life, the thrill of excitement, as well as the obligations of patriotism, that had sent Frederick on the path he had taken?

The dainty ormolu clock on her mantel chimed the hour, and Aurelia realized that she'd been sitting motionless for more than half an hour. Her moment of near panic had vanished as quickly as it had come. She looked down at the letter on her lap. She would never know for certain what had driven Frederick. He had told her all he could or would, and now he was gone.

She folded the letter again and replaced it in her jewel casket, then flung open the armoire in search of a gown suitable for a luncheon where the conversation would be less frivolous than usual. Cecily Langton's husband was a bishop, a somewhat worldly bishop let it be said, but he encouraged his wife to espouse good causes, and she threw herself into the business with a happy heart. She was renowned for her refusal to take no for an answer when she was dragooning her society friends into parting with their money, time, and energy. Cornelia, Livia, and Aurelia had always enjoyed Cecily's deft manipulations of the reluctant givers, a category in which they could not themselves be counted.

Aurelia picked out a gown of dove gray silk with a brown velvet pelisse trimmed with gray fur. Suitably sober, she decided, but undeniably elegant. The costume had been through various transformations, and she was fairly certain only her closest friends would recognize it in its present manifestation. The pelisse was now belted beneath the bosom with a brown silk cord instead of the tasseled gray that had previously adorned it. The fur trimming replaced a dark gray taffeta, and the gray silk gown now had darker gray flounces and little puff sleeves instead of the elbow length of before.

She rang the bell for Hester, who had added lady's maid to her general laundress and seamstress duties, and took off the simple cambric gown she'd worn to Mount Street.

"Good morning, m'lady." Hester, slightly breathless from running up the stairs from the basement, appeared in the doorway. "Should I press the gown, ma'am?"

"I don't think it needs it, Hester. But I'd like you to help with my hair. You're a wonder with that curling iron."

"Oh, thank you, ma'am. I does me best." Hester flushed with pleasure at the compliment. She helped Aurelia into the gown, then took the curling iron to the fire to warm it while Aurelia unpinned her hair, letting the corn-silk locks tumble free. Ringlets required a lot of attention to maintain, and her coiffure now was beginning to lose its curl.

She had very straight hair and unfortunately curly hair was the fashion, so she must submit several times a day to the hot iron in Hester's skillful hands. She'd always envied Livia her mass of dusky curls that could effortlessly be teased into any number of styles.

The smell of singeing hair made her wrinkle her nose, but Hester seemed oblivious, twisting, twining, pulling at the corkscrews she created until the soft, pale hair clustered in shining ringlets on either side of Aurelia's face.

"Lovely. Thank you, my dear." Aurelia reached for the hare's-foot brush to apply a little rouge before getting up from the dresser. Hester helped her into the pelisse.

"Will you wear the little velvet hat, ma'am. The brown one?"

"Yes, perfect." Aurelia took the hat and arranged it over the ringlets. The dab of a hat with a wisp of a veil looked very well atop her pale hair. Aurelia examined herself in the mirror and gave a little self-deprecating smile at the knowledge of her own vanity. She looked elegant, a figure to draw the eye. Of course as a widowed matron with a six-year-old daughter, such matters should be of no interest to her at all. But they were, and if that was a sin, then so be it.

She gathered up her gloves and reticule and left the house to walk the short distance to Hanover Square where the bishop had his residence. The day had warmed a little and a pale sun shone weakly from a light blue sky whenever the scudding clouds permitted. The square was quiet and Aurelia decided to walk through the garden to Holles Street on the far side.

She entered the cool, damp garden through the little wrought-iron gate. The daffodils were in full bloom and the forsythia was beginning to bud. The grass was a rich green after the winter rains, and the air had a wonderful moist, earthy scent. There was a sense of freshness, of new beginnings, and her step quickened with a renewed surge of that earlier energy.

The garden appeared deserted, not even a gardener tending to the shrubs. The children who usually played in the verdant square were presumably at their lessons, but it was unusual not to see a nursemaid giving a baby an airing. Aurelia strolled down the gravel pathway between privet hedges interspersed with macrocarpa. She took off a glove with her teeth, then broke off a macrocarpa twig and rubbed it between her fingers. The lemony fragrance of the cyprus oil took her back to her childhood and the tall hedges that surrounded the house where she'd grown up.

And the olfactory memory brought Frederick clear as day into her mind's eye. He had proposed to her one hot day in the shade of a macrocarpa hedge while she'd been doing just what she was now doing, rubbing the oil into her fingers and inhaling deeply of the scent. Everything about that day had seemed right. His proposal was far from unexpected. It was no secret to anyone that the families of Frederick Farnham and Aurelia Merchant had promoted the connection since their children were small. Their children had obliged them by falling in love. Aurelia couldn't now remember exactly when she'd realized that her feelings for her childhood friend had deepened into something much stronger than friendship and the shared experiences of growing up. But when Frederick proposed, she had felt such happiness, such a sense of fulfillment, of the absolute rightness of the future that lay ahead for her. Now, as she inhaled the lemony fragrance on her fingers, she wondered if Frederick had felt the same on that bright sunny afternoon. Perhaps his feelings had not run as deep or as strong as hers and she had not allowed herself to see it.

With a tiny sigh she tossed the twig aside and replaced her glove as she walked on down the path. As she emerged onto the grassy space in the center of the garden, a strange feeling hit her. The fine hairs on her nape lifted and her scalp crawled. She stopped and looked around. There was no sign of anyone. But she had company, she knew it. Her skin knew it. Or maybe it was simply the random goose prickles of someone walking over her grave. Her thoughts had been occupied, after all, with the dead.

She paused for a second on the path, hearing the reassuring rumble of traffic just a few yards away on the other side of the iron railings. There was nothing to fear in the middle of London on a bright morning. But the silence in the garden seemed unnatural. Even the birds were quiet. She jumped at a rustle behind her and twisted to look over her shoulder. A squirrel was digging in the rich soil beneath an oak tree. Nothing else.

Tentatively she called out, "Who's there?"

There was no answer. She began to walk quickly towards the street, and its pedestrians and carriages. Her back felt exposed, as if it had a target printed on it. This irrational fear was surely explained by the events of the last day. Frederick had somehow risen from the dead, then been buried again, and it was no wonder her nerves were on edge.

Her fingers were clumsy as she fumbled with the latch on the gate, but at last she was outside the dim, green shadows of the garden and in the bright and busy street. She drew another deep, steadying breath, settled her shoulders, smoothed down her skirt with a little comforting pat, and started walking towards Holles Street. *But someone was following her.* She stopped, looked behind her. Plenty of people were around, all apparently going about their business. No one she recognized.

She swallowed convulsively. She was being ridiculous. What possible reason could someone have for following her, and what possible harm could anyone do her in the middle of the busy street?

A hackney carriage stood against the curb a few feet ahead of her, and instinctively she increased her pace towards it. A passenger was just getting out on the pavement side. With a murmured apology, Aurelia climbed up into the carriage as he stepped to the ground, then without thinking slid across the bench and out of the opposite door into the thronged street, narrowly avoiding a passing curricle. The jarvey stared at her sudden appearance, opened his mouth to shout something, but she was already dodging traffic as she made for the far side of the street back towards Cavendish Square. She had no idea where she was going now, only that she needed to get rid of this fearful intuitive sense of being stalked.

She found herself breathless on Henrietta Place and stopped, listening, looking around. Again, nothing sinister was to be seen, and slowly her panic faded as her heartbeat returned to something approaching its normal rhythm. *What on earth had possessed her?* For the life of her, Aurelia couldn't imagine what lunatic impulse had driven her in the last few minutes. Now she was going to be late and she was facing the opposite direction from her destination.

She shook her head vigorously in an attempt to clear away the cobwebby residues of her fear and set off quickly in the right direction. Once again on Holles Street, she was walking briskly towards Hanover Square when someone stepped up beside her and a familiar voice said, "I must congratulate you, ma'am. You nearly lost me. That's a professional trick, dodging though a carriage like that. Where did you learn it?"

Aurelia stopped dead and stared at Greville Falconer, who was smiling at her with a cool serenity that made nonsense of her panic. *"You?"*

"Yes, me," he agreed with his unwavering smile. "I'm

sorry if I startled you, but I suddenly had the irresistible urge to see if you remembered the games you used to play as a child."

"Games?" she repeated, aware that she sounded like a parrot. "What games? You scared me half to death. How *dare* you do such a thing?"

He raised his hands in a gesture of surrender, and his smile became even more disarming. "Forgive me. But Frederick told me of a particular game you used to play, a kind of hide-and-seek, I can't remember what . . ."

"Hunt the hare," Aurelia said slowly, still staring at him. "One of us set off across the countryside and had to be in a certain place by a certain time, while the others hunted us." She remembered the excitement and the trepidation of being the prey on those long-ago days. Sometimes it had felt almost real, that desperate need to evade, to hide, to trick. That was exactly what she had felt in the last few minutes.

"Yes, that's right. Frederick told me about it. He said it had laid some groundwork for the kind of tricks he needed in the trade that became his." Greville put a hand lightly on her arm. "It was unforgivable of me to frighten you. Please believe that I truly didn't intend to."

Aurelia looked blankly at him. She could think of nothing to say. But she didn't brush his hand aside.

Greville said swiftly into the silence, "To tell the truth, I didn't really think you would even be aware that you were being watched. Many people wouldn't have felt an instant's unease. Most people are oblivious of their surroundings much of the time. And if you hadn't known you were being watched, you wouldn't have been frightened."

"A somewhat disingenuous excuse, don't you think, sir?" Aurelia demanded with heavy irony. She had found her tongue and her composure, and lightly and dismissively, as if it were a fallen leaf, she brushed his hand from her sleeve.

He let his hand fall away and bowed. "I won't intrude upon you further, ma'am."

"For which I am grateful." With a twitch of her flounced gown, she turned from him and continued on her way.

Greville watched her until she reached her destination. She had a right to her anger, he reflected somewhat ruefully. He certainly hadn't been playing fair. But he had learned something useful. Aurelia had the necessary instincts. Instincts that could be honed. But did she have the inclination? Or the willingness to consider incentives that might overcome a lack of inclination?

Aurelia spent the next two hours wrestling with her anger, which was directed as much at Frederick as at Colonel Falconer. What right had Frederick had to discuss something as intimate as those childhood games with *anyone,* let alone the man he worked for in such dubious circumstances. By sharing such an intimacy it seemed to her that he had given tacit permission to the colonel to use that information. But what was he using it for? Some cat-and-mouse game, just for the sake of it? That seemed ludicrous. Unless the man was deranged, and that, she decided, was a distinct possibility.

She forced her mind back to the conversation at the luncheon table. "How many new beds did you say the infirmary building will provide, Cecily?"

"Sir John Soane says eighty," Cecily responded. "Little enough, barely a drop in the ocean these days, with the number of casualties coming back from the war."

"Oh, they're all over the streets," Letitia declared with a fastidious shudder. "Begging for a penny, or a crust. One can't walk along Piccadilly anymore without being accosted. It's a disgrace. They look so dreadful, with no legs, or arms, and those filthy bandages. They should be put somewhere out of sight. Who needs to be reminded of those horrors?"

"Then I'm sure you'll make a very generous contribution to the infirmary, Letitia," Cornelia said with a silky smile. "It will take some of them out of your view."

"Yes, indeed. I shall put you down for five hundred guineas, Letitia," Cecily declared briskly. "If you're lucky, such a sum might clear one side of Piccadilly of such offensive sights."

Letitia blinked a little as she sipped her wine. Sometimes it seemed to her that she was being excluded from a joke. "I shall have to ask Oglethorpe," she said, a mite plaintively. "Such a sum would rob me of most of a quarter's allowance."

"I'm sure you'll find a way to persuade Lord Oglethorpe to assist such a worthy cause," Aurelia said, smiling. "Everyone knows you have him wrapped around your little finger, Letitia."

Letitia bridled, looked smug, and murmured, "Well, that's as may be, but I do have a trick or two up my sleeve when it comes to persuasion."

"I fear I can manage little," Countess Lessingham said with an apologetic smile. "You must forgive me, ladies, but so much of my own resources go to help my own countrymen in London. So many of them flee the tyrant with only the clothes they stand up in. I do what I can for them. But I could manage perhaps twenty guineas for the infirmary."

"That would be most generous, Countess," Cecily said. "We know how deeply you are involved in relieving the plight of your countrymen in exile."

"I will do what I can for anyone suffering from Napoléon's tyranny," the lady announced, her Spanish accent becoming more pronounced under the strength of her emotion. "Poor King Carlos and his family, forced into exile. It's such a dreadful time." Her voice quavered a little, and she dabbed at her eyes with a dainty scrap of embroidered lace.

The luncheon broke up soon after. "Will you come back to Mount Street, Ellie?" Cornelia asked as they gathered wraps and gloves. "You could collect Franny."

"Yes, yes, of course," Aurelia said somewhat absently. "That would be convenient, Nell. D'you have your carriage?"

"Mmm. The barouche. Of course, if you have something you need to do at home, I could drop you off in Cavendish Square and Daisy can come and fetch Franny later."

"No, I have nothing in particular to do this afternoon," Aurelia said with perfect truth. She had no desire to be alone with her thoughts, although it would be a strain to watch her tongue with Cornelia. They were not accustomed to having secrets from each other. But the more practice she had with this secret, the easier it would become.

They bade farewell to their hostess and walked down the steps to the barouche, which awaited at the curb. "Cecily certainly has a talent for organization," Cornelia observed, climbing up into the carriage with a nod to the footman who held the door.

"She's one of the few women I know who can keep the discussion on track," Aurelia agreed, grateful for this innocuous conversation. "Even Letitia can't budge her when Cecily's bee is buzzing in her bonnet."

Cornelia laughed and arranged the lap robe over both of them. "I was quite drawn to Countess Lessingham. Did you like her?"

"She certainly has a passion for her émigré countrymen," Aurelia said, tucking her hands beneath the robe. "And one can only respect that. This wretched war is causing so much suffering across the Continent. So many lives lost, so many wounded . . . so many families left destitute, homeless." She looked helplessly at her friend.

"Sometimes I wonder if we're doing enough, Nell."

"We gave two husbands to the war," Cornelia said quietly. "I know that could be considered a small sacrifice when one looks at what others have lost or have now to endure, but it's not insignificant, Ellie. Neither of us tried to persuade our husbands to stay safe at home. We knew the risks, but we embraced them, as did Stephen and Frederick."

Aurelia could only murmur assent. However Frederick had died, he had died for his country. Her eyes darted left and right as the carriage bowled through the streets. She half expected to see Greville Falconer lurking, although if he was lurking, she doubted he would make himself visible.

"Something troubling you, love?"

"No, whyever should there be?" Aurelia said with a laugh that she hoped sounded convincing.

Cornelia shrugged. "You seemed rather distrait at luncheon, and you seem on edge now."

"I'm a little tired."

"Ah." Cornelia nodded, unconvinced, but she would not probe in the absence of any encouragement. She changed the subject. "I must show you the color scheme I've decided on for the ball."

"Black and silver, you said."

"Yes, but with little hints of white and crimson. The flowers will be white lilies, and stripped honesty, for the silver. And then . . ." Cornelia looked expectantly at Aurelia. "Can you guess?"

Aurelia shook her head, amused despite her preoccupation.

"Black tulips."

"Where on earth . . . ?"

"Alex," Cornelia stated. "I mentioned my idea in a letter to Liv last week, and Alex came up with the notion of black tulips."

"Lord," Aurelia murmured. "Is there no limit to the miracles our Prince Prokov can perform?"

"Apparently not. He knows a tulip grower in Amsterdam who can let me have ten dozen. I know it's not many, but just imagine the effect, Ellie."

"Oh, I am," Aurelia breathed. "And what about the hints of scarlet?"

"Tulips again. They'll be at their best in May." Cornelia beamed with satisfaction. "It will be perfect, and Liv is adamant that she will be strong enough by the end of May to be there."

"Will you carry the color scheme onto the supper table?" Aurelia was fascinated, and more than happy to explore this unexceptionable subject.

"Harry thinks black-and-white food might be a little off-putting," Cornelia said. "He suggested tripe and onions for the white stuff, raw beef for the red, and black pudding for the black."

Aurelia burst into laughter. "Trust Harry to bring matters down to earth."

"Oh, I'll think of something," her friend said cheerfully. "But we have to liaise on our gowns." She regarded her friend with an assessing eye. "Silver and gold, I think for you, Ellie. So perfect with your hair."

"Oh, I've a hankering for a hint of scarlet," Aurelia retorted with a chuckle.

The carriage turned onto Mount Street and her laugh died in her throat. Harry Bonham was coming towards them. Sir Greville Falconer was at his side.

Aurelia began to feel stifled, trapped in a web spun by this man who'd marched uninvited into her life with what seemed the sole purpose of destroying all the equilibrium she had.

As the men approached, Harry raised a hand in greeting. "Good afternoon, Aurelia." He reached the carriage and stood one hand on the door, his eyes only on his wife. "Wife of mine," he murmured.

"Husband," she returned, her voice as low as his as she gave him her hand to alight. Aurelia was accustomed to the sensual charge between these two, but she couldn't help noticing with some satisfaction a slight surprised narrowing of the colonel's eyes, and she hoped he was discomfited. It would certainly be the first time in their brief acquaintance.

She stepped out of the carriage as Harry held up his free hand. "Forgive the intrusion, Harry," she said lightly. "I come merely to fetch Franny."

"You could never intrude," he said, and she knew it was not mere politeness speaking. "Allow me to introduce Colonel, Sir Greville Falconer." He gestured to his companion.

"Falconer . . . Lady Farnham . . . and my wife, Viscountess Bonham."

Aurelia met the dark gray eyes with a steadiness that surprised her. She extended her hand. "I'm delighted to make your acquaintance, Colonel."

He took her hand, raised it to his lips in a courtly gesture that surprised her as much as her own composure. "Lady Farnham, I'm honored." He gave her his smile again, and his gaze seemed to linger a moment longer than necessary on her countenance, before he turned to greet Cornelia.

"Colonel, are you new to town?" Cornelia asked.

"Colonel Falconer has just returned from Corunna," Harry said. "He's been out of England for some years now."

Cornelia understood immediately that the colonel was in some way involved in the business that kept her husband so occupied in the dark corridors of the War Ministry, business best not examined too closely. So she nodded and said, "I trust you'll take tea, Colonel. How long are you in town?"

"I hope to stay for several months, ma'am," he replied, following her up to the front door. "I'm looking for suitable lodgings."

"Oh, I'm sure Harry's agent could help you there," she said. "Don't you think, Harry?"

"Certainly," her husband said, standing to one side so that Aurelia could precede him into the house. "I'll ask Lester to arrange it."

"Come into the drawing room, Sir Greville." Cornelia led the way. "Will you take tea, or would you prefer something from Harry's cellars?"

"The latter, I'm sure," Harry declared. "Aurelia, a glass of Madeira?"

"No, I'd love tea, thank you," Aurelia said. "So, Colonel Falconer, what brings you to London? It must seem very tame after the rigors of the battlefield."

"Sometimes tame is welcome, Lady Farnham," he replied, taking a seat beside her on a small sofa.

His thigh seemed very close to hers, and Aurelia shifted slightly towards her arm of the sofa. She had the urge to discompose him, to play with fire a little. "I was rereading some of Frederick's letters from Oxford this morning, Nell," she said. "You know how he and Stephen used to write to us regularly during term. He was describing an evening when he and Stephen dodged the beadle and climbed in over the wall at dawn . . . do you remember?"

Cornelia hid her surprise at this strange conversational turn. "They were a pair of rakehells, weren't they? In their youth," she added with a small smile, gesturing to the footman that he should put the tea tray on the table in front of her.

Aurelia turned to the colonel. "Forgive the reminiscence, sir. My husband was Lady Bonham's brother. He and her first husband were childhood friends. They did everything together. Harrow, Magdalen College, Oxford, and then the navy." She met his eyes. "And they died together at Trafalgar." She took the cup Cornelia handed her with a bland smile.

Harry was looking at her strangely and Aurelia didn't care. She was no marionette to be danced at the end of Greville Falconer's strings. The colonel's gaze sharpened with a glint of surprise, and she felt a surge of satisfaction. He inclined his head in an infinitesimal movement that only she, sitting so close to him, would notice. But it was an absolute acknowledgment of a hit. This round she had won.

"It was a great naval victory," he said gravely. "Despite the many lives that were lost."

The unspoken name of Admiral Nelson hung heavy for a moment, and Aurelia reflected that her moment of satisfaction hadn't lasted very long. There was no countermove to the invocation of that particular hero's death at Trafalgar. Harry and Nell bore the look of someone prepared to support an old friend but completely at sea as to why it had to be on this particular tack.

"Where were you thinking of looking for lodgings, Falconer?" Harry asked, pouring Madeira in two glasses.

"Wherever I can find them. Thank you." Greville took the glass. "I'd like to be within comfortable walking distance of Piccadilly."

"You'll set up your stable, of course?" Harry took a seat and gestured to Greville to do the same.

"In a minor way. A decent riding horse . . . a good

pair for a curricle. No more than that." Greville sipped his Madeira. "Do you ride, Lady Farnham?"

"I enjoy riding, Colonel."

"Then perhaps you would accept my escort one afternoon. I am so new to town, and if you would be willing to introduce a newcomer to the rituals of a Hyde Park trot along the tan, I would be eternally in your debt." Greville smiled as he spoke, his eyes only on her countenance, giving the impression that she was the only person in the room.

What game was he playing now? Aurelia had no idea, but she knew she needed to bring it to a close quickly. Cornelia and Harry were far too sharp-witted to watch this byplay without wondering what was going on. She said pleasantly, "That would be delightful, Colonel, but I find little enough time for such exercise these days. My daughter occupies so much of my day."

"You leave me desolate, ma'am," Greville murmured. "But I understand that the needs of your child must be paramount."

She set down her cup and got abruptly to her feet. "If you'll excuse me, I must go up to the schoolroom. I wanted to ask Miss Alison some things about Franny's progress."

"I'll come with you," Cornelia said. "I'm sure you and the colonel can entertain yourselves for a few minutes, Harry."

"You'll be missed, my dear," Harry said with a quiet

smile. The two men both rose to their feet and bowed as the ladies left the drawing room.

"Have you met the colonel before, Ellie?" Cornelia asked as they ascended the stairs.

"Of course not. What gave you that idea?" Aurelia tried for a light dismissive laugh, telling herself that it *would* get easier.

"I don't know exactly," her friend said, shooting her a sideways glance. "Just something about the way he behaved with you. There was just something between you both that seemed to give that impression."

"Oh, perhaps it was just one of those instantaneous dislikes we all form occasionally," Aurelia said carelessly. "I own there's something about him that puts my back up . . . a certain presumption . . . arrogance, if you will."

Cornelia considered this as they climbed the nursery stairs to the children's apartments. "I can't say I noticed it," she said finally. "But he's a soldier, they all have something of the habit of command about them. I suppose after years in the service it's hard to moderate it in civilian life."

"I'm sure you're right," Aurelia agreed, opening the door into the schoolroom. "And I'm sure I'm being unreasonable. He'll improve on acquaintance, I expect."

Cornelia left it at that as they turned their attention to their children's clamorous greeting.

It was half an hour later when they returned downstairs with the children. Harry and the colonel came out of the drawing room as they reached the hall.

"I thought I heard the children's dulcet tones," Harry observed, bending to scoop up Susannah, who had hurled herself at his knees. He kissed her, hitching her onto his hip, and ruffled Stevie's hair. "Had a good day, then?"

"We found the backbone of a snake," Stevie began importantly. "And—"

"When Stevie picked it up, it broke," Franny interrupted. "But I fixed it all together an' we carried it upstairs on a piece of paper, an' then we drew around it."

"Franny did," Stevie said with an almost adult sigh. He was a year older than Franny and had in the last year shot up two inches, a height advantage that gave him a much needed illusion of superiority in the company of his bossy and precocious cousin.

"You inked it in," Franny reminded him kindly. "You keep inside the lines better'n I do."

Stevie looked gratified by this testimonial, and before anything could be said to destroy the moment of harmony, Aurelia said, "Say good-bye, Franny darling, we must hurry home before it gets too chilly." She kissed Cornelia and accepted Harry's salute on her cheek.

"You'll take the barouche, Ellie," Cornelia said. "It won't take a moment to bring it around again."

"No . . . no, thank you. The walk will tire Franny," Aurelia said hastily, raising a speaking eyebrow.

"Of course," Cornelia said, stifling a smile as she looked at the little girl, who was performing some elaborate dance of her own as she chattered to Stevie.

"I trust you'll permit me to escort you home, Lady Farnham."

Aurelia glanced briefly at the colonel and said with cool dismissal, "How kind, sir. But it will not be necessary, I assure you."

"I would consider it a great privilege," he said, bowing over her hand.

Aurelia was aware of Harry and Cornelia regarding her with a degree of interest. To refuse such a gentlemanly offer would be completely inexplicable to her friends. "I'm sure Cavendish Square is out of your way," she demurred.

"Not at all," he denied. "It's barely a step from Brook Street, and it will be my pleasure." He turned to Harry. "My thanks for the hospitality, Bonham."

"I trust you'll make one of my party at the Daffy Club on Thursday," Harry said, shaking his hand.

"I'd be honored," Greville murmured, well aware that Harry had been asked to smooth the colonel's return to society with the right introductions. The loosely formed aristocratic social and sports club that met at the Castle Tavern would not have been a personal choice, but then his sojourn in London was not for pleasure, and such a venue could well attract the kind of men who were his business.

He turned back to Aurelia, who was adjusting her daughter's bonnet. She was a very graceful woman, he noted, not for the first time, and there was something very appealing about her peaches-and-cream complexion framed in the corn-silk ringlets. As if aware of his gaze she looked up sharply, and he caught the flicker of uncertainty in the glowing brown eyes. She was off-balance and that would make his task easier.

Perhaps this assignment might hold some unexpected pleasures, after all. Instantly he dismissed the unbidden thought. He lived by the rules of his trade, and the cardinal rule was that all personal relationships carried unacceptable dangers. True, he had considered Frederick Farnham a friend as well as a partner, but the friendship had not taken precedence over the partnership. Frederick had been his subordinate, and there had never been any confusion as to the moments when friendship could be allowed to dominate.

"Lady Farnham." Greville offered his arm as a footman opened the front door.

Aurelia rested her hand lightly on his sleeve, holding Franny's hand firmly in her own free one as they walked down to the street.

"Who's the man, Mama?" Franny's piercing whisper brought a reluctant smile to her mother's lips.

Greville answered gravely before she could respond, "My name is Colonel Falconer, Franny." He paused to speak directly to the child. "I'm a soldier in the army."

Franny frowned. "My papa was a sailor in the navy. But I don't remember him. He died."

"Yes, so I understand," Greville responded. "I am very sorry for it, Franny."

"It's sad for Mama." The child swooped sideways to

pick up a pebble. "This is pretty . . . isn't it pretty, Mama?"

"Very," Aurelia agreed. "Put it in your muff. We must hurry now. Miss Ada will have your tea ready."

"Boiled egg and soldiers . . . I asked her this morning specially," Franny said, beginning her dancing step down the street.

"*Soldiers?*" Greville inquired softly.

"Bread-and-butter fingers . . . to dip in the egg yolk," Aurelia informed him. "Not part of *your* childhood, I gather." Her voice still held the residual anger at his earlier game.

"No, I was clearly deprived."

She looked at him. "Somehow, Colonel, I doubt that. I find it very difficult to imagine anyone succeeding in depriving you of something you wanted."

He exhaled a little puff of air. "I *have* made a bad impression. Which is a shame, since it was the last thing I wished to do."

"You should try harder," she said with acid-tipped sweetness. "There's no need for you to accompany us any further. We shall be quite safe . . . as long as no one decides to play stalking games."

Greville bowed. It was time to take his leave. He knew well when discretion was the better part of valor, and the lady had clearly had enough of his company for one day. He would return to the front tomorrow. "If you're sure?"

"Certain."

"Then I will do as you wish." He bowed again, taking her hand in a firm clasp, before solemnly bending to shake the child's hand. Then he turned aside and strode off towards Brook Street.

Aurelia resisted the urge to watch him go and instead walked quickly, swinging Franny's hand, towards Cavendish Square.

Chapter Five

Aurelia was at breakfast the next morning when Morecombe appeared soundlessly in the doorway to the breakfast room.

"Someone to see you," he announced.

"At this hour?" Aurelia glanced at the clock on the mantel. It was barely nine o'clock. "Who is it, Morecombe?"

The elderly retainer shrugged. "Don't rightly know. Didn't give a name, but he's been 'ere afore . . . yesterday, or thereabouts."

Aurelia frowned. Ordinarily a visitor this early in the day would betoken some kind of emergency, or at the very least an urgent errand. But in such a case the visitor would have declared his business. It could only be one man. And such an unorthodox arrival would not in the least be out of character for Colonel, Sir Greville Falconer.

She could refuse to see him, of course. But that wouldn't do much good. If he wanted to see her, he'd make sure he did, one way or another. And once again that strange frisson lifted the fine hairs on her skin, and her heartbeat accelerated.

Aurelia debated keeping the colonel waiting while she changed her clothes. A faded morning gown that had seen many better days was perfectly suitable for a quiet, solitary breakfast but not really for receiving visitors. But then she decided a visitor who insisted on such uncivilized hours would have to take her as he found her.

She took a sip of her coffee and returned the cup carefully to its saucer. "Show him in here, Morecombe."

Morecombe sniffed his disapproval but shuffled away, and within a minute Greville Falconer entered the breakfast parlor. He was dressed for riding and his tousled dark hair and wind-freshened complexion bore witness to the exercise. In the instant before he bowed, top hat in hand, Aurelia thought she caught a flash in his dark gray eyes, a glint of something that she couldn't quite read. Amusement, or something else?

"Ma'am, forgive the intrusion on your breakfast. It's outrageously early for morning calls, but I hoped to catch you before you went out, or other morning callers started banging the doorknocker."

Amusement was definitely in his voice, and that glint was still in his eye, but Aurelia didn't think that was pure amusement. It sent that strange and disconcerting prickle down her spine again. She wasn't certain for a moment how to respond to his disarmingly frank acknowledgment of this inappropriate visit, but then opted for a cool, matter-of-fact tone.

"Well, you certainly succeeded in that, Sir Greville. May I offer you coffee . . . or perhaps you'd care for breakfast. I could try to persuade the kitchen to rustle up something a little more substantial than toast. I'm afraid I have little appetite in the morning."

"That's very kind of you, Lady Farnham. I own a kipper or a chop or a plate of bacon wouldn't come amiss. I've been riding since six." He pulled out a chair and sat down with a serene smile.

Aurelia had hoped to discomfit him by an ironic invitation that was designed to emphasize the uncivilized nature of the visit. However, it seemed that discomfiting Greville Falconer was an art form she had not yet mastered.

Saying nothing, she rang the little silver bell by her plate and waited, wondering how long it would take Morecombe to appear. It was Hester, however, who popped her head around the door. "What can I get you, mum?"

"Sir Greville would like some breakfast, Hester. Could you ask Miss Ada or Miss Mavis if they could manage to find something suitable."

The girl stared at her mistress's visitor. "I'll ask, ma'am. But it's bakin' day an' Miss Ada's busy with the bread, an' Miss Mavis is makin' steak an' kidney puddin'."

"See what they can manage, Hester." Aurelia smiled her dismissal and the girl backed out of the room.

"If I'd realized it would be such a trouble, I would never have accepted your invitation. I'm sure a piece of toast will suffice." Greville reached for a piece of now cold and leathery toast in the rack.

"Oh, believe me, sir, it will not suffice," Aurelia declared. "Having disturbed the even tenor of my kitchen, you'll eat what comes out of it and enjoy every mouthful."

He bowed his head with mock humility. "As you say, ma'am. I'm suitably grateful, and equally remorseful for having put you out." His eyes sparked with laughter, and Aurelia couldn't hide her own amusement at this ludicrous cat-and-mouse banter. Two little dimples danced in her cheeks and her brown eyes were alight.

Greville regarded her now with frank appreciation. Her hair hung loose and straight to her shoulders, enlivened with a few hardy ringlets that had survived the night. Her cheeks were becomingly flushed, and her casual dress gave her an air of delightful informality.

"Where is the talkative Franny this morning?" he inquired with a smile.

"On her way to the schoolroom. Do you care for coffee? Or would you prefer ale?"

"I no longer have the temerity to express a preference, ma'am. Whatever will be the least trouble."

For answer, Aurelia got up from the table and went

to the door. "Make yourself at home, Colonel. I won't be long."

She returned in five minutes with a tankard of ale that she set down at his elbow. "Our Ada is prepared to offer you ham, eggs, and mushrooms."

Greville was powerfully aware of the curve of her breast brushing his shoulder as she set down the tankard, and even more powerfully aware of the scent of her skin and the loose ringlet curling over her ear. A hint of verbena and lemon. It had been many weeks since he'd been physically this close to a woman, and he would guess Aurelia Farnham had not breakfasted so informally with any man other than her husband. And yet she showed no sign of feeling at a disadvantage. Quite the opposite. She was playing the perfect hostess.

Either she was a superb dissembler, or she genuinely had no difficulty adapting to circumstances that should disturb her. Either talent would suit his purposes most excellently.

"Our Ada?" he queried.

"Morecombe's wife and his sister-in-law take care of the household in the absence of Prince and Princess Prokov and their own household," she told him, returning to her own seat across the table. "They're institutions here and have the right to remain either working or as pensioners for the rest of their lives. So far they prefer to work . . . according to their own lights," she added with a half smile.

"But the twins . . . Ada and Mavis . . . are superb cooks, and Morecombe . . . well, Morecombe is Morecombe," she continued. "They have a mutual adoration compact with the children, Nell's and mine, and . . ." She shrugged and reached for the coffeepot. "And with me, Lady Bonham, and Princess Prokov."

"I see." Greville wasn't quite sure that he did, but he was more interested in the ease with which she was treating him. It was almost as if she'd decided that he was a fixture who had to be accommodated. Either that, or she was preparing a nasty surprise for him.

Hester's reappearance with a laden platter interrupted his speculation, and he addressed himself to breakfast with a keen and appreciative appetite. Aurelia sipped her coffee and watched him eat. Despite her surface calm she was on tenterhooks. He had business with her. He hadn't declared it in so many words, but there was no other explanation for this interest in her. He had come for the document that Frederick had sent to her, and he had told her the truth about her husband's death. Both pieces of business had been accomplished. So why was he still here, popping up unexpectedly, behaving as if they were in some way already connected to a shared purpose?

Greville looked up from his plate and met her gaze. He took a deep draft of ale, then said, "That was an interesting piece of information you gave me yesterday."

Her eyebrows lifted. "Oh? What was that?"

"That Frederick's sister is married to Viscount Bonham. I didn't know that."

Aurelia leaned an elbow on the table and propped her chin in her hand. "Frederick told you nothing about himself?"

"It's not sensible in my business to share personal information with one's colleagues. Such information leaves one vulnerable." Greville's expression was calm but Aurelia thought she could detect a hint of bleakness in his eyes.

She frowned. "How? What do you mean?"

He forked a mushroom and ate it slowly as if considering his answer. "The work we do can only take place under a cloak of the utmost secrecy, as I'm sure you understand. One must keep one's own counsel at all times. It's an activity no one can afford to acknowledge, and certainly those who are engaged in it are very careful not to broadcast that fact."

"That doesn't appear to apply to you, Colonel."

A glint shone again in the gray eyes as he looked sharply at her. "Frederick did tell me a little about you, Aurelia, but he didn't tell me what a bee-sting tongue you have."

"I don't suppose he knew it." Her eyes never left his. It was as if they were engaged in swordplay, and every thrust and every feint was a matter of life or death. "I had no need to use it when I was with Frederick."

Greville inclined his head in acknowledgment. "I suspect he guessed, nevertheless."

"How so?"

"He told me there was a great deal more to you than appeared on the surface."

Aurelia smiled, not a particularly nice smile. "Hidden depths, you mean? How original."

Greville was beginning to feel a little scalded. "As I was saying, I didn't know anything about Frederick's sister except that he had one, and I certainly was unaware that you and she were such good friends."

"And does that in some way affect your . . ." She gestured randomly as she tried to find the correct words. "Your intentions, I suppose? Whatever it is that's behind this persecution."

He whistled softly. "*Persecution.* That's a mite strong, is it not?"

"I hardly think so. You spring yourself upon me with devastating information, then you follow me, scare me witless, pursue me into my friends' drawing room, and then turn up in my own breakfast parlor at an ungodly hour of the morning." She shrugged. "Can you think of a better description of your behavior, Colonel?"

"I wish you would call me by my name. Since we are engaged in this rather intimate conversation, formality seems a little de trop."

"I find it keeps a necessary distance, Colonel," she retorted. "I believe I heard you to say that developing personal relationships in your *business* is unwise."

"*Touché,* ma'am." He acknowledged wryly as he returned his attention to his plate, carefully slicing a piece of ham.

Aurelia allowed the silence to develop. To her astonishment she realized she was enjoying herself. She thought she had for the moment gained the upper hand, just as she thought she had the previous day in the Bonhams' drawing room. Not that that moment of ascendancy had lasted too long, she reminded herself. She sipped her coffee, leaning back a little in her chair, and cast a casual eye over the *Gazette* that lay beside her plate.

Greville watched her covertly with amusement and satisfaction. Frederick's widow was a lady of parts. He knew that she had relished that cut and thrust and had to acknowledge that he had, too. He had one simple purpose, to recruit her to his cause, but he was under no illusions about the difficulty of doing so.

He laid down his knife and fork, wiped his mouth on his napkin, and took another draft of ale.

"I trust you enjoyed your breakfast, sir," Aurelia said, looking up from the paper.

"It was delicious, thank you, ma'am. I hope you'll convey my thanks to the lady in the kitchen . . . Ada, I believe you said."

She nodded. "I'll ring for Morecombe to show you out."

He grinned appreciatively at the speed of her response. "Not yet, ma'am. I have yet to declare my intentions, as you put it." He crumpled his napkin beside his plate. "I have much to say to you . . . much that I am hoping you will wish to hear."

So the time for games was over. Aurelia wasn't sure

whether she had been trying to prevent the moment of revelation with her defensive tactics, or whether she'd been playing them simply to prove that she was not a dupe to be easily manipulated.

"Very well. What have you to say?"

"Frederick was a brave and dedicated man." Greville's manner had changed. His tone was stripped of all nuance, even his posture seemed more upright, his gaze more deliberately direct, as if with a fierce need to convince her. "He was the best partner I have had . . . and I've had many."

"I daresay they don't survive very long." Aurelia heard the sardonic note but was unable to control it.

"No," he agreed flatly. "We fight a well-trained, well-provisioned, and highly motivated enemy. Bonaparte has but one aim, complete dominion over the known world. You understand that?"

"My husband gave his life in that fight."

"Yes, and he did not die in vain."

A glaze of tears filmed Aurelia's eyes, and she turned her head away from the direct gray gaze across the table. "I wonder what difference it would have made to the war if he'd chosen not to give his life. He would have known his daughter and she him, and I would be sitting opposite my husband at the breakfast table instead of . . ." Her words stuck in her throat and she waved a hand impatiently as if to dismiss the incipient tears and the emotions that had brought them.

She got up from the table and walked to the window,

holding the looped-back curtain with one hand as she looked out at the small square of walled garden, the trees still leafless.

"It's not possible to quantify one man's sacrifice," Greville said quietly. "I can only tell you again that Frederick did not die in vain. He completed his mission by getting the document out of Portugal and into the right hands at the War Ministry. It was an achievement of resounding importance. The service can ill afford to lose such men."

"And what do you want of me?"

He chose his words carefully. "You have access to certain situations . . . certain people in particular . . . an access that can be very useful to me."

She whirled back to him, hand still on the curtain. "I beg your pardon?"

"My present mission in London requires me to circulate in the social circles that you inhabit so naturally." His voice was unwavering, his gaze as steady as ever. "It would help me greatly in my work if you would facilitate my access into those circles."

"What mission?" She was holding the curtain so tightly that her fingers had gone numb.

"I will tell you, but I must ask you for your solemn undertaking that you will not mention a word of what's said in this room to anyone."

She looked at him. "I've already agreed to keep all talk of our dealings to myself."

"True enough. But trust is something one cannot

take for granted in my business. And so I ask you again to honor your husband's memory. And his wishes. He would want you to hear me out . . . and he would trust you to keep my confidence."

She turned back to the window, seeing nothing of the garden beyond the glass, seeing only Frederick's words clearly on the page of his letter. To betray the colonel's trust would be the same as betraying Frederick's. And to dismiss the colonel without hearing him out would be to ignore her dead husband's last request. "Go on."

"We suspect that the Spaniards are establishing an espionage network in London. The information that we have is that they will infiltrate the upper echelons of society. Obviously, we, in turn, intend to infiltrate their network."

He found it disconcerting to talk to her back. Her back was rigid, her shoulders set, but her posture gave him none of the feedback that her face and eyes would have afforded. But he could not command her to turn around. And neither at this delicate stage could he take those slender shoulders as he wanted to do and turn her to face him.

"What has this to do with me?"

"It's been many years since I lived in London and played any part in society. I'm out of practice and I'm sure many customs have changed since I was last here. Now I need to establish myself as a man-about-town, if you like. I need to set up a household, a base of operations. I need someone well-placed in society to help me move naturally and easily in the right circles and to make sure I don't inadvertently break any unspoken rules. I need someone who knows how to talk to the right people, to ask the right questions, to listen to the right conversations, all the while providing me with an unexceptionable social front for my own activities."

Slowly Aurelia turned to face him, her hand still clutching the fabric of the curtain, almost as if were a lifeline to the reality she understood. "And you think I would be willing to do that?"

"I'm suggesting a business proposition." He rose from the table. He crossed to the fireplace and leaned one arm along the mantel, one foot propped on the fender. His tone was now brisk and businesslike. "The government paid Frederick well for his activities, but, of course, he was in no position to claim his earnings while he was abroad. That back pay should be paid to you. And there is also some prize money from the capture of two French ships while he was still serving in the navy. It's a not inconsiderable sum, but the government is willing to offer you rather more than that if you would be willing to work for them for a very limited period of time. It would be paid into a private account at Hoare's Bank at regular intervals." He watched her expression carefully.

Aurelia tried to make sense of this. There seemed to be too many strands to untangle. "You'll have to be more specific about what I would do," she said finally, releasing her tight grip on the curtain. She folded her arms across her breasts, absently caressing her elbows, a deep frown creasing her brow.

"Very well. We would start by seeming to develop an understanding, a certain romantic interest in each other, which would make it natural for us to be in each other's company. I would escort you to various social engagements that I might otherwise not be invited to, and you would introduce me to certain people that I might not otherwise meet."

"That doesn't sound particularly arduous," Aurelia said slowly. "Hardly sufficient to earn a lifetime's pension."

"You would also be acting as my eyes and ears in certain situations. I would tell you what information I was after and you would endeavor to acquire it."

"So, in plain terms, spying."

"No more than many women have done, and many still do." The fire spurted and a glowing coal fell onto the hearth. Swiftly he stamped it out before continuing. "There are women engaged in this gentle form of espionage in all the courts of Europe, my dear. Women tend to be better placed than men to hear some kind of whispers, the kind that can be vital to the success of a mission."

And women who worked on the front lines, too, she reflected, thinking again of Frederick's letter. He'd said his life had been saved by such women on many occasions. And only yesterday she and Cornelia had wondered if they were doing enough to help the war effort. If, by helping the colonel in this simple enough fashion, she helped save even one life, shouldn't she agree to it? It would not disrupt her way of life particularly, except for the need to keep it secret. But as she already had to carry the truth of Frederick's death to her grave, this would merely be a part of the same secret. If Harry had asked her for her help, she would have agreed without a second thought. But Harry was a very different prospect from Greville Falconer.

"A romantic interest?" she queried, looking directly across at him. "And where would that lead?"

"Maybe to an engagement in a few weeks," he said, returning her steady gaze. "It would smooth the path, give us an unexceptional reason to spend time together."

"And how would this end? How long is this charade to continue?"

"Once I have identified the Spanish network, I would hope to have our own infiltration in place within a few weeks . . . by the end of the season, if at all possible."

"Around three months, then," Aurelia said, absently chewing her bottom lip.

"It may take longer, but I would hope it doesn't."

"And then what? What happens to this fictitious engagement of ours?"

"Once this mission is complete, I'll be sent abroad again." He shrugged a little. "I will make sure to give you a good reason for calling off the engagement. If we time it well, the announcement of its end can be made when most people are out of town. By the time society returns after the summer, it'll be almost forgotten. I will have left town, and you will have Frederick's pension to augment your present funds."

Aurelia turned back to the window. She didn't want those uncomfortably piercing eyes on her face as she thought over his proposition. Even a small addition to her funds would enable her to manage a modest household of her own in town . . . with the right economies, of course, but she was already expert at making those. And if her friends wondered how she was managing to fund an independent lifestyle, she could always hint vaguely that Markby had been persuaded to disgorge more from the trust . . . either that or some distant relative could leave her with a small windfall. It could be done.

Once again she thought that if Harry had asked her, she would have agreed instantly. But Harry didn't send prickles up her spine or cause that strange pulsing energy that seemed to have no rhyme or reason. There was danger in the colonel's company, she knew it instinctively, but she couldn't identify what form it took. Certainly the work he was asking her to do had little enough of danger about it. Or, at least, not the way he was presenting it. For the sake of her country, she should do this. But something held her back.

Finally she turned round to face him again. She steepled her fingers at her mouth, frowning at him. "I need time to think this over."

A flash of disappointment crossed his eyes, then he stepped away from the fireplace. "Of course. But I would ask that you do not think overlong. Time is of the essence, and there are advance preparations we have to make." He picked up his hat and whip from a chair by the door and bowed. "I bid you good morning, Aurelia."

"Good morning." The door closed behind him and she listened for the sound of the front door signaling his departure. Then she left the breakfast parlor and went upstairs to her chamber, where she sat on the window seat and reread Frederick's letter . . . over and over.

Chapter Six

AURELIA SPEND THE REMAINDER of the morning in a haze of reflection. What exactly would be involved in a romantic interest between her and the colonel? Could she play such a role convincingly enough to fool her friends, sharp-eyed Nell in particular? There would have to be an appearance of developing intimacy, of growing affection. She wasn't even sure if she could remember now what that had felt like with Frederick. They had known each other since either could remember, and she couldn't identify a particular moment when the affection of close friendship had deepened into love. She couldn't for the life of her decide what she felt about Greville . . . or so she must get used to calling him if she was to do this thing. Her attitude to him was so mixed up with her hurt and anger at Frederick, but surely it wasn't entirely just to blame Greville? Frederick had had a mind of his own. He was no man's puppet. If she was to see her way clearly, she must find a way to separate the colonel from her dead husband.

When Morecombe opened the parlor door, she was so startled she dropped her embroidery needle. "What is it, Morecombe?"

"That Lady Langton and some other folk is 'ere to see you."

"Oh . . . well, show them into the drawing room, please."

"Done that," the elderly retainer declared. "Don't know what else t'do wi' 'em."

"Thank you. And ask Hester to bring tea, please." Aurelia retrieved her needle and secured it in the embroidery frame before going to greet her visitors.

"Cecily, how delightful to see you." Aurelia managed a warm smile as she entered the drawing room, hand extended. She bowed and smiled to the three other women. "Ladies, please, take a seat."

"Well, we're on another begging mission, my dear," Cecily said with an apologetic smile, drawing Aurelia down beside her on the gilt-edged sofa. "Although strictly speaking we're begging from Livia. You must be our intermediary."

"Yes, indeed, Lady Farnham," Margery Allenton declared, settling her ample frame into an armchair. "The foundling hospital in Battersea."

"Margery had the wonderful idea of a flower show," Cecily said. "Do you think dear Livia and Prince Prokov would allow us to use their conservatory. It's such a delightful hothouse, and filled with so many interesting specimens. We will ask donations to the hospital from all those who attend." She patted Aurelia's hand in her enthusiasm. "What do you think?"

"I'm sure that Livia and Prince Prokov will be more than happy to oblige," Aurelia said. "Prince Prokov has such a particular interest in his conservatory, he'd be delighted, I'm certain, to share his pleasure in such a good cause. I'll write to Livia this evening . . . oh, thank you, Hester." She smiled at the maid, who staggered under a laden tea tray that she placed on a low table in front of Aurelia.

"Miss Mavis made a seedcake, ma'am, an' there's a lardy cake if any o' the ladies would like some."

Lardy cake was a rich and somewhat greasy confection popular in the north of England. Aurelia thought her guests would probably not find it to their taste. "The seedcake will be sufficient, thank you, Hester." She poured tea, handing the cups to Hester to pass around. "Will you take a slice of cake, Lady Severn?"

"No, I thank you, Lady Farnham." The lady leaned forward, the ostrich feathers lavishly adorning her bonnet wafting over her eyes. She dropped her voice conspiratorially. "I find the seeds stick in my teeth, and one spends all afternoon and evening trying to suck them out without anyone noticing."

There were sympathetic murmurs in response interrupted by voices from the hall. "Ah, you have more callers," Cecily said gaily. "We always say how popular you are, the ladies of Cavendish Square as we used to call you when you all lived here. Oh, it seems so long ago."

"It does, doesn't it?" chimed in Nell from the now opened door. "See whom I've brought for you, Aurelia. Nick and David have just returned from a week of shocking dissipation in Brighton and are in sore need of rest and recuperation among the fleshpots of London."

"Such nonsense you talk, Nell," Sir Nicolas Petersham declared with the ease of old friendship. "Aurelia, ladies . . ." He bowed to the company. "I beg you will take no notice of such calumny."

"Yes, indeed, souls of propriety . . . always . . . you know us, Ellie." Lord David Foster bowed over Aurelia's hand. "You are in looks, my dear ma'am, if I may say so," he added softly.

Aurelia smiled. She was accustomed to David's extravagant compliments, but they did no harm to one's self-esteem. "Flatterer," she accused lightly. "But pray don't stop."

He chuckled, kissing her hand again. "No flattery, I swear it." He turned to pay his respects to the other ladies. "Lady Langton, about your charitable business as usual, I daresay?" He took a seat on her other side.

Aurelia dispensed tea, and when everyone seemed at ease, she rose from the sofa and crossed the room to rescue Nell, who was smiling bravely through a minute description of the valetudinarian Lady Severn's latest, most intimate health crisis. Aurelia was about to move the conversation into a different channel when Morecombe intoned from the door, "That other gentleman is 'ere again, mum."

Aurelia caught Nell's startled look at this but smiled brightly, turning to greet the newcomer. "Colonel Falconer, how kind of you to call."

"How kind of you to allow me to do so, Lady Farnham." He stepped into the room, his eyes moving swiftly around the assembled company, seeming to take special note of each one, before he acknowledged Cornelia with a bow and a murmured "Lady Bonham, your servant."

"Colonel." She gave him her hand. "Are you acquainted with Lady Severn?"

"I have not had the pleasure," he said, bowing over the lady's plump hand. "Your servant, Lady Severn."

She put up her glass and regarded him curiously. "New to town, are you?"

"I've been abroad for the last few years. At present I am staying with my aunt, Lady Broughton."

"Oh, you must be the nephew she says she never sees," her ladyship declared, shaking a reproachful finger, a somewhat incongruously coquettish smile on her rouged countenance. "You've been neglecting your relatives shamelessly, sir."

"I hope to make amends, ma'am." He bowed over her heavily beringed fingers, giving her a charming smile before turning slightly to where Aurelia stood just behind him.

"Do you care for tea, Colonel?" she inquired. "Or is

it perhaps too bland a drink for a dashing soldier home from the wars?" Her voice was light and teasing, but her eyes were serious enough as she met his gaze.

"Oh, yes, Ellie, give the man a glass of something from Prokov's excellent cellars," David declared. "I own I'd be glad of a drop of port . . . how about you, Nick?"

"Tea's not really to my taste," Nick said. He came over to Greville, his usual frank and friendly smile on his lips. "Falconer, I don't believe we're acquainted."

"No, I'm relatively new to town," Greville said, shaking hands.

"But Harry knows him," Cornelia chimed in with a chuckle, "and vouches for him. So you may safely know him."

"Well, that's all right then," David said with a mock sigh of relief. "May I fetch you a glass of Prokov's most excellent port, Falconer?"

"Please," Greville said.

"Yes, help yourselves." Aurelia gestured to the sideboard with a soft laugh. "Alex won't begrudge you."

"When do you expect the prince and princess to return to London?" Greville asked, drawing her slightly aside.

"Not for about two months," she replied, aware of the warmth of his fingers on her elbow, wondering why he was somehow separating them from the others. Or giving that impression, at least.

His eyes were fixed upon her, his mouth curved in a warm smile, as he said, "I do hope you will walk with me in the park one afternoon, Lady Farnham. Now that the evenings are growing longer."

Very well, Aurelia thought, *let's see if I can play the game.* She offered him her own warm smile and said with convincingly soft sincerity, "I should be delighted, Sir Greville. Do pray call upon me."

"If I suggest tomorrow, would you consider me incorrigibly importunate?" he asked, his hand still on her elbow, his tone lightly flirtatious.

Aurelia was aware of other eyes upon them. The eyes of her friends, who would be most interested not so much in the exchange itself, as in its manner. "I should consider you delightfully attentive, sir," she responded with a creditably flirtatious chuckle of her own. *Not so hard, after all,* she thought. Then came the reminder that she had not formally agreed to his proposal. But after this little play, he would know her answer. In truth, after hours of wrestling with the decision, she couldn't see how to refuse. It was a small enough service for her country, and she couldn't ignore the fact that she would be paid for it. Morally and practically, there really was only one road to follow.

"Port, Falconer." David handed Greville a glass, his tone a little chilly, a question in his eyes. Greville instantly let his hand fall from Aurelia's elbow and took the glass with a smile of thanks. He moved away with a murmur of excuse.

"You seem to know the fellow well enough, Ellie," David said, his eyes following him.

"No, not so well. He was a friend of my husband's however." Her smile was constrained, her voice dropping. "He called on me earlier today because he thought Frederick would have expected it of him."

"Oh, I see . . . I'm sorry. It must be difficult for you."

"It's been a long time, David," she said, looking up at him. "The reminder was a little painful at first, but now I find a comfort in the company of one who knew Frederick so well."

"Of course. Any way I can be of service, Ellie . . . you know that."

"Thank you, David. You're a good friend." She smiled and walked away to tend to her guests.

The company drifted away in twos and threes soon after, but Greville lingered in the hall, giving the impression of being on the moment of departure, about to follow the last guest, but when the door was finally closed, he was still there.

"You have an answer for me?" he asked quietly as they stood in the salon amid the detritus of teacups, cake crumbs, and port glasses.

"It seems my duty to help you if I can," she said simply.

Greville regarded her in silence for a long moment, and she had the uncomfortable feeling that he could see into her mind. Then he said, "I am glad you feel that way. Many people will be grateful for your assistance."

She shook her head in a vague disclaimer. "How do we proceed?"

He matched the businesslike clip in her voice as he replied, "We need to spend a few days alone. There are some essential skills you have to learn, and they're not the kind of skills that can be learned in Cavendish Square or its ilk."

"I have a daughter," she stated drily. "That won't be possible."

"It must be," he said with quiet insistence. "You must find a way to extricate yourself from her for five days."

Aurelia stared at him, frowning. "Is it really necessary?"

"I wouldn't say it was if it were not," he stated with the same quiet insistence.

For the first time Aurelia had a sense of what it would mean to work for this man. He would be controlling every step of the play, and she would have little or no say in the moves. But then, what else had she really expected? She knew nothing about this business, but if she was going to do it, she might as well do it properly.

While she still hesitated, Greville suggested, "Your daughter already has lessons at Mount Street. Could she stay for a few nights?"

"Yes, of course she could," Aurelia said, flattening her fingertips against her cheeks as she frowned in thought. "My difficulty is finding a reason for needing her to do so."

Greville tilted his head to one side, a quizzical gleam in his eye. "I'm sure you can think of something convincing." He reached for her hands, drawing them away from her face. He held them lightly in his as he looked at her closely, once again seeming to read her innermost thoughts. "We will work well together, Aurelia." It was a statement of intent. "And I look forward to it."

She pulled back a little, but then let her hands lie in his clasp. But she made no response to his statement and after a moment he said, "Be ready to leave in three days. I'll let you know the arrangements in plenty of time."

"Where am I going?"

"I can't tell you that."

"And how is anyone to contact me then?"

"They can't . . . they may not."

"I have a daughter," Aurelia repeated.

"Five days, that's all it will be. Franny will be well taken care of in Mount Street for five days."

She was doing this largely for Frederick, Aurelia thought with a resurgence of anger. But Frederick hadn't had to worry about smoothing the path for *his* disappearances. He hadn't had to trouble himself with concerns for his daughter . . . or his wife.

"I'll manage," she said grimly, withdrawing her hands from the light clasp.

"Of course you will." He reached up and touched the point of her chin with his fingertip. When she jerked her head in surprise, he said with a half smile, "A little familiarity is generally considered a necessary component of a romantic interest, my dear."

"Maybe so. But perhaps we could confine such a component to the public arena, where I can understand its necessity."

At that he chuckled softly. He bowed and turned to the door. "I'll see myself out. You'll receive instructions very soon."

Aurelia said nothing as he left the room. She stood in meditative silence, one fingertip pressed absently to the point of her chin where she could fancy she still felt the warm pressure of his playful touch.

Three days later her instructions arrived in the form of a succinct note. *The Bell, Woodstreet, Cheapside, eight a.m. tomorrow.* Aurelia read and reread it, looking in vain for some hidden meaning. There was no signature, no salutation. Not that she needed either to know its provenance. And there was definitely no hidden meaning. It was a straightforward instruction. Of course, she reflected, in the colonel's line of work written communication would naturally be kept to a minimum, and as anonymous as possible. And presumably the correct response in the circumstances would be to destroy it instantly. She crumpled the note and threw it in the fire, half laughing at herself for entering into the spirit of this enterprise.

She put on her pelisse and bonnet and set off to Mount Street, hoping to find Nell at home. She caught Nell on the doorstep, just leaving the house.

"Nell, I need to ask you a favor," she said, hoping she sounded convincingly flustered. She'd decided a sudden emergency would be easier to explain and require little detail, whereas a carefully thought-out story ahead of time would be much harder to stick to.

"Of course, love, anything." Cornelia looked concerned. "Come in."

"This won't take a minute," Aurelia said swiftly. "You're going out, I don't want to keep you."

"Oh, I'm not going anywhere special," Cornelia declared with a dismissive wave of her hand. "I was going to try on a hat, if you must know. A purely frivolous errand. Come in, we can't talk on the front steps." She turned and retraced her steps to the front door, banging the knocker once.

The door opened with enviable speed, Aurelia thought, as she followed her friend inside, acknowledging Hector, the butler, who bowed her in with a murmur of greeting.

She followed Nell into her sitting room at the rear of the hall. "You remember my elderly aunt in Bristol. . . ? Well, I've just received a letter from her companion. Apparently Aunt Baxter is seriously ill. Matty seemed to imply that she could be on her deathbed, but she's something of an alarmist. But just in case I think I need to go for a few days. I *am* her only living relative."

"Of course you must go, love," Nell said, pouring two glasses of sherry. "And of course Franny and Daisy shall stay here for as long as necessary."

Aurelia smiled her relief. She hadn't even needed to express the request. "I'll hire a post chaise and leave early tomorrow morning. If it's really all right, I'll send Daisy later this afternoon with Franny's clothes and the little things she can't do without. She won't sleep without that scruffy rag doll."

Aurelia was talking swiftly, almost breathlessly, and her agitation was not feigned. This tangle of lies tripping off her tongue was making her horribly uncomfortable. Even more so as she saw how readily her friend believed her. She took a restorative sip from her sherry glass. "I'll pop up to the schoolroom now and explain it to Franny."

"I'll come with you."

Much to Aurelia's relief, Franny seemed quite unperturbed by the news of her mother's imminent departure. The prospect of staying with Stevie and Susannah had all three children dancing excitedly around the schoolroom, and Aurelia had to beg for a farewell kiss. She left the schoolroom with Cornelia, saying as they reached the hall, "Thank you again, Nell. I must hurry home and make preparations. Daisy will come around five o'clock."

"Of course," Cornelia said, accompanying her friend to the door. "As a matter of interest, have you seen that Colonel Falconer recently?"

"Not since that afternoon, a few days ago," Aurelia said with a creditable imitation of carelessness. "Why?"

"He seemed very attentive that afternoon." Nell regarded her friend with a slight smile. "We all noticed it. David said he'd known Frederick."

"Yes, he'd met him once or twice before Trafalgar," Aurelia said, aware that her palms were growing moist.

"I don't think they were friends particularly. I did ask him if he'd met Stephen too, but he said not." *How she hated lying, but how easily the fabrication tripped off her tongue.*

Cornelia gave a casual nod of acceptance and leaned in to kiss her friend good-bye. "Good luck with Aunt Baxter."

"Thank you." Aurelia hurried away with a bright wave of farewell, feeling guilty but relieved. And somewhere amidst that guilt and relief lurked a quiver of excitement.

Chapter Seven

T HE NEXT MORNING AURELIA slipped out of the house just after dawn and walked briskly towards Wigmore Street in search of a hackney. She carried only a small cloakbag. It was a brisk morning, overcast, a touch of frost on the grass in the square garden, and she drew her fur-trimmed pelisse closer around her and changed hands on her bag so that the other hand could warm up in her fur muff.

No one had been around to see her leave. She had told Morecombe the previous evening that she would be going to the country for a few days on urgent family business, and the old man had shown no curiosity. Aurelia hadn't expected him to. If he bothered to answer the doorknocker in her absence, he would tell any visitors that Lady Farnham had gone out of town and he had no idea when she would be back.

As luck would have it, a hackney was standing at the

curb as she turned onto Wigmore Street, and when she raised a hand to call him over, the jarvey clicked up his horses and brought the conveyance up beside her.

"Where to, ma'am?" His voice was muffled in the thick folds of his woolen scarf, and the horses' breath steamed in the cold air as they shifted their hooves on the cobbles.

"The Bell, Woodstreet, Cheapside," she instructed.

The man peered down at her uncertainly. "The Bell . . . Cheapside . . . you sure, ma'am?"

"Positive," she said briskly, opening the door to the carriage. "As quickly as you can, if you please."

"Right y'are." He still sounded doubtful, but once she'd slammed the door on herself, he cracked his whip and the horses moved forward at a brisk pace.

Aurelia settled back on the worn and cracked leather squabs. She sympathized with the jarvey's surprise. Ladies accustomed to the elegance of Mayfair did not in general frequent Cheapside.

But neither did they head into the unknown on a clandestine adventure at the behest of a man they barely knew, she reflected wryly. But then Mayfair ladies did not in general find they'd been married to a man they barely knew either. She closed her eyes, trying to conjure Frederick's presence as he'd been when she last saw him. He and Stephen had been filled with the fever of patriotism, the passionate need to serve their country as they'd stood so proudly on the deck of the man-of-war as it steamed out of Portsmouth harbor down the river to the quiet waters of the Solent. She could hear the drums and pipes of the marine band playing them away and felt again that vicarious thrill that had touched her that afternoon, raising goose prickles on her skin, her eyes glazing over with a mist of emotion.

It was her turn to do her part now.

The hackney swayed sharply as it turned a corner, and the iron wheels bumped unevenly over the cobbles before it came to a halt. Aurelia drew aside the leather flap that served as a curtain and peered out. They were in the courtyard of an inn.

"'Ere y'are, ma'am. The Bell, Woodstreet. Just as ye asked," the jarvey said a trifle belligerently in case she should accuse him of making a mistake.

"Thank you," she said, alighting from the carriage. "What do I owe you?"

"Sixpence," he said, reaching down a mitten-clad hand.

Aurelia gave him sixpence halfpenny and he gave her a gratified tug of his forelock. "You want I should call the landlord from the inn, ma'am?"

"No, thank you. I can manage quite well." She smiled a dismissal, picked up her cloakbag, and turned resolutely towards the inn.

The back door led directly from the stable courtyard into the taproom. It was crowded, even at this hour, the long benches filled with folk eating breakfast. The sound of a post horn brought instant activity, people leaping up from the benches, cramming last mouthfuls, draining ale tankards, as they surged to the yard.

It was a staging inn, Aurelia finally realized. The public stages came in here from all over the countryside and left again with full complements. Well, she reflected, it was certainly the ideal place to be anonymous. No one she knew would ever dream of frequenting such a place. *And where was the colonel?*

She looked around, searching for his tall, large frame somewhere in the crowd. He would be easy to spot with that commanding presence, the restrained elegance of his dress. Perhaps he wasn't here yet. Maybe he'd been held up. Maybe he wasn't coming . . . the last thought brought a stab of disappointment that surprised her.

The taproom was quieter now as the stagecoach passengers departed. Others were waiting for the next stage to wherever they were going, but the initial chaos had quietened. Aurelia went back to the door and stood looking out into the stable courtyard. He would come in this way. Either by carriage or on horseback he would turn in beneath the archway from the street into the yard.

Then she felt her scalp prickle and a current of excitement ran up her spine. He was here, and of course he wouldn't look as she was expecting him to look. The man was a spy. He was on a mission. Colonel, Sir Greville Falconer was not going to stroll under the archway into the yard. He would be somebody else.

Slowly she turned back to the taproom and looked around, this time with new eyes. She saw him almost immediately. He was hunched over an ale mug at a table close to the inglenook. An old cloak trailed on the ground, gnarled hands in fingerless gloves curled around the tankard. A greasy cap was pulled down low on his forehead. But she knew him immediately.

Quietly she crossed the sawdust-littered floor. She didn't greet him, however, merely took a seat on the bench opposite and surveyed him. Those deep gray eyes were unmistakable, and she wondered if he ever needed to disguise them and, if so, how he did it.

"Well done," he said softly. "I expected it to take you rather longer." He reached into the pocket of his stained waistcoat and took out a key. "Go up to the second floor . . . the second door on the left." He slid the key across the table. "Dress yourself in the clothes in the armoire. I'll wait here."

Aurelia took the key. Part of her wanted to laugh at this cloak-and-dagger game, but the strange flutter of alarm in her gut told her it was definitely not a laughing matter. There was only one explanation. Greville Falconer didn't want anyone to know where he was. There were people in this world who wanted him dead, Frederick had said as much. It seemed such a dramatic thought, but drama had entered her life with a grand fanfare when she'd learned the truth about Frederick.

Without a word she rose from the table and made for the staircase at the corner of the taproom. It twisted and creaked its way to the second floor, where she found the door, fitted the key in the lock, and turned it. The door swung open onto a small chamber, lit by a smelly tallow candle on a rickety table under the window. A sullen fire smoldered in the grate, but she was grateful for what little warmth it gave as she surveyed the contents of the armoire and contemplated removing her own warm garments in favor of the worn serge dress and cloak hanging in the cupboard.

Was he testing her again with this disguise? Or was it truly necessary?

If it *was* necessary, she thought with another flutter of alarm, she was getting into deeper waters than she had bargained for. She'd agreed to help ease his social path, not racket around the countryside dressed in rags pretending to be someone she wasn't. But she found some comfort in the knowledge that in this disguise no one would recognize her. She held up the clothes with a grimace of distaste. They seemed clean enough, for which she was grateful, and she could keep her own underclothes and woolen stockings. She had to change her boots, however, for a pair of down-at-heel and ill-fitting leather clogs with paste buckles.

She made the transformation as rapidly as she could, shivering the while. She thrust her own clothes into her cloakbag, reluctantly relinquishing the pelisse. Clearly, the rest of this journey would be accomplished by public stage, with no hot bricks to alleviate the cold. The awful thought occurred that he might be expecting them to ride as outside passengers on the roof.

That would be too much, Aurelia decided, setting off downstairs again. She had enough money of her own to insist on an inside seat, and if it upset the colonel, or whatever he was in his present guise, then so be it. Heartened by this somewhat militant frame of mind, she reentered the taproom. He was still sitting where she'd left him, tankard and a plate of bacon in front of him.

She took a seat opposite again. "I think it's your turn to provide breakfast, sir."

For answer he turned and growled in the general direction of a potboy who was scurrying between the tables. "Bread an' bacon do ye?" the colonel demanded of the wench sitting opposite him.

"Aye, if'n you please, sir," she returned with a faint country accent to match his own. Rather convincing she thought. If she could manage to see her part as a game, in a competition of some kind, it would provide distance and maybe she would stop envisaging dangers where there were none.

He waved at his plate when the lad dodged across to them. "Same again fer the wife."

The boy went off and Greville looked at Aurelia, one eyebrow slightly lifted. "Quite the actress you are."

For some reason the compliment pleased her, but she did her best to hide it. "Does it surprise you?"

"A certain amount. I wasn't sure how good you'd be, but I see I need have no fears."

"And if I was terrible, what would you have done?" She regarded him closely.

He took a deep draft of his ale and set the tankard down. "If you had not managed to work out who I was, or if you had in any way balked at the costume, or the part you must play, I would have sent you back to Cavendish Square," he stated flatly. "I have no intention of endangering you in any way, or of making you uncomfortable. Not everyone is suited to this work."

"I see." She drummed her fingers on the stained table. He was telling her that she could still back out, even now. But if she didn't, then Aurelia knew there would be no turning back, because she would not allow herself to do so. Did she have sufficient courage to see this through?

She drew in a sharp breath. "So, who are we?"

If he felt relief, he gave so sign, merely answered, "A poor tenant farmer and his wife coming back from London. You've been staying with your sister, helping her with her children during her confinement, and I came to fetch you back because the chickens and the kitchen garden are going to rack and ruin in your absence, and I've enough on my plate with my own farmwork and the hours I have to put in on the landlord's fields." His voice was his own, but so soft as to be almost impossible to hear outside the immediate area around their table. "Clear enough?"

"Clear enough. But, poor or not, we'd better not be traveling as outside passengers."

At that he grinned, a quick flash of white teeth and

a laughing glint in his eyes. "No, ma'am, that won't be necessary. We may be humble folk, but I've coin enough for an inside seat."

She nodded, but said nothing as the lad came up with a hunk of barley bread on a plate piled high with fried bacon, and a tankard of ale, and set both in front of her.

"I suppose coffee is out of the question," she murmured when the boy had gone off.

"Remember your part," he admonished, taking another swig of ale.

Aurelia shrugged, broke off a piece of bread, piled it with bacon, and took a large mouthful. It was surprisingly good, and so was the ale. The bacon was salty, the ale thirst-quenching. "Where is our farm situated?" she inquired, wiping her mouth with the back of her hand in the absence of any napkinlike refinements.

"Barnet . . . it's only a day's coach journey."

"I'm relieved." She took another sip of ale. "And our exact destination? Or am I to be kept in the dark about that?"

"I see no reason why you should be," he said mildly. "We are going to a farm . . . you will not, however, be expected to assume the duties of a farmer's wife any more than I will be bringing in the cows from the corn."

He pushed back from the table as the clock in the yard struck the half hour. "The stage will be here in five minutes. It might be wise to find the outhouse. I believe it's at the end of the kitchen garden."

He swung a leg over the bench and stood up. "I'll settle up here."

Aurelia nodded and rose to her feet. The outhouse of a coaching station was not an appealing proposition, but it was probably a wise precaution. The public stage kept to a schedule and wouldn't stop to order. Or so she assumed.

The experience was every bit as unpleasant as she'd expected, and she couldn't help a flash of envy when she saw Greville emerge from behind one of the stable buildings in the innyard. He had had no need to wrestle with skirt and petticoats over a stinking hole in a crusted wooden plank.

The coach was in the yard, passengers piling in as the coachman and ostlers fastened baggage to the roof. "Quick," Greville said in an urgent whisper. In the same breath he lifted Aurelia up into the carriage with a deft maneuver that left a stout dame with a birdcage muttering imprecations.

Aurelia saw the point immediately. There was a single corner seat left by the window on the far side. She took it, refusing to consider for a second whether someone else had a prior claim. Greville had stood back with a courteous hand to help the stout woman and her birdcage into the coach. She huffed, but took the seat next to Aurelia, settling her skirts and her birdcage.

"Pretty bird . . . is it a parrot?" Aurelia inquired, trying to remember the slight rustic twang.

"Bless you, no, m'dear. 'Tis a parakeet," the woman

declared, suddenly all smiles. "Belongs to my Jake . . . he's on a ship, an' he brought 'im back from Jamaica." She pushed her fingers through the bars of the cage. "Eh, birdie . . . birdie . . . say good mornin' to the lady."

"Does he really talk?" Aurelia was fascinated despite the disconcerting sense of living in a dream. In her wildest fantasies she would never have seen herself on a public coach chatting amiably with a peasant woman about a caged bird.

"Never stops when 'e gets the mood on 'im, bless 'im. So where's 'ome, m'dear?" Her neighbor wriggled comfortably into her seat and seemed settled for a cozy chat.

Greville had climbed in last and accepted perforce one of the middle seats. He leaned back, arms folded, and immediately closed his eyes. To Aurelia's astonishment he seemed to be sound asleep before the carriage had clattered and rattled through the archway onto the street.

He stayed asleep, unmoving, breathing silently and rhythmically while the coach left the town streets.

"Eh, I can't stand the racket. Can you, dearie?" Aurelia's neighbor inquired comfortably as the noise of the streets faded and they began the climb to Hampstead Heath. "Give me the peace o' the countryside, eh?"

"Aye," Aurelia agreed, both weary and wary. "All that racket gives me the headache."

"Me too, dearie." The woman patted Aurelia's knee. "So what took ye t' the city, then?"

"My sister." Aurelia produced the required story, and as she did so, she became aware that Greville was wide-awake, although his eyes remained closed. Yet she would have sworn he'd been sound asleep until she'd begun to spin her narrative. Presumably he could hear in his sleep. He could probably see behind closed eyelids, too, she reflected somewhat sardonically. She wouldn't put anything past him.

The long day wore on. They crossed Hampstead Heath with much anxious mutterings about highwaymen, the parakeet kept up an endless succession of whistles, Greville kept his eyes closed, and sometimes Aurelia was certain he was sound asleep, and at others he would be wide-awake . . . if the movement of the coach changed, if the speed altered. She began to play a game. Every once in a while she would say something that went a little adrift from the script, just a small comment that no one would really notice, but every time, Greville awoke. She could see it in the slight stiffening of his shoulders, a tiny flutter of his eyelids, even though his breathing didn't change.

Fascinating . . . but also enviable, because he was most definitely sleeping the rest of the time, even if he was sleeping like a cat with a secondary sense to alert him to danger. And Aurelia could not imagine sleeping in the miserable discomfort of this crowded, jouncing vehicle, with a whistling parakeet, and a fellow passenger eating pickled onions, and her neighbor who produced a smoked-eel pie that she generously offered to share.

Faintly Aurelia refused the generosity and closed her own eyes. Sleep was not forthcoming, but eventually the coach drove through a village and turned into a coaching yard. It was midafternoon. Ostlers raced forward to change the horses.

"This is Barnet . . . this is Barnet . . . ," the coachman intoned. "'Alf an 'our, ladies an' gennelmen. Get yer victuals 'ere. Next stop Watford."

Greville uncurled himself and staggered as stiffly as his fellow passengers out of the coach. Except that Aurelia, as she accepted his hand to the cobbles, could see that he was not in the least bit cramped and was enviably rested. She resisted the urge to wince as her own cramped muscles objected.

"What now?" The spirit of adventure was lacking in her voice.

"The worst is over."

"You relieve my mind."

"Come." He picked up her cloakbag, took her arm, and led her towards the inn.

The establishment was as crowded as the one in Cheapside had been, and their fellow passengers surged into the taproom calling for ale and food. "Are we staying here?" Aurelia asked, trying not to show how the prospect dismayed her.

"No," Greville replied, relieving her mind. "Just long

enough for me to find a pony and trap somewhere. Sit down here." He propelled her towards a spindly chair in a dark corner of the taproom and set the cloakbag down on the floor. "I'll order some refreshment."

"I'd rather stand," Aurelia said. "I've been sitting cramped for an eternity, I need to stretch my legs."

"As you wish." He turned and plunged into the gabbling throng. He held himself more upright now, Aurelia noticed. Presumably he felt fairly safe from recognition in an ordinary coaching inn so far from town.

She rolled her shoulders to get the cricks out and paced the floor for a few minutes until Greville came back with two overflowing tankards. "Porter," he declared, setting them down on the table by the chair. "Do you a world of good."

Aurelia surveyed the dark brown contents of the tankard with disfavor. She associated the drink with laborers and farmhands, which was, of course, entirely appropriate to her present guise. She lifted the tankard and took a cautious sip. It was bitter and tasted of burned malt.

"It's an acquired taste," Greville said, watching her with amusement as he drank his own with evident enthusiasm.

"I'm not sure I wish to acquire it." She set the tankard down. "Besides, I have other, more pressing needs." She turned and went reluctantly in search of what would inevitably be another noxious privy.

When she returned through the stable yard, Greville,

holding her cloakbag, was talking to an ostler. He raised a beckoning hand when he saw her and turned away from the stable hand as she came over to him. "The landlord has a gig for hire, so if you're ready, we'll be on our way."

"More than ready. How far must we go?"

"Five miles . . . an hour, perhaps." He looked over to where the ostler was emerging from one of the outbuildings, leading an emaciated nag. "On second thoughts, maybe two, if he's intending to put that beast between the traces."

It seemed that he was. In ten minutes Aurelia was ensconced on the seat of the landlord's gig, Greville beside her, holding the nag's reins. He clicked his tongue and the horse moved forward, pulling the light, two-wheeled carriage onto the post road.

A stage coach was bowling down the road towards the inn, and Greville yanked the gig to the side of the road just in time as the heavy vehicle clattered past, the postilion blowing his horn.

"The sooner we get off the highway the better," Greville muttered. "I'm fairly certain we turn left at the crossroads up ahead."

"How do you know where we're going? I thought you'd been out of England for years."

"So I have. But I still know the countryside."

"And you know people around here?" Aurelia pressed.

"That would seem the obvious conclusion."

"Yes, it would," she agreed with a snap. "But since you claimed to have been in the country only a few days when you descended on my doorstep, after an absence of quite a few years, I wonder how you've managed to arrange for this country sojourn . . . or whatever you wish to call it."

He glanced sideways at her with an amused smile. "You're fatigued," he said as if soothing a fractious child. "It's hardly surprising after such a day."

"No, it's not," she returned, exasperated. Annoyance took the edge off both fatigue and unease, she discovered. "But my question is not unwarranted."

"True enough. It's been four days since I last saw you, and much can be accomplished in four days, as I'm sure you understand."

She left it at that and drew the horse blanket, which true to its name smelled strongly of horse, up over her knees, trying to make herself comfortable on the narrow bench perched over the iron wheels.

"We're going to a farm in a little village called Monken Hadley," he told her, turning the nag to the left at the crossroads.

"And what are we going to be doing there?"

"I'm going to teach you some of the basic skills of my trade. Communication in particular."

"Why couldn't we do that in London?"

"Because we will have to spend a lot of time together, and I rather imagine that would draw unwelcome attention in town . . . a widow living alone in the constant company of a bachelor colonel?" He raised an interrogative eyebrow, and she had to concede the point.

"Are there people living on this farm?"

"Certainly . . . very *discreet* people," he said cheerfully. "They were tenant farmers on my father's estates until they came into a small windfall and were able to buy their own farm."

Aurelia said nothing to this, interesting though she found it. Surely someone who'd known him as a child would have some enlightening insights to offer if gently prodded. She was quite good at gaining people's confidence and there was a great deal she'd like to know about Colonel, Sir Greville Falconer.

They went the rest of the way without further conversation. Greville seemed content whistling softly between his teeth as he guided the nag down the narrow country lanes. Aurelia huddled into the horse blanket and watched the countryside go by. She didn't know the county of Essex at all and was struck by how flat it seemed after the hills and forest of her native Hampshire. She was used to the salt tang of the sea as well when in the countryside, but here there was only the loamy smell of the turned fields on either side of the lane. Flocks of starlings chattered, rooks circled cawing in the treetops preparing to nest as afternoon yielded to the early dusk.

They drove through several tiny hamlets where lamplight began to show in cottage windows. A herd of cows being driven for the evening milking blocked the narrow lane at one point, and Greville drew back on the reins and brought the nag to a halt. He seemed untroubled by the delay, which surprised Aurelia. She would have expected this man of action to be impatient about moving on to the next stage of his plan.

"Hungry?" The question, breaking their strangely companionable silence, startled her.

She considered the matter. "As it happens, I'm ravenous. We haven't eaten anything since breakfast."

"No. But if you look under the seat, there should be a basket. I asked the innkeeper to provide something in case we were delayed on the road."

A man of action who thought ahead. Aurelia reached under the bench and drew forth a small hamper. She put it on her lap and opened it. "Pork pies," she pronounced with satisfaction. "And apples."

"Will it do, d'you think?" He glanced at her with that same smile, and again she felt a little frisson of excitement that could have nothing at all to do with sitting on the bench of a gig at a standstill in a country lane behind a sea of ambling cows.

For answer, she handed him one of the pies and took a hearty bite of the other. "Yes," she pronounced. "It will do very well indeed."

"It'll hold off starvation until we get to Hadley. Mary will have supper ready and waiting, but I expect you'll want to wash off the dust first."

"Are you always this considerate of your partner's needs?" she inquired through another mouthful of pie.

He shrugged. "When I can be . . . although it's not

always necessary." That flashing smile again. "I don't often have female partners."

"So this consideration is because of my sex?"

"Why not?"

"Why not indeed. I'm not too proud to appreciate it."

"Good."

Aurelia lapsed into silence, eating her pie and apple, letting her body flow with the rhythm of the gig on the uneven lane, falling into a kind of trance that was not quite sleep, but refreshing nevertheless.

"Here we are at last." Greville gestured with his whip to a cluster of lights up ahead. "Journey's end."

Or rather, journey's beginning, Aurelia reflected. She had no idea what the next few days would hold, but for the moment her uncertainty held no fear. Something about Greville Falconer gave her confidence, a sense of security, and a sense of rightness in what she had agreed to do.

As Greville drew rein in a small yard behind a thatched-roof farmhouse, a young boy bounded out of the house, a path of light from the open door streaming ahead of him.

"I'll take yer 'orse, sir," he cried eagerly, running up to seize the harness.

"Thank you, lad." Greville tossed the reins onto the nag's back and jumped down. He reached up a hand to help Aurelia alight.

She stepped down rather stiffly onto the cobbled yard, murmuring, "I am so weary of traveling." Presumably a real spy would never complain about such a mundane hardship, but she didn't really care at present. She was cold, stiff, and hungry despite the pork pie.

"Ah, there you are, Sir Greville . . . madam, you must be perished with the cold. Come you in now by the fire." A stout woman in a flowered apron hurried out of the open door and across the yard. She bobbed a curtsy and blushed fiery red when Greville took her hand and kissed her weather-roughened cheek.

"No need for ceremony, Mary," he said warmly. "Aurelia, this is Mistress Mary Masham, who has known me almost from the cradle. . . . Mary, this is Lady Farnham."

Aurelia came forward, hand outstretched. "It's a pleasure to meet you, Mistress Masham. I own it's been a long and tedious day."

"Aye, I can believe it, ma'am. Come in now and we'll soon have you comfortable again." Mistress Masham bustled ahead of them into a large, stone-flagged kitchen dominated by a long deal table and a massive range from whence came the most enticing aromas.

A man, as stout as Mistress Masham, sat at the deal table, a tankard in front of him. He was whittling a piece of wood, his large, rather stubby hands wielding a small knife with incongruous delicacy. He looked up as the newcomers came into the kitchen and nodded a silent greeting before returning his attention to his task.

"That's my man, Bert," Mistress Masham declared. "He don't say much, but he's a good man."

Bert made no response to this encomium, and Aurelia wasn't sure how to respond herself. She glanced at Greville, who said simply, "Evening, Bert."

"Evenin', sir." Bert didn't look up from his whittling.

And that seemed to be that. Aurelia wondered absently what the woman must think of her visitors' strange garb, but Mary didn't appear to have noticed anything out of the ordinary. She was ladling the fragrant contents of a saucepan into a pewter bowl.

"There now, a goodly drop o' posset will do ye the power of good."

Aurelia cast off the old cloak with a sigh of relief and took the warm porringer that the woman handed her.

"Thank you, Mistress Masham." Gratefully Aurelia buried her nose in the steamy fragrance of the warm spiced wine.

"Eh, *Mary's* good enough for me," the woman said comfortably. "There's not many folks around 'ere that calls me anythin' else. . . . Now, Master Greville, will ye take the posset, or would you rather a pot of Bert's strong ale?"

Aurelia hid a smile. *Sir* had yielded to the *master* of Greville's boyhood in a very short time. Greville didn't appear to notice the change as he said he'd settle for Bert's strong ale.

Bert rose heavily from the table and disappeared into

a scullery, reappearing with a foaming tankard that he set down on the table with a satisfied thump. "There," he declared, and returned to his seat opposite. Greville, with a word of thanks, straddled the bench as if he was quite at home in this kitchen and raised the tankard to his lips.

"Ye'll be wantin' a nice wash in some 'ot water, I'll be bound," Mary now said, turning back to Aurelia. "You come along a'me, m'dear, everything's ready for you. . . . Bring the posset." She picked up Aurelia's cloakbag and bustled to the door of the kitchen, and Aurelia, rather reluctant to leave the warm, cheerful room, followed with her porringer.

They climbed a narrow staircase rising from a corner of a small, stone-flagged hall. Every piece of furniture was agleam with beeswax, and the scent of lavender oil perfumed the air. Mistress Masham clearly kept an immaculate house.

"Here we are, m'dear." At the top of the stairs, Mary opened a door wide and Aurelia followed her into a square chamber lit by oil lamps and a bright fire in the grate. The hangings were chintz, the colors faded from frequent washing, but they were crisply starched and pressed. The bed coverlet was a patchwork quilt of intricate design, the furniture solid and well crafted. Once again the scents of beeswax and lavender oil filled the warm air.

"Now, there's 'ot water in the ewer." Mary gestured to the marble-topped washstand. "An' I'll pop a bed warmer between the sheets while y'are at supper. Nice an' cozy, you'll be."

"Yes, I will," Aurelia said warmly, looking with longing at the four-poster bed with its piled pillows that were scattered with lavender. An uncomfortable day had certainly ended in a delightful haven.

Chapter Eight

Mary set Aurelia's cloakbag on the chest at the foot of the bed. "Anythin' you want laundered, m'dear? 'Tis wash day tomorrow an' I can do it in a trice."

"Oh, no, thank you," Aurelia said. "Everything's clean . . . except for what I'm wearing." She brushed disdainfully at her serge skirt. "This is somewhat travel-stained."

"Leave it out an' I'll sponge an' press it tomorrow," Mary said, going to the door. She swept one more critical glance around before nodding her satisfaction. "Make yourself at home, m'dear. Supper will be served in the front parlor."

It was on the tip of Aurelia's tongue to say she'd much prefer the kitchen, but then she thought that Mary and her family might find it uncomfortable to eat with their visitors. For all Mary's apparent informality, the social chasm between them remained a fact.

Aurelia opened the cloakbag and took out the gown she'd been wearing that morning before assuming the guise of the tenant farmer's wife. It wasn't too badly creased. She shook it out and laid it on the bed, then unhooked the serge gown. In her chemise and petticoat, she poured hot water on a washcloth and sponged her neck and arms.

A knock at the door startled her. She looked at the door, washcloth poised over the crook of her arm. "Who's there?"

"Greville. May I come in?"

"Just a minute. I'm not dressed."

"Well, put something on quickly. There are a couple of things I would like to discuss before we go down to supper."

Aurelia took the muslin gown from the bed and dropped it over her head, buttoning it swiftly. She smoothed down the skirt and went to open the door. "Come in." She moved away immediately into the middle of the room.

Greville closed the door behind him. For a moment he leaned against it, regarding her closely, his mouth quirked in a half smile. Gleams of light danced in the dark gray eyes as he murmured, "You look quite charming, my dear, not in the least fatigued, despite the rigors of the day."

"Looks are deceiving," she said, attempting to brush aside the compliment. But she felt strangely vulnerable, suddenly acutely aware of the ramifications of what she had agreed to when she'd agreed to help him. It seemed emphasized by their isolation in this country retreat, by her complete separation from the life she knew and understood. In that life, she would not have been in an unfamiliar bedchamber alone with a man who was neither relative nor close friend. She wouldn't have thought twice if Harry or Alex were standing where Greville now stood, but they would not have been looking at her with that gleam in their eyes. It was very much the look of a man seeing a woman in a particular light. And his thoughts were definitely on something other than the mundane.

Her heart started to jump around behind her breastbone, and her fingers quivered slightly. She sat down on the bed, clasping her hands tightly in her lap. "So, what do you wish to talk about?"

"I want to prepare you with the right story." He came farther into the room and took up what seemed to be his favorite position in front of the fire, one arm leaning along the mantel. "Mary knows nothing of my extracurricular activities. She knows me only as Colonel Falconer, and she believes that in that role I am escorting you to Scotland. You are the wife of a fellow officer presently stationed abroad who, when he knew I would be returning to England on leave, asked me to ensure that you reach your Scottish relatives safely."

"Wouldn't she think our arrival in that hired gig, dressed like peasants, somewhat odd in that case?" The conversation was effectively calming Aurelia's overheated blood, and she rose from the bed, going across to the dresser to adjust the loosened pins in her hair.

"She believes your circumstances are somewhat straightened," Greville said, watching. The curve of her arms was deliciously sensual as she raised them over her head, and his breath caught in his throat.

He cleared his throat and continued in a brisk tone, "She knows that's why it's necessary for us to travel by stage, and our somewhat eccentric attire is designed to make us inconspicuous among our fellow travelers. Less likely to be robbed, or hassled in any way. Perfectly reasonable explanation, and I don't believe that she's given the issue a second thought."

"But are we staying here for the full five days?" She twisted a ringlet around her finger, encouraging it to curl tighter, before affixing a pin.

"Yes . . . you find travel debilitating . . . you're recovering from an illness and a few days in the fresh air before we continue our journey will be beneficial."

Aurelia shook her head in mock admiration. "My, my, you have been busy in the last four days. What a fabrication."

He raised his eyebrows. "I should watch that hornet's tongue of yours, if I were you. It could get you into serious trouble one of these days. As it happens, the fabrication, as you call it, is purely for your benefit. I thought you might be more comfortable in this situation with an unimpeachable explanation for it."

Aurelia turned slowly on the dressing stool, her expression a little rueful, as she regarded him with her head slightly tilted. "I'm grateful for your consideration, Colonel."

He bowed in acknowledgment, his eyes uncomfortably penetrating. "I have told you already, Aurelia, that your safety and well-being are of paramount importance. I will do nothing to jeopardize either."

She met his gaze steadily for a moment, then said slowly, "I know that I need your protection and I have no intention of making light of it. I don't have your experience at manipulation and deception, but I have a healthy sense of self-preservation, believe me. For my daughter's sake, if not my own. She's not going to lose two parents to this wretched war."

"Then we understand each other." He moved to the door. "Let us go down to supper."

Aurelia walked past him as he held the door and walked downstairs.

"Ah, there you are." Mary popped out of the kitchen as Aurelia reached the hall. "Go into the front parlor, ma'am. I'll bring supper directly." Aurelia opened a door to the right of the stairs onto a bow-windowed room, comfortable but shabby, warmed by a blazing fire and well lit with oil lamps hanging from the rafters. A round table in the bow window was set for two.

"May I help you carry something, Mary?" Greville asked.

"Bless you, no, Master Greville. Our Billy can lend a hand, and I've taken little Bessie Cobham on . . . you remember the Cobhams, I'm sure . . . anyway, it was doin' them a favor to take the little maid on. They can barely feed the mouths they 'ave, an', while she's small, she can still 'elp out a bit with the light work."

Greville murmured something appropriate and came into the parlor as Mary returned to the kitchen. "Now, I sent down a case of some rather fine claret . . . I wonder if Mary remembered . . . oh, yes, of course she did." With a nod of satisfaction he went to the sideboard, where a bottle of wine and two glasses reposed on a pewter tray.

He opened the bottle and poured wine into the glasses, bringing them both over to the fireplace, where Aurelia stood pleasurably warming her backside.

She took the glass with a nod of thanks.

"To our enterprise." Greville raised his glass in a toast. His eyes gleamed, his crooked mouth curved in a smile as he touched his glass to Aurelia's.

Something about the smile made her heart race again. He was looking at her as if he'd never seen her before. She took a deep draft of her wine and turned with relief to the door as Mary came in bearing a laden tray, accompanied by a young girl of around nine, who carried a bowl of potatoes.

"Set 'em down here, Bessie, there's a good girl," Mary instructed as she began to unload her tray on the table. The rich scents of oxtail and parsley dumplings filled the room.

"Master Greville said as 'ow you needed fatten' up a

bit, m'dear," Mary said comfortably, beginning to serve from the steaming cauldron. "Not been well, I gather. Come an' sit down now."

Aurelia took the chair Greville held for her and surveyed with comical dismay the mountain of food placed before her. Greville flicked an eyebrow in amused comprehension and sat down in front of his own laden platter.

"Now, there's a dish of buttered cabbage an' some braised onions, as well as the spuds," Mary said, gesturing to each dish in turn. "You 'elp yourselves now. We've 'ad ours in the kitchen, so there's no need to save a mouthful. Eat hearty now." She cast one last glance over the table to satisfy herself that all was in order, then bustled out, sweeping little Bessie before her.

"I couldn't possibly eat all this," Aurelia said. "It smells wonderful . . . oh, and it tastes even better," she declared, after a forkful.

"Don't worry, I'll eat what you can't," Greville said, piling potatoes onto his plate and mashing them into the gravy with his fork. "I have a hearty appetite."

"Well, there's rather a lot of you to feed," Aurelia observed, spearing cabbage on her fork.

"Certainly more than there is of you." His eyes darted at her, lingering for a minute on her bosom.

She felt her cheeks warm. Could he be imagining her naked? What an absurd thought. But her nipples hardened beneath the dark gray gaze and hastily she reached for her wineglass. "So what are some of these things I need to learn?" she asked with an attempt at insouciance.

His white smile flashed, then he seemed to compose his features, turn his mind inward, almost to become someone else. "Yes, it's time to get to work," he said rather briskly. "Tomorrow we shall look at some of the methods of communication . . . fairly basic for the most part, I doubt we'll need to become too arcane. But you should know about plain code, and we'll need to develop some simple body signals that will convey information in a crowd."

Aurelia was fascinated. She leaned forward, her food forgotten. "Do you mean at a party, a social event of some kind? What kind of information?"

"Certainly in a public place. Have you finished . . . shall I help you out?" He reached for her plate, and impatiently she pushed it across to him.

"I don't understand why it might be necessary to communicate something secretly to you in public."

He finished transferring the contents of her plate to his own, then added more potatoes and cabbage before saying, "If, for instance, you're talking to someone who is of interest, shall we say, I might need to know if he's getting ready to leave the party, or theater, or wherever. And you may well be in a position to give me that information."

"Oh, I see." Aurelia considered this. "So we'll be operating, if that's the word, most of the time?"

"*All* the time." He leaned across to refill her glass before refilling his own. "Once we begin, my dear Aurelia, you will never not be working." He looked hard at her. "I have no intention of making this sound easy. It is not. All the time you will be on your guard. All the time you will be listening, absorbing, choosing and discarding snippets of conversation as relevant or not. And you will be looking over your shoulder *always*."

Aurelia felt another chill of apprehension, of doubt. *Could she do this? Really, could she do this?* Frederick had done it . . . but Frederick had not had a child to worry about. Frederick had gone swanning on his merry way, knowing that *she* would take care of their child.

Greville continued with his supper, but he was aware almost physically of her thoughts, the doubt that jumped at him across the space separating them. He said nothing. Aurelia had to overcome this herself.

Aurelia waited for him to continue, and when he didn't, she spoke. "I won't do anything that will put Franny in danger. Can you guarantee that won't happen?"

He put down his knife and fork. "I can guarantee nothing, Aurelia. But can you guarantee that one day a hackney won't ride up on the pavement and run you down? Can you guarantee that you won't fall ill?" He reached a hand across the table and laid it over hers. "My dear, there are no guarantees in this world. I can promise, as I already have done, that I will do everything possible to keep you away from danger. And as far as I can see, the work I'll require of you won't bring you anywhere near danger."

"Except that I'll be inextricably associated with *you*," she pointed out, letting her hand rest beneath his, somehow comforted by the warm but undemanding pressure. "You must be known, somewhere, somehow, in the shadows."

He nodded. "Unfortunately that's always a possibility. But I'm fairly confident that Greville Falconer, a colonel in one of His Majesty's cavalry regiments, is not associated with any of my many aliases. My identity changes with every mission, and no one's exposed me yet, to my knowledge. But I will promise you this one thing . . . on my life and my honor. I will protect Franny."

"Even if something happens to me?"

"It won't . . . but, yes, even if anything happens to you, whether it's connected to our business or not. I will take responsibility for Franny's welfare." His smile was somber. "I owe it to Frederick, too."

The door opened and without fuss he withdrew his hand from hers as Mary and the little girl came in. "Finished?" Mary asked as she surveyed the dishes on the table. "I hope you ate something, m'dear. I know Master Greville, he'll 'ave the last morsel off your plate if you looks the other way for a minute."

Mary shook her head reminiscently as she piled the dirty dishes on her tray, handing some to the girl. "Now, there's a good apple crumble to follow. Tasty winter apples what Tom's been a-keepin' in the apple loft, an' a good pitcher of cream from old Bluebell . . . best milk cow we got," she added to Aurelia. "Set you up nicely, it will."

"Yes, I'm sure . . . thank you, Mary," Aurelia responded, wondering how huge the apple crumble would be.

But then Greville would eat what she couldn't, she remembered. Strange that he didn't seem to have any fat on him, his powerful frame was all muscle and long limb. And what would he look like in the skin? Dear God, what was happening to her? Where in the name of all that was good had that thought come from?

Greville said nothing further until the apple crumble and a big bowl of rich, yellow cream was set upon the table, then he refilled their wineglasses and said, "Have you ever fired a gun?"

Aurelia, serving the crumble, dropped the serving spoon back into the dish. "A gun? Of course not . . . why on earth would I?"

He shrugged. "You grew up in the country, it's not impossible that you learned how to shoot pheasant or starlings or some such."

"I'm not a farmer's daughter," she said a shade tartly, passing him a laden plate. "I wasn't taught to wring the necks of chickens either."

"The question wasn't intended as an insult," he protested mildly, ladling cream onto his pudding. "I've known many women who are adept with a firing piece."

"In your line of work, maybe," she said, remembering Frederick's letter. "Derring-do is not a feature of life in the New Forest. I can sail a boat, though, and ride a horse with more than competence. If that's of any use."

"Frederick was a good sailor. Was it a pastime you enjoyed together?"

"As children we all learned, Nell, Stephen, Frederick, Livia, and I, how to sail on the Keyhaven River. Once we were old enough to put up our hair, however, it was pronounced a forbidden pastime for the girls. Most unfair, we thought it." Her eyes were suddenly unaccountably misty, and she blinked hard. They had been happy times, those long, carefree summer days on the river.

"Well, I doubt you'll have a use for the talent in our present enterprise," Greville said, reaching to help himself from the dish of apple crumble.

"But I *will* have a use for the ability to fire a pistol?"

"I hope not, but it's a precaution, so we'll have a few lessons while we're here."

That chill of apprehension once again lifted the fine hairs on her nape. She took a sip of her wine and pushed aside her half-eaten pudding.

"I'm tired," she said abruptly, getting to her feet. "If you'll excuse me, I think I'll go up to bed."

"Of course. It's been a long day." He rose politely and went to open the door for her. As she passed him, he laid a hand lightly on her shoulder.

A shiver ran down her spine at the touch. She stopped and looked up at him. His face seemed to waver before her eyes, to lose its sharp, defining contours. Her eyes were fixed on his mouth, that crookedly sensual curve, and when he lowered his head and kissed her mouth, she knew she had been expecting it. His mouth tasted sweet and spicy, as apples and wine mingled on his tongue, and her belly lurched, her blood surged.

Then it was over. He raised his head, let his hand fall from her shoulder as he moved aside, and with a mute nod, she slipped past him through the door.

Greville closed the door on her departure and returned to the table. He took up his wineglass and stood gazing down into the ruby depths of his goblet. He had made love to many women, in the field and out of it, at work and at play. But he had never once lost his objectivity, however seductive the woman. Except of course for Dorothea, but he had been a mere stripling in the throes of calf love in those heady days. And damn it all, Aurelia Farnham reminded him more and more of Dorothea.

He found her as alluring, exciting, and challenging as he had found his long-ago mistress. But since Dorothea, he had found many other women all those things and still maintained an objective distance. There was one cardinal rule in his trade, trust no one. Never let down your guard.

And yet he could feel that guard slipping a little when

he was with Aurelia. As if his emotions were in danger of dictating the course rather than his head. He could not allow himself to get too close to her.

He drained the contents of his glass and went to a corner cupboard, where he knew he would find a bottle of apple brandy.

Chapter Nine

AURELIA ENTERED HER BEDCHAMBER and closed the door firmly behind her. She leaned against it, gazing around the welcoming firelit chamber. Someone had turned down the quilt and plumped up the pillows, and she could see the shape of a warming pan beneath the covers. Her nightgown had been removed from the cloakbag and was lying across the end of the bed, her slippers ready and waiting on the floor below.

An overwhelming fatigue washed through her. All she wanted to do was curl up in that warm, deep feather bed and close her eyes on everything. Time enough in the morning when she was rested and refreshed to wonder what that kiss had meant, if indeed it had meant anything. It was probably simply intended to underscore the nature of their mission. The world had to be convinced of a romantic attachment between them, and a little practice seemed entirely in keeping with the reason for this clandestine retreat. That was surely all he intended. Or was that all?

She pushed herself away from the door with an effort and turned to lock it.

She awoke to a firm tapping on the door and for a moment lay half-awake, disoriented. Then she heard Greville's voice from the hall outside. "Are you awake, Aurelia? We need to make an early start."

She groaned and struggled up against the pillows, blinking in the pale light of early morning. The grandfather clock in the corner of the bedchamber said six o'clock.

"Aurelia," he called again. "Let me know you're awake."

"I'm awake," she muttered, then said louder, "All right, I'm *awake*."

"Good. Unlock the door now, Mary wants to see to your fire." His tone was light, and enviably energetic. "I'll see you downstairs for breakfast in half an hour."

Aurelia lay back against the pillows again, trying to summon up the necessary will to swing her feet to the floor. Finally she did so and padded to the window. A rime of frost clouded the glass, but she unlatched the window nevertheless. It creaked open reluctantly and she shivered in the blast of crisp air. It was a lot colder in the countryside than in the city.

She went to the door and turned the key, opening it

a crack. Mary stood outside, patiently waiting. "I tried the door, ma'am, not wanting to wake you when I saw to the fire. It was locked so I was going to leave you to your sleep, but Master Greville said as 'ow you needed to be up and about," she explained apologetically as she entered the room. "Eh, good 'eavens, ma'am, what're you doin'?" she exclaimed, scandalized. "You be lettin' all that good warm air out. Close the window, now."

Aurelia obeyed, pulling the window shut with another shiver. "Forgive me, Mary. It looked so pretty outside, I didn't realize how cold it is." She came over to the fire where Mary was piling kindling on the ashy embers. "It's almost spring."

"Not 'ereabouts," Mary declared, lighting a taper and putting it to the kindling. "Not until April, at least not this year. Uncommon harsh winter we 'ad." She pushed back on her knees and stood up with a creak and groan. "'Ard on the joints it is, 'n' all. Right glad I'll be when the summer's 'ere."

"Yes, I'm sure it must be," Aurelia agreed with quick sympathy.

"An' you needs t' be careful, m'dear," Mary stated. "Master Greville told me as 'ow you've not been too chipper."

"Oh, it was nothing much. Just a touch of fever."

"Well, you'd best keep in the warm."

"Yes, yes, I will." Then, after an instant's hesitation, Aurelia said, "I understand you knew Sir Greville well as a child, Mary."

The woman's gaze softened. "Oh, aye, that I did, m'dear. Poor little mite."

Aurelia's attention sharpened. "How so?"

"Oh, he was left on 'is own to make shift as he could." Mary shook her head. "Roamin' the estate at all hours, 'angin' around Bert an' me whenever we had a moment to spare, while 'is mother . . ." She stopped, closing her lips firmly. "I'll not say ill of the dead."

She went to the door. "There's tea on the tray an' I'll send Bessie up with some hot water. Breakfast in the front parlor. Master Greville likes to break his fast early."

Absently Aurelia murmured her agreement, her mind occupied with what little insight Mary had given her into the child Greville had been. Neglected, lonely, it appeared. And what was it about his mother that had silenced Mary so suddenly? Interesting questions, but Aurelia was certain she needed to probe slowly and carefully if she was to discover more from Greville himself.

Bessie appeared with hot water and shyly offered her services to help miss dress. Aurelia declined the offer with a smile of thanks. Somehow she didn't think Bessie would be too adept with a curling iron. Alone, she stripped off her nightgown and sponged herself from head to toe. She dressed in one of the two linen gowns she'd brought with her. The muslin seemed a little flimsy for shooting pistols, or whatever the colonel had in store for her.

She hadn't known what to pack when she'd received the cryptic summons to Cheapside, but it had occurred to her that since they were going somewhere unknown to anyone in her circle, silks and satins would be surplus to requirement.

She drank her tea as she dressed, wrapped herself warmly in the paisley shawl she'd had the foresight to bring, and went downstairs as the long-case clock in the hall at the foot of the stairs struck six thirty.

Greville was already in the front parlor, where the fire blazed. Weak sunlight showed through the bay window and the candles were still lit. He was standing at the window when she came in and turned immediately, his gaze running down her in one all-encompassing sweep. He offered a small bow. "Good morning, ma'am."

"Good morning." She came over to him, standing beside him to look out of the window. "A cold one, it seems."

"Yes. But it will warm up soon enough."

He was standing so close to her she could feel his body heat, smell the soap on his skin. The memory of that kiss flooded back, the sweet, salt taste, the feel of his mouth on hers. Surely it had meant more than a simple practice run? It had certainly felt like it.

"Here's breakfast then." Mary's cheerful voice brought her back to earth. She stepped swiftly away from Greville and went to the table, taking dishes from the woman's tray and placing them on the table.

"This is a feast, Mary," she said, hoping that she was not blushing, that she'd given no indication to Greville of that moment of arousing memory.

"Aye, it should do you." Mary gave a satisfied nod as she surveyed the laden table, then took the empty tray and left.

"So what are we doing today?" Aurelia sat down and reached for the toast.

Greville glanced at the window, where the sun was shining with more strength. "Some outdoor exercise, I think. We might as well take advantage of the good weather, it's bound to rain one of these days, it always does. We'll save the indoor lessons for then."

"What kind of exercise?"

"A little target practice to start, then I want to show you how to recognize if you're being followed, and some avoidance techniques."

It was the strangest day she had ever spent, Aurelia thought in the waning light of late afternoon. She was standing in a narrow country lane, quite alone. Or so she believed. Had she managed to lose Greville in the little village behind her? He'd been following her. Although she hadn't seen him, she'd felt his presence. But now she couldn't sense him at all.

A little smile played over her lips. It had been an inspiration to climb into the back of the carter's wagon tethered outside the village inn. She'd buried herself among sacks of cabbages, and not even the carter, who admittedly was somewhat the worse for his sojourn in the inn's taproom, had known about his passenger. Once safely through the village and into the lane, she'd slid from the back of the wagon undetected. Fortunately the carter had been dozing on the driver's seat and the horse had been plodding along slowly, heading for home on his own instincts.

Her goal was to dodge Greville and reach Mistress Masham's farm alone. The farm was on the outskirts of the next village, easily reached by the lane. But she stood out like a sore thumb on the well-traveled road. She looked around, chewing her lip. A stile gave access between high bramble hedges onto a field. It was a matter of a minute to climb over. If she followed the hedge running parallel with the lane, she would surely find the farm.

Aurelia glanced anxiously around the field, hoping a rampant bull wasn't watching her. A herd of cows were peacefully chewing the cud in the middle of the field, watching her with typical bovine curiosity. But cows did not alarm her, and she could see no sign of a bull.

She set off along the hedge line, drawing her pelisse closer around her as a sharp gust of wind whistled around a corner of the field. It had been a strange day, indeed, but she was now more than ready for it to end. The farm couldn't be more than a mile away, as long as the hedge ran straight bordering the lane.

She reached the end of the field and climbed a gate into

the next one. She was hurrying along the hedge, thinking of fire and her dinner, when her scalp contracted and her heart jumped against her breastbone. Someone was walking on the lane on the far side of the hedge. She stopped, and the footsteps in the lane stopped, too.

Disappointment rose in her throat. She'd so wanted to succeed. She started off again and the footsteps kept pace with her, then speeded up. At the end of the field another stile gave access to the lane, and Greville appeared, leaning his folded arms on the top bar, smiling as she approached.

"Well done," he said.

"It wasn't well done at all," she retorted, unable to hide her annoyance. "You found me after all."

"Yes, of course I did." He offered her his hand over the stile. "What did you expect?"

He sounded so coolly self-confident, so complacent, that Aurelia wanted to hit him. She ignored his hand and clambered over on her own, saying nothing. After a minute he said, "Don't be annoyed with yourself, Aurelia. You did very well. I didn't see you get in the wagon. I spent a good ten minutes searching the village for you before I realized what you must have done."

She looked at him. "Really?"

"Yes, really." He took her hand and tucked it into his arm. "This was your first day out, dear girl, and you surprised me."

That made her feel a lot better, but she was more than relieved to see the lights of the farmhouse just ahead.

They went in through the kitchen, and Mary, tending a roast on a spit over the range, clucked her tongue at them.

"You shouldn't be keeping madam out this late in the cold, Master Greville. The night air's not healthy."

"I didn't intend to stay out so late, Mary," he said with a conciliatory smile. "But then I didn't expect Lady Farnham to surprise me as she did."

"I'll go and change for dinner," Aurelia said, slipping her arm out of his and heading for the door.

"There's hot water above, m'dear." Mary turned back to her roast.

In her own chamber, Aurelia closed the door and stood with her back to it taking stock of the day. She drew off her gloves and examined her hands, flexing her fingers, remembering how it felt to hold the pistol, to pull the trigger. Mentally she went through the steps of cleaning the fired weapon and reloading it, as Greville had shown her with painstaking patience.

He was a good teacher, she reflected, tossing her gloves onto the chest and unfastening her pelisse. Patient, although somewhat didactic at times. Infuriatingly sure of himself most of the time, but then he would give her that crooked grin that was utterly disarming, as if mocking himself.

And, sweet heaven, there was no denying how attractive she found him. As attractive as he was intriguing. She'd been attracted to a few men since Frederick left, but not sufficiently to be disturbed by the sensation. It had been pleasant while it lasted, and not particularly distressing when it had ceased. But something about this felt different. As if it wasn't simply superficial. But it could not be anything else, she told herself firmly. There had been no repetition of last night's kiss, no seemingly accidental touches, nothing that was not strictly business. They had a task to complete, just that and no more. She found him attractive and that was fortunate considering the charade they were to play. It would be easier to convince her friends of a sudden romantic attachment if indeed there was some truth in it. A lot easier to play the part for public consumption.

With a brisk, confirming nod of her head she went to the armoire to find her other linen gown. She saw that Mary had, as promised, sponged and pressed the dull, farmer's wife serge that she'd worn yesterday. She would wear it for any future scramblings around the countryside, she decided, and save her London wardrobe for indoor activities.

A deep yawn surprised her as she dropped her grubby gown onto the bed, and she realized how exhausted she was after the day's exertions. But she was also stimulated, mentally energetic, even if her body ached. And she was famished.

The wonderful aroma of roasting meat met her on the stairs as she hurried down to the front parlor. Greville was waiting for her in front of the fire, a glass of wine in his hand. "Wine?"

"Please, although it'll probably send me straight to

sleep." She took the glass he handed her. "If I weren't so ravenous, I'd be asleep by now." She turned aside to a small table in the window and picked up the sheaf of papers that lay there. A column of words was on one side, a column of numbers on the other.

"What's this?"

"I thought we'd look at some simple codes after dinner."

"Ah." So much for fatigue, Aurelia thought, laying the sheet back on the table. "How well do you know Harry Bonham?"

"Not well at all. We've run into each other once or twice," he answered vaguely.

"In the way of business, I suppose," she said, watching his expression.

"In the way of business. How long have you known about Bonham's work for the ministry?"

"Since before he married Nell." She shrugged and came over to the fire. "We don't discuss it."

"I should hope not." The comment was a trifle acerbic.

"You sound as if you disapprove." Her own voice had a snap to it.

"I do," he said shortly. "Bonham's work is highly secret. I'm surprised he took his wife into his confidence, and even more surprised that he allowed her to share the information with her friends."

"Perhaps you should ask him for an explanation then," Aurelia said coldly. "The circumstances were exigent to say the least."

"They would have to be." He frowned at her over the lip of his glass. "There will be no such exigent circumstances with this enterprise."

"I have already given my word."

He turned and placed his glass on the mantelpiece. "Forgive me, I don't mean to doubt it. But there is only one cardinal rule in this business, Aurelia. Never trust anyone. *Ever.*"

"Not even you?" She stared at him.

"You may trust me to protect you as best I can, but I cannot promise in all other respects that you will hear only the truth from me. There may well be circumstances when it will be necessary for me to deceive you, and you should be prepared for that."

Aurelia was cold suddenly. His gray eyes were dark and unreadable as they looked steadily at her. Harry and Nell trusted each other, she thought. Alex and Liv trusted each other, and both Harry and Alex were involved, albeit in different ways and in Alex's case for a different master, in the same dirty business of this war that held Greville in thrall. But then she thought how, in the beginning for both couples, there had been no trust, no confidences. Harry and Alex had gone about their business, using Nell and Liv for their own ends, keeping the women in the dark. Until the truth had exploded into the light. And Nell and Liv had had to reconcile themselves to the knowledge that their lovers had not trusted them until trust was forced upon them.

Greville had told her the truth from the outset. He had sought her partnership in his enterprise from the outset. She was under no illusions about their relationship. Perhaps this was better. An open acceptance of reality. No pretense. No emotional traps. She did what she did with full knowledge.

"So you don't trust *me*." It was a flat statement.

"I *never* trust anyone."

"So you didn't trust Frederick?"

Greville sighed and picked up his glass again. He sipped and frowned into the fire for a moment before turning back to her. "I liked Frederick very much, but he understood the rule. One must sever oneself from past ties. In our business we must avoid all talk of family, of our past lives, of emotions. We have to learn to be ciphers as far as possible, men with no history and no friendships. Why else do you think I did not know that his wife was his sister's best friend?"

"I would have thought that might have been useful to know."

He smiled, that rueful, slightly self-deprecating smile that never failed to disarm her. "Yes, in this instance, it would have been useful to break the rule."

"I would have said that it's always worth accepting that sometimes rules must be broken."

He inclined his head in acknowledgment, his eyes hooded as he looked at her. "I seem to be breaking one of my cardinal rules already," he said softly.

Aurelia put her head on one side, her eyes narrowed. "Oh? Which one is that?"

He shook his head as if dismissing a comment that he certainly hadn't intended to make and drank his wine, glad when the door opened to admit Mary and Bessie with dinner. "Come to the table."

Aurelia took her seat hungrily, but wondering even through her preoccupation with the offerings on the table which cardinal rule he was breaking.

Greville sliced roast pork onto her plate and placed a crisp, golden wedge of crackling beside it. He served himself and took his own seat. He should not have made that last comment, it was yet further evidence that his guard was slipping. It was all very well to dictate the rules, but it was not all very well to ignore them oneself.

Chapter Ten

THE REST OF THEIR TIME IN Essex passed in a daze, for which Aurelia was grateful. She was too busy, too mentally stimulated, to allow herself the time or energy to dwell on inconvenient sensations around her companion, and Greville seemed to withdraw a little, to create a distance between them. He was the master, she the pupil, and there was so much to learn, so many minute details to be mastered.

By their final evening, she felt in many ways as if she'd become a different person, one who saw the world very differently. Greville had taught her to notice things, tiny details she would probably never have registered in the past. He'd taught her to use certain words and phrases that, while sounding ordinary to anyone else, would convey a specific meaning to him. He'd shown her a range of gestures that he could read across a room. She still disliked using a firearm, but she was no longer squeamish and believed that if it was ever necessary, she could and would pull the trigger. And she was becoming adept at dodging pursuit. True, so far he always came up with her before she reached safety, but he admitted he was finding it harder every time.

The real test would be on the streets of London. She'd have to hope that her now more refined perception would tell her if someone was following her in that maze. Greville had shown her some of the more common practices of surveillance to recognize a follower, but she was by no means confident that she would always get it right. However, as far as she understood this partnership, her role would be merely an extension of the life she lived now. She would be going to the same activities, mingling in the same social circle, but with a specific purpose, as Greville's eyes and ears. She was as unlikely to be dodging pursuit down the back alleys of London as she was to need to fire a pistol.

"You'll be able to sleep in a little tomorrow if you wish," Greville said over their last dinner in the shabby parlor. "We don't need to be on the road until nine. That will give us ample time to catch the noon coach to London."

"Not the stagecoach again?" Aurelia grimaced over the lip of her wineglass. "Surely we could hire a post chaise."

"You may," Greville said, cutting himself a wedge of cheese. "But I must return by stage."

"Oh." Aurelia was conscious of a faint stirring of dismay. "We're to separate now?" So this was the end of the training. From now on she was to be on her own.

"Only temporarily." He nibbled at the cheese. "You will take a hired post chaise back to Cavendish Square, having come hotfoot from Bristol, where your aunt has made a successful recovery. I will return to London as anonymously as I left it. And Colonel, Sir Greville Falconer will pay a formal call in Cavendish Square the day after tomorrow."

Aurelia nodded. "And then what?"

"The first thing I am going to do is sign a lease on a furnished house on South Audley Street. That will serve as my base." He took a sip of wine. "It would be appropriate for you, once our engagement is announced, to show some interest in its redecoration, furnishings, et cetera. So it will give us a discreet meeting place. It's not as grand a mansion as Cavendish Square, or, indeed, Viscount Bonham's establishment on Mount Street, but it's not without elegance."

"I'm sure it will suit you very well," she said, since it seemed the only appropriate thing to say. "And then what?"

"A whirlwind courtship, I think. We won't have enough freedom of movement until we've made things official. We've already been formally introduced by Viscount Bonham, so that hurdle is overcome. From now on I shall haunt your door and you will let it be known discreetly that you are not averse to my attentions. In three weeks my aunt is giving a rout party in my honor. I suggest we use that occasion to make our intentions public."

"Three weeks . . . that's such a short time," Aurelia said with a grimace. "How am I to convince my friends that I've fallen hook, line, and sinker in love with a man I've only known for a month?"

He said nothing for a moment, looking at her as he sometimes did, as if he were seeing her for the first time, then pushed back his chair and slowly rose to his feet. He came around the table, took her hands, and drew her to her feet. "Perhaps I've neglected one aspect of preparation for this mission," he murmured.

A heady rush of excitement fizzed in her veins, and her belly and thighs tightened involuntarily as she felt her nipples peak against her linen bodice.

He took her face between his hands, stroked the curve of her cheek with a fingertip, traced the contours of her mouth. He bent and kissed her right ear, grazing the lobe with his teeth, one finger moving now to press against the pulse in her throat as her head fell back, offering her mouth for his kiss.

Her arms slid around his waist, her hands flattening against his buttocks as he brought his mouth to hers. She gloried in the taut muscles that seemed to tighten even more beneath her stroking, kneading fingers. His tongue was in her mouth and her own was joined with his in a wild dance of thrust and parry. Her body was on fire, her blood surging wildly in her veins, and the calm and collected widow of Cavendish Square belonged in some other world. Aurelia exulted in the sensation and the knowledge that no one, but no one, from the ordinary world knew where she was or could begin to imagine her as she was at this moment.

At last Greville released her mouth and raised his head. He drew a deep breath and ran a finger over her swollen lips, a rather rueful smile in his gray eyes. "Oh, dear," he murmured. "I have a feeling I'm going to find it difficult to be as objective as I would like in this enterprise."

Aurelia stepped back, letting her hands fall from him. She drew a deep breath, trying to regain some composure. Not only had she been unprepared for that flood of physical arousal, she couldn't remember ever experiencing anything like it before. She had enjoyed lovemaking with Frederick, but that sense of being caught up in a wild, tumbling whirlwind of desire was quite new.

"If we're to make this romantic interest convincing, perhaps we shouldn't aim for too much objectivity," she managed to say.

"Perhaps," he agreed with a slight twitch of a frown. He stood still, his eyes fixed on her countenance, but this time she had the disconcerting feeling he wasn't really seeing her.

"What is it?" she asked involuntarily.

He seemed to snap himself back into the room. "Nothing . . . nothing at all. But you should get some sleep. It grows late."

"Yes," she agreed, moving away from him to the door. "I'll be down by eight in the morning."

"Good night, then. Sleep well." He opened the door.

As she passed, he seemed to draw back deliberately, creating space between them. Aurelia gave him a brief smile and left the parlor.

Abovestairs, she packed her portmanteau before preparing for bed, but her thoughts were not on her packing. Greville had been as passionately responsive to that kiss as she had been, he had admitted as much. So why was he afraid to yield to that passion and desire? Was he afraid it would interfere with his work? Was he afraid of any involvement that was not strictly concerned with his mission? She had no answers now, but sometime during the next three months that he expected this mission to last, she would find them. She would be on familiar ground, operating in familiar situations among familiar people, and she would be all the stronger for it.

She went to bed and surprised herself by sleeping soundly. Clearly an unquiet mind was no match for an exhausted body, she reflected when she awoke to birdsong and sunshine. She dressed quickly and went downstairs, only to be told by Mary that Master Greville had already breakfasted and gone out. She was to break her own fast and be ready to leave in half an hour.

Greville appeared in the parlor within twenty minutes, dressed in his farmer's garb. "Your cloakbag is in the gig, so as soon as you're ready . . . ?"

"I'm ready now." It seemed the only appropriate answer. Aurelia abandoned her toast and honey. "I'll fetch my pelisse."

"It's in the hall." He gestured as he opened the door for her.

Clearly there was to be no hint of a reminder, covert or otherwise, of the previous evening. "If you don't mind waiting just a few more minutes, I'd like to use the privy," she said deliberately. "It's a little more salubrious than those I will encounter on the way to London."

"Hurry up then."

Aurelia shot him a look of irritation and brushed past him. Ten minutes later she was sitting in the gig and they were on the way back to the inn at Barnet.

"You have the story clear?" he asked as he turned the horse into the lane.

"Yes. We met by chance in Bristol, where you were on family business, and I was taking care of my aunt. We'd already been introduced in London, so it was natural enough for us to spend some time together," she recited. "And, of course, in those circumstances it will be perfectly understandable for you to call upon me in Cavendish Square as soon as we both return to London."

Greville nodded but said nothing. They journeyed the rest of the way in silence. At the coaching inn, Greville handed back the gig to the innkeeper and went to make arrangements for a post chaise to take Aurelia back to London.

It was a much more comfortable conveyance than the stage and, with several changes of team, would accomplish the journey in a fraction of the time. Aurelia set one foot on the footstep preparatory to climbing into the vehicle, then turned back to Greville, who stood holding the door for her.

"I'll see you tomorrow?"

"Look for me before noon." He took her hand and kissed it, his fingers tightening for an instant before he released it.

"I will." She climbed into the carriage and he closed the door. Greville gave the coachman the order to start. The man cracked his whip and the chaise lurched forward out of the innyard.

Aurelia sat back in the swaying gloom of the chaise, absently caressing her hand where she could still feel the impress of his fingers as they had closed over it.

They reached Cavendish Square at six that evening. Aurelia climbed down rather stiffly, glad that she'd resisted the urge to tell the coachman to take her first to Mount Street. She could barely wait to see Franny, but a half hour of preparation before she faced Cornelia was necessary. The last five days had changed her, and she had to find a way to hide those changes from her friend's perceptive eyes.

She also had to introduce Greville Falconer into the conversation naturally, while at the same time conveying the impression that their encounter in Bristol had somehow become more than a mere chance meeting.

In fact, she thought as she put her key in the lock of the front door, her covert life of deception was about to begin. She just wished it would begin with someone other than her best friend. But if she could fool Cornelia, she could fool anyone.

She pushed open the door and stepped into the deserted hall. Only one lamp was lit, in a sconce by the staircase, and the house was as quiet as the grave. "Morecombe," she called, dropping her cloakbag on the parquet floor. "Morecombe . . . anyone there?"

A door at the rear of the hall opened, sending a welcome shaft of light across the floor. "Eh . . . what's goin' on then? Oh, 'tis you, is it. Back wi'out a word o' warnin'." Morecombe shuffled in his carpet slippers into the dim light. He wiped his hands on his baize apron and peered at Aurelia. "Couldn't manage to send notice then?"

"No," Aurelia agreed with a conciliatory smile. "I couldn't. I'm sorry if my return discommodes you, Morecombe, but would you send Jemmy to light the lamps in the parlor and my bedchamber, and a few more in here and on the stairs wouldn't come amiss. And I'd like Hester to bring hot water up to my chamber as soon as possible."

"Oh, aye," Morecombe muttered. "We're 'avin' a bite o' supper right now." He turned back to the kitchen. "I'll send Jemmy."

Aurelia shook her head. Nothing else had changed even if she had. She went into the parlor and stood shivering in the doorway. No one had lit a fire in here while she'd been away. Reasonable, of course, but if the prince and princess had temporarily been absent, their major-domo would have kept the fires and lamps lit throughout the house in readiness for their return at whatever hour of the day or night. But Boris, of course, was with his master and mistress in the New Forest.

"I've a scuttle of 'ot coals 'ere, m'lady." Jemmy came running across the hall carrying a brass coal scuttle. "I'll 'ave a fire lit in a trice, ma'am." He hurried to the cold grate and worked swiftly. Within a few minutes a blaze was beginning to take hold. He lit a taper and put it to the candles on the mantelpiece before drawing the curtains. "Nice to 'ave you back, ma'am. Hester's gone upstairs to your bedchamber."

"Excellent, thank you, Jemmy. You go back to your supper." Aurelia went to the sideboard to pour herself a glass of sherry, which she took upstairs with her.

Hester had drawn the curtains in her bedchamber and was fiddling with the fire. She looked up as Aurelia entered. "Oh, ma'am, we wasn't expectin' you."

"No, how should you have been?" Aurelia said with a smile. "I didn't send word, after all." She discarded her pelisse, noticing how grubby it seemed after five days of fairly solid wear in rather more rigorous circumstances than usual. She unpinned her hat and grimaced at her reflection in the dresser mirror. Her hair had no curl at all.

There wasn't time for Hester to curl it before Aurelia went to Mount Street, if she was to get there before Franny was put to bed. She glanced at the clock. It was gone six thirty already. Reluctantly, she realized that Franny would have to wait until the morning. Cornelia and Harry could be getting ready to go out, or preparing to receive guests. Aurelia looked a fright and she had no time to repair the damage. She wasn't prepared, physically or mentally, to jump back into the world. A quiet evening, a good night's sleep, and she would be knocking on the Mount Street door in time to have breakfast with her daughter.

Discretion, always the better part of valor, she reflected, asking Hester to bring up a bath for her. "I'll take a light supper in the parlor when I've bathed. Could you ask Miss Ada to poach an egg for me, or something that's not too much trouble for her."

"Aye, ma'am." Hester hurried away, and Aurelia sipped her sherry as she undressed.

She woke early the next morning and rang for Hester. Within half an hour she was walking briskly through the early-morning chill to Mount Street. As she reached the steps, the front door opened and a wiry man emerged, wrapped in a greatcoat, cap pulled low over his eyes.

"Why, Lady Farnham, what brings you here so early?" He took off his cap politely.

"I've been out of town, Lester. I got back last night." Cornelia always referred to Lester as Harry's right-hand man, his aide-de-camp. Certainly, Harry did little in the shadowy side of his life without Lester at his side.

"Oh, aye, come to see the little miss then, I'll be bound. Right glad she'll be to see you, too, ma'am." Lester stepped back, holding the door for her.

"I can't wait to see her." Aurelia smiled. "You're out and about early, too."

"Oh, aye," he agreed placidly, replacing his cap. "Good day to you, Lady Farnham." He loped off down the steps and seemed to vanish into the street as if he'd been swallowed up.

Aurelia shook her head with a smile. Lester always played his cards close to his chest. She thought only Harry ever really knew what he was up to. And since whatever it was would be Harry's business, that was probably only as it should be.

"Good morning, Lady Farnham, I didn't hear the knocker, my apologies." Hector, the butler, hurried across the hall, buttoning his waistcoat. "I wasn't expecting such an early visitor."

"I'm shockingly early, I know, but I only returned to town last night and I'm very anxious to see Franny."

"Breakfast was sent to the nursery ten minutes ago, m'lady. If you'd like to go on up, I'll send coffee for you." Hector coughed discreetly. "I don't believe Lord and Lady Bonham are about yet."

"No, of course not," Aurelia said swiftly. "I wouldn't dream of disturbing them. I'll just run up to the nursery."

She suited action to words, knowing that Hector

would somehow find a discreet way of informing his mistress that Lady Farnham was in the house.

Franny was overjoyed to see her mother, snuggling into Aurelia's lap, prattling nonstop. Aurelia let the stream wash over her as she enjoyed the remembered feel of her daughter's small body. What would Franny make of Greville? She would by the nature of this enterprise see him much in her mother's company and, being Franny, would inevitably ask questions that might be hard to answer.

And what of Greville? she wondered. He had seemed perfectly comfortable with Franny on the occasion that he'd met her, but Aurelia had no sense of what he thought about children in general. He'd made it perfectly clear that he had no personal ties, no emotional commitments outside his work. She had learned that his childhood had been lonely. Mistress Masham had made it clear she disapproved of his mother. Did he have siblings? Aurelia guessed not. But it was impossible to be sure of anything. He erected such a wall around himself that even thinking of asking personal questions seemed impossible.

Well, there was no need for him to become close to Franny. This was a three-month mission. The child would forget all about him once he'd departed for whence he came.

Aurelia looked up from her wondering contemplation of the soft and vulnerable back of her daughter's neck as the door opened. "Ellie, you're home." Cornelia came into the nursery in a swirl of damask dressing gown, her honey-colored hair still tousled from sleep. She bent to kiss Aurelia.

"I didn't want them to wake you," Aurelia protested, returning the hug. "But I couldn't wait until a more civilized hour to see Franny."

"No, of course you couldn't." Cornelia kissed her own children, pausing to wipe a smear of jam from Susannah's mouth. She poured herself coffee and sat down by the fire next to Aurelia. "So, how's your aunt?"

"Much better. She decided soon after I arrived that her heart palpitations had probably been a touch of indigestion and proceeded to consume prodigious amounts of turtle soup liberally laced with Madeira. Which quite put her to rights again." The aunt in question was far from fictitious, and Cornelia knew enough about her eccentricities to find this catalog of falsehoods perfectly believable.

"So it was a wasted journey," Cornelia said, stretching her slippered feet comfortably to the fire.

"Maybe . . . maybe not," Aurelia said with what she hoped was a mysterious smile.

"Oh?" Cornelia looked at her sharply, her eyes inquisitive. "And just what does that mean?"

"What does it mean, Mama . . . what does it mean?" Franny chimed in, her voice repeating the mantra in ever-rising cadence.

"It only means, darling, that I was able to comfort Great-Aunt Baxter, even if she wasn't really unwell,"

Aurelia said, shooting Cornelia a warning look designed to increase her friend's curiosity.

Cornelia sipped her coffee and changed the subject. "I really needed you this week, Ellie. The Duchess of Gracechurch insisted on our attendance at a ghastly dinner party, and then Harry backed out at the last minute . . . urgent summons to the ministry, of course. . . . I didn't see him for days. So I had to go to his great-aunt's alone. If you'd been in town, I could have dragooned you into accompanying me. "

The conversation continued in this vein for half an hour, then Miss Alison, the children's governess, murmured about beginning the day's lessons, and Aurelia stood up, setting Franny on her feet. Adroitly Aurelia cut off the rising protestations with a preemptive bid. "Be good for Miss Alison, love, and I'll come and fetch you myself this afternoon. And we'll have supper together in front of the fire tonight."

"In your parlor . . . not in the nursery," Franny bargained.

"In Aunt Liv's parlor," Aurelia corrected, bending to kiss Franny.

Soon, once these three months were over, she would have her own parlor. It was a most satisfying prospect even if the route she had to take to achieve it was circuitous to say the least.

"Let's take breakfast in my sitting room," Cornelia said as they left the nursery. "Harry's gone riding with David and Nick. They were up half the night playing hazard at White's, and they've gone to clear their heads."

Aurelia was glad that Harry was not around. She wasn't sure how confident she would feel about bringing up Greville Falconer and their chance encounter in Bristol, or her surprising reactions to such an encounter, in front of a man who knew at least something about Greville's work. Harry would, of course, assume that Aurelia knew nothing of the colonel's involvement with the shadow world of the ministry, and she suspected he would try quite hard to dissuade her, either personally or through his wife, that such a connection was most unwise for such an innocent and unwary friend.

She would deal with the situation when it arose, but the longer she could put off facing Harry Bonham, the better prepared she would be.

Cornelia wasted no time once they were ensconced at a round table in her sitting room in front of the fire. "Maybe . . . maybe not?" she inquired with raised eyebrows.

Aurelia smile was rather secretive as she poured coffee for them both. "When I was not attending at Aunt Baxter's bedside with cups of gruel, I was walking those ghastly pugs of hers."

"So?" Cornelia said impatiently when Aurelia, instead of continuing, began to butter a piece of toast.

"So, I happened to meet someone . . . someone I had met only briefly before." Carefully Aurelia sliced her toast into quarters. Her eyes gleamed as she cast a quick conspiratorial glance at her friend across the table. She popped a quarter into her mouth and watched Cornelia with the same mischievous gleam. "Can you guess, Nell?"

Cornelia abandoned her own toast and sipped her coffee, frowning in thought. She was perfectly happy to play Aurelia's game. Then her gaze widened. "Not that colonel . . . the one who'd known Frederick? The one who seemed rather . . . how shall I put it? Rather interested in you?"

Aurelia nodded and reached for the marmalade. "The very same."

"What was his name . . . oh, I know." Cornelia snapped her fingers. "Something to do with hawks . . . *Falconer*. Colonel Falconer . . . crooked mouth, but attractive, a rather striking presence . . . graying temples . . . tall, big man . . . good eyes, very dark gray . . . astonishing eyelashes. Am I right?"

Aurelia laughed. "Yes, quite right. Colonel, Sir Greville Falconer, to give him his full title. I bumped into him in Bristol while I was walking the aunt's pugs."

"Oh . . ." Cornelia nodded significantly. "I thought you said he was arrogant when you met him here."

Aurelia shrugged, astonished at how easy this was. "I thought he was. But in Bristol he was a port in a storm. I was so bored, so tired of reading periodicals to Aunt Baxter, so utterly wearied of walking those wretched dogs for my daily exercise, I would have welcomed the devil incarnate.

"Anyway, he came to call once or twice, and then we went to a concert together. Somehow he was always in the park when I arrived with the dogs . . ." She smiled what she hoped was a mysterious if self-deprecating smile. "I don't suppose I'll see him in London, after all we were companions in the Bristol desert, but here, I'm sure he has many friends and many pursuits more exciting than walking pugs."

"As do you," Cornelia pointed out shrewdly. "Will you mind if you don't see him again?"

Now for it. "Yes." Aurelia dropped her eyes to the napkin in her lap. "Yes, Nell, I will." She looked up with a rueful shake of her head. "What am I to make of that?"

"Only that we have to ensure that you do meet him again," Cornelia said, her eyes alight with purpose. "This is excellent, Ellie. We will make Colonel, Sir Greville Falconer our project. I'll enlist Harry, since he knows him . . ." Her voice trailed away.

"Are you thinking what I'm thinking?" Aurelia said steadily.

"If it's that he's quite possibly engaged in Harry's line of work, yes."

Aurelia nodded. "Yes, I've already thought of that. I can't really ask him, though."

"No," Cornelia agreed drily. "It's not something they care to talk about." She frowned at Aurelia. "Would it matter to you?"

"It doesn't seem to matter to you and Liv."

"It's not easy, though."

Aurelia's smile had a touch of irony to it. "I think I can manage what you both manage."

"Of course," Cornelia said hastily. "I didn't mean you couldn't . . . merely . . ." She shrugged helplessly. "Merely that it's hard not knowing where they are, or what danger they might be facing. Most of all, it's so hard knowing there are huge areas of their lives from which we're essentially excluded. However much love and commitment there is, nothing changes that one essential fact."

And you think I don't know that? Aurelia half laughed. If anything, she knew it better than either Nell or Liv. She hadn't known about her husband's activities until after his death. And he would happily have left her in ignorance her entire life if he could have done so. But she had one advantage over her friends. She knew from the outset what she was getting into with Greville Falconer.

Chapter Eleven

"As you can see, Sir Greville, everything is in the first style of elegance . . . all newly refurbished," the agent said somewhat anxiously. His client had given nothing away in the final tour of the house on South Audley Street. Not so much as a quirk of an eyebrow or a twitch of his mouth. "And I think you'll find the lease very reasonable."

"Yes," said the colonel without expansion. He walked from the drawing room into the dining room. The mahogany table would seat twelve comfortably. He could see no reason why he would wish to entertain more than twelve at his dinner table. The dining room in Cavendish Square would seat more than twenty, and the cavernous room in his aunt's mausoleum of a house would better that by at least ten. But the more intimate the gathering, the more information could be gleaned.

He strode up the staircase to the upper floor. It was quite a handsome staircase with an elegant sweep and nicely carved banisters. Two corridors ran off a square landing at the head of the stairs, lined with doors on either side. Light poured into the corridors from long windows at the end of each. Double doors off the east corridor opened into the master bedroom, looking out over the front of the house, with a good-size dressing room beyond. A connecting door led to a second suite of rooms, looking out over the small rear garden, with a modest but rather pretty boudoir adjoining. Presumably the apartments designed for the lady of the house.

He returned downstairs, cast a cursory eye over the kitchen regions, the butler's pantry, the housekeeper's sitting room. He had absolutely no idea what servants in a London town house expected, never having needed to give the issue any thought before, but Aurelia would know whether they were adequate and what improvements if any should be made.

"It'll do," he stated.

The agent looked relieved. "Will you sign the lease then, Sir Greville? It's for just one year."

"Yes, but with the option to renew." Greville took the document from the agent and carried it into the drawing room. He doubted he would be in a position to renew, but the charade demanded an impression of permanent residency. He found pen and ink on a secretaire and signed the lease. He handed the paper back to the agent. "If you will give me the keys in exchange, our business is concluded, I believe."

"Yes, Sir Greville. With pleasure, sir." The agent handed over a heavy bunch of keys. "They're all there, sir, all marked. Keys to the cellar and the pantries as well . . . of course, I imagine your butler and housekeeper will take charge of those."

"I would imagine so," Greville said, weighing the bunch in his palm, before extending his hand to the agent. "Good day to you, Charteris."

"Good day, Sir Greville." The man shook hands with unmistakable relief. "I'll see myself out." He hurried into the hall and Greville heard the front door close on his departure. The house settled around him as he stood in the drawing room stroking his chin.

Aurelia could help him with the hiring of staff. It would be considered perfectly appropriate once they were engaged. But in the meantime he was anxious to move in, or rather, anxious to move out of Lady Broughton's establishment. His aunt had taken to lying in wait for him, ambushing him on his way in or out of the house with some new facet of her preparations for the rout party. Why she thought he was interested in the color of the champagne, the choice of dinner service, or whether it should be partridge or pheasant in the game pies was a mystery to him.

With a dismissive shake of his head he left the house, locking the door behind him. Whistling to himself, he strolled off in the direction of Cavendish Square. He'd told Aurelia to look for him before noon, and it was almost that now.

Aurelia was in the drawing room, watching the street from one of the long windows. She'd taken the precaution of telling Morecombe that she was not in to visitors this morning because she was expecting someone in particular and she would answer the door herself when he arrived. Morecombe's response had been typically laconic. He'd disappeared into the back regions, and apart from the appearance of the occasional maid with beeswax and duster, Aurelia had the front of the house to herself.

She saw Greville approach the house from the garden in the center of the square. He was swinging the slender cane that she now knew concealed a deadly weapon, and the now familiar prickle of excitement ran up her spine as she watched him cross the street.

She liked the restraint of his dress, he seemed to have no interest in the vagaries of fashion, and indeed his powerful frame needed no augmentation. He had no need of fancy stitching or shoulder pads to improve his figure. His coat of charcoal gray wool sat snugly across his large shoulders, the dove gray buckskin britches clung to his powerful thighs, the corded muscles rippling with each long stride. His starched white stock was of only moderate height, but he didn't need the exaggerated height so much in favor among young men to lengthen his neck and strengthen his chin.

Greville Falconer exuded strength and power in every inch. He paused on the pavement outside the house and looked up at the facade. His gaze moved to the windows and he saw her standing in the shadow of the curtains. He raised a hand in greeting, then came up the steps to the front door.

Aurelia hastened across the hall to the front door, pulling it wide. "You came."

"Did you doubt that I would?" He stepped into the hall, his gray gaze sweeping her countenance, running slowly down her body, almost as if he was checking to make sure everything was still there, she thought. But the appreciative gleam in his eyes, and that sensual smiling curve to his mouth, sent a jolt of arousal through her belly.

"You've curled your hair again" was all he said.

For some reason the comment flustered her, and she felt herself blush like an ingenue. "Ringlets are in fashion." She struggled to sound matter-of-fact, as if her skin wasn't on fire and her belly churning. She turned away to the drawing room. "One can't be seen in fashionable London with straight hair."

"Oh, I think you could," he declared, following her into the salon. "Your hair is delightful au naturel." He took up his usual position by the fireplace and stood smiling at her, his eyebrows slightly raised in quizzical inquiry.

Aurelia ignored the compliment as she could think of no response that wouldn't sound false or facetious. "May I offer you sherry . . . or Madeira, perhaps?" she asked, moving to the decanters on the sideboard.

"Sherry, thank you." He watched her move across the room, enjoying the fluid grace of her walk. "So, are you ready to begin our enterprise, Aurelia?"

She turned, decanter in hand. "What, now? Today?"

"I have just this morning signed the lease on the house in South Audley Street. Do you care to see it? I would appreciate your opinion on a few matters."

Aurelia poured sherry into two glasses. She felt as if time had speeded up somehow. For some reason she had thought there would be a few days of normality, time to settle in again before work started in earnest. But not so, it seemed. "Shouldn't we spend a few days getting society accustomed to the idea that we seem to enjoy each other's company?" she suggested tentatively, bringing the glasses over.

"Certainly," he agreed, taking the glass she offered him. "Looking the house over won't prevent that."

"But won't it cause raised eyebrows if we're seen together, particularly going into an empty house?"

He shook his head at her in mock reproof. "Come now, have you forgotten all the lessons of last week so quickly? Why should anyone see us going into the house together?"

"Oh . . . I see what you mean." She smiled ruefully

and sipped her sherry, taking a seat in the corner of the sofa. "I'll go in by myself, of course."

"Having, of course, made certain no one who knows you is around to see you enter."

"Of course. How will I get in?"

"The usual way. You'll knock on the door and it will open for you."

She nodded, already enjoying the sense of challenge, intellectual and physical, that she had so relished during the previous week with each new test. "Shall we go now?"

He raised his glass to his lips. "We're not in that much of a hurry." His eyes were laughing and she couldn't help a chuckle in return. "Did you talk to Lady Bonham about your visit to Bristol?" Greville inquired casually.

"It came up, naturally. When I went to see Franny."

"Yes, I imagine it would." He waited, eyebrows quirked.

"I told her what we'd agreed. She didn't appear to find anything strange in it."

He nodded. "What else?"

"Nothing really. Nell's my friend, my interests are her interests. If I happen to like someone, she'll be prepared to like them, too, unless given a good reason not to." She frowned down into her glass.

"Go on," he prompted, well aware that there was more here.

Aurelia sighed. "Well, Nell is no fool, and well aware that anyone she meets through her husband could be involved in War Ministry business. She asked me if I thought it likely."

"And what did you say?" He was watching her closely now.

"I said it had occurred to me. She'd think it very odd if it hadn't. I'm not generally considered a fool either."

"With good reason." His white smile flashed. "This is something of a hurdle, I admit. Bonham knows full well that he and I obey the same master, although he has no idea what I do. It's company etiquette to avoid discussion of company business outside the ministry itself, so he won't probe too obviously. But you should be prepared for some covert opposition."

"I am prepared. Harry doesn't know about Frederick?"

"Good God, no. Only three people know about Frederick. You, myself, and my master. And even he does not know the connection between Bonham's wife and my late partner. It will stay that way."

She nodded in silent acceptance. "Nell and Harry won't stand in my way," she said after a minute. "They might, in fact probably will, try to dissuade me from this marriage, but in the end they'll stand behind me, if I'm resolute."

It was her turn to look at him closely now. "Harry knows nothing to your detriment . . . nothing that would make him think, apart from your involvement in his own world, that you would make me an unsatisfactory and dangerous husband?"

"No more unsatisfactory and dangerous as he is himself."

"Then I'm confident that's a hurdle I can jump without too much difficulty." She set down her glass and stood up energetically. "Shall we go and see the house now?"

"I'll leave first." He rose in more leisurely fashion, draining his glass as he did so. "When you reach number Twelve South Audley Street, what will you do?"

"Walk past it twice, then if I'm satisfied, knock on the door."

"Good." He glanced at his fob watch hanging from his waistcoat. "Can you be there in half an hour?"

South Audley Street was close to Grosvenor Square. If she took a hackney to the square, then walked to the house, she could make it. "Barring traffic, or anything unexpected."

"I'll be waiting . . . no need to see me out." He strode into the hall and Aurelia ran upstairs to fetch her pelisse, hat, and gloves.

She let herself out and hailed a passing hackney. "Grosvenor Square, please."

"Any particular address, mum?"

"No, just in the middle somewhere."

The driver gave her an odd look but cracked his whip, and the conveyance trundled forward. Halfway around the square, he drew rein. "This do you, mum?"

"Perfectly." Aurelia descended, paid the man, then walked off to the south side of the square. She walked up South Audley Street casually, glancing up at the houses. They were for the most part stately, double-fronted mansions, but every few houses there would be a pair of smaller, narrower, attached single-fronted houses. She guessed someone had divided a mansion into two at some point, maybe to accommodate a second branch of a family.

Number 12 was one of these houses. A narrow flight of honed steps led up to an oak front door with a glowing brass knocker and handle. The iron railings were freshly black-leaded, and the windows to the left of the door winked in the sunlight. A pretty fanlight had been installed over the door, together with a brass lantern. Two stone flowerpots, at present empty, flanked the door. The house's adjoining twin was as well kept.

Aurelia walked past the house. Several houses down, she stopped to adjust her boot. A few people were around, mostly tradesmen as far as she could see. A nursemaid with two small children in tow hurried by towards the square. One child was playing with a top that threatened to spin into the street at any moment. The nursemaid needed to take charge of the top until they reached the square garden, but Aurelia closed her eyes and fought the urge to intervene. She couldn't draw attention to herself under any circumstances, or at least,

she amended, not unless the child was about to spin itself under the wheels of a carriage.

After a hundred yards or so she crossed the road and
sauntered casually on the opposite side past the house.
She saw no one she knew, even vaguely, and as casually
as before, she strolled over the road and up the steps
to the house, banging the knocker once, resisting the
compulsion to look over her shoulder to see if anyone
familiar had appeared on the street.

The door opened and she stepped swiftly inside, the
door closing instantly at her back. "No one saw you?"
Greville stood with one hand leaning against the door
he had just closed, his gaze searching her face.

"No, I'm certain."

"I'm certain, too, you did a good job." He laughed
softly. "But I own I thought for a minute you were going
to start berating that nursemaid."

"How could you tell?" She stared at him, astonished
as always by his powers of observation.

"I'm getting to know you, my dear," he said with a
mock bow. "I could read you very clearly at that moment, and I applauded your restraint."

Aurelia was delighted by the compliment but tried
not to show how much. She looked around the hall. The
house faced south and the pale sunlight shone bravely
onto the oak floor through the one long window beside
the door and the fanlight above it.

"Let me show you the rest of it," Greville said, leading the way to double doors on the left of the hall.

She followed him into a reasonable-size drawing room, high ceiling, attractive moldings, a lovely Adam's fireplace. Long windows looked onto the street and there was plenty of light. The furniture was fashionable, not particularly ornate, the draperies neutral as befitted a leased house. But with books and pictures, and a few little decorative touches, it could be made quite personal. But did Greville own such personal objects? Somehow she doubted it. He wasn't a man who spent much time in any one place.

"What do you think?"

She turned back to him. "It will do you very well. In your place I'd move things around a little, make a few adjustments, add a few personal touches, but . . . yes, it seems perfect for your purposes. Not too large for a bachelor, but plenty of room for entertaining."

He stroked his chin thoughtfully as he looked around, seeing the room with fresh eyes. "I'm not very good at making places seem like home. Could you do that for me?"

"Do you have any books, pictures, ornaments . . . anything like that?"

He laughed. "No, my dear girl, I do not. What would I do with such fripperies . . . carry them around in a knapsack as I jaunter around the world?"

"Of course not." She shook her head. "You'll need to buy a few bits and pieces."

"Would you consider acquiring them for me? In the interests of our enterprise."

"Certainly. I'd enjoy it," she said frankly. "Tell me how much you wish to spend and I'll happily make a nest for you. Obviously, since it's only for three months or so, you won't wish to be extravagant, but I'm sure I can find a few odds and ends for a relatively small sum, and we need only work on the public rooms."

He nodded, but made no other response. "Let me show you the rest of the house."

They toured the ground floor, and Aurelia had no objections to the dining room or the cozy library at the rear of the house. It would be a perfect house for herself and Franny, she thought, looking around the library, imagining her own books on those shelves. "How much is the lease?" she asked suddenly.

Greville looked surprised. "Twenty-five guineas a week. Quite reasonable for its size and location I thought. Why do you ask?"

She frowned at him. "This pension I am promised as payment for my services . . . you have not told me how much it will be."

"Oh, I understand." He nodded his head. "You will be wanting your own establishment of course. Unfortunately I cannot give you an exact figure as yet. The issue is being considered by those whose job it is to consider such things. But I could make a recommendation if you care to give me an idea of what you need."

"I'll have to think about it."

"Do that and let me know." Simon Grant had agreed in principle to pay a pension to Frederick's widow, both in recognition of Frederick's services to his country and in payment for his widow's forthcoming services. But practical matters tended to slide out of Simon's overworked brain, and he would need reminding and a gentle prod to sign the necessary authorizations.

Aurelia felt a little surge of satisfaction as she went up the stairs. Twenty-five guineas a week would probably stretch her finances too far, but there was also that not inconsiderable sum in Frederick's back pay and prize money that Greville had said would be paid to her. That might bridge the gap. The idea of paying her own way through the sweat of her own brow was eminently gratifying. No one could control that money or dictate how it was spent. She was answerable to no one, finally free of Markby's yoke. And all she really had to do was pretend to have a romantic interest in a most attractive man. Not a particularly arduous task. Not in the least.

She almost flew up the stairs, her step powered by the swift and exultant tumble of her thoughts. She arrived on the landing a few steps ahead of Greville. "So, where does the master of the house lay his head?"

Greville paused just below the top step. Something in her voice arrested him. He looked up at her, his eyes narrowed, and slowly her expression changed, her eyes looked startled, as if by a sudden, extraordinary thought, and her mouth became different, sensual and inviting. The air around them in the silent, deserted house seemed suddenly to come alive. The very emptiness of the space around them became charged with significance. She held out a hand to him and slowly he took it, coming up the last step to stand beside her.

He drew her in front of him, his hands resting on her shoulders as he looked into her eyes, deep golden brown eyes that held his gaze, and he felt the hard certainty that ruled his every moment, informed his every action, losing shape, becoming fuzzy around the edges. Then Aurelia smiled at him, a slow smile that brought a luminous shimmer to her eyes, like sunlight on a forest pool.

"Heaven help me," Greville murmured. "This is madness, and I am helpless against it." He lowered his mouth to hers, crushing her against him as he devoured her mouth, ran his hands down her back, pressing her to him, his hands hard on her hips, fingers digging into the soft, yielding curves. She murmured against his mouth, caught his bottom lip between her teeth, pressed her loins into his. He moved her backwards, his mouth still cleaving to hers, along the corridor to the double doors to his bedchamber. He reached around her waist and flicked up the latch, propelling her into the room.

Only then did he step back from her, but his eyes remained locked with hers as he loosened his stock, throwing it from him as he shrugged out of his coat and waistcoat, sending them in the same direction. In shirt and britches he caught her up by the waist. He held her

above him and she laughed down at him in sheer exultation, her eyes deep and sensuous as the richest brown
velvet.

He carried her to the bed and dropped her into the
middle of the deep feather mattress, then lifted her feet
one by one onto his thigh so that he could unbutton her
boots. He tossed them unceremoniously to the ground
and slid his hands up the silken length of her stockinged
legs, molding her knees into his palms, fingertips dancing in the soft hollows behind her knees.

Aurelia unbuttoned her pelisse, her fingers clumsy in
their haste. Urgent need filled the hushed silence of the
empty house, her loins were hot, the deep furrow in her
body moist with anticipation. She struggled to free her
arms from the pelisse, and Greville half lifted her, pulling the confining garment away from her. Her gown
was a simple jonquil crepe affair that clung to her bosom
and hips. She tugged at it, yanking it up to her waist, her
legs curling around his hips as her fingers struggled with
the buttons of his britches.

He reared back for a moment, looking down at her
flushed face, her glowing eyes, her parted lips. Then
with a swift motion he yanked loose the ties of the lawn
drawers she wore beneath the thin crepe, pushed a hand
beneath her to lift her so that he could pull the garment
clear over her hips. She lifted her hips high on the bed,
her legs still curled around his waist, pulling him into
the hot cleft of her body.

But with a wicked smile he held back, just inserting

the tip of his penis within her, holding himself there, moving slowly, stimulating the exquisitely sensitive opening of her body before finally sheathing himself within her. She sighed as she took him deep inside her, and he lay still, feeling himself enclosed in the silken warmth, content for the instant to feel just that.

Aurelia moved her hand down his back, stroking the hard-muscled curve of his backside, pressing her hand against him as he began to move within her, setting up a slow rhythm that increased in pace as their passion grew. The silence of the house around them added to her excitement, they were alone, utterly private, no one knew where she was, no one, not even her dearest friends, could guess at what she was doing.

She arched her back, rising to meet his thrusts, tightening around him, her hands pressing into his buttocks, and he gave her what she wanted, his head thrown back, the strong column of his throat bared, his hips plunging, his penis so deep within her it touched her womb, and she cried out, a triumphant, exultant scream of delight as the world spun off its axis, and she clung to him as to a lifeline as his own cry joined with hers.

Afterwards, as Aurelia came back to herself, she realized that they were lying entwined in a tangle of clothes. Her drawers were around her ankles, her gown and petticoat caught up at her waist.

Greville hitched himself onto both elbows above her and shook his head in a dazed wonder. "I can't remember when I last made love in my boots." His britches were around his knees, his shirt half-unbuttoned.

Aurelia only smiled weakly. There were no words to describe how she felt. Sated with delight, astounded at the suddenness of that excess of pleasure, stunned at the realization of how much she had missed the simple act of love since Frederick had sailed away.

Greville slid backwards until his boots touched the floor again and he could stand upright. "What a gloriously immodest sight you are." He chuckled, bending over her to kiss her, one hand resting over the damp mound of her pubes, twisting a dark curl around his forefinger. "Put yourself together, before I ravish you again."

"I'm willing to be ravished," she murmured, making no attempt to cover herself.

"Clearly, you don't know much about the harsh anatomical realities of the male." Greville hauled up his britches. He did up the buttons before bending over to take her hands and pull her to her feet.

He held her with one hand, pushing up her chin with his other. He said nothing, but something in his eyes penetrated her daze, sending a little chill into the warm aftermath of loving. Then he released her and the moment passed.

Aurelia bent to pull up her drawers. She adjusted the light folds of her dress over her hips and sat down to put on her boots. What had been behind that strange, almost forbidding look? Should she bring it up? But she realized she didn't want to. She didn't want to analyze what had happened between them, not at this moment.

"Will you move in here soon?" It was such an ordinary question after the intense communication of the last half hour, but it was all she could think of. The world was back, and there were questions and situations that had to be discussed.

"As soon as possible," Greville said. "But I'll need to hire a staff."

"You'll need a housekeeper, and cook. And a butler, valet . . . batman . . . don't army officers have batmen?"

"Regular army officers, yes." Greville bent to the low dresser mirror to retie his stock. "But by no stretch of the imagination do I fall into that category."

"No, I suppose not." She nudged him away from the mirror so that she could see to her sadly tumbled hair.

"I'm quite accustomed to taking care of my own needs," he said, stepping back to pick up his waistcoat.

"You can cook?"

"Probably better than you." He pushed his arms into his coat.

Aurelia gave a rueful laugh. "That would not be difficult. I don't know the first thing about cooking."

"Frederick learned."

"I assume because he needed to. I don't see how, in this play of ours, that I should ever need to."

"No," Greville agreed. "Shall we continue the tou of the house? You need to know the layout, since we'll be using it as a base for operations." He walked over to a door in the far wall and flung it wide. "This bedchamber belongs to the lady of the house."

Aurelia came up beside him and glanced around the room. It was similar in size to his own, unexceptionably if unimaginatively furnished. "Pleasant enough." She walked through the room and opened the door to the boudoir. This would suit her admirably, she thought longingly. If she could afford a house like this, she and Franny would want for nothing.

"You're thinking how much you would like this for your own," Greville said, catching her chin on a fingertip and turning her face towards him.

"Is it that obvious?" Her smile was faintly rueful.

"I'm aware that finances are much on your mind." He traced her mouth with his thumb. "And where you and your daughter are to live. It's not difficult to read your mind in such an instance."

"No, I suppose not. But I've always had my own sitting room, my own private room, and I think I would find it hard to live in a house without it." She gave a slight self-deprecating shrug.

"I would have thought a bedchamber and a drawing room sufficient," he said, sounding genuinely puzzled. "Why would one person need so much space? I've lived for many years with nothing to call my own but the clothes on my back, and what I can carry on my back. I count a solid roof over my head a luxury."

"Well, you are a rather unusual individual," Aurelia responded with more than a hint of irony. "I'm sure your mother had her own sitting room." Even as she said it, Aurelia realized it was the first time she had touched upon his personal history. And Greville didn't know that she had had some tantalizing inkling from Mistress Masham.

"Oh, yes," he said, his voice suddenly cold and distant. "She had an entire wing of the house to herself. She was not one for company."

Well, that fitted with what little Mary had let fall. But it still told Aurelia nothing of any significance. However, it meant a lot more than the surface words implied, Aurelia was convinced. He looked utterly forbidding, his tone icy, his eyes like gray stones, and she could no more bring herself to question his statement than she could swim the English Channel.

"It's time we left." Greville moved past her and strode down the corridor to the staircase. Aurelia followed more slowly. It was difficult at this moment to remember the passion they had shared such a short time ago.

In the hall, he went to open the front door, but stopped before doing so. He held out his hands to her and she walked forward, placing her own in his. He clasped her hands tightly and drew her towards him.

"I find you irresistible, Aurelia," he said softly. "Somehow you've slipped beneath my guard, and it makes me a little uneasy. If that causes me to behave curtly, or to distance myself, then I ask your forgiveness and your understanding. I would not make you unhappy for the world. And I don't want your anger or annoyance, I want your warmth and your passion, and that lovely smile. We will work well together, and all the better for what happened this afternoon. I believe that. Will you forgive me?"

"There's nothing to forgive." And there wasn't. If he didn't want to talk about his childhood, that was his business.

He studied her expression for a moment, then nodded as if satisfied. "We'll walk in the park at five o'clock," he told her, slipping back easily into the role of senior partner in the enterprise. He opened the door and stepped behind it so he was invisible to the outside world. "Meet me just inside the Stanhope Gate. It's time we started to be noticed together."

"I'll be there." She stepped through the door, pulling it shut behind her. She glanced up and down the street, saw no one she knew, and quickly went on her way. Her mind was in turmoil. The glories of the afternoon were one thing, one wonderful thing, but they had brought her closer to the man himself. Was that what he had been afraid of? What had produced that sudden coldness? He was afraid that physical closeness would engender a need on her part for emotional closeness? If so, he'd been right. He'd warned her that he never discussed personal matters, that there was no place for private emotions in the world of the spy. But he had to have them even if he didn't discuss them. It wasn't human to have no emotional relationships, no personal history.

Had his lonely childhood scarred him in some way? Had there been something that made emotional withdrawal natural for him?

Had something in his early life groomed him for the isolated, dangerous world of the spy?

Chapter Twelve

T HE FISHING KETCH DOCKED at Dover in the late afternoon. A heavy shower dampened the quayside, and the two gentlemen who stepped from the deck of the ketch carried umbrellas. The quayside itself reeked of fish and tar, the stench accentuated by the rain. From the wide-open door of a tavern came raucous laughter and the odor of spilled beer, sawdust, and tobacco.

The taller of the two men examined his surroundings through a quizzing glass with an air of fastidious disapproval. He was richly dressed, his chin supported on a highly starched, elaborately folded neckcloth, his dark coat and waistcoat of the softest wool, legs encased in skintight pantaloons, feet in glimmering top boots. His tall, lean, athletic build spoke of a man of action. He sported a neat spade beard, a high-crowned beaver hat, and carried a silver-knobbed cane.

His shorter companion was stocky, clean-shaven, with

a rather round face, and dressed in the dull black coat and britches of a factotum. They both looked around, clearly expecting some kind of welcoming committee.

A sailor came down the gangway with two portmanteaus that he dumped unceremoniously at their feet. "There y'are, gents." He held out a callused, grimy hand.

The tall gentleman, with a flare of his nostrils, gestured imperiously to his companion, and the other hastily felt in his pocket and took out a copper coin. He dropped it into the waiting palm. The sailor looked at the coin, spat derisively onto the cobbles very close to one shining boot, and returned to the ketch.

"So, it would seem we are not expected, Miguel." The voice was clipped, impatient, the man's expression conveying the hauteur of one not accustomed to being kept waiting.

"He'll be here, Don Antonio," the other man reassured, looking around. "Carlos has never failed yet."

"So, we should stand here in the rain?" A sculpted eyebrow lifted as Don Antonio turned his well-bred countenance to his companion.

"Would you prefer to enter the tavern?" The suggestion was tentatively made.

Don Antonio gave him an incredulous stare, then began to pace the cobbled quay, picking his way through the puddles. "At least we can make absolutely certain our arrival does not go unnoticed. Whoever's watching for a stranger's arrival will make good note of two sodden gentlemen who clearly have nothing to hide, hanging around miserably on the quayside in the rain." He gave a scornful laugh.

"Ah, here he is," Miguel declared, as a coach pulled up at the edge of the quay. The door opened and a man jumped down, hurrying across the cobbles towards them.

"Forgive me for not being here to greet you on your arrival, Don Antonio, Senor Alvada. But one of the horses threw a shoe on the road from London." The man bowed low, the rain pattering onto his bare head. "If you would care to take shelter in the coach, I'll bring your luggage." He was a small man and struggled with the two portmanteaus.

Neither of the gentlemen offered him any assistance, however, both hurrying across the quay and into the dry confines of the coach.

"Miserable country and its miserable weather," Don Antonio observed, settling into a corner of the vehicle. He rubbed at the window with his gloved hand. "This damp gets into a man's bones."

"Yes, indeed," responded Miguel, taking the opposite corner. "Carlos should have a snug parlor reserved for us, though. We'll have a good dinner, a good bottle, and a comfortable night's sleep before we continue to London."

"A good dinner?" Don Antonio scoffed. "In this benighted country? The English don't know the first thing about food. They cook like peasants."

Miguel said nothing, merely hunched his shoulders

into his coat. Don Antonio Vasquez had a vehement loathing of the English and all things English, and Miguel had no intention of exacerbating that loathing with any words of excuse or defense. Only a fool would risk annoying Don Antonio, a man without remorse, without conscience, and he was very, very good, a master of his profession with no equal in Miguel's eyes. Don Antonio chose his associates with the greatest care. On each enterprise he would pick someone who had a particular skill or penchant for a certain type of action. Miguel, trained by the Inquisition, had no illusions as to why he had been selected for this mission. He considered it an honor of the highest order.

"I took the liberty of booking bedchambers and a private parlor at the Green Man, on the road to London, Don Antonio." Carlos, rain-sodden, clambered into the coach. Don Antonio withdrew farther into his corner with a grimace of distaste at the puddle forming beneath the other man's boots.

"The kitchen has a good reputation," Carlos offered hopefully. "And quite a decent cellar, I'm told."

"That remains to be seen," said the gentleman. "Let's just get there, shall we, before we all drown?"

Carlos rapped on the roof to signal the driver, and the carriage lumbered forward. "The *asp* has leased a house on South Audley Street, Don Antonio. I have found very pleasant lodgings for you on Adam's Row, very close by." Carlos spoke fast, as if afraid he would be cut off at any moment. "I will act as your majordomo, of course, and have taken the liberty of hiring a chef who comes highly recommended. Senor Alvada"—Carlos nodded politely to Miguel—"will be acting as your secretary."

"Do we have an entrée at court?" Don Antonio asked.

"Doña Bernardina y Alcala is now the Countess of Lessingham. But she remains loyal to her Spanish blood. She will ensure you have all the entrées necessary, Don Antonio."

"Good." He nodded, his mouth twisting in a sardonic smile. "Her loyalty to poor King Carlos in exile will be put to good use, although not perhaps to the use she imagines." He smiled a little. "I do enjoy a double-headed mission," he said almost to himself. "Such an economical use of effort and resources. We shall set up our network and flush out the *asp* at the same time."

He swiped his glove against the window again. "I have waited a long time for that, gentlemen. Now, how soon before we get to this paragon of an inn?"

"Half an hour, Don Antonio." Carlos exchanged a glance with Miguel, who shrugged with fatalistic patience.

❧

"How well do you know that colonel, Sir Greville Falconer, Harry?"

Harry knew his wife too well to assume she was making idle conversation. He put down his pen and looked across the desk at her as she crossed the carpet in the library. "We're slightly acquainted, why do you ask?"

"Aurelia met up with him in Bristol." Cornelia perched on the arm of a chair, smoothing down her blue silk skirt. "They spent some together."

"Ah. I see." Harry toyed with the feather tip of his quill pen, frowning slightly. "And you think Aurelia might be interested in Falconer?"

"Maybe." Cornelia lifted her shoulders in a graceful movement. "Is there any reason beyond the obvious why she shouldn't spend time with him?"

"And what's the obvious?"

"You know perfectly well. I'm assuming he's involved in the same business you are."

"To be quite honest with you, my love, I have no idea exactly what it is that Falconer does."

"But it's something to do with the ministry?"

"As far as I know." Harry leaned back in his chair, linking his hands behind his head. "You know perfectly well, Nell, that if I did have any specific information, I couldn't discuss it with you."

His wife sighed. "I suppose I understand that."

"Does Aurelia suspect he might have anything to do with the ministry?"

Cornelia nodded. "She thinks it's possible. I just wondered if you could give me a hint as to the kind of work he does."

"Well, I can't, my dear. I'll say only that in general he doesn't haunt the ministry corridors. To my knowledge he doesn't even have an office there."

"Which means he works abroad." She frowned when her husband said nothing to confirm or deny the statement. "I suppose if that's the case, then he won't be around for much longer."

Harry sighed. He tried not to have too many secrets from his wife, but another man's business was not his to divulge. Yet he knew that Falconer was on some mission in London that would require a longer-than-usual stay. "If I were you, I would discuss it further with Aurelia. If she's really interested in Falconer, then she's going to be asking him questions."

"Which, if he's anything like you, he'll find a way to deflect," Cornelia said tartly. She stood up. "I'll leave you to your correspondence."

"Nell, love, I can't discuss someone else's work." Harry stood up and came around the desk. He put an arm around her. "If you like, I'll talk to Falconer about Aurelia. Maybe I can get an idea of his intentions. I'm sure he has no more than a flirtation in mind, and Aurelia's more than capable of looking after herself in such matters."

"True. But I wouldn't want her hurt."

"I'll talk to Falconer." Harry kissed her, his mouth lingering on hers. Then he said rather ruefully, "He's going to tell me to mind my own business, of course, and I wouldn't blame him either."

"It's a small price to pay for my peace of mind," Cornelia said with a smile. "I'll talk to Aurelia some more.

After all, they only met a couple of times in Bristol, it probably means nothing at all."

At five o'clock Aurelia entered Hyde Park through the Stanhope Gate and glanced around casually. There was no sign of Greville. Waiting for him would merely draw attention to herself, and if she had learned one thing in her time in the country, it was never to be conspicuous unless she wanted to be. It was unusual for a woman to walk or ride alone in the park at the social hour of five o'clock, particularly without a groom or footman in her wake, so she turned back to the street, strolling purposefully in the direction of Piccadilly, her hands clasped inside her muff.

She heard his step the instant before he came up beside her. "Lady Farnham . . . well met." He swept off his beaver hat and bowed. "Shall we take a turn around the park?" He offered her his arm.

"I was wondering what kept you," Aurelia murmured, slipping her gloved hand into the crook of his elbow.

"Forgive me, I had some business to transact and it took me rather longer than I'd expected." He lowered his head towards her ear as he spoke barely above a whisper. His lips hardly moved, but Aurelia heard every word.

They entered the park and Greville looked around, a smile of greeting on his lips. "Now, let's see how much attention we can attract."

Aurelia followed his lead, examining the pedestrians, carriages, and riders thronging the tan, the carriageway, and the grassy walking path alongside it. Greville kept up an animated stream of chat as they walked, doffing his hat to anyone who gave them a second glance.

Aurelia was hailed several times and on each occasion stopped to talk, introducing Greville when necessary. Then she saw the one person who would ensure that word of this perambulation in the company of a near stranger to the ton would spread like the proverbial wildfire.

"Letitia Oglethorpe," she murmured in a voice that only Greville could hear. "Just the lady we need." She waved vigorously at a barouche bowling down the carriageway towards them.

"Why, Aurelia, how delightful to see you . . . isn't it a charming day." Letitia leaned over the door of the barouche as it drew to a halt beside them. Her eyes gleamed with predatory curiosity as they swiftly assessed Aurelia's companion. "What a pretty hat, my dear." Her eyes were still on Greville.

"Thank you," Aurelia said. "May I return the compliment." She wasn't sure she wanted to. Letitia's hat was a monstrous concoction of black taffeta with tulle flowers and six white plumes. It looked to Aurelia as if the first slight breeze would take it aloft like an eagle in full flight.

Letitia patted a plume with a complacent smile. "I am rather pleased with it . . . but come, my dear, won't you introduce me to your escort . . . a new face, I believe. So refreshing . . . it's such a bore in town these days, only the same old faces."

"Allow me to present Colonel, Sir Greville Falconer," Aurelia said, her smile fixed. "Sir Greville, Lady Oglethorpe."

"Ma'am . . . I'm honored." Greville swept off his hat with another flourish as he bowed over the hand languidly extended over the barouche door.

"How long have you been in town, Sir Greville?"

"A week or two, Lady Oglethorpe."

She nodded, her eyes sparkling. "Colonel . . . my goodness, how brave. Are you just back from fighting that tyrant?" She put a hand to her breast. "Just the thought of the savage gives me palpitations."

"Then I suggest you don't think of him at all, Letitia," Aurelia said with a sweet smile. "Leave such matters up to the colonel and his friends."

"Oh, but how could a sensitive soul not be tormented by the idea of the monster?" Letitia exclaimed. "Don't you agree, Colonel?"

"His name certainly strikes fear into the bosoms of most of the fair sex, Lady Oglethorpe," Greville said, his voice dripping with honey. "But pray don't alarm yourself. Bonaparte will not set food on England's shores."

"Oh, so brave . . . so strong." Letitia fanned herself with her hand. Then she turned to Aurelia, and her eyes were sharp. "Shame on you, Aurelia, for keeping Sir Greville to yourself."

"Sir Greville and I are but recently acquainted, Letitia. I happened to meet him in Bristol last week while I was visiting a relative. Believe me, I had no intention of . . . of *keeping him to myself.* That would be a little fast, don't you think?" Aurelia's smile didn't waver, but there was no hiding the sting in her voice.

A slight flush crept up Letitia's neck. Somehow, whenever she was in the company of Aurelia or Cornelia or, indeed, Livia, they managed to imply some failure of breeding on her part. She turned her head away sharply and smiled upon Sir Greville. "I do hope you will call upon me, Sir Greville. Everyone knows where to find me." She wagged a finger at him. "I shall look for you before the week is out. . . . Drive on, Leonard."

"I should be honored, ma'am." Greville bowed again and stepped back as the barouche moved forward. "No love lost there, I gather," he observed, offering Aurelia his arm again.

"She's odious. None of us can abide the woman. But she's the worst gossip in town, so the tale of this meeting, much embellished, will be flying around the salons and boudoirs of Mayfair before noon tomorrow."

"Then our work here is done. I'll escort you back to Cavendish Square."

It was strange, Aurelia thought, how he could put that afternoon's gloriously wild tangle of lust behind him so completely. Of course at this delicate early stage of the charade they couldn't risk anything that would raise eyebrows. They had not been seen in public before,

and they had to conduct themselves according to protocol, and society's conventions in such cases were rigid. A
romantic interest moving towards an engagement was a
pas de deux where each step was set in stone. No public
displays of affection until an engagement had been announced.

But he could have murmured a personal word or
squeezed her hand, he was an expert at covert communication. Instead, at her doorstep, he kissed her hand
punctiliously, wished her a good evening, and waited
until she had let herself into the house.

She went up to her bedchamber, reflecting that it was
only what she should have expected. When Greville was
at work, he was only at work, she had learned that much
in the week they had spent together.

Greville had one last task for himself that day. He
went in search of Harry Bonham. He tried the ministry first, hoping that his quest would end there, but he
was out of luck. No one had seen the viscount for two
days. He was reluctant to call in Mount Street for this
particular errand. He needed to talk to Harry well out
of eye and earshot of Frederick's sister. At least on this
occasion.

He trawled the clubs of St. James's and on his second
visit to White's was finally rewarded. The viscount was
sprawled in a deep wing chair by the fire, a glass of claret
at hand, his eyes half-closed.

Greville sat down in a chair opposite with his own wineglass and waited until the viscount chose to wake up. Greville was accustomed to the half sleep that refreshed almost as much as a long night of unconsciousness and was loath to disturb a man in the throes of recuperation.

After a minute, though, Harry's green eyes opened and regarded Greville with full awareness. "You must have read my mind, Falconer. I was hoping to have a word."

Greville nodded, sipped his wine. "I thought perhaps you might have been."

Harry pulled himself out of his slouch and reached for his own glass. "Thing is . . . it's a trifle awkward."

"Your wife has set you a task, I take it."

"Precisely, dear fellow. Precisely. And when Cornelia gets an idea into her head, it's the devil's own job to get it out again." Harry sipped his wine. "Well, to the point. Do you have an interest in Lady Farnham?"

"Not one to beat about the bush, are you, Bonham?" Greville's eyes gleamed in the firelight.

Harry shrugged. "What would be the point?"

"Quite so. Well, I could tell you it was none of your business . . ."

"You could . . . indeed, my dear chap, I wish you would."

Greville laughed softly. "But I won't. Aurelia's friends are entitled to their interest in her well-being, and I'd make a poor fiancé if I ignored that."

Harry was now wide-awake. *"Fiancé?"*

Greville laughed again. "My dear Bonham, you wouldn't suspect me of dishonorable intentions, I trust?"

"To tell you the truth, I have no idea what to expect of you," Harry stated flatly. "I don't know you . . . I know that you do vital work and the less I or anyone else knows about it the better. But if you're talking of becoming engaged to Aurelia Farnham, then that puts you in a different category altogether. You become the business of her friends . . . as I'm sure you understand."

"Which is why we're having this conversation." Greville gestured with his glass to a footman passing through the salon with a decanter of claret. He waited until their glasses had been refilled and the footman had moved on, then said, "I've a mind to settle down and . . . ." He shook his head with a slight self-deprecating smile. "I believed myself a hardened bachelor until I met Aurelia. She . . . she has touched me in a way I've never experienced before." He shrugged helplessly. "It sounds ridiculous, doesn't it, a man of my age and experience being swept off his feet like a stripling?"

Harry smiled. "Not really. Does Aurelia reciprocate your feelings?"

"She has said so," Greville responded simply.

"Forgive me . . . but you don't think an engagement is somewhat precipitate?" Harry asked somewhat awkwardly.

Greville raised his eyebrows. "I think we're both of

an age to know our own minds, Bonham. And to trust our instincts."

"Yes . . . yes, of course," Harry said hastily. "I had no intention of implying otherwise." He lapsed into frowning silence, twisting the stem of his wineglass between finger and thumb.

"There are other considerations," Greville said into the uncomfortable silence. "I can give Aurelia a comfortable life, provide more than adequately for her and the child. I've lived without a home for the better part of fifteen years, Bonham, and I'm tired of it. To find a woman like Aurelia, a woman who stirs me deeply, whose company I enjoy as I've never enjoyed another's, to find such a woman with whom I can share a fireside seems like a stroke of God-given fortune that I can only embrace."

Harry nodded. He understood perfectly. He knew little about the colonel's work, but he did know it had kept him on the move and away from his own country for close to fifteen years. A man could indeed grow tired of such an existence. And it was true that such a marriage would give Aurelia many benefits. She would never take such a step merely for financial stability, Harry knew well, but if that promise went hand in hand with a real liking, love even, for the man who offered it, then her friends could only rejoice with her.

"Forgive the question, but does this mean that you intend to leave the ministry?"

Greville shook his head. "You know I'm on an operation at present, one that gives me the opportunity to settle in London."

"I know that Simon asked me to ensure that you had the right introductions to pick up the threads of London society again. I don't know why."

"No, of course not. Suffice it to say that if this mission succeeds, then I will probably remain in England, and the ministry will use me as they see fit within the boundaries of our fair isle."

Harry regarded Greville closely, not certain that he believed him, but it was possibly true. Either way he had no right to challenge the declaration.

"Well, I offer my congratulations," Harry said after a minute. "I should warn you, though, that I can't guarantee my wife won't ask some seriously searching questions of Aurelia. You should be prepared for some questions from Aurelia once Cornelia brings up her suspicions that you might be more . . . or less . . . than you appear. And she *will* bring them up."

"I'll tell Aurelia myself all that she needs to know," Greville said. "Rest assured, she won't enter into this engagement without knowing everything that is important for her to know." He let this sink in before continuing, "Aurelia knows her own mind. She won't be swayed against her convictions by anyone, even her best friend."

"You appear to have learned rather a lot about Aurelia Farnham in a few chance encounters. I daresay finding yourselves in Bristol, so far from stimulating society, hastened your acquaintance."

"I daresay it did." Greville uncurled himself from his chair, ignoring the slightly pointed edge to his companion's statement. "I'm glad we had this little chat, Bonham, and all's square between us. I won't ask you to put in a good word for me, but I'd be grateful if you refrained from a bad one."

"I'll not queer your pitch, Falconer." Harry raised a hand in farewell and watched the colonel leave the salon. There was more there than met the eye, but then there always was in their business. Cornelia would warn Aurelia, with his encouragement, but both Cornelia and Livia had managed to make peace with husbands who worked in the shadows. There was no reason why Aurelia shouldn't. Besides, if the colonel was to be believed, he was going to be doing much less dangerous work in the future.

And there was a pig flying down St. James's Street.

What the devil was a man to do?

Cornelia listened to her husband's carefully edited retelling of his conversation with Greville Falconer. "But do you believe he's giving up his activities for the ministry?"

"I don't know, Nell. And it's none of my business, or yours. Say whatever you wish to Aurelia, warn her off if you like. But bear in mind that she might resent your interference, particularly if her feelings run deep for Falconer."

"I won't be interfering," Cornelia said with a touch of indignation. "I'll merely be giving my best friend the benefit of my opinion . . . my *informed* opinion, as you know very well. And I'm going to Cavendish Square right now."

Aurelia was getting ready for a visit to the theatre when Cornelia entered her bedchamber without ceremony. "Nell, is everything all right?" Aurelia jumped up from her dresser stool in alarm.

"Yes . . . yes, I just need to talk to you about something." Cornelia was unusually agitated, pacing the bedchamber. "But you're going out . . . I'll come back tomorrow."

"No, you won't." Aurelia caught Cornelia's arm and pushed her into a chair. "I'm early anyway, and one can always miss the farce." Aurelia pulled the dresser stool around to face Cornelia. "Hester, that will be all for now."

"Yes, 'm." Hester disappeared, and Aurelia leaned forward, her elbows folded on her knees.

"Greville?"

Cornelia laughed a little self-consciously. "I'm sorry, Ellie. I shouldn't interfere."

"You're not. You have something to say to me, and I know it will be something I want to hear. So, say away."

"He does work for the ministry."

Aurelia nodded. "Harry knows that?"

"Yes . . . but he doesn't know what he does."

"I wouldn't expect him to." Aurelia regarded Cornelia with a quizzical smile. "My love, I've watched you and Liv wrestle with these complications. Do you think I haven't learned a thing or two? Even if Harry knew exactly what Greville does, he couldn't tell you. But it's highly unlikely that he does."

Cornelia looked as relieved as she felt. "So it really doesn't matter to you? Harry said Greville was going to propose."

"Is he?" Aurelia didn't sound in the least surprised, and her glimmering smile told her friend the same. "I am really attracted to him, Nell." When something was so true, it was easy to be convincing, she reflected. "But it's more than that. I enjoy his company, I love to hear him laugh . . . I look forward to seeing him, and I miss him when he's gone." Smiling, she extended her hands palm up in a gesture of helplessness. "What else can I say?"

"Nothing else at all, love." Cornelia rose to her feet and leaned over to kiss her. "If you feel like that about him, then you have my blessing and that of all your friends. It seems rather quick, but . . ." She shrugged. "Love either grows slowly or it hits one between the eyes. It certainly did the latter with Alex and Liv."

"Yes, and look at them," Aurelia said with a soft chuckle. "And, be honest, Nell, how long did it take before you knew in your heart that Harry was the man for you?"

Cornelia laughed. "A little longer, but not much." She went to the door. "I'll leave you to your dressing. I'll give a small dinner party for you and Greville and some of our close friends, the word will soon spread that there's an understanding between you." She blew her friend a kiss and left.

Aurelia swung her dresser stool back to the mirror. She propped her elbows on the dresser and rested her chin in her cupped hands, looking at her reflection in the mirror. That had gone smoothly. She had been utterly convincing, so convincing in fact that when this sham engagement was concluded, she was going to find it hard to persuade her friends that she was not brokenhearted. She sighed, picked up her hare's-foot brush, and smoothed a little rouge on her pale cheeks.

Chapter Thirteen

"So that's the woman who's caught Greville's fancy," Lady Broughton observed to her companion, raising her lorgnette as she looked across her drawing room to the double doors, where a small group of guests were congregated. Her butler had just announced the arrival of Lady Aurelia Farnham, in the company of Viscount and Viscountess Bonham.

"Quite a handsome woman on the whole," her ladyship muttered, watching her nephew make his way swiftly towards the new arrivals.

"Yes, indeed, Agatha." Her companion nodded her vigorous agreement. She was a somewhat impoverished cousin of Lady Broughton's and made it a point of principle never to contradict Agatha, who could be generous to a fault to those who pleased her. "Quite handsome."

"It's a wonder she hasn't snagged a husband before this," Agatha said, still scrutinizing Lady Farnham and

Greville through her glass. "She's been in town for some time, I gather. How long ago was she widowed, Martha?"

"Four years, I believe. Dear Greville told me she lost her husband at Trafalgar."

"Hmm." Lady Broughton dropped her lorgnette. "I daresay she has no fortune, then. Everything else about her is unexceptionable. Decent breeding, nothing in her appearance to disgust. Fashionable, but not extreme. But if she has no prospects . . ."

"Dear Greville has no need to marry a fortune, Agatha," her cousin put in rather timidly.

"Maybe not, but if he's finally decided to take a wife, and he's not interested in making a love match, why wouldn't he choose a woman with money? It can never do any harm, you know."

"No, I'm sure it can't," murmured the impoverished cousin with a sigh.

"Well, you should know, Martha," Agatha declared somewhat heartlessly. "Greville's no pauper, but even so he should be looking to improve his situation like any sensible man."

"Perhaps it is a love match, Agatha," Martha ventured to suggest. "It's been less than a month since he returned from his army service. Perhaps he's been swept off his feet." She uttered a sentimental little sigh.

Agatha turned her lorgnette upon her cousin, regarding her in astonishment. "*Greville!* You're suggesting Greville would throw his hat over the windmill for a woman. Good God, Martha, the man's thirty-five years old. He's never lost his head, let alone his heart. He thinks of nothing but duty. It's always been duty to his country until now, but I believe he's finally accepted that he also owes a duty to his family. He's decided this Lady Farnham will fit the bill admirably, and she won't interfere with his priorities."

Agatha nodded her head vigorously, diamond eardrops swinging wildly. "Trust me, Martha, I know my nephew. Once he decides to do a thing, he wastes no time about it. He decided to find a wife on this trip home, and he went about it in his usual speedy and efficient manner."

"I'm sure you're right, Agatha."

"Of course I'm right. And the woman has a child, I understand. A girl child."

"I believe so."

"Hmm. Well, you can be sure he took that into account. Proven childbearing is an asset greater than a fortune, and he can have every hope that she'll give him an heir. I'm sure he weighed the pros and cons thoroughly . . . Greville is nothing if not thorough."

Lady Broughton began to move towards the group at the door. She presented a magnificent figure in a clinging gown of striped-crimson-and-turquoise satin that showed off her ample curves to best advantage. She wore the Broughton diamonds, her throat encircled by a scintillating collar, long drops dangling from equally long earlobes, a tiara fastened to her pearl-encrusted black lace mantilla, her wrists gauntleted with gems.

"Lady Farnham," she declared, extending her white-gloved hand. "I'm delighted to make your acquaintance."

Aurelia fought to maintain a neutral smile as she took the hand. Greville had prepared her well for this encounter, and she had been expecting no surprises. But he had not prepared her for Lady Broughton's appearance, which was striking to say the least. It was impossible for the gaze not to linger on the ample bosom spilling from the low décolletage of her colorful gown, or the wide swell of her hips accentuated by the hourglass shape of the dress. The gown fitted snugly over her thighs and knees, then flared into a train at the hem. The cut hobbled its wearer, obliging her to teeter on her impossibly high-heeled, diamond-studded satin slippers.

Greville had told Aurelia his aunt was generally well-meaning but tended to be overbearing. He'd told her that Lady Broughton was firmly of the opinion that she knew better than anyone, Greville included, what was best for her nephew. And he'd advised Aurelia that as long as she ventured no opinions of her own, responded modestly to all inquiries, however impertinent they might seem, and gave every impression of being thrilled at her good fortune in attracting the attention of Colonel, Sir Greville Falconer, then Aunt Agatha would approve the connection. Such approval, while not necessary, would make life a lot simpler. But he had not prepared Aurelia to be struck dumb by the lady's costume.

She found her tongue at last. "Good evening, Lady Broughton." She inclined her head in a courteous bow. "I'm honored to be here. . . . Are you acquainted with Lord and Lady Bonham?" She fought to avoid Cornelia's eye, knowing that one shared glance and they would both be lost.

"Only by name," her ladyship said, turning to greet the couple. "Of course, you young people move in different circles from those of us in our dotage." She laughed, and after a stunned moment, her guests joined in the laughter with appropriate disclaimers. No one could call Lady Broughton in her present guise in her dotage.

"But I do know the Duchess of Gracechurch," her ladyship declared, tapping Harry on the arm with her fan. "Your relative, I believe, Lord Bonham."

"My great-aunt, ma'am," he responded with a bland smile.

"Yes, I knew her when I was but a slip of a girl myself," her ladyship said. "Of course, the duchess can give me at least ten years, but we moved in similar circles when I had my first season." She turned her attention back to Aurelia. "I understand you reside in Cavendish Square, Lady Farnham."

"Yes, in the house of some friends. They are at present in the country. Princess Prokov gave birth to a healthy boy three days ago." Aurelia smiled. "A matter for great celebration amongst her friends, as I'm sure you understand, ma'am, but they will remain in the country until the princess is deemed fit to travel. Until then, I'm staying in Cavendish Square."

"Oh, rather in the manner of a caretaker," her ladyship said, frowning a little. "Do you not have a London residence of your own?"

Aurelia's smile was unwavering. "No, ma'am. I am very fortunate in my friends."

Lady Broughton nodded. "You would be anxious for your own establishment then."

"I own it would be agreeable, Lady Broughton." Aurelia's smile remained cool and composed.

Lady Broughton looked at her sharply. Aurelia regarded her with the same composure. Greville's aunt was accusing her of being a gold digger, but she would find it very difficult to discompose Lady Farnham. She held the elder woman's stare and suddenly Agatha chuckled and nodded. "Yes, yes, of course it would be, my dear. Well, if you can make this wandering nephew of mine stay home once in a while, we shall all be grateful to you."

When Aurelia said nothing, her ladyship turned aside, putting up her lorgnette. She swept the room, declared, "Oh, my goodness, there's Dorrie Garfield. She's looking remarkably well for someone rumored to be on her deathbed." She teetered off, managing her heels and her train with practiced dexterity.

"Nicely done," Greville murmured, speaking for the first time since his aunt had borne down upon them. "You handled her very well."

"What did you expect?" said Cornelia. "Lady Broughton accused her of marrying you for your money. You didn't really think Ellie couldn't handle such an impertinence? Actually it was more than an impertinence." Cornelia's blue eyes were flashing with indignation.

"You must forgive my aunt . . . she's not accustomed to considering the feelings of others," Greville said, glancing at Aurelia, his gaze as always penetrating, seeing much more than the surface. "She's been indulged her entire life."

Aurelia laughed. She had read Greville's scrutiny easily. He was anxious to see if she had in any way been distressed by his aunt's outrageous if covert accusation. His concern warmed her and she said, her eyes smiling at him, "She doesn't trouble me in the least. There's no need to look daggers, Nell. I'm not upset." Aurelia had ostensibly spoken to Nell but the reassurance was for Greville.

Cornelia looked unconvinced but allowed herself to be carried away on her husband's arm.

"Let's move away from the door." Greville took Aurelia's arm, tucking it into the crook of his elbow. "Do you care for some refreshment . . . champagne, perhaps? I believe it to be pink. Although the significance of that escapes me." He smiled down at her. "You do look utterly delectable in that gown, my dear. Emerald is a wonderful color for you. I must remember that."

Aurelia smiled her pleasure at the compliment. The emerald green gown of flowing crepe was new, one of her few extravagances, bought specially for the evening, and she knew how well it suited her. It was confined beneath the bosom with a band of gold lace, matched by the edging to the flounced hem. She wore a fragile gold fillet in her hair, the gold gleaming against the pale corn-silk ringlets, and a simple gold chain at her throat.

"Why must you remember it?" she asked playfully. Tonight they could be as publicly affectionate and flirtatious as they wished because tonight they were to show the intimacy of a betrothed couple. Notice of their betrothal had been sent to the *Morning Post* and the *Gazette*. It would appear in print in the morning, and it should come as no surprise to those of the ton who'd witnessed the couple at Lady Broughton's rout party. It was a relief for once to behave naturally in public in Greville's company. There was no part to play at this function, what their fellow guests saw was all there was to see.

"Oh, I might find the urge to buy you a present from time to time," he said with an airy wave, releasing her elbow. He took two glasses of pink champagne from the tray of a passing footman and handed her one. "A toast," he said softly, his gaze holding hers as he touched her glass with his. "To our partnership." He raised his glass to his lips, his gray eyes still holding hers, and they drank, for a moment seeming to stand alone in the crowded room. It felt as if people had moved back to give them space.

Aurelia sipped her champagne, aware of many eyes upon them. There could not have been a more public declaration. "Partnership," she agreed as softly as he. For a moment she was filled with a yearning, an overwhelming wish that it was a real declaration. That there was no charade. The air around her seemed brittle as crystal, and she had to do something before it shattered.

Deliberately she sipped her champagne with a critical frown. "It tastes just like the ordinary stuff . . . but I daresay my palate is not sufficiently discriminating."

"There really isn't much to distinguish it." His eyes sharpened at this abrupt change of topic and mood. "Do you care to dance?"

"Yes, thank you." Her smile was slightly strained, but she was regaining her equilibrium and looked around her, nodding at acquaintances, murmuring greetings, as they walked into the next room where a set was forming for a country dance.

Her feet performed the steps of the dance automatically, and she was only slightly surprised that Greville was a good dancer. He was surprisingly light on his feet for such a big man, or it would be surprising if one didn't know what else he was. In their games of pursuit in the country she had seen him move through a thicket as stealthily as a cat, spring from the roof of a byre to the roof of an outhouse, landing with barely a sound, crawl on his belly through a ditch. He had not expected such tricks from her, but he had been teaching her to look for escape routes, to see her surroundings with fresh eyes, to look for and find opportunities. And she had watched his maneuvers with helpless envy, wishing she could emulate them.

But she was a lot more at home on the floor of a ballroom moving gracefully to the strains of the orchestra, smiling, conversing, never worried for a moment about where to put her feet. And this, after all, was the arena in which she was to operate. She needed no lessons here. She smiled the smile of a woman who was about to announce her betrothal to the most attractive man she had ever met. The man who twirled her beneath his arm and moved her on down the dance with practiced ease.

As the music ended, she curtsied to her partner's bow, and he led her off the floor. "Come and join us at supper," Nell invited, waving them over to where she stood with Harry. "Harry's famished for some reason."

"I had no dinner," her husband murmured plaintively.

"And whose fault was that?" Nell retorted. "You weren't home in time."

Harry grinned. "True enough. I was riding with friends in Richmond and we stopped on the way home for ale, and . . . well, time passed . . . you know how it is, Falconer."

"Indeed," Greville said easily. "All too well, Bonham."

Aurelia very much doubted that. She couldn't see Greville idling away an afternoon in an alehouse with friends unless he was there for some other purpose. But then she had similar doubts about Harry. It was easiest with these men to accept their explanations and move on. "Shall we go to the supper room then?" she suggested.

"We'll join you in a moment," Greville said. "I have something I wish to show Aurelia."

Cornelia looked as surprised as Aurelia, but said only, "Of course. We'll see you in a minute." She linked arms with Harry and they moved away in the direction of the supper room.

"Show me what?" Aurelia asked, looking at Greville in puzzlement. "Is there something in the house I should see?"

"No," he said with a wicked smile. "No, it's on my person actually."

Aurelia's eyes widened. "That sounds almost indecent, sir," she murmured. "And I can't believe you would venture . . . in your aunt's house, no less."

For answer he eased her ahead of him with a hand in the small of her back into the corridor. She obeyed the pressure as he guided her into a small, deserted antechamber. "The picture over there is of one of my more disreputable ancestors," Greville pointed out casually. "He was a pirate, I believe. But that was probably putting it politely. Handsome devil, though, don't you think?"

Aurelia was feeling quite out of her depth, but obediently she looked up at the portrait of a perfectly attired

Elizabethan gentleman. "Oh, he has a gold earring! Was that usual in those days?"

"I have no idea," Greville said from behind her. Something about his voice made her turn around.

"Oh." Her mouth formed a perfect *O* of surprise. He held a small box on the palm of his hand, outstretched towards her. "What is that?"

"Open it. I can't believe how clever I was." He sounded very pleased with himself.

She took the box, looking at him in a mixture of puzzlement and alarm.

"It won't bite," he said, watching her with a curious little smile.

She opened the box. A perfect square-cut emerald ring rested against the black velvet. "Oh, oh, it's beautiful . . . what a perfect stone." She took it reverently from the box and held it to the light. The stone glowed deepest green against its surround of tiny diamonds set in white gold.

"How perfect that you should be wearing that color tonight," he said, taking the ring from her. "Give me your hand." He took her left hand and slipped the ring onto her ring finger. "Good, I sized it correctly."

She turned her hand this way and that as the emerald caught the light. "I hadn't thought . . ."

"Hadn't thought what?"

"Oh, that we would . . . would do things properly, like this," she finished, shaking her head.

"We don't do things by halves in my business, Aurelia." He was still smiling, but the comment had an underlying note of seriousness.

"Yes, but a counterfeit stone would do the job just as well, and I know this is not counterfeit."

"No, it's not." He took her hands in his, holding them tightly. "I would not disparage you or your contribution to this work by such an insult. You are my partner, and I respect and honor you as such." Then his eyes took on that sensual glow and he said softly, "And you are far too beautiful a woman to wear anything but perfection."

"I did not believe you given to extravagant compliments, sir," she said, attempting to smile through the sudden mist of tears, to make her voice light even though her throat was thick with emotion.

"Oh, believe me, my dear, I am not. Shall we show the world the evidence of our engagement?"

"Yes . . . yes, of course. This is the perfect occasion, isn't it?" She blinked the incipient tears away and swallowed the emotion. Of course he had chosen this evening to give her this because of the greater impact the ring would have in this gathering. But even as she allowed him to escort her to the supper room, she knew that however pragmatic the occasion, there was nothing pragmatic about the gift.

Cornelia saw it first when they sat down at the supper table, and her eyes widened. "What a magnificent stone," she breathed, reaching for Aurelia's hand. She looked across at Greville, who was smiling slightly. "You have an eye, sir."

"Thank you, ma'am." He bowed his head in acknowledgment.

Harry picked up Aurelia's hand with all the casual informality of old friends and examined the ring. He whistled softly. "Congratulations, Colonel."

"How about me?" Aurelia asked, laughing.

For answer Harry leaned sideways and kissed her cheek. "That goes without saying, my dear. I wish you every happiness."

"What's going on here?" David Foster came over to the table, eyes gleaming with curiosity. "Are you talking secrets?"

"Not in the least," Aurelia said, holding up her hand for his inspection. "Quite the opposite in fact."

David nodded his approval in Greville's direction and kissed Aurelia. "So when's the happy day?"

"We haven't discussed it," Aurelia said with a vague gesture. "I'm enjoying this moment far too much to look ahead."

"As you should, love," Cornelia said. "David, go and bring Nick, and on your way do us a big favor and try to head off Letitia before she smells gossip and sails on over here. She'll only say something malicious and envious. You know what she's like."

"All too well. At your command, ladies." David bowed and strode away through the crowd.

Aurelia sat back on the little gilt chair and sipped

her champagne. For a moment she wondered how she would be feeling if this were a genuine engagement. Then she dismissed the thought, it only spoiled this moment, which was too good to spoil.

"Lady Farnham." Lady Broughton loomed before them, her quizzing glass up. "What's this I hear about a ring? Have you declared yourself, Nephew?"

Greville rose to his feet with the rest of the gentlemen at the table. "I have, indeed, ma'am. Lady Farnham has graciously agreed to be my wife."

"Well . . . well . . . I knew it was in the wind, and I'm heartily glad of it," the lady said, taking the chair beside Aurelia that Harry held for her. The delicate piece of furniture seemed to quiver beneath the layers of satin and the weight of diamonds.

"Let me see, my dear." The lady examined the emerald through her glass and nodded. "I approve the setting, Greville. A pretty design. Your dear mother's was too heavy for the stone." She released Aurelia's hand. "There are one or two other family pieces that belonged to my late sister. I have had them in my charge since her death. You shall have them on your wedding day, Lady Farnham."

Aurelia smiled, too stunned to think of appropriate words. *Greville had given her his mother's ring.* She smiled her way through the congratulations that continued for the rest of the evening, but at one o'clock she was more than ready to go home when Cornelia announced that she was dead on her feet.

"I'll be with you directly," Aurelia said, rising from her chair. She had arrived with the Bonhams, it seemed natural that she would leave with them.

"I'm taking you home myself," Greville said swiftly, coming over to her, carrying her fur wrap. "I have a carriage waiting." He draped the wrap over her shoulders.

"Then we'll bid you good night, Ellie." Cornelia kissed her. "Come shopping with me tomorrow. Let's look at some materials for our gowns for my ball. I'm determined we should complement each other."

"Tomorrow afternoon," Aurelia promised. Cornelia went off on her husband's arm.

"Come." Greville took Aurelia's arm in a light clasp and escorted her down to the hall. A town carriage stood at the curb and he opened the door for her.

"I didn't realize you kept a carriage," Aurelia said, settling into the corner, drawing her wrap closely around her.

"It's a hired conveyance," he said easily, sitting beside her. "I could have borrowed my aunt's, but that would not have worked with my plans for the remainder of the night."

"Oh?" She peered at him in the dim light from the single oil lamp swinging from the roof. "And how's that?"

"Can't you guess?" He drew her into his embrace, tilting her chin for his kiss. "I've a mind to celebrate our engagement."

Aurelia let her head fall back against his shoulder, savoring the warmth of his mouth, the pliant lips, hard and then soft against hers. Her lips parted for the light probe of his tongue, and her eyes closed as the carriage rocked and she lost herself in the scent of his skin, the feel of his face against hers, the taste and feel of his mouth as her tongue went on its own voyage of exploration.

Then the carriage halted, and reluctantly she struggled up against him. "So soon?" The disappointment was clear in her voice.

"Not exactly," he said with a low laugh. "We shall say good night. I shall see you to your door. You will go inside and unlock the side door. I shall tell the coachman I wish to take the night air and will walk the rest of the way to my house. I shall take a turn around the square, making sure there are no watchers, then let myself in through the side door. You will be waiting for me in bed." His dark eyes glittered with sensual amusement. "Your bedchamber is the second on the left, to the right of the upstairs landing. Am I right?"

She nodded, for a moment speechless, then said, "How do you know about the side door? How do you know which one in that mansion is my bedchamber?"

"All these houses have side doors, and a discreetly casual question to young Jemmy gave me the answer to your second question."

She shook her head. "Stupid of me to ask."

"Just a little. Now, let us begin, or it will be dawn before we've had any time together, and . . . and I have to tell you, dear girl, I am consumed with hunger for you." His voice was a low throb, and his gaze seemed to swallow her whole as he held her face for a second between his hands. Then he released her, opened the carriage door, and sprang to the ground. "Come."

Greville held out his hand and she stepped down beside him. Her body was now on fire with anticipation, all traces of fatigue vanished. Punctiliously he kissed her hand at the door and saw her inside, waiting until the door closed and he heard the lock turn. Then he went to dismiss the carriage.

The feel of him gave her so much pleasure, Aurelia thought an hour later, as she drifted out of a trance-like doze, her body languid and fulfilled. Greville had come to her, throwing off his clothes even as he crossed the room to the bed. He had made love to her with an urgency and a passion that had caught her up in a tidal wave and left her beached and breathless, unable to move.

Greville had his arms around her and she turned sideways, digging her chin into the angle of his shoulder and neck, licking the salt sweat on his neck. He was so big and powerful, so full of weightiness, of the solidity of power. It made her feel small, yet somehow empowered by connection. She could feel the muscularity of his shoulders, the rippling muscles of his back as he moved his thigh to cross it over hers. He rolled her onto her back and leaned above her, his lower body pressing hers into the mattress.

"So, ma'am," he murmured, his eyes holding hers. "How would you like to be pleasured now?"

"However it pleases you," she returned, shifting languidly beneath him.

For answer, he slid his hands beneath her buttocks, lifting her on the shelf of his palms as he slid very slowly into the warm, moist furrow of her body. He moved with tantalizing slowness, pausing, drawing himself back to the brink of her body so that she caught her breath in an agony of anticipation, then slowly sheathing himself within her again. It seemed he could continue like this forever.

This was only the fourth time they had made love, but Aurelia was learning that Greville Falconer had extraordinary staying power when it came to the pleasures of the bedchamber. He could bring her again and again to ecstasy and save himself for one final throbbing release when he sensed that she had strength for but one more orgasmic explosion.

Now he moved his hands to the backs of her thighs and lifted her legs onto his shoulders. He sat back, holding her ankles as he drove deep inside her, deep to her core, a deeper intrusion than she would have believed possible.

She held his gaze as he hung above her, moving swiftly now, his eyes sparks of gray light. She arched higher, trying to take him even farther within herself, tightening her inner muscles around him, suddenly determined that she would control this finale. He would reach his climax at her dictation. And when he threw back his head with a muffled cry, she tightened herself around him once more, and the hard length of him pulsed and throbbed within her. Then, as always, he pulled himself out of her body the instant before his orgasm engulfed him and lay heavily on her, his seed pumping against her thigh.

Aurelia ran her hand down his sweat-dampened back, feeling warmth and tenderness as well as triumph that she had at last succeeded in breaking her lover's iron self-control.

Greville finally raised his head from her breast and rolled sideways onto the mattress. "Wicked woman" was all he said before his eyes closed and he seemed to sleep.

Aurelia was never sure when he was truly asleep or when he was merely drifting in semi-awareness. She turned her head on the pillow to look at him. He seemed unconscious. But then his arm moved and his hand came to rest on her belly and his eyes flickered open. "Wicked woman," he murmured again.

Aurelia smiled to herself and closed her own eyes under a wash of lethargy. The sky was graying beyond the window, but it would be half an hour before dawn began to break.

The half hour was over too soon. Greville sat up, flung aside the covers, and got to his feet. He stretched once, then was instantly awake. He turned to the bed and leaned over her, running a caressing hand over her turned flank.

"Good morning," he murmured, kissing her ear.

"Morning," she mumbled into the pillow.

"You have to get up, I'm afraid, and lock the side door after me," he whispered.

Aurelia groaned but struggled up, blinking. "I would have thought you'd have a way of doing that for yourself, master spy," she grumbled, reaching for her peignoir as she swung her legs over the side of the bed.

He only chuckled, dressing swiftly. "Hurry now. We're cutting it fine as it is."

Aurelia flitted ahead of him down the corridor, pausing to listen for sounds. The household still seemed to be asleep, but not for much longer. At the head of the stairs, she stopped, looked around, then ran on silent bare feet to the hall. Greville followed, making no sound. The side door was in the corridor that ran behind the stairs to the door to the kitchen regions.

Greville slipped through and vanished into the gray light of dawn, one hand raised in farewell. Aurelia locked the door. She heard sounds coming from the kitchen now and sped to the stairs. It wouldn't matter if someone came upon her wandering the house, she had every right to do so, but she had absorbed enough of Greville

Falconer's maxims to want to make a clean escape to her bedchamber.

She closed her chamber door behind her with an exultant little chuckle. She climbed into bed, snuggling into the nest she had already made, and lay wide-eyed and wide-awake, savoring her memories of the night.

Chapter Fourteen

Simon looked up as Greville came into his dingy office in the War Ministry. "Good morning, Greville." He half rose from his chair, extending his hand across the desk. "You've been busy I hear."

"Matters move apace." Greville shook the offered hand. "I have established my household on South Audley Street, and with the engagement made public, Lady Farnham will act as my eyes and ears, cultivate the acquaintance of those who are of interest to us, and report back to me. Our spending an unusual amount of time together now we are betrothed will cause no raised eyebrows." He perched casually on the arm of a rickety wooden chair across from the desk.

Simon regarded him narrowly. "Forgive the bluntness, Greville, but Lady Farnham has had no previous experience of our particular business. You are confident that she will be able to—"

"Perfectly confident," Greville interrupted him

brusquely. "Aurelia is quite capable of holding up her end. Her tasks will be quite simple and she understands them to perfection."

Simon nodded. "Of course . . . of course. You will, of course, have made sure of everything." But a frown still lingered in his eyes.

Greville regarded him with a slightly rueful smile. "As we agreed, this engagement will provide exemplary cover. Better than any other device."

"Indeed . . . indeed." Simon pulled at his chin. "I own to a slight misgiving, though. It seems so . . . so convenient, if you will, that Frederick's widow should present herself to you as the perfect partner."

Greville shrugged. "As you know, Simon, in our business one takes one's partners where one finds them. I would not have recruited Aurelia had I thought for one minute that she was unsuitable. She has responded well to her training and since her work will be confined to doing what she's been doing most of her adult life, entertaining, social mingling . . ." He shrugged again. "I see no possible reason for concern."

Simon looked down at his cluttered desk. He trusted Greville Falconer absolutely; he would happily put his own life in the colonel's hands, but he couldn't shake off a vague unease. Undoubtedly the betrothal would provide the perfect stage for Greville's work in London, but it was difficult, even for an agent as experienced as Falconer, to involve a person with whom he had emotional ties. Not that Falconer was giving the impression of having such ties with his fiancée, indeed he'd implied that Aurelia was as detached about their relationship as he was himself. That she had her own reasons for agreeing to serve her country in this way.

"I've discussed the matter of the pension for Lady Farnham with my masters," Simon said, following his last thought. "They are all agreed that her services and those of her late husband should be rewarded financially, but with a single lump sum rather than a pension. A sum of two thousand guineas has been approved. I hope Lady Farnham will find that satisfactory."

It might not put a house like that in South Audley Street in her price range, Greville thought, but carefully invested and combined with the funds she had at present, it would certainly support a more modest independence. "I'm sure Lady Farnham will be pleased," he said. "There is still the matter of her husband's back pay and prize money."

"Yes, that will be paid at once in whatever form she chooses. A bank draft . . . or ready cash . . . Now to business." The subject thus dealt with, Simon opened a drawer in the desk and drew out a sheet of paper. "It seems possible that the games are about to begin." He slid the paper across the desk to Greville. "Two Spanish gentlemen were observed landing at Dover. Very open they were about it, too, as I understand. They spent a good ten minutes pacing the quayside, showing themselves off to any interested observers."

Greville nodded. "Making certain their arrival was noticed then." Every major seaport in the British Isles was watched day and night by the agency. Any foreign visitor would know that it would be almost impossible for someone to land without attracting attention, unless at a secluded beach in the middle of nowhere.

"Indeed," Simon agreed. "So they're either legitimate émigrés or anxious to be thought so, which fits with our earlier intelligence that they're intending to infiltrate society at its highest levels. Anyway, they'll bear watching, and perhaps cultivating. They arrived in London last night and took up residence on Adam's Row."

"Convenient," Greville murmured, scanning the information on the paper he held. "Number fourteen. I should be able to contrive an accidental meeting when I take my morning's constitutional." He laid the sheet back on the desk. "Don Antonio Vasquez? Do we know anything of him?"

Simon shook his head. "Not at present. The name is unknown to us, but it could be an alias. I've sent instructions to our man in Madrid to do some digging, and with luck we might get something in a week or so. In the meantime, I suggest we approach with caution. As we've just said, he could be perfectly innocent, following his deposed king into exile. Simply an aristocratic fugitive from Bonaparte's Spanish dependency. There are plenty of them all over the Continent as Napoléon puts his own relatives on the thrones of Europe."

"I'll make his acquaintance," Greville stated, getting to his feet. "Presumably this Senor Miguel Alvada is a henchman of some sort."

"Presumably." Simon, too, got to his feet, leaning his hands flat on the desk. "You might start with Countess Lessingham. She's the center of the Spanish exiles in London . . . offers support, introductions, help with lodgings, that kind of thing. Her house is always a first port of call for any new émigré. If she doesn't know Don Antonio now, she soon will."

Greville nodded. "She was Bernardina y Alcala, if I remember right."

"Exactly so. She married Lessingham five years ago, but is well-known for her patriotic efforts on behalf of her countrymen."

"I'll follow it up . . . make my own assessment." Greville shook his companion's hand in farewell and left the ministry. As her first mission, he would ask Aurelia to pursue an acquaintance with the countess.

His curricle was waiting for him in the ministry's courtyard, a groom attending the handsome pair of bays, who shifted restlessly on the cobbles as Greville approached. He took the reins from the groom and took his seat on the box. "Let go their heads."

The groom released his hold on the bits and jumped up behind as the curricle headed for the big wooden doors that stood open onto the street. Greville nodded at the guardsmen on either side of the doors as they saluted him, then drove towards St. James's Park. He crossed the park and turned onto St. James's Street, heading for Piccadilly. Two men stood deep in conversation as he passed White's club and he drew rein.

"Good afternoon, Bonham, Petersham." He greeted Harry and Nick Petersham.

"Nice pair, Falconer," Nick said approvingly, examining the horses through his quizzing glass. "They look familiar."

Greville laughed. "That's because they are. They're Eden's breakdowns."

"Ah." Nick nodded wisely. "I heard he was selling up. All to pieces I gather. Did you hear that, Harry?"

"Aye," Harry agreed. "Lost a fortune at hazard in Pickering Street . . . young fool."

"Well, if he will play in a hell, what can he expect," Nick stated, then caught his friend's astounded eye. Nick flushed a little. "All right, Harry, no need to look at me like that. I know I've played there m'self, once or twice." He turned back to Greville. "You're not one for the tables, are you, Falconer?"

Greville shook his head. "Never seen the appeal, which is fortunate since I have little aptitude and less money to waste."

"And now you're to be a married man," Nick said with another sagacious nod. "Nothing like a wife to encourage a man to keep the purse strings tight."

"Which is presumably why you remain a bachelor," Harry stated. "Are you going home, Falconer? Could you take me up?"

"With pleasure," Greville said with alacrity.

Harry climbed into the curricle beside him. Nick Petersham waved them away and went up the steps to the hallowed portals of White's.

"Convenient that we're such near neighbors now," Harry remarked. "Nell and Aurelia will certainly find it so once the marriage has been solemnized."

Greville's only response was a flickering smile and an accepting nod as he turned his horses into the cacophonous throng on Piccadilly, concentrating on weaving his way through the carriages, coaches, street barrows, and drays.

"Have you and Aurelia set a date as yet?" Harry asked nonchalantly.

"I await Aurelia's word on that subject. It is customary, I believe, for the lady to set the date."

"Of course." Harry hesitated, then decided to take the plunge. "You have said that you expect to work mostly in England now, but should that change, have you thought how to explain such an absence to Aurelia?"

Greville gave him a sideways glance, then said in a tone that stated quite clearly that it was none of his passenger's business, "Should that time come, I'll deal with it."

"Of course. I'll say no more, except that if I can be of service where Aurelia is concerned, Falconer, you have only to say. She does not lack for friends."

Greville cast him another sidelong look, his lips

slightly pursed. So that was the reason behind this shared drive. He'd guessed it had to be something more than mere companionship and convenience. "I'll bear it in mind, but I assure you, Bonham, you have no cause to worry about Aurelia. She's my responsibility, and I don't take such responsibilities lightly."

"No . . . no, of course not." Harry made haste to deny any such implication. He turned the conversation to mundane matters until Greville drew rein outside Bonham's house on Mount Street.

"Thank you for the lift, Falconer," Harry said, jumping down.

"Anytime." Greville raised a hand in salute and drove the few yards back to South Audley Street. Outside his house he handed the reins to his groom, with instruction to take the curricle back to the mews, and went into the house. The man who emerged from a side entrance half an hour later bore little or no resemblance to Colonel, Sir Greville Falconer.

The man in a rough homespun jerkin, patched leather britches, his face obscured by a woolen hat pulled low over his eyes, seemed to slink up the street towards Grosvenor Square, hugging the shadows as if afraid of the light. Just before the square he turned right onto Adam's Row.

It was a street much like any other in this part of Mayfair. Elegantly fronted tall row houses, white steps, gleaming black iron railings. He strolled head down to the end of the street, glancing around every now and again as if on the watch for something. Few people were on the street, but those avoided him, even going so far as to cross the street at his approach. Everything about the man seemed to speak of a nefarious errand.

The afternoon shadows lengthened and a chill breeze rattled the branches of the plane trees where the pale green of early spring was beginning to show. Outside number 14, Greville's step slowed as he cast a seemingly swift glance at the house. In fact he had taken in everything of note. Casually he crossed the street and leaned against the railing of a house some way down the street that still had a clear view of number 14 across the road. He took a clay pipe from his back pocket and stuffed it with foul-smelling tobacco, struck a piece of flint against the iron railing, and lit the pipe. He puffed reflectively, a cloud of noxious smoke surrounding him, as he watched the house. He looked like any laborer having a well-earned smoke and a rest at the end of a day's work.

After half an hour his vigil was rewarded. The door opened and a man emerged, dressed impeccably in a fawn coat and cream pantaloons, his tasseled Hessians gleaming in the late-afternoon gloom. His complexion had an olive tinge to it and his neat spade beard was in the Spanish style. He held his cane under his arm as he drew on his gloves, standing on the top step of the house, glancing up and down the street. If he noticed the scruffy figure farther along on the opposite side of the street, he gave no indication. He took his cane from his armpit and set off down the street, swinging it lightly.

Greville didn't move, just watched closely. He could feel the fine hairs on his nape lifting with the conviction that he had seen the man before, somewhere, and in circumstances that were not at all pleasant. But he couldn't chase down the elusive memory that was almost more of a feeling than a concrete recollection. It was something to do with the man's posture, his walk, the set of his head. *Where had he met Don Antonio Vasquez before?*

He was about to turn away when a movement at the side of the house caught his eye. Another man emerged. A short, stocky figure, dressed all in black, stepped into the street from the narrow passageway that separated this house from its neighbor. He had the appearance of a secretary of some kind, but Greville, watching closely, his eyes narrowed against the veil of smoke around him, knew the gait and the build of a fighter when he saw it.

He extinguished his pipe with relief. Though a useful prop, he disliked it intensely. He returned it to his pocket, feeling the heat of the bowl against his thigh, and set off after the black-clad figure. He made sure the man knew he was being followed, pausing when his quarry paused, hurrying after him when he turned abruptly into George Yard. The man stopped in the deserted yard and turned around sharply. Greville glanced around. No one was around; it was a perfect place for a little daylight robbery.

"Whatcha doin' 'ere, guv?" he called out, stepping closer, feeling in his pocket for the short, weighted club he always carried in his present guise. "Lost yer way, 'ave yer?"

His quarry stood foursquare, rocking slightly on the balls of his feet. "You'll find me a hard man to rob, my friend." His accent was heavy but his language fluent. His hands were balled into fists at his side as he waited for the would-be assailant to approach.

Greville swung the weighted club with clear menace, staring at his quarry malevolently, as if of two minds whether to initiate his attack or turn tail. The Spaniard saw the hesitation and, as Greville had hoped he would, took advantage of it. He sprang forward, two rigid fingers outstretched towards Greville's eyes. *A street fighter,* Greville thought grimly, one who knew all the dirtiest tricks.

The man was light as air on his feet and covered the distance between them in two leaps. Greville sidestepped the jabbing fingers not an instant too soon and dropped into a defensive crouch, the club hanging loosely from his right hand. He circled his quarry and the Spaniard followed his movement, turning on the balls of his feet, his fingers still outstretched.

He would have another weapon, Greville thought. This was no secretary. Knife or pistol? His gaze ran over the figure looking for a telltale bulge, anything that would tell him what to prepare for. He guessed it would be a knife. The man had the air of a knife fighter, a man who liked to get up close to his quarry, a man who liked to attack in silence.

Greville saw the flash of silver and jumped sideways in almost the same moment. The Spaniard muttered an imprecation and spun around, the hilt of the stiletto blade between his fingers. Greville recognized his way of holding the blade, which was particular to a certain group of people, and he had heard and recognized the imprecation. He knew who and what he was dealing with now, and exactly how the man would attack.

The Spaniard raised his knife hand, and in the instant before the knife flew towards him, Greville threw the weighted club. It hit the Spaniard square in the forehead. He teetered, his eyes glazing, and the knife fell to the cobbles, but amazingly he remained upright. Greville swooped low, picking up the club as he dodged behind the man. He brought the club down with cracking force across his skull, and slowly his opponent crumpled to the ground.

Greville stood quite still for a second, catching his breath. The yard was still deserted, and now in near darkness. Little enough light penetrated at high noon, and it was now well past sunset. He bent to pick up the knife, turning it slowly in his hands, looking for the mark he was certain he would find. It was there, just inside the carved hilt. The insignia of the Inquisition.

That put a different complexion altogether onto this enterprise. They would not send an agent of the

Inquisition on a mission to set up an intelligence network. His usefulness lay in quite other arenas. So what *was* he here for?

He bent down again and felt for the pulse in the man's neck. It was faint but still there. It would take more than a blow on the head to finish one of the Inquisition's own. He ran his hands through the man's pockets. If this was to look like a robbery, he needed to steal something. He took the fob watch and a purse containing three silver sovereigns. Then he walked quickly out of the yard, leaving the scene of the crime behind. No one would think it had been anything but one of the many footpad attacks that plagued the alleys and dark corners of the city.

He returned home and changed his clothes, resuming once again his customary persona. Then he went out again, hailed a cab to the ministry, and went directly to Simon Grant.

"Back so soon, Greville?" The chief looked up in surprise from a pile of papers. "I could have sworn you were here not three hours past."

Greville acknowledged the witticism with a faint smile. "I wasn't sure I'd still find you here at this hour, Simon."

"Oh, I live here." Simon sighed and leaned back in his chair, linking his hands behind his head. "So, why the return visit?" His eyes, although tired, were shrewd.

"An interesting encounter." Greville swung a wooden chair around and straddled it, resting his folded arms along the back. "It would seem that the Inquisition has something to do with our Spanish friends' arrival in this fair city."

Simon sat up abruptly, his hands falling to his desk. "How d'you know?"

Grimly Greville related the events of the last hour. "We have to assume that there's more to their enterprise than the simple establishment of a network. Why else bring the Inquisition?"

"Troubling," Simon said, pulling at his chin. "We might know more when we hear from our man in Madrid. In the meantime, we shall have to play a watch-and-wait game. Keep a close eye on them." He regarded Greville thoughtfully. "How does this affect Lady Farnham's involvement in this enterprise?"

Greville frowned. "I've been thinking about that," he said slowly. "I see no alternative to changing the plan. I'm not prepared to take any risks with her safety with the Inquisition around."

"No . . . no, I can see not. Well, do what you think best, Greville."

"I shall, have no fear, Simon." Greville swung off the chair, shook hands, and left. He hailed another cab to take him to Cavendish Square.

He banged the knocker vigorously, tapping his foot on the top step, unable to conceal his impatience. But the door opened quickly, and Aurelia stood looking up at him in surprise. "Greville . . . Isn't it a little late for an afternoon visit?"

"I need to talk with you." He stepped adroitly past her into the hall. "Are you alone?"

"Yes, but I have to go up to Franny in a moment. I always sit with her while she has supper."

"Can she wait for a few minutes?" He couldn't hide his impatience, his gaze flicking around the hall.

"Yes, of course," Aurelia said quickly, puzzled. Greville was never impatient. "Come into the salon." She led the way, then turned to face him as he closed the door behind him. "What is it, Greville?"

He went to the window, where the curtains were already drawn against the encroaching dark. He moved to one aside, looking out onto the street before letting it fall back. "We have to modify our situation, Aurelia," he said directly, turning to face her. "I want you and Franny under my roof for the duration of this enterprise."

Her jaw dropped. "Under your roof? Whatever do you mean?"

"I have learned some new details about this Spanish network that make me think they might find my fiancée interesting," he said bluntly. "I cannot protect you adequately if you're here and I'm more than half a mile away."

She paled, looking at him, her hands clasped against her skirt. "You said you expected no danger to me and certainly not to Franny."

"I did not. But that was before some new information was brought to my notice." He came towards her, taking her hands in his, turning his penetrating gaze onto her upturned countenance. "I swore I would protect you and your child, and I will do so. But you must accept that I know best how to do that."

"How serious is this threat?" she asked, withdrawing her hands and turning away to the fire.

"I don't know. But I do know that the very possibility of there being a threat of any kind is enough to make me act. So, our engagement needs to become a marriage without delay."

She turned back to him. "And how do we break a marriage after three months? It's a very different matter from an engagement."

"I shall be sent on a mission abroad, and my death shall be reported soon after. It wouldn't be the first time."

"But then you could never come back, never be Greville Falconer again."

He gave a short laugh. "My dear Aurelia, that would be no great loss to me. I have had many aliases and will have many more. There's nothing here to keep me. I have no interest in London's social scene. No family, no ties of any description. This is the first time in fifteen years that I've been back for more than a fleeting visit. I can slip in and out of England for my work as and when necessary with no one being any the wiser. I will leave the country, and you will be free within a matter of months, once the news of my death is verified by the ministry."

His words fell like a cold stone into the pit of her stomach. *Nothing here to keep me.* It was such a negative statement, and it seemed to underscore the temporary nature of their relationship. The times he'd looked at her in a certain way, said things in a certain tone, and the way he made love to her, had made her fancy that perhaps there could be more to their romantic interest than a game to be played for the public eye. She stared down at the emerald ring on her finger, twisting it around so that it caught the candlelight.

"This was your mother's ring?" To her it was not a non sequitur.

"Not exactly. The emerald was part of a set that had belonged to my grandmother. My mother to my knowledge never wore any of it. That ring itself was made specifically for you. Your fingers are far too slender and dainty for the original setting." He looked puzzled. "Why do you ask?"

Such a matter-of-fact explanation of what could have had some significance. It was pointless to deceive herself, to imagine he might feel some inkling of what she felt herself. "No particular reason, just curiosity," she said with a dismissive gesture, bending to poke the fire. "Wouldn't it be better if I just withdrew now? If our engagement is broken, I would no longer be of interest to whoever these people are, and Franny and I would no longer be in danger."

He shook his head. "Apart from the fact that I need you in this work, Aurelia, now more than ever, until I have dealt with this threat, and completed our enterprise, they will still find you of interest, even just as a way to get to me."

"I see." She felt chilled all over, as if she'd just stepped out of an ice bath. "But how are we to accomplish a wedding so swiftly? We've only just become engaged."

"At least we *are* engaged," he said, moving to his customary position by the fire. "And very publicly. Everyone expects a wedding. If it takes place sooner rather than later, there might a little talk but not much. We're both past the age of discretion."

Aurelia said nothing for a moment. She'd already invested so much time and emotional energy in this enterprise; she'd learned so much, and she loved what she'd learned. It excited her. This change of plan was merely a tweak of the original. And she couldn't deny the little frisson that the prospect of sharing a roof with Greville for the duration of this enterprise gave her. She had never denied to herself his attraction, or the amazing pleasure he gave her in bed. Why not embrace the opportunity to explore both further in the most natural of circumstances? There was nothing to stop her, and she'd deal with the eventual parting one way or another. She was used to dealing with hurt.

She went to the sideboard and poured two glasses of sherry. She handed him one, then sipped her own, still standing in the middle of the room. "We could pretend to elope, I suppose," she said. "As you say, it won't come as a complete surprise since people are used to the idea of our marriage, eventually. I could say I didn't want any ceremony. I didn't want to be reminded of my first wedding, perhaps . . ."

She looked into the amber liquid in her glass, wondering if she could persuade Cornelia and Livia that she'd succumbed to the wildly romantic notion of an elopement out of impatient passion. She'd certainly gone out of her way to imply that she found Greville thrillingly attractive, that she'd fallen in love with him almost at first sight, and the emerald ring had only proclaimed with public emphasis the idea of a passionate attachment between them. She could probably pull it off. It wouldn't be that difficult to be convincing, she recognized wryly.

She became aware of Greville's silent scrutiny and looked up to meet his steady gaze. "When?" she asked simply.

"Can you and Franny be ready to move to South Audley Street in two days?"

"As soon as that?"

"Sooner if it were possible."

Chapter Fifteen

IN THE PARLOR OF A SUITE of rooms at 14 Adam's Row, Don Antonio Vasquez stared at the battered figure standing in front of him. A bandage was wound around his head and his swarthy complexion had a yellowish tinge to it.

"You were robbed?" Don Antonio said in disbelief. "By a mere street felon? How could that happen?"

Miguel winced. The light in the room hurt his eyes, and a full marine band seem to be clashing cymbals and banging drums behind them. He swayed a little, nausea swamping him, and with a murmur of apology sank into a chair. "It was no mere street felon, Don Antonio," he croaked. "The man fought like a soldier. He knew all the tricks."

His master gave a snort of derision. "Have you seen how many soldiers are on the streets of this godforsaken city? Deserters, pressed men on leave, wounded on furlough. The lucky ones are on half pay, the rest destitute, fleeing the authorities. Of course they know a trick or two when it comes to robbery. They're desperate and they learned the tricks of survival in His Majesty's armed forces. You were robbed by one of them, make no mistake. You must have been half-asleep to let such a one get the better of you."

Miguel put his head in his hands. Don Antonio was mistaken, he knew it in his bones. His opponent had been a trained fighter, not just a disaffected, desperate soldier on the lookout for easy prey. But he couldn't summon the energy to argue with Don Antonio, who was looking at him with a snarl of derision on his well-bred mouth.

"I need to rest, Don Antonio," he muttered, fighting the nausea that threatened to overwhelm him. "I am concussed."

"Well, you're certainly no good to me in your present state," Don Antonio declared with a dismissive wave of his hand. "Get to your bed."

Miguel staggered to his feet and stumbled to the door, his hand over his mouth.

❦

"Is she in bed?" Greville looked up from his book as Aurelia entered the drawing room of the house in South Audley Street three days later.

"Yes, and almost asleep," Aurelia said, settling into a chair opposite him. "Franny's not a creature of habit."

Her smile was fond. "It can be a nuisance on occasion, but sometimes, like now, it can be very useful. A new house, new nursery, new furniture . . . she's happy as a clam."

"And you?" He set down his book.

"Relieved, now that everything's all right with Cornelia and I've written to Livia. It was surprisingly easy actually. Cornelia just accepted the fact with a murmur of annoyance that she hadn't been a witness, and that was it."

"I'm glad. I wouldn't like you to fall out with your friends over this."

"It would take more than this for a real rupture. But I'm glad it's over nevertheless."

Greville crooked a finger at her, his eyes narrowed. She rose, iron filings to his magnet, and went to him, allowing him to pull her down into his lap. He slipped a hand around to caress her breasts, lightly flicking at the nipples beneath the fine cambric of her gown. They rose instantly to his touch, and he chuckled, nuzzling the nape of her neck. "So wonderfully responsive. I could spend all day touching you."

She leaned back against him, thinking that she could probably spend all day being touched by him in a world of sensual fantasy. She could feel him growing hard beneath her and mischievously shifted her hips a little, grinning at his groan of mingled pleasure and protest. Then she jumped up.

"Dinner, sir, will be served in half an hour."

"Oh, God," he moaned. "Look what you've done to me. I won't be able to move for ten minutes."

Aurelia laughed. "A glass of claret will cool your ardor." She poured him a glass and brought it over to him. "You will not wish to miss dinner, I promise you. Our Mavis has prepared scalloped oysters, followed by roast duck with apple sauce, and Ada's prepared a Rhenish cream and a gooseberry fool."

Greville sipped his wine, eyes half-closed. "I still don't know how it happened that in the space of twenty-four hours, in addition to young Jemmy, Daisy, and Hester, we have acquired two formidable identical twins in charge in the kitchen and a doddering gentleman failing to answer our door."

"They decided it for themselves. When Liv and Alex return to Cavendish Square, it's inevitable that the old friction will arise again between Morecombe and the twins and Alex's rather stuffy household staff. But Morecombe and the twins don't want to leave their apartment there; it's their home, they've lived there for decades, but they do want to work. They won't take payment from anyone because they have Aunt Sophia's pension and their own apartment in Cavendish Square. They just like to do what suits them. And when I told them I was married and moving here, they didn't bat an eyelid, simply decided it would suit them to follow me. So, they'll come here in the morning and leave in the evening. Jemmy will answer the door at Morecombe's bidding."

She poured herself a glass of sherry and sat down again. "The arrangement will suit everyone very well, and I know Liv will be relieved that she doesn't have to negotiate anymore between Boris and Alphonse, the chef, and the old guard."

"Well, I have no objections." Greville raised his glass in a toast. Then a glimmer of humor appeared in his gray eyes. "I have a wedding present for you." He left the drawing room, a spring in his step.

Aurelia leaned her head against the chair back and closed her eyes, wondering what on earth he was going to give her. Something presumably that would facilitate the part she had to play.

She heard the door open again and kept her eyes tight shut, a smile dancing over her lips. She felt his approach across the room, felt his presence in front of her. "Should I open my eyes?"

"It might help," he said drily.

She opened her eyes. At first she saw only Greville, but then her gaze moved to the door and she gasped. It was the most beautiful animal she had ever seen. Huge, like a small pony, powerful shoulders a perfect match for Greville's, she thought with a long exhalation. "He . . . she . . . ?"

"She," he said, clicking his fingers at the animal, which padded gracefully towards them and sat down at Greville's feet. "She's called Lyra, after the constellation. And she will be with you everywhere you go, and most particularly when I cannot."

So she hadn't been far wrong after all, Aurelia reflected, reaching a hand to touch the dog's magnificent head. But even a useful present could be as beautiful as it was welcome. "Lyra," she greeted softly. The dog lifted her head beneath her caressing hand, and the great brown eyes met hers. "Oh, you beauty. What is she, Greville?"

"An Irish wolfhound," he said, radiating his pleasure in her reaction to his gift. "Cornelia told me that you loved dogs . . . *real* dogs, she specified."

Aurelia laughed. "Oh, Liv's silly pink dogs . . . of course."

He looked puzzled. "I don't understand."

"You will when you meet them." She moved her hand beneath the wolfhound's chin. "She's beautiful, Greville, and I thank you."

He pulled the hound's ears. "She's beautiful, but she's also been trained to protect. I can't be at your side always, and I'm not very confident that you'll use a pistol if you have to. Lyra is gentle as a lamb most of the time, but there are words she understands. When you and she know how to work with those words together, then you'll be as safe as I can make you when I'm not beside you."

Aurelia felt a familiar shiver cross her scalp. The chill of reality crept into the warm, lamplit drawing room. "You haven't told me exactly where this danger is coming from."

"I don't know exactly. And quite probably it will not touch you at all. But I'm not prepared to take any chances."

"No," she agreed, caressing the wolfhound's neck in

long strokes. She looked up at Greville. "I understand the risks."

He drew her to her feet, holding her hips, his expression grave. "And do you trust me to protect you, Aurelia?"

"Oh, yes," she said softly. "In as far as you are able."

He kissed the corner of her mouth. "I *am* able," he promised. "I will not put you in the way of danger, understand that, Aurelia."

She kissed him, relaxing into his embrace. It was impossible to imagine the kind of danger that had killed Frederick, here in this house in this quiet London street, among the well-regulated households, the social conventions and rigid rules of Mayfair society. And that was where her contribution to her country's cause would lie.

"Dinner is served, Lady Far—Lady Falconer," Jemmy announced from the doorway, averting his eyes from the embracing couple.

They moved apart. "Thank you, Jemmy." Aurelia took Greville's arm and they went as sedate as any married couple into the dining room.

Midmorning a few days later, Aurelia left the house on South Audley Street, Lyra padding at her side. On this beautiful April morning, the sun had some warmth and the air a spring freshness.

Aurelia was dressed for walking in an olive green pelisse over a gown of tawny gold silk with a deep flounced hem, and a pair of rich brown leather half boots. She wore a close-fitting brown velvet hat with an ostrich plume curling over the brim, and her hands, one of which held Lyra's lead, were buried in a sable muff.

She walked briskly, aware of her own pleasure in a costume that was fresh from the dressmaker rather than in the latest manifestation of a series of refurbishments. No one looking at this fashionably dressed lady walking her dog towards Green Park would guess that beneath the smiling, assured surface her heart was beating fast and every sense was stretched. Tucked into the muff was a sealed paper that Greville had given her with the instruction that she was to deliver it to a certain point in Green Park. It was her first courier job, and excitement warred with the apprehension that she might somehow fail to complete the mission.

The man polishing the iron railings of a house opposite watched her go. When she turned the corner of the street into Audley Square, he shoved his polishing cloth into a deep pocket of his greatcoat and set off, whistling carelessly to himself. She had left the square when he got there, but he could just make her out along Charles Street. He quickened his step, anxious to keep his quarry in sight without coming too close to her. The *asp*'s newly acquired wife was a matter of considerable interest in 14 Adam's Row.

Aurelia wasn't certain when she first felt the prickle on the nape of her neck. It was before she reached the gate into Green Park. She paused, bending to adjust the lace of her boot while Lyra sat patiently beside her.

Aurelia glanced behind her as she busied herself with her boot, but could see nothing and no one out of the ordinary. But of course, as Greville had told her many times, she wouldn't see anything suspicious. If she was being followed, her pursuer would be too experienced to give himself away.

However, she knew a trick or two of her own. She straightened, turned completely full circle, and raised a hand in enthusiastic greeting to someone behind her. She waved more vigorously, standing on tiptoe, as if trying to attract the attention of someone who hadn't seen her yet. And a man turned around and looked behind him. A man in an ordinary, rather scruffy greatcoat, with a muffler around his neck, and a cap with a brim pulled low over his forehead. A man indistinguishable from many others on the street, strolling past the park railings. But no one else paid any attention to her vigorous gesticulations.

Why should they if they had no interest in *her*?

"Well, well, Lyra," she murmured. "We have company it seems." She bent as if to adjust the dog's collar and whispered, "On guard." The dog's ears pricked for a second, then the hound stood and pressed herself against Aurelia's legs.

They walked into the park and Aurelia made no attempt to look behind her. She knew she was being followed, there was no need to confirm it. She took one of the winding promenades that led to the reservoir in a corner of the park and walked in leisurely fashion around the lake. It was bounded by shrubberies, and off to one side lay a small copse dominated by a copper beech in its center.

The copper beech was Aurelia's destination, or, most particularly, a small hole in the trunk that made a perfect poste restante for unorthodox mail. However, she ignored the copse and continued on her way around the lake towards the Ranger's Lodge. Lyra kept close to her legs and every now and again emitted a low-throated growl, which told Aurelia that the hound had now picked up the follower on their tracks. Presumably he was closer now, but she made no attempt to check.

Her mind was working fast now. She could abort the mission, and no one, least of all Greville, would blame her. Caution was always the first watchword. But the idea of being balked of success on this her first time out made her furious, as disappointed as she'd been in the country when she had been so certain she'd evaded Greville, only to find him waiting for her at the stile.

She would find a way to elude her present follower. As she rounded the lodge at the end of the lake, she came upon the broad swath of grass where grazed a herd of cows tended by a group of milkmaids, who would, for a small sum, provide a cup of milk fresh from the cow to a thirsty pedestrian.

Aurelia smiled suddenly, a mischievous gleam in her eye. She strolled casually onto the grass and into the middle of the herd of cows, Lyra at her side. She whispered softly to the wolfhound, and instantly Lyra put back her head and howled, a long, mournful howl that lifted scalps, sent shivers down backs, and threw the herd into a milling, lowing panic.

The milkmaids and the cowman rushed into the herd to try to calm them. Lyra continued to howl, and the cows blundered about, lowing and bumping into each other. Aurelia took a firm grip of Lyra's lead and darted through the warm and heaving flanks and out the other side of the herd, which effectively blocked both a view of her and any possibility of pursuit. A crowd had gathered to watch the spectacle, and she had a clear path to double back to the copse.

Once among the trees, she stopped and listened, remembering Greville's words: "Do nothing in haste. You may think you don't have time to pause, to listen and look, but you do."

So she paused, listened, and looked—and heard nothing but the trill of a songbird welcoming spring, and the rustle of a squirrel in the grass beneath the trees. It was the matter of a moment to slip the document into the hole in the beech, artfully concealed by a square of moss, and in no more than three minutes, she and Lyra were strolling towards the gate that led to Piccadilly.

She was certain now that she had lost her pursuer. There was no sign of the man in the greatcoat behind her, and she felt no sixth sense. Lyra was walking beside her, showing none of her own instinctive awareness of danger. Aurelia skipped a little, then laughed self-consciously at such a childish display of delight.

Greville was waiting for her when she came home. He came out of the library as he heard her in the hall, and one look told him all he needed to know. Aurelia was glowing with satisfaction, her brown eyes alight, her cheeks pink, her slight frame radiating energy.

"You had a pleasant walk, my dear?" he inquired with a smile.

Aurelia, aware of Jemmy's presence, responded with a demure "Yes, indeed, it's a beautiful morning. Green Park was delightful." She bent to release Lyra's lead as she spoke.

Greville gestured to the library behind him. "Will you join me?"

"Of course." She drew off her gloves, following him into the library, Lyra at her heels. She closed the door and stood smiling at Greville, triumph exultant in her gaze. "I'm sure I was followed."

His expression darkened. "Tell me."

She gave him a full account, trying to make an unembellished narrative of the sequence of events, but she couldn't conceal her delight in her successful ruse. When she had finished, she regarded him expectantly.

Greville stood with his back to the fire, hands clasped lightly behind him. "You did well. But tell me again exactly what happened when you reached the gate to Green Park."

Aurelia frowned. "You don't believe me? You think I might have missed something?"

"Not necessarily. But you're excited, understandably,

and I want you to tell me again, step by step, now that your triumph is not quite so fresh."

Aurelia bit her lip, trying to conceal her annoyance at what felt like an admonition. An unjust one. "Very well." She reached up to unpin her hat and laid it carefully on a drum table by the door, together with her gloves and muff. She unbuttoned her pelisse, letting it hang open as she walked slowly to the window seat and sat down, folding her hands in her lap.

"A plain unvarnished tale, then." And she told it again. And as she did so she realized that Greville was right. It wasn't that she'd missed anything out the first time, but that she *could* have done when she was glorying in self-congratulation and in the expectation of Greville's admiration. She ought to have known, she thought wryly, that expressing admiration in these matters was not Greville Falconer's way. Greville Falconer, the colonel running a covert operation in London, was a very different man from Greville Falconer the lover.

"So there you have it." She shrugged and regarded him without a smile.

He didn't seem to see her as he stared frowning at the carpet. He had hoped his suspicions about the inhabitants of Adam's Row had been wrong. He had hoped that their proximity to South Audley Street did not indicate that he was the object of their presence in London. He had said nothing of this suspicion to Simon, waiting for some proof one way or the other before acting on it. But it seemed he had his proof. Somehow they knew that Greville Falconer was the *asp*. There was no other explanation for why they would follow Aurelia. She could be of no interest except in her association with him. If they had simply been setting up an intelligence network, they would have had no interest in Greville or his wife unless Greville got in the way of their network. And there'd been no time for that.

It explained the presence of a servant of the Inquisition, too, he thought grimly. They were after a highly sought prize who would have many secrets to divulge. Under the right pressure, the *asp* could be induced to break open the entire European intelligence network of England and her allies. And who better to apply that pressure than a graduate of the Inquisition's training?

"What is it?" Aurelia asked, alarmed by his expression. "Did I do something wrong?"

He tore himself from his sinister train of thought and shook his head. "Not at all. You did very well. That was a neat device with the cows."

"Yes, I thought so, too." She looked at him, still puzzled. "Something's troubling you?"

He gave a short laugh. "Only the fact that you were followed."

"Oh. Yes, of course." She could have kicked herself for stupidity. "It means that someone's watching the house . . . which must mean that someone suspects that you are not what you seem."

"That is rather the conclusion I had come to myself,"

he said aridly. "But there's nothing to be done for the moment except maintain constant vigilance. Now, tell me, have you thought any more about pursuing an acquaintance with Lady Lessingham? I mentioned it a couple of days ago."

"Oddly enough, that's exactly what I'm going to be doing this afternoon. Lady Lessingham is to be at Lady Buxton's card party this afternoon. She's known to be a demon at the whist table." She made a move towards the door, unable to conceal the deflation that came with anticlimax. Greville's flat reaction had been like a dousing under the stable-yard pump.

He spoke suddenly as she put her hand to the doorknob. "You enjoyed yourself this morning, didn't you?"

She turned back to the room. "Yes," she said simply. "Probably I shouldn't have. It probably means I'm not taking the work seriously enough." Without waiting for a response she opened the door and left.

Greville remained in the middle of the library staring at the closed door, absently tapping his mouth with his fingertips. He'd made a mistake, taken a false step. Aurelia was disappointed. She'd tried to hide it, but her eyes as always spoke the truth. They'd been so full of delight when she'd arrived home and had quickly lost the glow, become as cool and flat as a forest pool in the shade.

It was not his habit to praise a job well done since he expected nothing less. If she had failed in her mission, returned home unscathed having made no attempt to elude her suspected follower, he would have had the same reaction. Satisfied that although she hadn't completed her mission, she had at least taken no risks. But Aurelia was not like his other partners, and if he had not been preoccupied with the truth of his grim suspicions, he would have reacted differently. He would have given her what she wanted . . . indeed, what she deserved. She was still a tenderfoot, but she'd done all and more than he could have expected, and she needed to know that.

He strode out of the library and up the stairs to her bedchamber. He tapped out a rhythm on the door and she invited him in immediately. She was sitting at the dresser while Hester arranged her hair, and she looked surprised as he came in. "Did you forget something?"

"Yes," he said, holding the door ajar at his back, a smile playing over his mouth, a gleam in his eyes. "Hester, Lady Falconer will call you when she needs you." He stepped aside, holding the door wide.

"Aye, sir." Hester, her mouth full of hairpins, bobbed a curtsy. Hurriedly she put the pins back on the little silver tray on the dresser and scooted past him into the corridor. Greville closed the door firmly and turned the key.

"So what did you forget?" Aurelia inquired, unable to conceal the prickle of sensual excitement as she read intent in his gaze.

"It seemed I was rather niggardly in congratulating my partner on her quick thinking," he said with a lazy smile. "I thought to remedy the omission."

"Oh," she said, her heartbeat speeding, a light flush blooming on her skin as anticipation grew.

He came up behind her, resting his hands on her shoulders, watching her face in the mirror, holding her gaze with his own. He slid his hands down over her shoulders, slipping beneath the loosened opening of her negligee. He cupped her small, firm breasts in his hands, one finger teasing each nipple until they rose to hard points. All the time he watched her face, saw the flicker of her tongue across her lips, the languid, sensual glow deepen in her eyes as her body came alive beneath his caress.

He leaned farther, sliding his hands down over her ribs to her belly, his breath rustling through her pale hair. One hand slid farther, down to the base of her belly, a finger twisting in the curly tangle of hair to reach into the warm, moist space between her thighs.

Aurelia took a deep, shuddering breath, but she found she couldn't move. She remained transfixed by the dark eyes in the mirror and the increasingly intimate exploration of his busy fingers. The negligee had fallen open, exposing her blue-veined breasts, her white belly, and now, as she shifted a little on the dresser stool, the last folds parted to reveal his hand disappearing into the dark nest at the apex of her thighs and the smooth, pale planes of her thighs, clutching convulsively around the pleasure-bringing fingers.

He smiled at her in the mirror as, deft and knowing, he brought her closer and closer to the brink. Beads of perspiration gathered on her lip, in the cleft of her breasts, in the soft hollow of her navel as her breath came swift between parted lips. Her head fell back against his chest as he leaned over her, and the pulse at the base of her throat danced to a wild beat until she felt herself soar over the cliff and into the maelstrom of delight, and the tension left her body. She slumped back against him, her eyes closed, her breathing rapid and uneven.

Greville kissed the side of her neck, slowly withdrawing his hand. He cupped her chin, turning her face sideways so that he could kiss the corner of her mouth. Slowly her eyelids fluttered open, and her eyes, languid and slightly bemused, gazed at him.

"It's the middle of the day," she said with a tiny chuckle.

"What difference does that make to the price of apples?" he asked with an answering chuckle.

"None at all." Aurelia turned on the stool and stood up, her opened negligee falling away from her shoulders. She reached behind him, pressing her hands into his buttocks, feeling the muscles tighten beneath the kneading fingers. She pressed her bare loins against the hard bulge of his penis straining against the butter-soft leather of his britches.

Slowly she slid to her knees on the carpet and swiftly unfastened his britches, slipping a hand into the opening to draw out his penis. She stroked down its length with finger and thumb, reached farther to cup his balls, squeezing lightly. It was his turn now to inhale sharply, to remain still to receive his pleasure. His hands twined in her hair as she bent to her task, her fingers scribbling gently up the length of the hard shaft she held, before she took him in her mouth. Her hands cradled his balls as her tongue flickered against the moist tip, and her lips moved up and down the shaft, her teeth grazing lightly, tantalizingly, against the rigid, pulsing flesh.

And when he cried out at the glory of climax she held him tight, resting her cheek against his belly until he gave a deep, shuddering breath and dropped to his knees beside her.

He caught her against him and stretched out on the carpet, cradling her in the crook of his arm. He reached a hand down her bare back and lightly stroked over her bottom as she lay turned against him, one thigh flung carelessly over his leg. "I seem to be building up a debt of gratitude," he murmured into her tousled hair. "I came to discharge one debt and now I find myself with another."

Aurelia laughed weakly. "Not so, sir. I merely served you with your own sauce."

He kissed her forehead, then sighed. "Delightful though this is, my dear . . ."

"Yes," she agreed, struggling to a sitting position. "Look at me. It'll take me hours to make myself presentable enough for a staid card party." She felt him hesitate, as if he was considering something, and wondered for an instant if he was going to suggest that they consign business to the devil for the rest of the day, but he didn't.

"Hester will soon put you to rights," he said, standing up, then reaching down to pull her to her feet, before fastening his britches.

He picked up her discarded negligee on the floor by the dresser stool and held it for her, then tied the girdle at her waist before examining her critically. "You do look a little tumbled," he conceded with a grin. "But if you pull a comb through your hair, Hester probably won't notice."

"She won't say anything if she does." Aurelia picked up her hairbrush and tugged at the tangle of once artfully arranged ringlets. "I'll just have to plait it and wear a cap."

"A cap . . . you most certainly will not." Greville sounded outraged. He was using her comb to tidy his own hair and dropped it onto the dresser. "You're not some middle-aged matron."

"Let me remind you that I am in my thirty-first year, the mother of a five-year-old, and as far as the world is concerned on my second husband," she stated, half-laughing, half-pleased at his indignant response.

"That is nothing to the point. For as long as you are supposedly married to me, Madam Wife, you will not wear a matron's cap. Understood?"

"But I have such pretty caps," she said with an innocent smile. "Dainty lace ones, a few with delightful starched ruffles and wide ribbons under the chin and—" She gave a shriek of feigned alarm as he descended upon her with a ferocious expression.

She fled across the chamber, putting the bed between them, and stood laughing at him. "The starched ribbons are most becoming. They help to support one's double chins when they wobble." She tapped beneath her own sharply defined chin in illustration.

"Vixen, just don't ever let me see you in such a garment." He blew her a kiss and went to the door. "I'll instruct Jemmy to bring the barouche in half an hour," he told her as he left her chamber.

Aurelia, still chuckling, rang for Hester.

Chapter Sixteen

DON ANTONIO VASQUEZ, stretched at his ease before the fire, a glass of port to hand, surveyed his visitor with an expression of distaste.

"I seem to be surrounded by fools. What do you mean, you lost her?"

The man twisted his cap between his hands, his gaze firmly fixed upon his shuffling feet. "Your pardon, Don Antonio, but it was the cows."

"*Cows.*" Antonio stared at him. "What nonsense is this. Miguel, what's he talking about?"

Miguel was standing discreetly and somewhat anxiously in the shadows during this interview. His head was no longer bandaged, but his forehead was covered with a deep purple bruise, and an angry knot throbbed just above his right eye. But he was back on duty, despite the dull, continuous headache. As luck or misfortune would have it, he had employed the man who had so signally failed in his task that morning, and that failure was bound to be visited upon his wounded head at some point. He was not in Don Antonio's best books as it was.

Miguel cleared his throat. "Apparently they keep a herd of cows in the park, Don Antonio."

"What's that to do with anything?" his master demanded, draining the contents of his glass. "Why would I be remotely interested in bovines?"

"Of course you wouldn't, sir. But the lady in question somehow became lost in the herd and disappeared. By the time Sanchez here had extricated himself from the fracas, there was no sign of the lady or her dog."

Antonio frowned, holding out his glass imperatively. Miguel rushed forward with the decanter. "Was this encounter with the bovines deliberate?" Antonio fired the question at Sanchez.

Sanchez shuffled even more uncomfortably. "I don't see how it could have been, my lord. It was the dog, see. It took against the beasts . . . dogs don't like cows in general, in the country—"

"For God's sake, man, I'm not interested in the relationship between dogs and bovines," Antonio interrupted. "What kind of a mad country is this, when they keep a herd of cows in a park in the middle of the city?"

"Something to do with public grazing rights, sir," Miguel explained stolidly, unsure whether the information was truly required.

Don Antonio's blasphemous response was answer enough. "What do we know of this woman?"

"A widow before her marriage to the *asp*. Nothing of note. Her first husband was killed at Trafalgar. One child, a daughter of five or six."

"Why would he marry her?" Don Antonio uncurled his lean, slender frame from the chair and rose to his feet. He was dressed in black, except for a shimmering white neckcloth, from whose starched folds glowed a massive ruby. A silver dagger was clipped to his belt.

He took a turn around the small parlor, his body as lithe and graceful as a panther's. "The *asp* amuses himself with women when it suits him, but there's never been a permanent woman in his bed before." He tugged at his square beard, frowning into the fire. "*Why?* Why would he take a wife *now*?"

"Perhaps because he chose to," Miguel suggested.

"*Idiot,*" his master declared. "Of course he chose to. The question is *why*?"

"Perhaps we'll discover if we watch her," Miguel ventured.

Antonio spun on his heel to face him. "That bumbling idiot who couldn't follow an elephant in a desert has made that impossible," he declared icily. "I told you to find me someone who would *never* be picked up."

"I thought I had, sir." Miguel glared at the unhappy Sanchez. "But perhaps it *was* an accident with the cows. There's no way to be certain."

"Which is precisely why we can't take the risk," his master stated. "The *asp* must not suspect anything. It's vital that he assumes his real identity remains unknown.

So all surveillance stops as of now. And from now on, I'll do the job myself. There are better ways to skin a snake than surveillance."

Miguel bowed, clicking his heels together. "As you command, sir."

"Get this clumsy oaf out of my sight."

Miguel gestured to the unfortunate man, who backed hastily and with obvious relief from the room.

Don Antonio stood in front of the fire, rising and falling on his toes and heels in the manner that Miguel knew denoted deep thought, the kind of thoughts that boded ill for their subject.

"What the devil does this marriage mean for us?" Don Antonio murmured finally.

Miguel did not make the mistake of responding.

"If, against all the odds, our friend has somehow succumbed to the softer emotions . . ." Antonio's thin lips twitched in a sardonic smile. "If he has feeling for this woman, then she'll prove very useful. And if he's using her in some way, then we shall also find a use for her. I look forward to making her acquaintance."

"Yes, Don Antonio." Miguel bowed again. "I see what you mean."

At that his master gave a short, unkind laugh. "Do you, Miguel? Do you indeed? If you do, it'll be the first time in my experience."

Miguel bowed his head beneath the contemptuous statement and made no attempt to defend himself. He turned to go.

"One minute." Antonio raised a hand. "What's her name?"

"I believe it to be Aurelia, sir."

"And of what countenance is she? What does she have that would attract the *asp*?"

Miguel considered. "In truth, sir, I don't know," he said finally. "I've only seen her briefly, but she seems nothing out of the ordinary. Pleasant enough countenance, rather small frame, no bosom to speak of . . . or at least that I could see. Nothing special, Don Antonio."

"And you don't consider that to be of interest?" Don Antonio inquired with a deceptively pleasant smile.

"I didn't, but I do now." Miguel bowed hastily. "If you'll excuse me, sir." And he beat a prudent retreat.

Aurelia stepped out of the barouche at the Buxtons' house in Stanhope Gardens and mentally gave herself a shake. The morning's adventure had left her feeling rather foggy for some reason. At the time she hadn't realized how much nervous energy it had taken, but she needed all her faculties this afternoon. Countess Lessingham, as Aurelia had told Greville, was a demon at the card table and she needed to impress her.

She ascended the steps and was welcomed by an austere butler, who escorted her to the back of the house and into a large salon that was set up with four card tables. Edith Buxton turned from a group of ladies by the fire as Lady Falconer was announced and came forward to greet her. "My dear Lady Falconer, welcome. I hope your wits are sharp for the cards." A warm and friendly lady, Edith was well liked even by the most malicious gossips, and she beamed with pleasure at the prospect of her afternoon's entertainment.

Aurelia responded with her own warm smile, even as she was casting a quick eye over the assembled company. It astonished her how she had learned to see in this way, to take in a scene in one sweeping glance. The hours with Greville, poring over pictures of complex scenes or groupings, absorbing the most minute details, learning mnemonics for memorizing trays of unrelated objects, had all enabled her to feel certain that one inclusive view of a scene would give her the salient facts.

Lady Lessingham stood out in the crowd. Aurelia had thought before what an imposing figure she cut, and she seemed to stand out like a peacock in full feather among the more subdued English ladies. A mantilla was fastened to her jet-black hair, her curvaceous figure encased in a dramatic afternoon gown of coffee and cream lace.

Aurelia moved towards the group of women, smiling, acknowledging greetings with a small bow and a handshake. "Lady Lessingham, how are you?" She shook hands. "Have you been out of town? I haven't seen you in a week or two."

"I was in the country, Lady Falconer . . . oh, do permit me to congratulate you." The lady spoke with a slight lisp as she fluttered her eyelashes behind a skill-fully manipulated fan. "Such a surprise. Is it true . . . an elopement? How romantic."

"We felt that a very quiet ceremony would be appropriate," Aurelia said calmly. She was getting used to the slightly scandalized questions, and quite adept at deflecting them, but they did grow tiresome and she couldn't wait for the nine days' wonder to be replaced with another. "You've been in the country, you said?"

"Oh, yes . . . I have been nursing one of my countrymen." The countess was happily diverted. "So ill, after the most dreadful journey, such a narrow escape from Spain, with the barbarian at his heels." She sighed behind her mantilla.

"Countess Lessingham . . . our dear Spanish friend, you are so good to your fellow countrymen," Edith declared, patting the lady's arm with her silk-mittened fingers. "And so welcome among us . . . poor King Carlos . . . to have been forced from his throne by that monster." She gave a well-bred shudder.

"I'm so glad to run into you here, Lady Lessingham," Aurelia said warmly. She slipped an arm through the countess's and adroitly drew her slightly apart from the circle around the fire. "I'm so curious about your country and I haven't had the opportunity to ask you any of the hundreds of questions I have. Do tell me about Madrid. I must own to a long-standing urge to see the Prado . . . such a beautiful palace, from everything one has seen and heard."

"Yes, indeed . . ." The countess sighed heavily, helped herself from a plate of sticky sweetmeats on a side table, and launched into a description of the exquisite marbles, frescoes, and paintings in the royal family's palace.

As soon as Greville had asked her to further her acquaintance with the countess, Aurelia had set herself to learn enough about Spanish customs and art to be able to pose intelligent questions and murmur sympathetically at the losses her companion had sustained. Within fifteen minutes the countess had insisted she call her Doña Bernardina and was announcing to their hostess that nothing would do but that she be partnered at cards with dear Lady Falconer.

Even if Greville thought two tours de force in one day no great achievement, she certainly did, Aurelia reflected, as she played to her partner's ace. Doña Bernardina's skill at the cards was everything she had been led to expect. They partnered each other well, and at the end of the afternoon were, to all intents and purposes, the best of acquaintances.

"My dear Lady Falconer, you must come to one of my soirees," the lady said as they made their farewells. "I hold a small salon for my unfortunate compatriots every Friday evening . . . they are so grateful to be able to talk with their own countrymen, and we have some most stimulating intellectual discussions . . . I'm sure you would find them so entertaining. You are so knowledgeable about the art and culture of my country."

"You flatter me, Doña Bernardina," Aurelia demurred. "I have but a smattering of knowledge, but I own to a great interest, and a desire to learn more."

"Then you will come?" Doña Bernardina clasped her mittened hands in front of her with an expression of delight.

"I should be delighted. Only . . . only, forgive me, Doña Benardina, but my husband is also . . ."

"Oh, splendid . . . nothing could be more delightful," the lady exclaimed. "I shall send you an invitation directly."

Aurelia's smile gave no inkling of her triumph as she made her farewells to her hostess and fellow guests. She rode home behind Jemmy with her blood singing in her veins, wondering how she could ever have reached the grand age of thirty without ever really knowing this astonishing exultation at performing a difficult task to perfection. She raised her head, smiling up into the sky, where the first faint glimmer of the evening star showed. Fanciful, foolish, an impulse born of this moment of jubilant self-congratulation . . . but she enjoyed the moment nevertheless.

She entered the house on South Audley Street still on wings. Morecombe was no longer in the hall, and she guessed he was having supper in the kitchen with the twins. She hurried to the library, flinging open the door with a dramatic gesture, standing on the threshold, one hand on her hip. Only the room was empty.

Ah, well, she should have expected it. With a shrug Aurelia turned back to the hall. She had rather hoped, after their play that morning, that Greville would have arranged to spend the evening with her . . . she had also rather assumed that he'd be waiting to hear the result of her afternoon's excursion. Not so, it seemed.

She went up to her bedchamber, feeling deflated for the second time that day. Quite clearly she had not fully grasped the importance of this work, she decided as she went into her chamber. It wasn't a game, where jubilation and congratulation at a win might be appropriate. In this business, one might be entitled to indulge such feelings if one succeeded against expectation. But she expected herself to succeed. And Greville certainly did. This morning he had indulged her need for praise, but she was fairly certain he wouldn't always do that. They were partners and she was no novice who could be allowed to make mistakes. And she couldn't expect a reward just because she didn't make mistakes.

A good lesson. Aurelia rang for Hester and unpinned her bonnet. Greville would have no inkling of her moment of weakness and subsequent revelation. She was going out for the evening, and if he came in before she left, then she would tell him what had happened, and if she didn't see him until later, then she would describe the afternoon's action in as cool and businesslike a fashion as he could wish for.

And he didn't return before Lord David Forster came to escort her to Almack's Assembly Rooms. Greville had made it clear from the beginning that standing idly around the Assembly Rooms with an insipid glass of lemonade or a dish of tea and a piece of wafer-thin stale bread and butter watching decorous couples circling the dance floor was not his idea of an entertaining evening. Aurelia had laughed and said he was not alone in that opinion, and she would not expect his escort on the occasions that she felt obliged to attend the weekly Wednesday ball.

Livia, before her marriage to Prince Prokov, had needed a chaperone to attend the Assembly Rooms, otherwise she would have incurred the powerful censure of the patronesses of Almack's, and Aurelia and Cornelia had faithfully performed their duty, but now there was really no need for either of them to expose themselves to the tedium. But occasionally they went together just to keep themselves in the social eye. They could always find some old friend to escort them, and this evening Lord Forster had volunteered.

Punctually at ten o'clock he was waiting for her in the hall, immaculately clad in the required uniform of black silk knee britches, white waistcoat, black coat, white stockings, and buckled shoes. He bowed with an appreciative murmur when Aurelia came down the stairs in a gown of orange-blossom crepe, an Indian muslin shawl draped over her elbows, her hair gathered into a knot on top of her head, a cluster of ringlets framing her face.

"Beautiful as always, ma'am."

"Flattery as always, David," Aurelia accused, smiling. "But don't let me stop you." She gave him her hand and he kissed it gracefully. "Is Harry escorting Nell tonight?"

"I believe so. Your husband is otherwise engaged, I take it?"

"He's made certain of it," she said with a laugh, allowing David to drape a fur stole over her bare shoulders. "He loathes Almack's."

"Can't say I blame him." David offered her his arm as Jemmy pulled open the heavy front door. "But we must show our faces lest society forget us." He gave an elaborate shudder at such a prospect.

Aurelia glanced once quickly along the deserted street before climbing into the carriage. Not a sign of a watcher anywhere. She settled into the closed carriage beside her escort and decided she was going to relax into the comfortably familiar, routine tedium of this evening and enjoy it. She had no need to be on her guard, no need to play a part.

"I'd as liefer be at the theatre, I own," David said, rapping on the roof to give the coachman the order to drive on. "What a piece of ill fortune that both Covent Garden and Drury Lane should burn to the ground within months of each other."

"They're being rebuilt, though," Aurelia pointed out. "And they'll be even more magnificent than before, I'm sure. Although it's said that Kemble and Sheridan will never recoup their losses."

"No, I'm sure of it. Sheridan, in particular, is close to bankruptcy, if I hear aright. But we'll see Siddons's Lady Macbeth again, mark my words."

"And that actor, what's his name . . . Kean, Edmund

Kean, there's much talk about him playing one of the new theatres."

"He's made a name for himself in the provinces, certainly."

They chatted pleasantly until the carriage drew up outside Almack's Assembly Rooms in King Street. A linkboy, holding a pitch torch aloft, opened the carriage door for them, and David jumped down to offer an assisting hand to Aurelia as she stepped out. Light poured from the open front doors of the building, and the discreet strains of the orchestra drifted into the night. Carriages were discharging their passengers, and Aurelia paused on the flagway for a moment looking for familiar faces. She couldn't see the Bonhams as yet, but a familiar voice separated itself from the generalized hum.

"It's Letitia, let's go in quickly," she whispered to David, who grinned and promptly offered his arm.

"She is certainly a pill," he murmured as he escorted Aurelia up the wide staircase to where Lady Sefton, one of the patronesses, stood scrutinizing the guests as they arrived.

"Lady Falconer . . . Lord Forster, I bid you welcome." A chilly smile accompanied the greeting, but since neither David nor Aurelia expected an effusive greeting from the lady, who was generally considered to be excessively high in the instep even for a patroness of Almack's, they merely bowed politely and walked on into the main salon, where the orchestra was playing.

"Refreshments, or would you care to dance?" David

asked cheerfully, as he raised his quizzing glass and examined the assembled crowd. "Or shall we do the promenade and greet our fellow revelers?"

"The latter," Aurelia said. "There's Nell, over in the embrasure with Nick."

They threaded their way around the wall, past the seated chaperones, who were watching their maidenly charges, eagle-eyed, making sure they didn't dance more than once with a partner or spend too long in conversation with any one man.

Cornelia greeted their arrival with relief. "Nick and I were wondering why we came. Harry's gone off to the card room, grumbling about having to play for penny stakes. The only good thing about the evening so far is the absence of Letitia Oglethorpe."

"She's right behind us," Aurelia said with a chuckle, opening her fan. "I heard her braying in the street."

"Vicious, aren't they?" David observed to Nick with a conspiratorial wink.

"Certainly not mealymouthed," Nick agreed.

"Then why don't you go and engage the lady in conversation?" Aurelia inquired with a sweet smile. "I'm sure she'd be delighted to regale you with her latest purchase."

"I have a better idea." David extended his hand with a bow. "May I have the honor, ma'am?"

Nick took Cornelia onto the floor for the country dance that was just forming, and the two couples chatted with all the ease and intimacy of long-standing friendship. But as David handed her up the dance, Aurelia saw Countess Lessingham enter the salon on the arm of a man some years her senior. A distinguished looked, white-haired gentleman whom she didn't recognize.

"Do you know who that is with Lady Lessingham, David?"

David turned her beneath his arm, before looking towards the door. "Oh, is that the countess . . . the Spanish lady I've heard so much about? She's with the Earl of Lessingham at any rate."

"What have you heard about Doña Bernardina?" Aurelia exchanged partners with her opposite number in the line and didn't get her answer for a few minutes until she returned to David.

"Only that she's rather flamboyant, rather exotic, an unusual choice for Lessingham, who's known for a somewhat scholarly bent and no interest at all in social frippery. I don't recall ever seeing him at Almack's before . . . not his thing at all."

"Perhaps he's obliging his wife," Aurelia suggested, stopping as the music died, fanning herself vigorously in the overheated room. "Do you care for an introduction?"

He looked surprised. "Are you acquainted with the lady?"

"Yes, not wonderfully well, but well enough for it to look strange if I didn't acknowledge her." Aurelia began to move towards the countess and her husband, then stopped suddenly. It was a minute before eleven o'clock, the hour beyond which no guest was admitted to the Assembly Rooms, and just as the clock was striking from the head of the stairs, Greville Falconer strode into the salon and stood on the threshold, quite clearly looking for his wife.

"I'll be damned," she muttered, thankful that only David could hear her. "What is Greville doing here? I'd have laid any odds he would never set foot here."

"Perhaps you should find out," David suggested.

Aurelia eased through the chattering throng to the door, David just behind her. Her husband looked his best in the regulation costume, she thought, surprised by a little thrill of pride. His height, the breadth of his shoulders, the assured air of control, made him, to her mind, the most powerful presence in the room.

As she watched, Lady Sefton approached him, and to Aurelia's amusement she saw that the sheer physical force of Greville's presence had affected that lady. She was simpering as she gazed up into the somewhat battered countenance that Aurelia found so attractive. When Greville gave her his white flash of a smile and that twinkling glint of his dark gray eyes, from beneath those impossibly lush, long eyelashes, Aurelia was not at all surprised to see Lady Sefton lay her hand on his black-clad arm and flutter her own much sparser lashes at him.

"Good evening, Husband," Aurelia said as she reached them. "I was not expecting to see you here tonight."

"I came home rather earlier than I had expected to,

my dear," he said smoothly, "and I thought to make the acquaintance of the charming patronesses of Almack's."

"Well, I'm afraid you must be satisfied with just me, Sir Greville," Lady Sefton said with another simpering smile. "My friends are otherwise occupied tonight."

He bowed. "Dare I say, ma'am, that their loss is hardly felt in *your* company."

"Oh, shameless man!" she declared, tapping his arm with her furled fan. "Lady Falconer, take your husband onto the dance floor before he puts us all to the blush." She floated away in a rustle of silk, her cheeks rather pinker than usual.

"You flirt," Aurelia accused with a bubble of laughter. "Outrageous, Greville. I would never have believed you would stoop so low."

"I was merely charming my hostess," he protested, raising her hand to his lips and lightly kissing her fingers, a wicked glint in his eye. "Would you have had me do otherwise?"

He turned with a smile to David. "My thanks for taking care of my wife, Forster."

David grinned. "I take it I've been declared surplus to requirements. In that case I shall follow Harry to the card tables." He bowed to Aurelia, offered a mocking nod of a bow to Greville, and strode off to the double doors at the far end of the salon.

"I hope he wasn't offended," Aurelia said.

"Good God, why should he have been?" Greville de-

manded. "I'm sure he's more than happy to receive his
congé and drink tea over the cards."

"You sound as if you would be." She opened her fan.
"Why are you here?"

"I wanted to know how your afternoon went." He
reached to take a glass of lemonade off the tray held by a
passing waiter. "You look a little warm, my dear."

"It's stuffy in here, and I've been dancing." She wondered why she felt annoyed. She had been pleased to
see him, but now he seemed to be deliberately putting
a damper on her pleasure. He might at least have pretended that he'd come to find her for her own sake.

"I'm sure the account could have waited until I got
home," she said coolly, sipping her lemonade. "But as it
happens, the countess is here tonight."

"Ah . . . where is she?" He looked over the crowd, an
easy feat given that he stood head and shoulders above
most of the patrons.

"Over by the windows, with her husband and Lord
and Lady Buxton."

"The rather ample lady in the scarlet mantilla?"

"Yes."

He let his gaze roam casually over the salon, and no
one would know that he had taken note of everyone
with whom he was acquainted even as in that one glance
he absorbed every aspect of Lady Lessingham's attire
and appearance. "Perhaps you should introduce me,"
he suggested, taking Aurelia's empty glass from her and
putting it on a small table.

"Yes, perhaps I should." She moved ahead of him, saying casually over her shoulder, "I'm guessing that's the real reason why you're here."

"One of them." His eyelid flickered in an unmistakable wink that banished her earlier flash of annoyance on a bubble of laughter.

It was no good, Aurelia thought. She couldn't slip as easily into this role as Greville could. In fact, she thought, he was never out of it, whereas she had to remember to put it on, and sometimes, such as now, it was a damnable nuisance. She just wanted to enjoy being herself, and she wanted simply to enjoy Greville's company. But there was no point taking umbrage at his businesslike attitude. What else could she expect of him? He'd never promised her anything else. Even in the glorious intimacies of their bed, he never pretended that their enterprise did not exist. He never lost sight for a minute of the real purpose of their short time together, even though she did. And if she allowed herself to forget it, the inevitable reminder always seemed to come as a shock.

"Lady Falconer, how delightful," the countess trilled as she saw them approach. "Allow me to present my husband, Lord Lessingham . . . my lord, Lady Falconer. I was telling you about our delightful afternoon at cards."

"Yes, indeed, my dear," the earl said with a benign smile. He bowed to Aurelia. "At your service, Lady Falconer."

Aurelia gave him her hand as she offered a small courteous bow of her own, before turning to Greville. "May I present my husband, Sir Greville . . . Lady Lessingham . . . Lord Lessingham."

Aurelia stepped slightly to one side as the courtesies of the introduction were completed and, when the moment was ripe, explained to Greville, "I was telling Lady Lessingham this afternoon about your own interest in Spanish culture, sir. We had such a fascinating discussion about the paintings in the Prado. How I wish I could see Ribera's *Jacob's Dream,* and the Velázquez . . . *Adoration of the Magi* is said to be among the most magnificent of his work."

Aurelia turned to the countess with a longing little sigh. "Of course, Lady Lessingham has seen everything there. She's been a frequent visitor to the royal palace."

"Not for a long time, alas," her ladyship said heavily. "Not since the tyrant drove King Carlos and his family from his own country and installed that puppet on the throne in his place. So many of us were obliged to flee our homeland." She dabbed at her eyes with a froth of lacy handkerchief.

"Indeed, ma'am, you have all our sympathies," Greville said in his warmest, most mellow tones. "To be an exile must be very painful."

"Oh, if only you knew, Sir Greville," Doña Bernardina said with another sigh. "I weep for my country every day. Is it not so, my lord?" She appealed to her husband beside her.

"Yes, my dear. But you do much for your compatriots, and you must take heart from that." His tone was bracing, as if he was anxious to forestall another episode of weeping.

The countess seemed visibly to take heart, her shoulders stiffening, the incipient tears vanished. "Yes, well, one must do what one can for those worse off than oneself, don't you agree, Lady Falconer?"

"Certainly," agreed Aurelia. "I'm sure you sustain your countrymen with your own courage."

"Well, I like to think so," the lady said. "It's true then, Sir Greville, that you share your wife's interest in Spanish culture, and our art? Lady Falconer is very well informed."

Greville shot a faintly amused glance at Aurelia as he said, "Don't I know it, ma'am. My wife is a regular bluestocking."

"I would hardly say that," Aurelia demurred. "Your knowledge far exceeds mine, Husband. You are so erudite, your scholarship quite puts my own fragments of knowledge to shame."

"You must come to my soiree on Friday," the countess declared. "I was telling dear Lady Falconer only this afternoon how I hold these little gatherings to bring my compatriots together. We all draw so much support and comfort from each other, but we also have most stimulating discussions, and sometimes a little music, that I'm sure you would both enjoy. Do tell me I may count upon you both."

"It will be our pleasure, Lady Lessingham," Greville said with a bow.

"At eight o'clock then." She smiled and accepted her husband's arm into the dance.

"Excellent," Greville murmured. "We move apace, Aurelia."

"So it would seem."

"Well, we've accomplished all we needed to here. Come, let us go home."

"I have to say good-bye to Cornelia, and to David," Aurelia protested. "It would be the height of ill manners just to disappear."

"Where are they then?" Greville peered across the room. "Oh, over there by the card-room doors." He took her arm and moved as swiftly as possible through the throng. "Cornelia, I give you good evening," he said as he reached Cornelia. "Bonham . . . you've abandoned the cards already?"

Harry grimaced. "There's no joy in playing for pennies." He kissed Aurelia's cheek. "You look radiant, Aurelia."

"Thank you," she said with a smile. "You always did have a smooth tongue, Harry."

"Calumny," he declared.

Greville listened to the light banter, so redolent of a long and close history. Aurelia had a gift for friendship, he thought. It was difficult to acknowledge, but sometimes the closeness of his wife's relationships made him uneasy, uncertain in some way. He couldn't avoid the knowledge that he was not overwhelmingly enthusiastic about meeting Prince and Princess Prokov. He didn't know anyone in whom he could confide as openly as Aurelia and her friends could. Even with Frederick, who had been the closest to a close friend he had ever had, he hadn't shared this level of easy intimacy. Too much had been at stake.

Sometimes, though, he approached it with Aurelia. And when he did, he was finding it harder and harder to distance himself.

Chapter Seventeen

"IT SEEMS WE HAVE NO CHOICE but to accept that the *asp* is known," Simon said, resting his chin in his linked palms with a weary sigh. "It's a damnable nuisance."

"It was inevitable one of these days," Greville observed, pacing the office restlessly. "But it means my operation here has to change its focus. I need to neutralize Vasquez before he gets to me."

Simon nodded. "Use anyone you need from here as backup. What of Aurelia?"

"She's safe enough under my roof. If they're interested in her as a way of getting to me, then they'll find her wherever we try to hide her." He didn't add that he would never know a moment's peace if he didn't have her directly under his protection.

"Quite apart from trying to explain her disappearance," Simon said in tacit agreement. "We don't want people asking difficult questions."

"Exactly." Greville ceased his pacing. "I'll continue

as planned. Make Vasquez's acquaintance and wait for him to set a trap . . . one I trust I shall be able to spring myself," he added with a grim smile.

Simon looked at him gravely. "We can't afford for you to fall into the hands of the Inquisition, Greville. You know too much, and no one has the power to withstand their persuasion."

"Have no fear, Simon, I'll fall on my sword first." Greville's tone was light, but his eyes were black holes, devoid of light or expression.

Simon Grant merely nodded, and Greville turned to the door. "Brief me daily, Greville."

Greville raised a hand in acknowledgment. "Send a couple of good men to watch my house and Fourteen Adam's Row."

"It will be done at once."

Greville nodded and left. He drove his curricle back to South Audley Street, deep in thought. The situation was no worse than many he'd encountered in the past, but he hadn't had anyone else to worry about then. It made it hard to keep a single-minded focus on his own safety.

He left the curricle with his groom and went into the house. Morecombe was nowhere in evidence, but Jemmy, looking smart in a new livery, appeared at a run from the back regions at the sound of the door opening. "Afternoon, sir." He tugged at his waistcoat. "Lady Farn—I mean, Falconer, Lady Falconer is in the library. Should I bring you summat, sir?"

Greville smiled at the lad's eagerness. He'd taken to his new duties like the proverbial duck to water. "Make sure the decanters are fully charged, if you please, Jemmy." Greville handed him his hat, whip, and gloves, then strolled to the library at the rear of the house.

The door was partially ajar and he pushed it open quietly. He stood for a moment on the threshold, unnoticed by all but Lyra, who, knowing there was no threat here, merely flicked her eyes beneath long lashes in his direction. Aurelia was sitting at the secretaire writing a letter, Lyra lay at her feet, and Franny was curled up against the dog's haunches frowning over a writing slate as she painstakingly formed the letters of the alphabet with a stick of chalk.

Greville felt the strangest sensation beneath his breastbone. He had no experience of family life, certainly not in his barren childhood, and had never expected to repair the omission, but something about this serene family scene in the lamplit, fire-warmed, book-lined room stirred him in a hitherto unknown fashion. Aurelia had put her stamp on the rented house. It had lost the anonymity of furnished accommodation. Personal touches were everywhere, from the jugs of early daffodils and sprays of forsythia to embroidered cushions, piles of books, her embroidery frame, and the stray possessions of Franny's that had escaped the nursery quarters.

Aurelia turned from the secretaire, pen in hand, and smiled. "I was wondering when you'd return." The smile conveyed recognition of recently shared pleasure, her brown eyes glowing in the soft lamplight. Her pale hair was braided neatly in a coronet around her head and her gown of fine dark green wool had a high neck that set off her small, shapely head to perfection.

Franny scrambled to her feet. "See what I've writ," she said, coming towards him. She seemed to accept Greville as a presence in her life without undue concern. In fact she saw little enough of him and her life continued much as it had before. Aurelia intended to keep it that way. This arrangement would be over in three months, less now, of course, and the smaller the impact it had on her daughter the easier the break would be.

Greville now examined the slate and the careful letters inscribed thereon with the required gravity. "Very neat, Franny," he pronounced, ruffling the top of her head. He stroked Lyra, who had gracefully risen and was pushing her nose into his hand. Then he crossed to his wife, who lifted her face for his kiss.

"Your face is cold," she said, laughing, touching his cheek with a slim, warm hand. "Is it cold out? I haven't set foot outside all day."

"It's chilly now," he said, turning to the sideboard. "Sherry?"

"Mmm, thank you."

"Why haven't you been out?"

"Oh, I had rather a lot to do here." She took the glass he handed her. "Menus for the week, bills to settle, a dressmaking session with Claire, who's making up a new evening dress for me with that Italian, figured silk that Liv sent me."

She stood up as she spoke. "I don't know where Alex gets these extraordinary luxuries from. He's immured in this little village in the New Forest with his wife and infant son, and he still somehow manages to acquire the most unbelievably exotic stuff. He's promised black tulips for Nell's ball." Aurelia laughed and sipped her sherry. "He's an amazing man."

"I look forward to meeting him," Greville said, glancing through the day's post on the desk.

Aurelia gave him a quick, slightly sharp look. He didn't sound as if he meant it. "Alex can be a little overpowering," she conceded.

He looked up from the letter in his hand, his eyes narrowed. "But you like him."

"Oh, yes. It's impossible not to, particularly when he's so good for Liv. She adores him and he worships the ground she treads on."

Greville grimaced and Aurelia couldn't help laughing. "Oh, dear, how horribly soppy that sounded."

"It did," he agreed drily. "When am I to meet this paragon?"

"Sooner than you think," she said, wondering at the sardonic tinge to the question. It seemed most unlike Greville. "I was just writing to Liv. I had a letter from her today. Alex has to come up to town on business next week, and Liv wants to make sure that we'll look after him."

Greville looked astounded. "He can't look after himself . . . in that mansion on Cavendish Square?"

"Oh, of course he can," Aurelia said impatiently. "And I'm sure Boris will come to make sure everything is in order for him. But Liv wanted us to know so that we can ask him to dinner." She paused, then said deliberately, "You'd be surprised at how much you have in common with Prince Prokov, Greville."

Greville met her steady gaze in silent comprehension. "You do seem to have moved in some interesting circles, my dear."

"Is Uncle Alex coming to stay, Mama?" Franny had been following the conversation between her elders with a puzzled frown.

"Not to stay, sweetheart. He'll stay in Cavendish Square, but he'll come for dinner one evening."

"Is he bringing the baby?"

"No, the baby has to stay with Aunt Liv, he's too small to travel."

"Oh." Franny lost interest in the subject and returned to her slate.

Greville glanced at Aurelia and she caught his meaning. She reached for the bell rope that hung beside the fireplace. "It's time for you to go back to the nursery for tea, Franny."

Franny pouted. "Not yet . . . it's too early."

"It's five o'clock," Aurelia said calmly. "When you've had your tea and your bath, you can come to my bedchamber while I change for dinner." It was sufficient inducement to send Franny off with Daisy without further protest.

Greville sat down in a winged armchair by the fire, twirling the stem of his sherry glass between finger and thumb. "Russian secret service?"

Aurelia shook her head. "I haven't been given the exact details. Liv knows the truth but obviously didn't feel free to tell Nell and me everything. But I believe Alex is, or has been, working against the czar. Alexander is proclaiming undying friendship to Napoléon—"

"Or giving that impression," Greville interrupted, stretching his booted feet to the andirons. "There are some who think he's playing a devious game. But you're right, I look forward to meeting Prince Prokov."

"And you'll talk to him about such things?" Aurelia inquired, curious to know if her husband was contemplating dropping his rigid guard.

Greville gave her a shrewd smile. "Not in so many words, my dear. As you should well know."

"I didn't think so," she said, sitting in a corner of a sofa, arranging her skirts around her. "Were you at the ministry this afternoon?"

He nodded. He crooked a finger at her, and with a resigned chuckle she set down her glass, got up, and came over to him, allowing him to pull her onto his knee. He palmed her scalp, bringing her face down to his.

She kissed him, tasting the cold freshness of his lips, the tang of sherry on his tongue, inhaling his special scent, a mélange of lemon and lavender, overlaid with the tang of horseflesh and leather and today a residue of tobacco smoke that she guessed came from the closeted offices of the ministry, if not from the taproom of a tavern or the smoky salon of one of the clubs on St. James's Street.

"Are we to be doing anything in particular at Lady Lessingham's soiree?" she asked, drawing back and resting her head on his shoulder, looking up at him with a sharp intelligence that belied the sensual glow in her eyes.

"There are Spaniards come to town," he said lightly. "They may or may not be the ones we're waiting for. I hope they'll be in attendance."

"Ah . . . now I understand." She straightened a fold in his cravat with a deft twitch of her fingers. "You assume they will make contact with their former compatriot."

"I believe it to be inevitable."

"Then we must waste no time." She made to stand up but he seized her waist and pulled her down again.

"There's nothing to be done tonight, my dear."

"No?" She looked playfully askance. "I assumed you would wish to drill me in the correct techniques for smoking out Spaniards from the drawing rooms of the ton."

"It can wait. . . . Shall we go upstairs?"

Aurelia half stood up, her hand in his, then she sighed. "I promised Franny."

He inclined his head in rueful acceptance. "Of course. But anticipation always makes the feast taste better." He stood up with her. "Do we have any engagements this evening?"

She considered the question. "Several . . . should we choose to attend . . . but none that are imperative." She regarded him with her head on one side, reminding him yet again of an inquisitive bird.

"Then let us spend a quiet evening at home."

Aurelia sighed heavily. "Must it be quiet?"

"Shameless hussy. No one would believe you were a respectable matron."

"I *used* to be," she said with a puzzled little smile. "At least I thought I was. Strange how little one knows oneself."

"Oh, I think you know yourself quite well, Aurelia." He caught her chin, tipping it up so that he could look into her eyes.

"Better now," she said simply. "And I'm beginning to feel that I know Frederick now, or certainly better than I used to. I can't believe there was a time when I thought there was nothing further I needed to know about him."

"He has my gratitude in more ways than one." Greville bent and kissed her ear.

Aurelia wondered if Frederick should have *her* gratitude. Would she have been better off if he'd followed the rules of his world and accepted the destiny that his lineage and position dictated? Instead of throwing convention to the four winds and embracing the extraordinary life led by Greville Falconer? She would have been safer, certainly, in the established rhythms and routine of that married life with Frederick. But happier . . . more content . . . more satisfied?

No. Whatever lay ahead, she would always have these memories. The excitement of not knowing what each day would bring, what would be required of her, while she played the part so familiar to her, all the while knowing that she *was* only playing the part, that she was engaged in some other quite different, astoundingly exciting, play.

"What's worrying you?"

She became aware of Greville's troubled gaze and shook her head. "Nothing . . . nothing at all. Just that my life has turned upside down in such a short time, and every now and again I'm reminded of it."

"Regrets?" His tone was expressionless, his countenance giving nothing away.

Aurelia considered the one-word question. She couldn't imagine dissembling with Greville, couldn't imagine that he wouldn't see through any smoke screen she could throw up. And she didn't want to lie to him. "I don't think so," she said finally. "But I do know that I won't let you down, Greville."

He nodded. "No, *I* know you won't." He laid a hand on her shoulder. "I will do everything in my power to keep you from harm, but you must remember the one cardinal rule . . . ?" He raised his eyebrows.

"Trust no one," she said, her nostrils flaring slightly. "I remember, Greville."

"Don't ever forget it."

"I won't." She tried to disguise the bitter edge to the assertion, but it was hard. "I must go to Franny." She offered him a small, hopeful smile and left the room.

Greville gazed at the closed door, his expression hard to read. He understood how difficult it must be for someone like Aurelia, unaccustomed to mistrust, to accept that in her dealings with others she had to work from a foundation of mistrust. But he could not keep her safe if she let her guard slip for an instant. He was not in the habit of considering the personal, emotional effects of his world on those he recruited to play their part in it. If they agreed, they accepted the consequences. It was how he had always operated. But it was different with Aurelia.

And he could not afford to acknowledge the reason. He drained his sherry glass and went up to his bedchamber.

When Greville strolled into his chief's dusty office in the War Ministry early the following morning, Simon Grant looked up from the map spread over his massive desk, a pair of compasses in hand.

"Ah, Greville, just the man I wanted to see."

"What's the significance of the map?" Greville came behind the desk without invitation and leaned over the map at his chief's side. "Ah, I see. The Tagus. You've marked the location of the guerrilla groups."

"Aye, and Wellesley has their coordinates, thanks to you and Farnham. He landed at Lisbon on the twenty-sixth." Simon glanced at the calendar on the wall. "It's

May fourth now, but I think we can expect a dispatch in the next two weeks."

"Pigeons?"

"Aye. Most of the posts are still operative across France. And we have two in the Channel Islands."

Greville nodded. The pigeon couriers were among the most important participants in this war. Their handlers more often than not were as much at risk as a soldier in the front line. "Any new information on our friend Don Antonio?"

Simon grinned tiredly. "There, at least, an unqualified success." He went to an armoire across the room and opened a drawer, extracting a sheet of paper. "Our man in Madrid did us proud and a pigeon landed at Dover yesterday evening. Much earlier than I dared hope. Guess who our friend is?"

Greville frowned in thought. "He has to be in the top echelons of their network for a mission this visible and important. And I have the strangest feeling that I've seen him somewhere before. But I can't for the life of me track down the memory."

Simon nodded rather grimly. "Well, you're right. You have certainly encountered him before. Do you recall that little fracas just before Junot occupied Lisbon last year? You were trying to get the Portuguese regent out of Portugal on his way to Brazil . . ."

"And nearly lost him," Greville said slowly. "Nearly lost him to an assassin's blade." He stared inward at the memory. He had caught only a fleeting glimpse of the assassin as the man had fled over the stone wall of the harbor, with Greville and his men on his heels. "El Demonio. No wonder I thought I'd seen him before."

"Just so." Simon nodded. "Antonio Vasquez and El Demonio are one and the same."

Greville nodded. "Well, well. A worthy opponent, indeed."

Simon regarded him closely across the desk. "Do you have a plan?"

Greville smiled, and it was not a nice smile. "Only to make sure I get to him before he gets to me."

"I know I've said this before, Greville, but we can't afford for you to fall into their hands."

"I don't believe I could afford it either," Greville said with a lightness that did not deceive his companion. He held out his hand for the paper that Simon still held. "May I take that?"

"Of course . . . of course, dear fellow. It concerns you more nearly than anyone else."

Greville glanced at the document and shook his head. "Do me a favor, Simon, and have two men on duty at my house. Whenever the child leaves with her nursemaid, make sure they're discreetly escorted by someone well able to protect them."

Simon nodded gravely. "Of course. And what of her mother?"

"I'll take responsibility for Aurelia's safety, but I can't take the risk of needing to be in two places at once."

"Understood."

Greville let himself into his house the following afternoon and stepped into the midst of a maelstrom. A small figure resembling nothing so much as a whirling dervish was dancing and shrieking in the middle of the usually tranquil hall, surrounded by a group of flapping, exclaiming individuals, all talking at once as they seemed to be trying to lay hands on the spinning creature.

Lyra bounded to his side and stood pressed against his legs as if for protection as the racket reached a crescendo.

"Quiet," Greville commanded in a voice that barely seemed to rise above its usual pitch. Nevertheless the whirling body came to a stop and the fluttering group ceased flapping. Into the now eerie silence the small figure gave a pathetic hiccup.

"What on earth is this circus?" Greville demanded.

"Make 'erself ill, she will, one of these days, you mark my words," one of the twins, Greville thought it was Ada, muttered. "Poor little mite to take on so about nothing at all . . . 'tain't natural, as I've said before."

Greville examined the assembled company with raised eyebrows. His entire household, with the exception of Morecombe, appeared to be gathered there. "Forgive my asking, but do none of you have any work to do this afternoon?" he inquired, striding across to where Franny stood, still hiccuping, her face blotched and tearstained.

The hall emptied rapidly of all but Daisy, who stood wringing her hands nervously.

"What on earth was all that about, Franny?" he asked, going down on one knee beside the child.

Franny sniffed and wiped her nose with the back of her hand. "I want to take Lyra to the square garden . . . Mama promised I could this afternoon . . . but they won't let me. Daisy's scared of Lyra. " Her voice rose alarmingly on this accusation.

Daisy said, "Beggin' your pardon, Sir Greville, but my lady didn't say nothing to me about taking that dog in the garden."

"Franny, that's enough," Greville said as the little girl's tears began to flow anew and her mouth opened on an incipient yell of protest. "Daisy knows that the only people who are allowed to take Lyra out are myself or your mother."

"Mama's not here," Franny protested. "An' she promised. She *promised* and you should never break a promise, she said so."

"Well, I'm sure she has good reason," Greville said. "But having a fit of hysterics is not an appropriate response."

Franny regarded him with wide-open eyes, curiosity now uppermost. "What's that? Hyst . . . hyster . . . ?"

"Hysterics. What you were doing just then, screaming and flinging yourself all over the place. It won't do, my child."

"She don't do it so often now, sir," Daisy ventured.

"Thank the Lord for small mercies." Greville got to his feet, brushing down the knees of his britches. "Where is Lady Falconer, do you know?"

"She went out after lunch, sir . . . didn't say where, leastways not to me."

Greville nodded and looked down at Franny, who sniffed vigorously but seemed considerably subdued. He took out a handkerchief and wiped her nose. "If you'll wait quietly for ten minutes, Franny, I'll take you and Lyra to the garden myself."

Franny hiccuped and nodded, and when he strode into the library, she trotted at his heels and sat on a low ottoman while he sorted through the post that had been delivered that afternoon.

It was rather distracting, he found, to have the child's huge eyes fixed upon him, watching his every movement as if in suspended animation until he should say the magic words. Lyra was sitting beside Franny, watching Greville with a similar air of expectation, and after a couple of minutes he gave up.

"Very well, let's go."

Franny instantly leaped to her feet and raced ahead of him into the hall, rather as if he'd turned the key to start a run-down clock, he thought, amused. He had no real experience of children and very little really to do with Franny. Aurelia didn't seem to expect any involvement from him, and nursery matters ran smoothly without impinging on his activities at all. At least, they had until this afternoon.

He fastened Lyra's lead and took Franny's hand firmly as they left the house. Aurelia hadn't said where she was going, but she would not be on foot or horseback since she'd left Lyra behind. It was unlike her, however, to fail to keep a promise to her daughter.

He glanced casually up and down the street as they walked to Grosvenor Square. A man sweeping leaves out of the gutter scratched his nose as Greville and the child walked by. Greville nodded briefly, acknowledging the man sent from the ministry to keep an eye on the house. Greville could pick up no sense of another, more sinister, observer. He remained on his guard, however, and Lyra, beautifully behaved as always, walked sedately beside him, only her raised head and pricked ears indicating that she was on the alert.

"The gate's here." Franny tugged at his hand as they crossed the street to the large railed garden in the middle of the square. Franny pulled her hand free of his and jumped onto the bottom rung of the gate to pull down the latch. "It's much bigger 'n the one we used to play in . . . in the old house," she informed him, swinging on the gate as it opened.

"Cavendish Square isn't quite so large," he agreed, waiting patiently until she'd decided she'd swung enough and jumped down. He closed the gate behind them, released Lyra, and followed child and dog as they raced down the path towards the grassy center of the garden. Franny was leaping and singing with sheer exuberance, the violent storm of half an hour past completely forgotten.

It surprised him that a woman as tranquil and even-tempered as Aurelia should have such a tempestuous child. Frederick, too, had given no indication of a volatile temperament. He had taken things as they came, handled situations as they arose with a calm practicality. What would he have made of his little daughter for whom life was either bathed in tropical sunshine or battered by winter gales?

He stopped at the grass and stood watching as Franny and Lyra chased and tumbled, the massive hound playing as happily as a puppy, and yet always with a degree of delicacy, careful not to knock the child over.

The first warning of a watcher took its usual form. A quick surge of energy in his chest, followed by a deep calm. He smiled fondly as he watched the child and dog at play, then casually glanced around, before bending to pick up a stick and throwing it for Lyra, who leaped after it. He moved towards Franny, his eyes everywhere, noting the man standing on the gravel path just to the side of the lawn.

A tall, well-dressed, bearded gentleman. Black eyes deep-set in a lean, hawkish, angular countenance. After a moment he walked off.

Greville gave a shrill one-note whistle, and Lyra instantly bounded back, dropping down on guard beside Franny.

"Is it time to go? I don't want to go yet," Franny complained as Greville came up with her.

"It'll be dark soon," he said, in no mood now to indulge the child. He snapped Lyra's lead onto her collar. "Come along." He held out a hand imperatively to Franny, who took it reluctantly, but without further protest.

Franny chattered cheerfully as they crossed the street and made their way home.

Greville had discovered early on that in the absence of a response Franny would continue chattering away, peppering him with questions to which it seemed she had no real interest in answers, leaving him free with his own thoughts.

Vasquez had not been watching Franny by coincidence.

Chapter Eighteen

Aurelia had just returned home when Greville came into the house with Franny and Lyra. "Oh, there you are. Daisy said you'd gone to the garden." Aurelia looked surprised, giving Greville a quizzical smile as she bent to kiss her daughter.

"You said you'd take me to the garden with Lyra," Franny accused.

Aurelia frowned. "Not today, love. I said I'd take you tomorrow."

"Well, I wish you'd made it a bit clearer," Greville commented, unfastening the dog's lead. "It might have saved quite a scene."

Aurelia looked up, puzzled. "What do you mean?"

"We'll discuss it later," Greville said, turning aside to the salon.

"Let's go upstairs to Daisy." Aurelia took Franny by the hand. "And you can tell me what you've been up to."

Aurelia came downstairs half an hour later having heard the full story from Daisy. She found Greville in the salon, sipping madeira and reading the *Gazette*. "I'm sorry you were embroiled in one of Franny's tantrums," she said, pouring herself a glass of sherry. "She's growing out of them, I think, but every now and again it happens."

"I own I was at something of a loss," he said, laying aside the paper.

"Not according to Daisy. To listen to her, one would think you were a hero who had triumphed over insuperable odds." Aurelia sat down in the corner of the sofa. "It was good of you to take Franny and Lyra after that scene. Have you had experience with children?"

"None at all, as it happens."

Aurelia inclined her head in surprise. "Then it must come naturally." She paused and, when he made no response, said, "You were an only child, of course."

"Yes," he agreed without expansion.

She persevered. "I sometimes worry about Franny being an only child. Do you think you would have liked siblings?"

He shrugged. "I've no idea, Aurelia. I didn't have them and I don't believe I ever gave the matter much thought."

"Of course Franny has Stevie and Susannah." Aurelia sipped her sherry. "I don't know how it will be when Stevie goes away to school. She'll miss him dreadfully."

Greville picked up his paper again as if the subject was of no interest to him at all. He always responded to any conversation about family ties in this way, a detached if polite air of boredom. For once, Aurelia found that she wasn't prepared to leave it at that.

"Tell me about your mother," she demanded. "You say very little about her."

"There's very little to say," he replied shortly, without looking up from the *Gazette*.

Aurelia, however, was convinced he wasn't reading. "Was she ill?"

"So they said." His eyes remained fixed on the newsprint.

"They? Your father, you mean."

He put the paper down with an impatience that crumpled the sheets. His face was closed, his eyes cold as he spoke with clear deliberation. "From the age of around two I probably saw my mother five or six times. She inhabited a wing of the house with her own staff and had absolutely no interest in me, and as far as I could gather, even less in my father. He was never at home and I vaguely remember being told of his death, but very much in passing. Does that satisfy your curiosity, Aurelia?"

She flushed. "I was not being inquisitive, Greville. We live together, we were talking about children, it was natural enough to ask you about your childhood. I'm sorry it was such a miserable and lonely one. Perhaps that explains—" She stopped and bit her lip.

"Explains what?" he asked, his voice very soft.

She sighed. "Oh, your detachment, your lack of emotional passion, I suppose. It's not normal, Greville, for a human being to be able to detach himself so completely from all human ties. I understand that it makes you good at your job. If you've never felt the need to trust in anyone, to believe in anyone and have them believe in you, then of course it's easy enough to exist in an emotionless vacuum. I just find it difficult."

He regarded her closely. "Are you saying you find it too difficult?" he asked quietly.

She looked at him in mingled exasperation, frustration, and dismay. "You haven't heard what I've been saying, Greville. I'm not talking about being unable to partner you in this London charade, I'm talking about who I am, about trying to understand who you are. It matters to me who you are, and why you are as you are."

She stood up abruptly. "It's ridiculous to have this conversation. You don't see the point of it at all. I have to change for dinner." She swept from the room, closing the door quietly behind her.

Aurelia lay in a copper tub before the fire in her bedchamber while Hester poured lemon-scented water over her freshly washed hair. She was feeling so dull and out of sorts that she could summon no enthusiasm even at the prospect of a music party at which Paganini was to be the guest violinist. She would be missed, of course, and her absence at such an event would bring Cornelia knocking at her door in the morning, but she'd find some excuse.

"I'll take dinner on a tray in my sitting room, Hester," she said, wringing out the long strands of pale hair between her hands. "Just pass me a towel and then go for your own supper. I can manage myself now."

"If you're sure, mum . . . sure you're not goin' out tonight?"

"I've never been surer, Hester. I have a slight headache and I'm going to have an early night."

"Right y'are then, mum." Hester passed her a thick towel that was hanging over a rail to warm in front of the fire. "Your dressing gown is on the chest." She indicated the garment at the foot of the bed.

"Thank you. Run along now." Hester left and Aurelia slowly stood up in a shower of water.

The adjoining door to Greville's chamber opened and her husband stood on the threshold. "Venus arising from the waves," he observed, crossing the room swiftly. "Allow me." He twitched the towel from her grasp and began to dry her vigorously, an appreciative little smile on his lips.

Ordinarily this would have been the prelude to a little love play, but to her surprise and chagrin Aurelia felt no such urge. "I'm sorry, Greville, but I don't seem to be in the mood," she said with a sigh, taking the towel from him and wrapping herself tightly before stepping out of the tub.

He stepped away, regarding her thoughtfully. "I've no intention of forcing myself on you, Aurelia."

"Of course you haven't." She took a smaller towel from the rail and wrapped it turbanlike around her wet head. "But for some reason I'm tired and dull and out of sorts this evening, and lovemaking is the last thing I feel like."

He frowned. "That's your prerogative, of course. Is there any particular reason?"

She shrugged. "Not that I can think of."

His frown deepened. "My dear, I don't think you're telling the truth. It has something to do with our less than satisfactory discussion earlier on. Am I right?"

"Maybe." She turned to pick up her dressing gown. She dropped the towel and shrugged hastily into her robe.

Aurelia tied the girdle of her robe around her waist with a final decisive tug and pulled the towel from her head. "Couldn't we just leave it, Greville?" She sat down and picked up her hairbrush.

"I don't think so." He took the brush from her. "Let me do this at least. I promise it's no prelude to anything else, but I do love to brush your hair."

She made no demur and he began to pull the brush through the pale cascade of still damp hair. The sensation was pleasant and soothing, and she allowed her eyes to close, her head to fall forward as the sweeping strokes caressed her scalp.

"So," he resumed after a minute of this tranquil silence, "what was it about my responses this afternoon that upset you so much?"

She opened her eyes and looked at him in the mirror. "I was only asking a perfectly ordinary question about your childhood. And you reacted as if I'd pried into the deepest personal secrets. Most people have no difficulty talking about their past lives, or at least something as innocuous as childhood. We live together, Greville. I know it's only for a short time, and I'm certainly not asking for any emotional declarations, I know that would be outside the parameters of this contract that we have."

If she had known what such a lack would mean, truly *mean, in this strange partnership, would she have entered it as willingly?*

She shied away from a question that she sensed could only bring painful answers and continued firmly, "Be that as it may, we *do* like each other, and in my book that means that I'm interested in what made you the person I like. Do you really have no interest at all in what made me, me?"

The smooth, rhythmic strokes of the hairbrush continued as Greville gazed down at the silken flow of hair beneath his hand. It was drying quickly in the warm room, and among the pale blond locks he caught little glimmers of a deeper gold, and once or twice in the flicker of lamplight even a hint of auburn.

"Such beautiful hair," he murmured almost unconsciously.

Aurelia raised her eyebrows in a gesture of theatrical frustration. "I'm flattered by the compliment, Greville, but it's hardly an adequate contribution to a discussion that, may I remind you, was at your initiative."

He nodded. "So it was . . . so it was. Well, my dear girl, I am very interested in what made you into the woman I like, and respect. It's vitally important to me to understand you in order to work with you. I need to know as far as it's possible how you will act and react in certain situations."

"And that's all?" She stared at him, her incredulous eyes meeting his in the mirror.

For a moment he couldn't move, transfixed by her velvet gaze. *Of course it wasn't all. But he couldn't admit that. Not without jeopardizing the detachment that had kept him safe all these years and made him such a superb operator. A detachment that would keep Aurelia and her daughter safe.*

"Is that all, Greville?" she repeated, reading the smoky whirls of confusion in the usually clear gray eyes.

He thought of Don Antonio watching Franny at play, that close-eyed, predatory stare. The Spaniard had been wondering how best to use a nugget of information, a potential weakness. Greville knew that he dared not allow such potential weaknesses in his life. He had seen what happened to men when they fell victim to the blandishments of affection. "It has to be," he said finally.

Aurelia stood up, whirling to face him, grasping his

upper arms in a hard grip. "No, Greville, it does not."

"Yes, Aurelia, it does." He took her hands from his arms and placed them firmly at her side. "That doesn't mean that I don't wish it could be otherwise. But you must accept that I know best how to do my job, and it's a job that does not permit any of the softer emotions. It's the job I have chosen, just as Frederick chose it."

"And you're trying to tell me that Frederick had put aside all warm and loving thoughts about us . . . about Franny and me?" she demanded, standing very still, her gaze locked upon his as if she would see behind those impenetrable gray eyes.

"He had no choice," Greville said simply.

"So you're saying that if he had not died, if he could have come home safely at some point, he would not have done so, because he had renounced all personal ties. He was no longer a husband or a father?"

She shook her head and took an agitated step towards the fire. "I don't believe it. Frederick could never have believed such a thing . . . never have forgotten his life, his friends and family, like that. He didn't enter a monastery." She turned to face Greville again, her hands cupping her elbows, her shimmering hair flowing over her shoulders, her brown eyes pools of angry distress.

"He might as well have done," Greville said quietly. "He knew that he had to be dead to you, to everyone in his past, if he was to be a successful agent. He made a decision that would make it impossible for him ever to resume his old life. Frederick Farnham died at Trafalgar. It was not Frederick Farnham who died in the streets of Corunna, Aurelia."

"And as far as your family are concerned, you are dead, too?"

His smile was ironic. "I was as good as dead to my family from the moment of my birth. I nearly killed my mother, for which my father never forgave me. Or at least he never forgave me for the consequences of that birth. My mother retreated into a world of her own and apparently forgot my existence . . . or ignored it. The effect was the same. And she forgot or ignored my father's existence in precisely the same manner."

He drummed his knuckles on the dresser. "There, Aurelia, you asked for it, and now you have it in all the words it takes . . . my entire youthful history."

Aurelia could think of nothing to say. He was angry, presumably because she had forced him to reveal the pain he had managed to bury so deep all these years. Or was he simply angry with himself because he had broken his own rules, weakened and succumbed to her, yielded to her need to break through his defensive shell?

"I'm sorry," she said simply, coming towards him. She put her arms around him in a fierce hug. "I'm sorry that you had such a miserable childhood, but I'm not sorry that you told me."

She let her hands fall when she felt no response from the rigid figure and stepped back. "I won't press you any further, it clearly makes you uncomfortable. Don't let me keep you any longer."

He seemed to hesitate. Then he ran a hand through his close-cropped hair in a gesture of frustration and said, "Are you coming down for dinner?"

"No, I told Hester to bring me a tray in my sitting room." She turned back to the dresser and picked up her brush, scooping her hair into a knot on the nape of her neck.

"I thought you were going to the Paganini recital."

"I don't feel well tonight."

"Oh." He turned halfway to the door, adding almost as an afterthought, "I had thought to accompany you."

He sounded so diffident, she thought. Extraordinarily so for such a man. As if he were completely at a loss, a feeling and experience with which he was totally unfamiliar.

"You could go alone and make my excuses," she suggested, fastening a netted snood around the knot of hair. "Cornelia will be there."

"No . . . no . . . I think I'll settle for a quiet evening, too." He paused with his hand on the door, glancing over his shoulder at her as she sat on the dresser stool. "Shall I look in before I go to bed?"

"By all means," she said easily. "I intend to seek my bed early, though, so I may not be awake."

"I'll take my chance then," he returned drily, and left her.

Aurelia sat for a moment longer wondering what had just happened. They had touched some sore spots, approached some emotional boundaries whatever Greville might say about avoiding them at all costs. She couldn't at the moment decide whether that had been an achievement or not.

"I'm assuming I don't need to wear formal evening dress for this event, Aurelia." Greville came into Aurelia's bedchamber on the Friday evening of the Lessingham soiree, brushing at the silk sleeve of a dark gray coat.

"Not Almack's formal, certainly," she said, turning to look at him while still holding out her arm for Hester, who was intent on fastening the row of tiny buttons at the cuffs of the long, full sleeves of her gown. "That will do nicely. You look very much à la mode." Indeed, the formfitting, dark gray silk coat and skintight, knitted, dove-gray pantaloons couldn't be faulted, unless, of course, one would rather one's husband did not display the masculine muscularity of his figure quite so blatantly in public.

"May I return the compliment," he responded with an appreciative smile.

Aurelia knew that the old gold damask gown, fastened at the waist with a tasseled cord, the décolletage accentuated by a simple collar of deep gold amber circling her throat, more than flattered her coloring. Hester had spent hours with the curling iron perfecting the cluster of pale blond ringlets framing her face, and she thought without an excess of vanity that she was looking her best.

Not an accurate reflection of her inner self, however. Since their unhappily fruitless discussion of the previous afternoon, Greville had behaved as if they had never come anywhere near such difficult emotional territory, and Aurelia found it impossible to do anything but follow his lead. But what had not been said yawned like a wasteland between them, or so *she* felt.

"Don't forget your fan." He picked up the delicate Japanese painted fan and unfurled its ivory sticks.

"I'm not about to." The fan was to be their medium of communication, most particularly if a Don Antonio Vasquez was one of the guests. Her role tonight was simply to engage the man in conversation, flirt with him, draw him out as far as possible, act as bait in fact, and Greville would make his own move when he judged the time right. She had a series of gestures with the fan that would impart basic information if she decided he needed it.

He nodded. "Shall we go then?" He took her evening cloak from Hester and draped it carefully about her shoulders, then as he reached his hands around to fasten it at the throat, he bent and brushed the nape of her neck in a warm whisper of a kiss.

His mouth as always sent a shiver of anticipation down her spine and a warm jolt to her belly. She stepped away from him quickly, slipping the fan into her beaded reticule. "Ready," she stated with a bright smile.

Greville's eyebrows flickered as he offered her his arm, but he said nothing.

In the carriage Aurelia sat back in a corner, idly playing with the drawstring of the reticule that she wore around her wrist. Greville sat opposite, watching her through half-closed eyes. Sulfur yellow light flickered across the windowpanes as they passed beneath the gas streetlights. The unpleasant light cast a sickly yellow glow across the interior of the coach.

"Are you apprehensive?" he asked finally.

"Not particularly." She looked up, surprised. "Should I be?"

"No. You've had enough training for this to be as easy as playing Lottery Tickets with Franny."

"It's a simple enough card game, I grant you," she said with a faint smile. "Unlikely to offer any complicated play."

"Well, tonight should be the same. But you seem a little distrait and I would not have you distracted. If there's anything that's troubling you, you should tell me now."

Dear God, Aurelia thought. *Don't you ever think of anything but the game in hand? You can't begin to imagine that I might be distracted by anything other than this evening's ploy.*

"Don't worry, there's nothing troubling me," she said. "Why should there be? All I have to do is engage a man in conversation, something I've been doing quite skillfully ever since I put my hair up."

"We are talking about a particular man, and a particular point to the conversation."

Aurelia shrugged. "It doesn't make any difference, Greville. One conversation is conducted essentially very like another."

"True enough. And I will never be out of your sight." He leaned back against the squabs, folding his arms. "Show me again what gesture will tell me that you want me to come over and join you."

Without expression, Aurelia took her fan from the reticule and flicked it open. She moved it to the height of her right shoulder and waved it with a twist of her wrist towards her face. "Good enough, spymaster?"

And suddenly she felt her spirit lighten. She loved this game for itself. She loved the sense of competency she felt, the knowledge that she was outwitting a roomful of people who thought she was one person, when she was quite another. And as a bonus tonight, none of her close friends would be there, so the deception had no strings attached.

Greville caught the flash of light in her eye, the sudden twitch of her lips, and felt himself relax. Whatever the unresolved issues between them, Aurelia would not let them get in the way of her role play.

"More than good enough." He reached across the narrow gap and took her hand. "I know you will be superb, my dear. You are made for this work."

He had said it before, but the repetition never failed to excite her, to fill her with a sense of power. For tonight, nothing existed but their partnership and the game they would play.

The carriage drew up in front of the Earl of Lessingham's mansion on Berkeley Square. A footman from the house ran up to open the carriage door before Jemmy could jump down from his seat on the box beside the coachman.

"Good evening, Sir Greville, Lady Falconer." The footman held open the door and offered a hand to Aurelia.

She stepped down to the street, puzzled that the man should have recognized the carriage, a fairly modest conveyance, bearing no livery on the panels.

Greville descended without assistance. "My thanks," he said with a nod at the servant. "You're an observant fellow."

"I was told to watch for you, sir," the man said, pocketing the coin Greville slipped into his hand. "Most of the guests at her ladyship's Friday soirees come on foot, or by 'ackney carriage."

Greville merely smiled in vague acknowledgment and gave Aurelia his arm as they followed the man into the lighted hall.

"Why on foot?" Aurelia whispered.

"Exiles . . . too poor to afford private carriages," Greville murmured. "Or unwilling to admit that they can . . . which would in itself be rather interesting.

Find out, if you can, Don Antonio's means of transportation."

Aurelia smiled a little, but nothing showed on her face as she ascended the staircase to greet her hostess waiting at the head. Doña Bernardina, her voluptuous curves accentuated by a gown of rose gauze over crimson satin, confined tightly beneath full breasts, flung open her hands as if she were an opera singer about to launch into an aria. Aurelia caught her breath, afraid that with the extravagant gesture the rich swell of the lady's bosom would spill forth like two overfed and excitable puppies. They stayed in their basket however.

"Lady Falconer, how good of you to come." Doña Bernardina's black mantilla was fastened to her décolletage with a ruby broach, massive diamond drops hung from her earlobes, and three strands of perfect pearls were wound around her neck.

She turned her radiant smile on Greville. "And Sir Greville. I bid you welcome."

Greville bowed low over the plump white hand, beringed fingers ending in long scarlet nails. "Lady Lessingham," he murmured.

The countess led the way through a set of double doors into a large apartment furnished with an opulence as conspicuous as her own. Swagged curtains, a multiplicity of silk cushions on deep velvet armchairs and gilded sofas, rich Persian carpets in a riot of colors, all contrasted with the massive, gold-framed oil paintings of generally somber-looking gentlemen, presumably the earl's ancestors, against dark and rocky backgrounds that adorned the silk-hung walls.

Two or three groups of people were scattered around the salon. A woman was seated at a pianoforte in the far corner of the room, the music providing a soft counterpoint to the buzz of conversation.

Greville took in the room's occupants. Don Antonio Vasquez was not among them. He turned with a smile to his wife. "Permit me, my dear." Solicitously he adjusted the tawny-toned paisley shawl over Aurelia's shoulders.

She understood at once that their specific quarry was not present, and she relaxed a little, accepting a glass of champagne from a footman's tray and responding to her hostess's introductions to their fellow guests.

For an hour she moved among the guests, exchanging pleasantries, accustoming her ear to their occasionally thickly accented English. She knew that she must absorb as much of the conversations as she could, listening for anything that might hint at an unusual activity or interest. Don Antonio's absence did not mean that the evening was wasted. One or two of these generally solemn and preoccupied gentlemen were more than possibly agents of Napoléon, and she might pick up something useful.

Greville kept to his own circuit, glancing only occasionally in Aurelia's direction to satisfy himself that she was holding her own in comfort. When Don Antonio Vasquez was announced in ringing tones by the butler, Greville didn't turn his head towards the door, merely continued softly with his conversation with an elderly matron, who was lamenting the loss of her treasures, which she'd been obliged to abandon when her son had taken his entire family into exile just ahead of the usurper.

The fine hairs on Aurelia's nape lifted at the sound of the name, but she didn't turn immediately, not until Doña Bernardina billowed over to them, the newcomer in tow. "Ladies . . . gentlemen, some of you know Don Antonio, I'm sure."

There were murmurs of agreement, hands shaken, bows exchanged, before it was Aurelia's turn to be introduced. She extended her hand to the tall, slender man with the spade beard and coal black eyes. His hair was longer than prevailing fashion dictated, curling a little on his broad forehead. Apart from his white shirt, he was dressed entirely in black, and it suited him, she thought, absorbing his appearance with an almost clinical detachment. His countenance was arresting, almost aggressively handsome, but his mouth was cruel, and his long nose resembled a hawk's beak.

Aurelia decided she would not care to meet Don Antonio Vasquez alone in a dark street. There was something predatory about him, and something intrinsically dangerous in his lithe, fluid grace. As the introductions were made, she sensed instantly that he had an interest of some kind in her. His hand as he held hers was cool and dry, the fingers long and white, a huge emerald set in gold on his right-hand ring finger. He lifted her hand to his lips and kissed it with a courtly flourish and a bow that was now so old-fashioned as to be almost archaic in London society.

"Lady Falconer, how delightful." His voice was soft and almost mellifluous, the accent faint and charming, and his mouth smiled, but his eyes did not.

"Don Antonio, I'm pleased to make your acquaintance," she returned with a warm smile. "How long have you been in London?"

"A mere three weeks," he said, taking a glass of champagne from the footman's tray. "Not long enough to feel at home as yet." He sipped his champagne. "And you, Lady Falconer, you are, of course, quite at home in London?"

"I have lived here for some time. But my family home is in the country. In the New Forest. Have you visited there? It's a most interesting and ancient part of England."

"No, alas, I have seen only the town of Dover, where I landed, and the area around my lodgings. Grosvenor Square . . . a pretty garden, but with none of the magnificence of our Madrid parks."

"Perhaps not, sir. I own I have long wished to visit Madrid." Aurelia tapped her closed fan against her mouth as if in thought. Greville would understand that while battle had been joined, she needed no assistance at this point. "But you say you have lodgings on Grosvenor Square?"

"Close by. Adam's Row, I believe it to be called."

"Yes, indeed. We are neighbors, it seems, Don Antonio. South Audley Street is but a step away, too close to warrant the use of a carriage."

"What a delightful coincidence, and so convenient since I do not maintain a carriage. Such an unnecessary expense when hackney carriages are so easy to obtain. Perhaps I may call upon you, my lady."

This was not a gentleman accustomed to the rough-and-tumble of a frowsty hackney carriage, Aurelia reflected. It was almost impossible to imagine that elegant frame reposing itself on the cracked and stained leather squabs of a hired vehicle.

She smiled an invitation. "I should be happy to receive you, sir. Are you acquainted with my husband, Sir Greville Falconer?"

"I don't believe so," he replied smoothly, turning his head to follow her gesturing hand. He turned his cold smile upon her. "Is your husband the tall gentleman talking to our host?"

She nodded. "He is."

"I think I may have seen him in Grosvenor Square gardens. He was with a small girl and a very large dog. They made a most charming spectacle."

"My daughter." Aurelia felt a shiver down her spine as if she was standing in an icy draft.

"A pretty child, ma'am. I congratulate you."

Keep away from my daughter. She had to bite her tongue to stop herself from shouting the words.

She managed a laugh, however, although it sounded rather hollow to her own ears. "I hardly think I can take credit, Don Antonio."

"Ah, but she takes after her mother, clearly," he responded with a gallant bow.

Play the part, she told herself. *Think of it as a game of charades.*

She batted her eyelashes and flipped open her fan, half covering her face as she offered a flirtatious smile and murmured, "You flatter me, sir."

Greville, aware of every movement of her fan from across the room, understood the message. She was telling him everything was going smoothly.

"Perhaps I could show you some of London, Don Antonio?"

"I would be honored, Lady Falconer." His eyes slid away from her across to her husband. "If your husband would have no objections."

Again her laugh sounded artificial to her ears, but she hoped a stranger wouldn't notice. "In London, sir, ladies do not live in their husband's pockets."

He bowed solemnly. "We live in a rather more rigid society in Madrid, Lady Falconer. Rather old-fashioned, I daresay, by London standards."

She twinkled at him over her fan. "Do you disapprove of our free and easy London ways, sir?"

"Not at all, ma'am," he said, his eyes hooded. "Just a matter of becoming accustomed, and with so many lovely and accommodating ladies, I don't believe it will take me long to become accustomed."

And once more, out of the blue, Aurelia felt an eerie breath of cold and thought suddenly that Don Antonio Vasquez was playing with her. She had thought she was doing the playing, but now she was not so sure. She was no longer sure she was in control. She moved her fan with a twist of her wrist to her right shoulder, wafting it leisurely towards her face.

Greville was at her side more quickly than she would have believed possible. "My dear, I don't believe I have made the acquaintance of your companion."

To her astonishment, she thought his voice sounded faintly slurred, and when she cast him a covert glance, she thought his eyes looked a little glazed. She performed the introduction, saying lightly, "It seems that Don Antonio is a neighbor of ours, Greville. He has lodgings on Adam's Row."

"I believe I may have seen you in Grosvenor Square the other afternoon," the Spaniard said. "You were accompanying a delightful child and her dog."

Greville peered at him over the rim of his glass, blinking as if unsure if he was seeing him aright. "Can't say I noticed you." He shook his head. "No offense, I hope."

"Not at all," Don Antonio said. "The dog drew my attention. One doesn't see an Irish wolfhound very often." His lips moved in the semblance of a smile.

Greville gave a bluff laugh and his hand shook, spilling a little of his champagne onto the carpet. "No, indeed not."

Aurelia was awestruck. She would swear on her parents' grave that Colonel, Sir Greville Falconer had never been the worse for drink in his life, but he was giving the most superb imitation. But why? He had, of course, succeeded in turning the Spaniard's attention completely away from her, and she had now regained the composure she had momentarily been afraid of losing.

She turned her full attention to Don Antonio, giving him a dazzling smile. "I do hope you will call in South Audley Street, Don Antonio. I am anxious to fulfill my promise to show you some of the sights of our city. I have my own barouche, so there's no need for you to concern yourself with a conveyance. I would be delighted to take you up." That should have given Greville one specific piece of information he'd asked for.

The Spaniard bowed. "I will be in your debt, my lady, and the envy of all."

She tapped his arm reprovingly with her fan, her eyes sparkling, something approaching a simper on her lips. "I do protest, sir. Such shameless flattery."

He took her hand and raised it to his lips, exclaiming, "It is for me to protest, my lady. You must absolve me. I am utterly sincere."

"Then I look forward to your call, Don Antonio. I am at home most mornings at eleven o'clock."

He bowed again to her, then offered a nodding bow to Greville, and with a word of excuse moved away.

Greville spoke into the air above her ear, in that whisper that only she could hear. "Leave now."

Why? But she didn't ask the question, instead stepped away from him and threaded her way through the room to where her hostess was holding court by the piano.

"Ah, Lady Falconer, come and join us." Doña Bernardina greeted her with an outflung hand. "Give us your opinion on Lope de Vega. We find so few English know any of our writers except for Cervantes."

"And much as they say they love the book, they cannot pronounce *Don Quixote* correctly," an effete young man stated with a laugh that bordered on a sneer.

"You must forgive us our ignorance," Aurelia said with a chilly smile. "The English are not known for their linguistic skill, I have to admit. I daresay it is because our language is spoken everywhere and we have grown quite lazy as a result."

"But you, Lady Falconer, you speak a little Spanish, no?"

Having done her patriotic duty in defending her countrymen's lamentably arrogant lack of interest in foreign languages, Aurelia was prepared to yield the ground. "Not really. Only French, and a little Italian."

It was a while before she could politely excuse herself from the conversation and make her farewells to her hostess. She could hear Greville's voice from the far side of the room, pitched a little too loud to be appropriate, and while he couldn't be accused of actually slurring his words, a thickness indicated a lack of control, and his tall frame seemed to waft a little as if he were a tree in a high wind.

Aurelia would have laughed at such a brilliant display, except she assumed that what lay behind it was probably not funny at all.

Chapter Nineteen

The carriage was waiting by the door in the same place it had dropped them off, Jemmy standing by the horses. But Aurelia noticed for the first time that there was an unfamiliar coachman on the box. Usually Jemmy managed the carriage with just the help of Greville's groom. Greville must have hired the new man without telling her. Not that he had any obligation to do so. Jemmy ran to open the door.

"I didn't realize we had a new coachman," she said as she climbed into the carriage.

"Just this morning, m'lady," Jemmy informed her in a tone that rang with disapproval. "Sir Greville said as 'ow there 'ad to be the two of us to drive you, even though I've been doin' it quite satisfactory for years."

It was presumably part of the protective net Greville had thrown over her, Aurelia thought. She smiled rather wearily at Jemmy. "I'm sure Sir Greville was not casting aspersions on your skill, Jemmy. He probably felt two coachmen were necessary for his wife. Husbands often think like that. It adds to their consequence."

"Mebbe," Jemmy said doubtfully. "The new bloke don't say much, that's fer sure." He closed the door and went around to jump up on the back step, clinging to the strap as the coachman started the horses and the carriage moved off at a fast clip.

Aurelia was astounded at how suddenly exhausted she felt, as if she'd been walking a high wire for hours. She leaned back in a corner and closed her eyes, wondering why Greville was staying on, and why he was putting on such an act.

She was almost asleep when the carriage drew up outside the house. Jemmy let down the footstep and opened the door, peering into the dark interior of the vehicle. "We're 'ome, mum."

"Oh, goodness, are we, Jemmy. I was almost asleep." She gathered herself together and stepped out into the street. The night air had a breath of warmth, a real intimation of spring at last, and the faint scent of early-May blossoms drifted from the trees in Grosvenor Square.

She let herself into the quiet, lamplit house and went into the library, determined to wait for Greville's return. The soiree would not go on for much longer by the unexciting nature of the entertainment offered, but Greville might go on somewhere if it suited his plan. But Aurelia decided to take her chance for an hour. She kicked off her satin slippers and curled up in a corner of the sofa with a small glass of cognac, thinking over the events of the evening, and particularly Don Antonio Vasquez.

He frightened her, she realized after a minute's careful thought. He was like a large cat with his eyes on unwitting prey. Was she a match for him?

Greville let himself into the house quietly an hour later. The lamps were still lit, and he saw that the library door was open. He trod quietly to the door and looked in. Aurelia was fast asleep in a corner of the sofa, her paisley shawl draped over her. The fire was almost out, the candles on the mantel guttering, the lamps burning low. He went over to the sofa and gently shook her shoulder.

"Aurelia, wake up, my love. It's late and you need to be abed." He touched the curve of her cheek with a fingertip and her eyelids fluttered, then her eyes opened and she looked up at him in bleary confusion.

"Greville?"

"Yes, it's me, as ever was." He bent and kissed the corner of her mouth. "Come, let me help you to bed." He slid an arm around her shoulders and half lifted her off the sofa. "Shall I carry you?"

"No," she said with a semblance of indignation. "Of course not. I'm quite capable of walking on my two feet . . . which, I might say, you did not seem to be earlier this evening."

He chuckled. "You noticed."

"Hard to miss." She gathered her shawl around her, decided to ignore her discarded shoes, and set off resolutely on stockinged feet to the door.

"Ah, and there I thought I was giving a good imitation of a drunk acting sober."

Aurelia laughed. "You probably fooled everyone but me."

"I hope so." He took her arm and led her to the stairs.

"Why did you want Don Antonio to think you were drunk?" she asked over her shoulder as he urged her upward.

He laughed a little. "A man who can't hold his drink is quickly dismissed. It never does any harm to encourage people to discount one, particularly those in whom one might have some interest oneself."

"Oh . . . smoke and mirrors."

"In a manner of speaking."

"I didn't like him," she said, turning towards her room at the head of the stairs. *And that was the understatement of the year.*

"With good reason." Greville followed her down the passage. "I believe him to be a very dangerous man."

"I wish he hadn't seen Franny." She gave voice to the amorphous apprehension that had gripped her earlier.

"My dear, I was with her and so was Lyra. You need have no fear for Franny, I swear that she is in no danger, and never will be."

Her feelings for this man were confused and often conflicted, but despite the fact that he had drilled into her the mantra that she must trust no one, she trusted his word in this instance. "The new coachman is in some measure a bodyguard?"

"Yes. He'll drive you everywhere if you're not with me. And there will be someone to escort Franny wherever she goes, unless she's with me."

It was sufficient reassurance and Aurelia willingly accepted it, yielding now to her fatigue. "Why am I so tired?"

"You had a hard evening," he said, propelling her to the bed and pushing her down with a hand on her elbow. "Harder than you realized at the time. Deception is not an easy business."

"Is that why you sent me away?"

"I judged you'd had enough. As I keep saying, you're still new to the business."

He bent over her as she sprawled on the coverlet and began to undress her with a deft efficiency that she thought through the tendrils of fatigue had less of the lover and more of the nursemaid about it. He helped her into her nightgown, offered her toothbrush and tooth powder, and while she brushed her teeth, he unpinned her hair and pulled a brush through it to loosen the curls.

Aurelia crawled under the coverlet, still astounded at how utterly exhausted she was. But when he bent over her to kiss her, she looked into his dark eyes that glowed with a strange warmth and she thought, *You called me "my love."* Never before had that word in any context passed Colonel, Sir Greville Falconer's lips in her hearing. Did he know he'd said it? Would he remember?

The words accompanied her into sleep, and when he slid in beside her, she turned into his embrace, burrowing into the hollow of his shoulder, falling into a sleep that she knew was safe and protected.

When she awoke in the morning to his soft, whispering touches beneath the coverlet, she smiled to herself in the dim light of the curtain-hung bed, thinking again of those words he had spoken. *He had called her "his love."*

Perhaps he hadn't been playing the drunkard after all, perhaps there'd been some truth to the charade. But, no, he had not been drunk when he'd helped her to bed, not one iota. And he had not been drunk when those words had passed his lips.

Of course, he didn't know she'd heard them. She'd been dead to the world as far as he knew. But he'd still spoken them.

She stretched languidly and parted her thighs to give his tongue and fingers access to her core, and her smile deepened as she curled her fingers in his hair and caressed his ears, lifting her hips to the rhythmic waves of delight.

"The woman never leaves the house without the dog if she's on foot or on horseback," Miguel stated, watching his master covertly. Don Antonio was unusually restless, pacing the drawing room of the house on Adam's Row as he listened to his assistant's report. "I don't follow her, of course, but I watch."

Don Antonio spun on his heel and walked to the window that looked down on the street. "Have we identified anyone else of interest in the house?"

"Apart from the child, no, sir. There have been no unusual comings and goings that would give us any indication of—"

"Don't be any more foolish than you must, Miguel," his master interrupted acidly. "Do you really think a man of the *asp*'s skill and experience would make it *obvious* that his house was a center for espionage? You're supposed to be skilled enough yourself to notice things that shouldn't be noticeable."

"Yes . . . yes, of course, Don Antonio." Miguel flushed. "But I swear there's nothing."

Don Antonio regarded him in speculative silence for a moment. Then he sat down in a winged chair beside the fireplace and said more moderately, "Very well. If you swear it, I'll take your word for it."

Miguel blossomed under the rare vote of confidence. "How do we proceed now, sir?"

His master frowned. "The *asp* has given no indication as yet that he has broken my cover. As long as he continues to believe that we're planning an information-gathering mission, according to the misinformation given to their network in Madrid, we will proceed exactly as intended. It's obvious that they would assume our very public arrival at Dover was part of that information-gathering operation. Looking for me at Doña Bernardina's soiree was an obvious step."

He tapped the ruby ring on his finger against the wooden arm of his chair in an unmelodic rhythm as he said softly, "But our friend has made things a little easier for us by this marriage. I have long thought that for all your undeniable skills at your profession, Miguel, it's possible that the *asp* will withstand your techniques. He is no ordinary man. Either that or he will ensure somehow that he is not alive to be broken by them. But a woman and child live under his protection. A strange burden for such a consummate professional to assume. And one that I hope will provide a chink in his armor. We work on the woman, not the *asp,* and we'll see if he can withstand her agony as well as he will quite possibly succeed in withstanding his own. When we have what we want from him, I will kill them."

He crossed one leg over the other, gently swinging a quizzing glass on its black velvet ribbon as he surveyed Miguel. "Can you perhaps deduce why *I* have been set this particular task, my friend?"

Miguel made no attempt to guess. "You are the best there is, sir," he offered simply.

Don Antonio nodded and agreed amiably, "Yes, my

friend, I believe I am. But that is not the entire reason, my dear Miguel. I choose my tasks with great care, and I have a personal reason for choosing this one." A grim expression crossed his face. "I do not tolerate failure."

"No, Don Antonio."

"Particularly my own." He pursed his lips. "Unlike many of my comrades in the service, I have never crossed swords face-to-face with the *asp*. But I would have done so had he not outwitted me once . . . and believe me, Miguel, no one ever outwits me twice." The very softness of his voice accentuated the ferocity of the declaration.

Miguel nodded in hasty agreement. "You are the best, Don Antonio," he repeated reverently.

His master didn't appear to hear him. Don Antonio continued in an almost musing tone, "The *asp* is one man I will never underestimate. Over the years he's cut a swath of destruction through our networks . . . which is why we can no longer afford to accommodate him," he stated with a flicker of a smile.

"The question remains, however: will Spain's best be more than a match for England's on this occasion?" Don Antonio watched the swinging quizzing glass with a distracted frown, as if mesmerized by it, but then he caught the ribbon and dropped it with the glass into the pocket of his waistcoat. "Don't trouble yourself to answer that, Miguel. It was purely rhetorical."

Don Antonio uncurled himself from the chair. "So I shall cultivate the wife. I still cannot understand why the *asp* would complicate his operation with a woman. But he must have some devious reason."

Don Antonio threw back his head and laughed. "*Madre de Dios,* there is no limit to what the *asp* will do for his work. It's the man's lifeblood."

Miguel found his master's laughter if anything more alarming than his ferocious contempt. He shuffled his feet and looked longingly towards the door.

"Go." Don Antonio waved a hand in dismissal, and Miguel bowed and left.

"Ah, yes," Don Antonio murmured softly into the silence. "Once a spy always a spy . . . until death brings the endgame."

Aurelia was returning to the house after walking Lyra in Hyde Park when a smart curricle bowled down South Audley Street from Grosvenor Square. She recognized the tall, fair-haired, blue-eyed driver immediately as he reined in the pair of blood chestnuts outside her house.

"Alex," she called, hastening her step, smiling with delight. "Liv said you'd be in town sometime this week."

"And here I am." He jumped down lightly, tossing the reins to his groom. He looked askance at Lyra, who was standing at Aurelia's side, her massive head at waist level, her deep brown eyes regarding Prince Alexander Prokov with mild curiosity.

"Is it safe to approach you?" he asked, extending an undemanding hand towards the hound.

"Perfectly." Aurelia gave a gentle tug on Lyra's left ear, and the dog visibly relaxed, pushing her head into Alex's hand.

Alex judged he'd established his friendly intentions and embraced Aurelia, kissing her warmly on both cheeks. "Congratulations, Lady Falconer. I bring letters and wedding gifts and all sorts of nonsense from Livia. But I brought only the letter today. I shall send the parcels round this afternoon. There are far too many to fit in the curricle. Shall we go in?"

He led the way up the steps to the front door as confidently as if it was his own house. "Will Morecombe answer the door, do you think? I can't tell you how grateful we all are at this arrangement. I was beginning to fear that Boris would hand in his notice before we returned to Cavendish Square. And that, my dear, would not do at all." He raised the doorknocker and banged it vigorously.

Aurelia chuckled as she and Lyra followed him up. Fatherhood hadn't changed Alexander Prokov. He still swept all before him.

"I have a key." She produced it. "But Morecombe doesn't answer the door very often. He leaves it to Jemmy . . . much speedier, as you might imagine." She fitted the key in the lock and swung open the door.

Morecombe, as it happened, was shuffling his way

across the hall as they went in. "All this bangin' an' thumpin'," he grumbled. Then he stopped, peered myopically, and declared with something akin to pleasure, "Eh, 'tis you, Lady Sophia's boy."

"It is, Morecombe. How are you? And Ada . . . Mavis . . . they're well?" Alex took the old man's gnarled hands gently in his. Neither of them would ever forget that Morecombe had given him the last push to put his father's history behind him and to forge his own future with Livia.

"Pleased enow to see ye, they'll be," Morecombe said. "I'll bring summat to the salon fer ye, an' the lassies'll be in t' greet ye shortly. 'Ow's our lady Liv then? An' the babby. The lassies can't 'ardly wait to set eyes on 'im."

"Soon enough," Alex reassured. "Livia and the baby will be returning to London in two weeks."

"Oh, in time for Cornelia's ball," Aurelia said, leading the way into the salon. "That's splendid. Nell will be so pleased."

"Livia wouldn't miss it for the world." Alex looked around the room. "This is a pleasant house."

"Not as grand as Cavendish Square," she responded with a smile. "But I do like it. It has a good feeling about it, and Franny has settled well."

Alex sat down without an invitation as befitted an old friend. He said with a hint of a rueful smile, "You do understand that I am expressly charged with taking a complete description of your husband back to Livia?"

Aurelia laughed. "Of course. Although I'm sure she's had plenty of detail from Nell. And I've not been unforthcoming myself." She'd left a lot out, however, and Livia would certainly have noticed the lacks.

"But Cornelia's eyes are not mine," Alex said, letting Aurelia's latter statement lie unchallenged.

"True enough." Aurelia rose to her feet to help Morecombe with the tray as he staggered slightly entering the room. "Let me take that, Morecombe."

"Put it down over there then," he said, "an' I'll pour for ye. 'Tis not a bad sherry, sir."

"It's as good as any Prince Prokov has in his cellars, Morecombe," Aurelia protested, hearing faint damns in the comment. Alex merely smiled and accepted the glass before the old man's shaking fingers spilled it.

"So, where is Sir Greville?" Alex inquired, sipping his sherry as Morecombe closed the door behind himself.

"He had some business." Greville was at the ministry, but she wasn't going to divulge that. If Greville felt comfortable taking Alex into his confidence in some part, then that was his business. It wasn't hers.

"I see." Alex leaned back in his chair and regarded her. "He's one of us, I gather."

"You'll have to ask him," she said with a half smile.

Alex nodded without further comment. "I have a miniature of little Alexander." He reached into his pocket and drew out a tiny portrait in a pearl-encrusted frame. He squinted at it before saying with a half smile, "Much as

I adore my wife, I don't think portrait painting is really her forte."

Aurelia went into a peal of laughter as she took the picture. "Liv did this?"

"Insisted upon it."

She examined the splodge of an infant in the jeweled frame. "Is it really a baby?" she asked doubtfully. "It could be one of Liv's silly pink dogs."

"Trust me, Aurelia, it is my son."

She nodded and held it to the light. "A bonny babe. I can't wait to see him in the flesh."

"I think you might get a better impression of his charms when you do," his fond papa declared.

At the sound of the front door, Aurelia jumped up. "Ah, that's Greville." She hurried to the door. "Greville. Come and meet Prince Prokov."

Greville knew Aurelia had been expecting her friend's husband for the last three days. He put aside the thoughts that had been occupying him since he'd left the ministry and entered the salon, hand outstretched in welcome. Lyra moved to greet him with a nudge of her head against his thigh, before sitting down again at Aurelia's feet.

Aurelia watched as the two men shook hands and offered the ritual phrases of greeting. But she could sense something beneath the conventional pleasantries. They were sizing each other up, too.

"I must congratulate you on the birth of your son," Greville said, moving to the sideboard. "All went well, I understand."

"Very well." Alex beamed and reached for the miniature in his pocket. "This is not a very good likeness, I'm afraid." He offered the little jeweled frame.

Greville studied it diligently and despite his obvious puzzlement said all the right things, until Aurelia laughed and said, "Alex isn't going to mind if you say it doesn't really look like a baby, Greville. It's Liv's attempt at painting a miniature. She's very good at a lot of things, but I don't think even she would say she's much of an artist."

"Oh . . . well, nevertheless, he looks a most handsome child," Greville said, handing back the miniature with barely concealed relief and changing the subject. "When did you arrive in London, Prokov?" He refilled his guest's sherry glass before pouring himself one.

"Yesterday. South Audley Street is my first port of call." Alex settled back into his chair. "My wife insisted that I waste no time in paying a wedding visit to Aurelia. Which reminds me . . ." He reached into his pocket and took out a fat letter. "This is for you, Aurelia. It will have all her news, much more fully described than I could manage."

"I doubt you'd even think of half the things Liv would consider vitally important to share," Aurelia said with a chuckle.

"I'm sure you're right, dear girl. Women do have different priorities," Alex agreed with a rather complacent smile. "So, Colonel Falconer, you've only recently returned to these shores, I understand."

Greville nodded easily. It was hardly a secret. "I've been in Spain and Portugal for most of the last two years."

"And you're enjoying some well-earned leisure, I trust." Alex smiled over his glass, raising an eyebrow in slight question.

"Up to a point," Greville agreed, taking a seat opposite Prince Prokov. "I'm sure your country sojourn affords you a little leisure also?" The question mark was clear in his voice, and Aurelia thought it contained a hint of a challenge, too.

"True enough." Alex seemed to hesitate, as if debating whether to respond to the challenge and open the subject up a little, but the door opened and Ada and Mavis came in, bearing plates of savory tartlets and honey cakes.

"Eh, we thought as 'ow ye might like a bite wi' yer sherry," Ada announced, setting the plates on a low table. "An' 'ow are ye, sir . . . an' 'ow's Lady Livia an' the babby?"

"Very well, both of them," Alex said, rising to shake hands. "I've a picture here painted by his mother." Once again he proffered the miniature, and the twins exclaimed over it, holding it up to the light.

"Why, the little lad's the image of 'is ma," Mavis pronounced. "Look at 'is nose there . . . just like our Lady Liv's."

"The very image," Ada agreed. "But the eyes are Lady Sophia's."

"Aye, that they are, just like 'is pa. When's Lady Liv and the babby comin' to town, sir?"

"In two weeks," Alex said, slipping the miniature back into his pocket.

"Oh, aye, well, we'd best be gettin' the nursery set up," Mavis said. "Or is that there Boris doin' it?" Disapproval was heavy in her tone.

"I think Boris would be more than pleased to leave such details up to you," Alex said diplomatically. "But now that you're working for Lady Falconer, how will you find time?"

"Oh, never ye mind about that, sir. We've plenty of time on our 'ands," Mavis said with a nod at her sister.

"Oh, aye, time on our 'ands." Ada nodded her agreement. "Won't take but an hour or two, anywise." Then, as if by silent communication, the two elderly women turned in unison and left the salon.

"I wonder how they saw the likeness to Livia," Alex said, peering closely at the miniature. "For the life of me, I can't even see his nose."

"And one would never accuse either Morecombe or the twins of being adept at the tactful white lie," Aurelia said, laughing. "I think their fondness for Liv probably colors their vision."

"Probably." Alex took a tartlet and savored it with a little sigh of bliss. "I'd forgotten how good these are. Is it all right with you if they do some work in Cavendish Square as well as here?"

"Perfectly," Aurelia stated.

"As long as we don't lose their culinary skills," Greville said, helping himself to a tartlet and consuming it with much the same expression as his guest's.

"Oh, Alex has his own French cook," Aurelia said. "He and the twins are chalk and cheese. But I'm sure if Liv expresses a desire for one of their specialties, they'll manage to produce it without depriving us of anything."

"Whatever you say, my dear. I leave all such matters in your more than capable hands." Greville reached for the sherry decanter again, then paused, his hand in midair, as the sound of the doorknocker reached them. "Are you expecting someone, Aurelia?"

"No, but I am home to *visitors* in the morning." The faint emphasis on the word and the look she gave Greville conveyed her message. Somehow she knew who her visitor was. Don Antonio Vasquez was paying his promised call, and her body was suddenly as taut as a bowstring.

Lyra rose to her feet and stood with ears pricked facing the door.

"Of course," Greville said calmly. "Is Jemmy around, or should we let our visitor wait on the doorstep until Morecombe gets there?"

Alex laughed. "Oh, that's such a familiar dilemma. Shall I go and play butler?"

"*No,*" Aurelia said, laughing herself. "Of course not. Jemmy will get it."

She was right. A minute or two later, Jemmy opened the door and announced proudly, "A gentleman to see you, my lady." He came in ahead of the visitor and proffered the card.

"Thank you, Jemmy." Clearly the lad couldn't quite manage to pronounce the name inscribed upon it, and she couldn't really blame him. He was hardly an experienced butler.

Aurelia took the card and went to the door, hand outstretched to greet her visitor, who was standing on the threshold of the salon with an air of impatience and a hint of incredulity at his unusually clumsy reception.

"Don Antonio, how delightful. I didn't dare hope you would honor me with a visit so soon." She gave him her hand with the slightly simpering smile she'd practiced at the countess's soiree.

The Spaniard bowed with a snap of his heels and raised her hand to his lips. "The honor is all mine, Lady Falconer." His black eyes met hers as he smiled, and once again the smile on his lips came nowhere near his eyes.

He turned to greet Greville, who stood now by the fireplace, one arm resting along the mantel, his sherry glass in his hand. He acknowledged his guest's greeting with a nod of a bow and a murmured "Don Antonio, welcome."

"Allow me to present Prince Prokov," Aurelia said, turning to Alex, who had risen from his chair and stood waiting expectantly. "Alex, this is a newcomer to our country, Don Antonio Vasquez."

"I know what it's like to be a newcomer to London society," Alex said amiably, shaking hands with a courteous bow. "How long have you been here, Don Antonio?"

"Several weeks only. Thank you, Sir Greville." Don Antonio accepted a glass of sherry from his host.

"Won't you sit down, sir." Aurelia sat on the sofa and patted the seat beside her in invitation.

He took the offered seat, and Lyra, who until now had not changed position or posture, came forward and sat at Aurelia's feet. Her ears remained pricked, and her head was lifted, her eyes alert. Don Antonio reached out a hand to touch her and a low growl came from deep in her throat. He took his hand back swiftly. "Not the friendliest of hounds. I would never have guessed, having caught sight of her playing so well with your daughter."

"She was trained as a guard dog," Aurelia said. "Of course, we have no need of such protection here in London." She gave a little self-deprecating laugh. "But my husband likes to have her around."

"How interesting," Don Antonio said in a tone that indicated he found it not in the least interesting.

Greville offered his bluff laugh. "I'm a country man, and I'm not comfortable without a dog at my side. I feel my wife and stepdaughter should have the same comfort."

Alex gave no indication of how interesting he was finding this exchange. Aurelia was behaving in a manner quite unfamiliar to him. In all the time he'd known her, he'd never encountered either the simper or the artificial little laugh. And unless his instincts were way off course, his host was up to something, too.

Alex knew from Harry that Aurelia's husband was connected to the War Ministry. And he knew that Harry assumed the colonel was working on something for their chief. But Harry had known nothing beyond this assumption and, of course, had followed protocol and not broached the subject with Falconer. Now Alex wondered if this Spaniard could be a part of whatever it was. It would be logical, given that the colonel by his own admission had spent the better part of the last two years in Spain and Portugal.

But none of that explained why Aurelia was behaving so oddly. She couldn't know anything of Falconer's business. An honorable man didn't involve his wife in his own dangerous missions. He himself had kept Livia as far away as it was humanly possible from his own mission.

And where had that got him? If it hadn't been for his wife, he'd have spent his last days in Arakcheyev's torture chambers.

He sat back, idly twirling his glass by the stem, and watched closely. After five minutes he was incredulously convinced that Aurelia and her husband were operating as a team and the Spaniard was their quarry.

At an appropriate moment Alex said casually, "Forgive me, Aurelia, but I must go. I have yet to visit Cornelia. I have a letter for her and she won't take kindly to it being too delayed." He rose to his feet.

Aurelia jumped up at once, only too glad for the opportunity to get away from such proximity to Don

Antonio. "No, of course not. Give Nell my love, and tell her I'll see her this afternoon. I'll fetch Franny myself."

"Of course." Alex kissed her on both cheeks, turned, and bowed to the Spaniard, who remained seated on the sofa. "Delighted to make your acquaintance, Don Antonio. Shall I see you at White's perhaps?"

"Lord Lessingham has been good enough to put my name up at White's and Watier's," Don Antonio said with a thin smile. "I daresay we shall meet at the tables. I look forward to it, Prince Prokov."

Greville said, "Let me walk you to the door, Prokov." He moved ahead, opened the drawing room door, and ushered his guest into the hall, closing the door firmly behind them.

"Thank you." Alex glanced back at the closed door. "I didn't get the impression that Aurelia cared over much for Vasquez."

Greville's dark gray eyes showed a glimmer of amusement. "Really? I understood from her that she finds him pleasant company." His lips quirked in a half smile. "Of course, you've known her rather longer than I."

"But perhaps not as well," Alex returned, holding Greville's gaze.

"No. Perhaps not. Aurelia and I understand each other very well."

"I don't doubt it." Alex gave a brief nod and offered his hand. "Thank you for your hospitality. I hope to return it in Cavendish Square soon."

"I look forward to it. And I look forward to meeting your wife." They both smiled the correct smiles as the pleasantries were pronounced and hands were shaken.

Greville opened the front door and held it wide. Alex stepped through it. Then he turned. "Aurelia is very precious to her friends, Falconer."

"She is also very precious to her husband, Prokov." Greville gave him a benign smile that was returned in kind, then stepped back and closed the door.

He had known Frederick's widow would have friends, but he hadn't expected the friendships to be quite so intense and protective. And he had certainly failed to anticipate that they would extend to the husbands of her friends, which, in the circumstances, given these particular men, could be either extremely annoying or very useful. He'd have to come to a decision on which way the dice fell on that one sooner rather than later.

He stood in the hall, gazing thoughtfully at the closed drawing room door. Then he turned and made his way to the library. He would leave Aurelia to her work with the Spaniard. She could come to no harm in her own drawing room, with Lyra at her side. And Greville had no intention of going anywhere out of the house until Don Antonio Vasquez had departed.

Maybe she would get a clue to his plans, maybe something would be said that would give Greville an inkling about the trap Vasquez was going to spring. If all else failed, if Aurelia became close to the Spaniard, she would be able to set the trap that would give Greville his chance to eliminate El Demonio once and for all.

In the drawing room, Aurelia refilled her guest's glass and offered him a honey cake. "I did so enjoy Countess Lessingham's soiree." She popped a cake into her own mouth with a little moue of pleasure. "And I do so adore sweetmeats."

"The ladies do in general," he said, taking a savory tartlet for himself.

"Oh, yes, a sweet tooth is our besetting sin," she tittered.

"I'm sure you have others," he said with a suggestive twitch of his eyebrow.

Aurelia dabbed at her mouth with a linen napkin. "I daresay, sir. Are you free of them?"

He shook his head. "No, alas. I have many."

"Dare I ask what they are?" She leaned into him a little.

He put his hand on her knee. "I fear they're too many to list." He increased the pressure of his hand for a moment, then withdrew it. "But I love to ride in the park, Lady Falconer. Could I persuade you to join me one afternoon?"

"How lovely, yes, I should be delighted, Don Antonio." Aurelia tried to disguise her relief that he had moved a little away from her. She had never been good at flirting, it always made her want to laugh at the most inconvenient moments, but for some reason Don Antonio frightened her to her marrow, and this game was so deadly serious that she had not the slightest urge to laugh.

He rose to his feet. "Shall we say tomorrow afternoon, then? I will call for you at five o'clock."

"I look forward to it, sir." She rose and led the way to the door, Lyra padding quietly beside her. "Let me show you out. Our butler is very old and his substitute is very young, as I daresay you noticed. Sometimes it's easier to do things for oneself."

"It would be considered very strange in my country, but when in Rome, as they say." He laughed lightly.

"Indeed," she agreed, opening the door for him and giving him her hand.

He kissed it, murmured, "Until tomorrow, my lady."

"Tomorrow." She managed to wait until he was halfway down the steps to the street before she closed the door. Then she shuddered, feeling as if a slug had crawled down her back leaving a slimy trail. She wondered for an instant if she was out of her depth, then put the doubt from her. Greville was her protector. She had nothing to fear.

Lyra pushed her nose into her hand and Aurelia tugged her ears gently.

She had nothing to fear.

Chapter Twenty

HARRY BONHAM WAS AT home when Alex arrived at Mount Street. He came out of the library at the familiar voice in the hall.

"Prokov, we were expecting to see you any day." Harry greeted him with genuine pleasure. "How are Livia and the baby?"

"Doing well . . . *very* well, in fact." Alex shook Harry's hand vigorously. "I'll be escorting them to town in two weeks in plenty of time for Cornelia's ball."

"Cornelia's not at home at present, some charity-visiting as I understand it. She'll be so cross to have missed you, but come into the library." He led the way into his bookroom. "Sit down." Harry gestured to a deep leather armchair beside the grate where a small fire burned. "Sherry?"

"Please." Alex sat down. "I've just come from South Audley Street."

"Ah." Harry handed him a glass, then took the opposite chair with his own glass. "Did you meet Falconer?"

"Yes, he came in while I was visiting with Aurelia. She's looking well."

Harry nodded. "Marriage seems to suit her." He sipped his sherry. "Let's not beat about the bush, Prokov. What were your impressions of the colonel?"

Alex didn't answer directly, asking instead, "Have you ever worked with him?"

Harry shook his head. "Different fields. I tend to be deskbound as you know. Falconer is a field agent. One of the best ever according to my chief . . . and believe me that's high praise coming from that quarter."

"Is he working now?" Alex asked directly.

Harry shrugged. "I believe so, but he won't confirm it and neither will Simon Grant. But I was asked to ease him back into London society if he needed it. A couple of invitations, a few introductions, that kind of thing. But he really didn't need my help. It took all of a week and the man had established himself comfortably. And then, of course, he married Aurelia, which opened a whole other circle for him."

Alex nodded, regarding Harry shrewdly. "How did that happen?"

"No one is entirely sure. Apparently they met in Bristol while Aurelia was at the bedside of some ailing relative. They took to each other, decided marriage would suit both of them, and got on with it."

"A marriage of convenience, do you think?"

"No, not at all. According to Cornelia, it's a marriage of wild, impetuous passion. So much so that they eloped overnight, almost as soon as the engagement was made public. And I've never seen anything to disagree with such an interpretation. Aurelia seems happy, and she's certainly happy to have her own establishment in town." Harry sipped his sherry again. "Did you not think she seemed happy?"

"Certainly. Rather more than that, in fact." Alex held up his sherry glass to the light, tilting it to catch the amber glow in the liquid. "There was a Spaniard there, a Don Antonio Vasquez. Mean anything to you?"

Harry shook his head. "Émigrés from the courts of Europe are in plentiful supply these days as Bonaparte knocks kings off their thrones with depressing regularity." Harry looked shrewdly at his visitor. "Why don't you come clean, Alex, and tell me what you're getting at?"

"It was just a feeling." Alex crossed one booted leg over the other. The tassels on his highly polished Hessians swished against the leather as he swung his foot idly. "A sense if you like that Aurelia and Falconer were working in concert. Something to do with the Spaniard."

"I haven't met the Spaniard, so I can't speak to that," Harry said thoughtfully. "But I, too, have had a sense once in a while that in public there's something more going on than a simple marital outing. Certain looks they exchanged, and certain mannerisms and gestures that seemed new to Aurelia."

"Exactly. I had the same impression this morning. But could the man actually be using Aurelia, Harry? It beggars belief."

"Does it?" Harry's eyebrows lifted. "I doubt he's using her without her consent. And Aurelia is hardly a naïf. She won't be doing anything she doesn't want to do. Or at least, that's Cornelia's firm conviction, and she knows Aurelia better than anyone, apart from Livia."

"So you've discussed this with Cornelia?"

"En passant. If Falconer's working undercover as we suspect, then it's not for us to probe, or even speculate. I've hinted several times, but he always freezes me off with a polite but utterly impermeable smile, and just a faint hint of menace."

Alex nodded grimly. "I noticed. So what do we do?"

"Nothing, of course." Harry refilled their glasses. "If Aurelia's working with him, then he'll have trained her himself and he wouldn't use her if he thought she wasn't up to it. I'll also lay odds he's safeguarding her with that wolfhound."

"We could at least make certain he knows Aurelia's friends are looking out for her."

Harry laughed a little. "Oh, I believe he's all too aware of that, Alex. I've even offered my own services somewhat obliquely. Politely declined, I might add, but he knows the offer stands."

"Then I suppose that must be—"

Alex broke off as the door flew open and Cornelia came in, the skirts of her russet riding habit whirling around her with the energy of her step. "Alex, Hector said you were here." She came forward hands outstretched in welcome.

He embraced her warmly, then sneezed as the black plume of her hat tickled his nose.

She laughed and unpinned the hat, tossing it onto the console table by the door. "How's Liv? Tell me all the news."

"You can read it in her own words." Alex gave her a fat packet similar to the one he'd given Aurelia, then produced the miniature of his son. Cornelia laughed when Alex told them that the twins had seen both Livia and himself in the baby's portrait.

"Come to dinner tonight," Cornelia said as Alex prepared to take his leave. "I'll make sure Ellie and Greville come, too."

Alex thanked her and promised to be there, then he said casually, "So, you approve of Aurelia's husband?"

"Of course," Cornelia said simply. "Aurelia does, so of course I do." She frowned at him. "Did Liv tell you to ask me directly?"

"Yes," he admitted with a rueful smile. "She said she couldn't be certain from your letters. They seemed a little ambiguous, but that if I asked a straight question, then you would give me a straight answer."

"And so I have. But I will admit that he's a little difficult to know. I think he keeps his real self well hidden. However, Ellie seems to understand him, and that's all that really matters." Cornelia gave him a half smile. "We didn't really know you all that well for a long time, Alex, but we followed Liv's lead."

He acknowledged the hit with a faint smile and a nod. "Until this evening then."

When Don Antonio left her, Aurelia went in search of her husband. She found him in the library as she expected.

"Our friend has left," Greville said as she came in. "I heard the front door."

"Yes, thank goodness." She crossed her arms over her breast, clasping her elbows. "He makes my flesh creep, Greville."

"I'm not surprised." He got up and came over to her. "Not to put too fine a point upon it, he's a deeply unpleasant man." Greville tilted her chin and looked closely into her eyes. "He frightens you." It was a plain statement.

"A little."

"It's good that he does." Greville ran a thumb over her mouth, his eyes grave. "It means you won't take any chances. And, trust me, my dear, you cannot afford to drop your guard with Vasquez for one moment."

Aurelia shivered a little. "It's his eyes. There's nothing there, nothing behind them."

"He works in espionage. It's the nature of the beast," Greville said as if it was an obvious point. "Did you make any arrangements to meet?"

He didn't appear to connect that statement with

himself, Aurelia reflected, wondering whether to point it out. Instead, she answered his question. "Yes, tomorrow afternoon. To ride in the park."

He frowned. "Your new coachman will accompany you. He'll keep a discreet distance, but he won't let you out of his sight."

"There'll be plenty of people around."

"Nevertheless," he said quietly, turning to the decanters on the sideboard.

Aurelia felt a little nugget of warm reassurance. "What do you want me to get out of him?"

"What we've discussed. Get him to talk . . . about the people he associates with, both English and Spanish. I need to find out what he's up to. If he's setting up a network, we need to know whom he's recruiting, and if he's interested in any particular individual, I need to find that out. So I want you to draw him in . . . ensure that he's a frequent visitor here, find out who his friends are, whom he's cultivating. Establish a flirtatious friendship with him, and we'll see where it leads."

His back was to her and she didn't see the grimace that crossed his countenance. The last thing he wanted to imagine, let alone encourage, was Aurelia flirting with Vasquez. But the closer she became to the man, the easier it would be for her partner to find a way in to set his own trap for the assassin before the assassin sprang his.

"It sounds simple." Aurelia sat on the window seat, tugging gently on Lyra's ears. "I just wish I didn't find him so distasteful."

"It's a good thing that you do, although it will make your task harder." He turned back to face her. "He's considered one of the best agents in Spain." He gave her a fleeting smile. "Which means we take him very, very seriously. You mustn't let your guard slip for one minute."

Why did she have the feeling that Greville wasn't telling her everything?

Of course, she told herself, he never did tell her everything, and he was quite open about it. Information was shared only if he felt she needed to know something, and she understood that. But this felt a little different, almost as if he was being evasive. And while he'd refused to answer her questions on occasion, he had never evaded them.

Greville caught her uncertainty; it was an almost palpable current in the air between them. He came over to her, taking her hands and pulling her to her feet. "Do you have any plans for the next hour that you can't put off?"

She looked up at him and saw the gleam of desire awaken in the dark eyes. And her body stirred in response. "No," she said, touching her tongue to her suddenly dry lips. "Unless you have something we have to do."

"I think I do," he murmured, drawing her tightly against him, kissing her mouth at first gently, then with increasing pressure, his tongue darting between her lips as his hands gripped her bottom, pressing her hard against him.

Aurelia closed her eyes on the red mist of arousal,

aware now only of the scent of his skin, the slightly rough texture of his chin and cheeks, the power of his body that seemed to engulf her, swallow her whole in his embrace.

He lifted her off the floor, holding her against him as he moved backwards to the door. For a second he set her on her feet, his mouth still dancing with hers, and reached behind him to turn the key. At the sound of the lock engaging, he raised his head and gazed down at her, his eyes filled with hungry passion.

"I have never had a woman who could fill me with such an intemperate need," he murmured, one hand roughly unpinning her hair, the other still gripping her backside, pressing her to his loins. He lifted her against him again, moving backwards to the chaise beneath the window. He sat down, settling her astride his hips.

She half rose from his lap to yank up her skirt and petticoat, fumbling with the laces of her drawers as he unfastened his britches, then she lowered herself slowly onto the hard, erect shaft of pulsing flesh. She sank down, her thighs against his, feeling him buried deep within her, and bent to take his mouth with her own, glorying in the sensation of controlling the kiss, and the rhythm and speed of their movements.

Greville rested his head against the back of the chaise and followed her lead. She rose and fell upon him, never releasing his mouth as she drew his penis high inside her, then slowly released her grip, before taking him in again. Then she sat back on his thighs, her hands behind her, balancing herself on his knees, as she lifted herself slightly and moved her sex around the very tip of his flesh in a tantalizing circle, until he moaned and pulled her down hard against him.

Aurelia laughed with the sheer joy of it. She played him like a violin, as he had so often done for her, bringing him closer and closer to the climactic notes, then easing down gently. She didn't know why she was glorying in this sense of control, but somewhere in the back of her head lurked the knowledge that she was in control in this partnership all too infrequently.

And then he raised his hips sharply, driving up inside her, and she was lost in sensation, riding him to her own climax. He held her hips, moving with her, watching her face, loving her as with a triumphant groan of completion she fell forward, her head resting on his shoulder, and his own orgasm pumped deep within her.

Greville held her against him as the world stopped spinning. But it didn't quite stop spinning for him. He *loved* this woman. He had never allowed himself to acknowledge anything more than a deep liking and respect. But for a moment then he had felt she completed him. That without her, he was half-finished.

Colonel, Sir Greville Falconer was rarely alarmed, and when he was, it was by something he could see and deal with. This strange, amorphous feeling was not visible, and he knew no techniques to defeat it.

He opened his eyes and she raised her head from his

shoulder. "That was good," she said with a little sigh of satisfaction.

He held her head between his palms, running his fingers through the cascade of ringlets. "Oh, it was a lot more than that, my dear," he murmured. "I would have described it as transcendent."

Aurelia smiled as he drew her head down so that their mouths engaged once more. "So would I," she whispered against his lips.

He held the kiss for a long time, relishing in the sensation of her sweetness, in his own presence, soft and now undemanding, still within her. Slowly his sense of being rudderless faded and he came back to himself. And to the realization that on this occasion he had neglected the one precaution he had always taken to prevent conception.

He patted her hip. "Lift up, now."

Aurelia raised herself and stepped back, adjusting her clothes, letting her skirt and petticoat fall around her. She put her hand to her hair, which was tumbling in a tangle to her shoulders. "I had better go and put myself to rights."

Greville stood up, fastening his britches. He caught her chin between finger and tip and kissed the tip of her nose. "When I'm with you sometimes, Aurelia, I lose touch with myself." His smile was rather puzzled.

It was one of the most beautiful compliments she had ever been paid, Aurelia thought, her blood singing in her veins. Greville had always been a spontaneous lover, it was one of things she loved about him, but he rarely spoke spontaneously about emotions. "It's a shared feeling," she said softly. She unlocked the door and slipped from the room, feeling as if she couldn't bear to disturb that moment, as if she wanted to leave it intact behind her.

But a minute later she opened the door again, reluctantly bringing domestic reality to break the spell. "Greville, there's a note from Nell. She and Harry want us to go for dinner tonight with Alex. You will come, won't you?"

He turned from the window to face her. "Of course. What time?"

"Eight o'clock." She closed the door again and stood for a minute listening to the ticking of the long-case clock at the foot of the stairs. He was still wearing that surprised, disconcerted expression when he'd turned to face her when she'd opened the door. Quite unlike the colonel's customary assurance.

Aurelia made her way upstairs to her bedchamber to repair the ravages of noontime loving in the library.

She awoke the next morning at light fingers patting her face.

"Mama . . . Mama . . . wake up." Franny was sitting on the bed beside her, tapping her anxiously. "Mama, I need you to wake up."

"And I am awake," Aurelia said, coming instantly to life. "Why do you need me, love?"

"Because I want to take Lyra to Stevie's house. He

doesn't believe I know how to tell her what to do, so I have to show him that I do."

Aurelia sighed and prepared for battle. "Lyra isn't a pet, sweetie. And she's not going to want to spend all day in the schoolroom with you and Stevie and Susannah. She needs exercise."

"We'll take her to the park when we go out with Miss Alison," Franny insisted. "We go an' play in the park. We'll take a ball an' Stevie can see how she runs after it when I throw it. Oh, please, Mama, *please*."

Sweet heaven, Aurelia thought. The last thing she wanted was a tussle with Franny first thing in the morning. However she girded her loins and sat up against the pillows.

"No, Franny, Lyra stays here with me. If you like, I'll bring her this afternoon when I come to fetch you, and you and Stevie can play with her in Aunt Nell's garden. But you cannot take her for the whole day."

Franny's lower lip wobbled. "But I want to show Stevie how she does what I say."

"She doesn't do what you say, Franny."

The child spun towards the door, which had just opened. Greville stood there, a cup of coffee in his hand.

"Yes, she does," Franny insisted.

"No. Lyra only does what she knows is expected of her. If she runs after your ball or comes to heel when you call her, it's not because *you* are telling her to do that, it's because of her training. If you tell her to do something outside the commands she knows, then she won't do it."

Franny regarded him suspiciously, but also with a degree of interest. "So who told her what she should do?"

"Her trainer," he said, coming into the room and sitting on the end of Aurelia's bed. "A man who understands dogs. You're not old enough yet, my child, to train a dog. And Lyra is a working dog."

"What's that mean? Dogs don't work."

"Yes, they do. They herd sheep. They guard buildings, and sometimes they guard people."

Franny's eyes widened. "And which does Lyra do? We don't have any sheep."

"Then you have your answer," Greville said, offering Aurelia his coffee cup.

She accepted gratefully, taking a revivifying sip. "So, you see, Franny, you can't take Lyra from her work. She wouldn't be happy."

"Oh." Franny slipped off the bed. "But you will come and fetch me this afternoon, and bring her so I can show Stevie."

"Yes, love. Now go and find Daisy. I'll come down in a few minutes and see you off." Aurelia reached for her daughter and kissed her. Franny hugged her and raced off.

Aurelia leaned back against her pillows and took another sip of coffee as Franny left the bedchamber. "It's good that you don't talk down to her," she observed.

"She's a bright child . . . somewhat challenging at times, I grant you, but she's quick-witted." He went to the window and pulled back the curtains, letting in the soft sunshine of the May morning.

"Do you see anything of her father in her?"

Greville turned slowly from the window. "I've never been good at noticing physical resemblances between small children and their parents. I don't see the point really. They are who they are."

It was a flat statement, and Aurelia recognized that her question had come too close to those invisible boundaries that encircled him. She shrugged. "Maybe so, but it's a conventional game people play as part of social intercourse. Parents like to be told their children resemble them in some way."

"Well, never having had a child of my own, I wouldn't appreciate the pleasure. But I did want to talk to you about Franny."

"Oh?"

He frowned, pulling at his chin. He'd been trying to think how to broach this subject without alarming Aurelia. He wanted her to get close to Don Antonio, and he didn't want her worrying about her child. He was certain he could protect the child, but it would be much easier to do if she was away from the scene of the intrigues in South Audley Street.

"What is it?" she said, disconcerted by his expression.

"I have been thinking that while you're working with Vasquez, it might be better if Franny were to go somewhere else. Maybe to your friend in the country."

She stared at him, saying quickly, "Why? Is she in danger?"

He shook his head. "No, I don't believe so. But I'd rather neither of us was distracted at this delicate stage of the operation."

"By neither of us, you mean *me*?" she said coldly.

"I suppose I do."

"Yes, I hardly think *you* would permit yourself to be distracted by the needs and welfare of a six-year-old." Aurelia's eyes were cold and angry. "I'll not be separated from my child. I told you at the very beginning that I would not have Franny involved in any way. Her life must continue as she knows it. How on earth would I explain why I have to send her away without frightening her?"

"It would be difficult, I agree," he said, surprised that he was hurt by her accusation that he cared little for the child, but at the same time knowing that giving the success of their mission as his concern would keep Aurelia away from the true reason for his anxiety about her daughter.

"So, are you saying that I'm not playing my part properly because I'm distracted by my child's needs?" she demanded, her face rather pale.

"No . . . no, I'm not saying that at all." He ran a hand through his close-cropped hair. "It was a suggestion intended to lessen the burden on you, that's all. I thought it might be easier on both of you if you had only one thing to concern you. Just until these early maneuvers are accomplished."

"I appreciate your concern," she said in the same icy tone. "But I assure you it's unnecessary. I'm quite capable of doing both, and as I've told you once before, I won't let you down." She pushed aside the coverlet and stood up. "I have to get dressed and see Franny on her way to Mount Street."

"Very well. I'll leave you then." He turned on his heel and returned to his own chamber.

Aurelia rang the bell for Hester and sat down at the dresser, pulling a brush through her tumbled hair. She was rarely angry, and if she really thought about it, she wasn't sure why Greville had angered her so deeply. From one viewpoint he had merely expressed concern for her well-being. But that wasn't what lay behind his suggestion. She knew him too well to believe that. His concern was for the success of his mission. He didn't want her maternal cares to get in the way.

Well, she'd prove to him that there was no possibility of that happening. And then she remembered. She'd just promised Franny that she would bring Lyra to Mount Street at the end of the schoolroom day, but she was engaged to ride in the park with Don Antonio at five o'clock.

"Hell and the devil," she exclaimed aloud just as Hester opened the door.

"Is summat the matter, mum?" the girl inquired anxiously.

"Not really," she said, glancing over her shoulder towards the half-open door to Greville's chamber.

She wasn't surprised to see him standing there, leaning against the doorjamb, regarding her questioningly. Her voice had been loud enough to wake the dead.

He crooked a finger at her and she swore again, but this time to herself. "I'll wear the striped muslin morning dress, Hester. Lay it out for me and I'll be back in a moment." She rose from the stool and followed Greville into his own room.

"What is it?" he asked as she drew the door shut behind her.

"I don't know whether to laugh or scream," she said, shaking her head in mortification. "I promised Franny I would take Lyra to Mount Street this afternoon, but I forgot I'd agreed to ride with the Spaniard at five."

"I wondered how long it would be before you remembered."

"*Damn you,* Greville. Are you telling me that when you heard me make that promise to Franny you remembered my engagement with the Spaniard?"

He nodded. "It's my business to remember these details."

"And it's mine, too," she said with a sigh. "And now you can crow all you like. You've proved your point . . . or rather I've proved it for you."

"I have no intention of crowing," he said mildly. "As I've said, you will have an escort on your ride this afternoon so Lyra's presence won't be necessary, particularly as it's a very public venue at the most popular time, and you will ensure that you ride only on the tan in full view.

I will take Lyra to Mount Street and fetch Franny myself this afternoon."

She looked at him askance. "You'd be willing to do that?"

"Of course. Why wouldn't I be? It's the nature of a partnership, dear girl." Now he was smiling with just a hint of teasing amusement. "If there are conflicting needs, then if possible one partner helps out the other."

"You are insufferable," she declared, but she was laughing nevertheless. "You could have reminded me about the Spaniard at the time I promised Franny, so that I could have come up with something else to satisfy her, and you deliberately chose not to, just to prove the point you were about to make."

He shook his head. "Believe that if you wish."

She looked at him uncertainly. "Didn't you?"

"No. To tell you the truth I didn't make the connection until after we'd had words. Of course, I should have done so, so that was my error. I should have known what an opportunity you had given me." He shook his head with a sorrowful air. "I must be losing my touch."

"I'm not letting her go, Greville," she said abruptly.

"No, you've made that clear."

There seemed nothing else to say. "I'll get dressed then." She went to the door to her own room, pausing to say, "Thank you for the compromise, Greville."

He bowed. "I am always the soul of compromise, ma'am."

Chapter Twenty-one

AURELIA CHOSE THE MOST DASHING of her riding habits for her ride with Don Antonio. The close-fitting jacket and skirt of dark brown, corded velvet, fastened with braided buttons, made the most of her bosom while accentuating her small waist. She wore her hair in a knot confined in a netted snood at her nape beneath a tall hat, like a shako, ornamented with an ostrich feather dyed emerald green.

She drew on her matching green kid gloves, giving herself a critical once-over in the long mirror before going downstairs to await her cicisbeo. A public ride in Hyde Park at the fashionable hour could hold no unpleasant surprises, but she was glad to see Jemmy waiting by the door, dressed in his groom's livery. She was to have more than one escort on this jaunt apparently. Greville was taking no chances.

"The 'orses are ready an' waitin', m'lady," Jemmy said.

"Good. I'll wait for Don Antonio in the salon." She

made her way to the drawing room and stood at the window, half-concealed behind the curtain, watching the street. Greville had already left for Mount Street with Lyra, and she felt strangely alone, even though plenty of people were in the house.

Don Antonio rode up on the dot of five, and to her relief she saw he was alone. There was no reason to be frightened of the man on this occasion. As long as she kept a cool head, acknowledged that he was the enemy, and remembered every conscious minute that she must never let down her guard, she would be quite safe. There would be someone discreetly following, someone presumably armed and ready for anything. It seemed melodramatic, but Aurelia was beginning to think that her life at present would fit well within the pages of a Gothic melodrama.

She went into the hall as the Spaniard dismounted, tethered his horse to the railing, and came up the steps to the front door. Jemmy opened it at the first knock and Aurelia went forward smiling. "Good afternoon, Don Antonio. It's a beautiful day for a ride."

"It is, indeed, ma'am." He kissed her fingertips. "How enchanting you look."

"Thank you, sir." She smiled her little simpering smile and allowed him to usher her down to the street, where her own horse and Jemmy's cob awaited them.

"Is your groom to accompany us?" Don Antonio looked a little put-out as Jemmy knelt to offer his palm to help Aurelia mount.

"But of course, sir. Is it not the custom in Spain for

ladies to be escorted by their own household on public outings?" Her voice was bland, her smile all innocent inquiry, even as her eyes darted up the street looking for the bodyguard. But, of course, he was nowhere to be seen. Greville's men worked in the shadows, but he was there. Greville did not make promises he would not keep.

"It certainly is, but our social rules are rather stricter than yours," Don Antonio said. "Or that, at least, has been my impression, Lady Falconer."

"Maybe so. But my husband is somewhat old-fashioned. He would look askance if I rode unaccompanied with a male acquaintance without a groom."

"I see." Don Antonio brought his horse up beside hers. "You are perhaps a nervous rider. In such a case, I quite understand your husband's need to provide you with trustworthy escort."

"You have the right of it, sir," Aurelia said with an anxious little titter. "Indeed, my husband is overly protective, I believe. But I confess I am not the most confident of riders, and I do believe the horse guesses it."

"I shall watch your mount very carefully, ma'am. Have no fear." He gave her his chilly smile.

He still couldn't be certain what she was. Was she Falconer's partner as well as his wife? But why a man as formidable as Falconer would fall for a woman who, in the Spaniard's opinion, had little out of the ordinary to recommend her was a question beyond answering. Although men did do the strangest things when it came to love and lust. He'd known several brilliant men who'd fallen helplessly into the toils of a woman who seemed to offer nothing more than a pleasant and undemanding personality, and a certain flair in the bedchamber.

It was not impossible that this was the case. Not impossible but highly unlikely. Either way, it mattered little. Whether she was merely lover *or* partner, or lover *and* partner, she could prove a useful tool in his fight with the *asp*.

They turned into the park through the Stanhope Gate and he set himself to be charming.

Greville arrived at Mount Street with Lyra just before five, the appointed hour for the schoolroom to cease the day's activities. Cornelia was coming downstairs as he was admitted and greeted him with surprise.

"Greville, this is unusual."

"Aurelia had some errands to run," he explained. "She had promised Franny that she could show off Lyra to Stevie and Susannah. So I volunteered my services."

Cornelia laughed. "Always wise to keep promises to Franny. The consequences of failure can be painful."

"So I've noticed," Greville replied somewhat aridly.

Cornelia looked at him with an arrested expression. "Forgive me, but do I detect a note of disapproval?"

He stepped back from the brink just in time, raising his hands in disclaimer. "I have no experience with children and am in no position to have an opinion, ma'am."

Cornelia looked as if she would have said more, but then

decided to take her own step back. She called to a hovering footman, "Will you take the dog up to the schoolroom, please, Gavin. The children are waiting for her."

The footman looked doubtfully at the massive hound, who returned the look with calm benignity. "How should I do that, m'lady?"

Greville said something quietly, and immediately Lyra rose and padded to the stairs. The footman went after her and they disappeared into the upper reaches of the house.

"Will you come into the drawing room, Greville?" Cornelia invited, unable to disguise the slight chill remaining in her voice.

"Thank you, but I was wondering if your husband was in? There's something I wished to discuss with him."

"He's in the library. I'll take you to him." Cornelia led the way to the back of the house, knocked briefly on the door, and put her head around. "Greville would like to speak with you, Harry. He's come to fetch Franny."

Harry rose from behind his desk and greeted Greville warmly. "Come in. Let me offer you a glass of claret. It's unusual for you to be doing nursemaid duty."

"It is. But Aurelia had conflicting plans. I had no plans, so . . ." An easy shrug completed the sentence, and Greville took the proffered glass of claret with a nod of thanks.

The door closed softly behind Cornelia, and Harry looked a question at his visitor. "Your visit is not purely social, I take it."

"No." Greville took the seat his host waved him to. "You offered your assistance and now I have a simple question for you. I ask that you answer it without asking for details, which I am not at this point in a position to give."

"Ask away." Harry sipped his claret and kept his intense curiosity in check.

"If I should need you to take Franny at a moment's notice . . . I may not even have time to bring her to you . . . can you guarantee to do it?"

"Yes," Harry said calmly. "Is that all?"

"Yes." Greville drank deeply of his wine. "I thank you."

"No need." Harry swirled the wine in his glass thoughtfully. "Can I assume that the dog is trained to protect Franny as well as Aurelia?"

"Yes. But she can't be in both places at once."

Harry nodded. "Forgive me, Falconer, but I must say one thing. If you allow anything to happen to Aurelia or Franny, you will answer for it to me."

Greville gave a short laugh. "Have no fear, there's nothing you could do to me, Bonham, that I will not already have done to myself." He stood up. "It's our business. You know the rules, you know the risks as well as I do. And believe me, Aurelia knows them, too. And that, my friend, is all I am going to say."

Greville set his glass down and walked to the door. "I must take Franny home before it gets dark."

"One minute, Falconer." Harry spoke sharply. "I need you to clarify just one point."

Greville paused, his hand on the door. "Yes?"

"Are you implying that Aurelia is working with you?"

"She has been pretty well from the first moment I met her. Aurelia is my partner, and she *knows* what she's doing. Good afternoon, Bonham." Greville opened the door and left the library.

Harry blew out his cheeks on a noisy exhale. He had suspected it, but had resisted the knowledge. As much, he recognized ruefully, because it pointed up his own failings in that regard. If he'd trusted Cornelia with the truth of his work, she and her son would not have become unwittingly and so nearly catastrophically involved. And he knew Alex Prokov would say the same about Livia. Prokov owed his life to his wife's courage and determination. If Aurelia shared those characteristics with her friends, and of course she did, then who were they to wax indignant that she willingly partnered her husband in his work?

But where did the marriage come into it? That would be Cornelia's first question, he knew. Was the marriage merely part of what they were working on together? Or was there more to it?

Harry hoped fervently for Aurelia's sake that it was the latter.

By the time Don Antonio and Aurelia were in sight of her house on South Audley Street at the end of their ride in the park, the Spaniard was ready to wring his companion's neck. She was a most accomplished flirt and the worst kind of tease. Every flattering advance he had made, she had turned aside with a suggestive smile and a conflicting murmur of maidenly distress. She led him on as she pushed him away, and her stream of inconsequential chatter, interspersed with an irritating titter, was driving him insane. She had given him absolutely nothing, and he had the infuriating conviction that she had been enjoying herself most definitely at his expense.

"What a delightful ride, Don Antonio," she said as they drew rein outside the house. "And you are such an entertaining companion." The simper and the titter were cleverly restrained this time, with just the inviting up-from-under look from those deep brown eyes.

"May I return the compliment, ma'am," he said, lying through his teeth. "And may I dare to believe that you would agree to another such excursion?"

"If you would dare to ask me, sir," she returned with a wicked smile that had none of the simper about it.

Oh, she was good, he thought. *Very, very good.* She knew exactly when to leaven the demure ingenue with the knowing sophisticate. If confusing her escort was her intention, she was an expert at the game. And if he had not had his own game to play, he might have enjoyed beating her at hers. But he would have his own back soon enough, and that victory would be particularly sweet.

"Perhaps something a little more daring than a ride in

Hyde Park?" he suggested with a flirtatious smile of his own. "I do believe, my lady, that you are not in the least a nervous rider." He wagged a mock reproving finger at her.

His smile gave Aurelia the shivers. It was trying to be inviting, and yet she found it utterly repugnant. She batted her eyelashes. "What are you suggesting, Don Antonio?"

"Richmond. Where better for a springtime ride? The trees will be in blossom, the horse chestnuts ablaze with their candles, bluebells in all the dells."

Aurelia managed with difficulty to produce a light laugh. "How poetic you are, sir. I could believe you to be very familiar with our English spring."

"I read your English poets," he said with an assumption of sincerity, leaning over to touch her gloved hand. "I admire your English culture as much as I understand you admire mine."

Here she heard just the edge of the knife beneath the gentle banter. "I do, indeed, Don Antonio." She slipped her hand out from his. "But it is quite unlike the English. There's a certain darkness to it, a touch of melancholy, don't you think?"

He smiled again. "If you would permit me, my lady, I could show you aspects of our culture where there is only light and pleasure."

"And perhaps I will, sir," Aurelia said lightly. "A ride in Richmond sounds delightful." She beckoned Jemmy, who had dismounted and was waiting at the bottom of the steps for her signal. He came hurrying over but not before Don Antonio had dismounted and was standing at her stirrup to help her down.

She accepted his hand, but as soon as her foot touched the pavement, she stepped away from him. "My thanks, Don Antonio, for a most pleasant excursion."

He took her hand and bowed over it. "Will you ride with me again tomorrow, Lady Falconer?"

"Sir, I may not," she said, trying for another light laugh. "What would the world say if they saw me ride in the park with you on two consecutive days? We do have our rules, you know. They may not be as strict as yours, but one breaks them at one's peril."

He gave her an accepting bow. "I understand. But you will consider the ride in Richmond?"

"With pleasure, Don Antonio." She gave him her hand.

He raised it to his lips. "Then I will call upon you tomorrow to arrange the date, ma'am."

"I look forward to it, Don Antonio." She took back her hand, smiled once, then went swiftly up the steps to her front door, her key already in her hand. She had it open before Don Antonio had remounted, and she was inside with the door firmly closed before he had nudged his horse into motion.

She stood for a moment, leaning against the door at her back, absorbing the familiar atmosphere of her home, the scent of beeswax and lavender, the peaceful glow of the oil lamps, the knowledge of people, *her* people, moving about the rooms and corridors of the house.

Franny was upstairs in the nursery. She headed for the stairs, taking them at a run, barely hearing Greville's voice in the hall, calling her name.

Greville followed Aurelia up to the nursery. He was on her heels as she greeted Franny, who, bathed and in her nightgown, was eating her supper of bread and milk sweetened with honey, and regaling Daisy with details of Lyra's splendid performance in the Mount Street schoolroom.

"Susannah couldn't believe her *eyes,* Daisy, when he told Lyra to lie down, an' she did, an' then when he told her to, she held up a paw to shake hands . . . it was amazin', really . . ." Franny accepted her mother's kiss. "Really amazin', Mama, you should have—" The rest of the sentence was lost in a mouthful from the porringer.

"I'm sure it was, sweetie," Aurelia said, gazing hungrily at her daughter. She wanted to enfold her, to hold her tightly against her, but Franny would find such a sudden and untimely impulse both strange and alarming.

"Lyra's not a pet, Franny." Greville spoke from behind Aurelia and she turned, wondering why she hadn't sensed his arrival. "Today was the only time I'll ask her to do tricks for you. She's a working dog, as we explained to you."

"All right," Franny said peaceably, taking another heaping spoonful. "Are you goin' to read me a story, Mama?"

"That's why I'm here." Aurelia welcomed the routine duty with open arms. "When you've finished your supper." She looked up at Greville, who still stood beside the door. "Did you see Nell when you went to Mount Street?"

"Briefly. I had a word with Bonham."

She looked at him. "Really? What kind of word?"

He smiled. "Just a word, Aurelia . . . Come to the library when you're ready. Good night, Franny." He bent over the child and kissed her brow, then left the nursery.

Aurelia stayed with her daughter for the best part of an hour, oddly reluctant to bring the bedtime rituals to a close, and when she finally left the nursery, she went to her own bedchamber before going downstairs.

She exchanged her riding habit for a casual robe of Indian muslin suitable for a quiet evening at home and went down to the library.

Greville was standing at the desk shuffling through a sheaf of papers, and he spun around instantly at the sound of the door opening. "Oh, there you are. I was beginning to wonder what had happened to you." His dark, intent gaze searched her countenance. "You look tired."

She smiled and shrugged. "I am a little. I don't find Don Antonio's company in the least restful."

"No, I imagine not." He leaned back on his hands, which were planted on the desk behind him, and continued to scrutinize her countenance until she began to feel he was actually reading her mind. "So," he said after a minute, "aren't you going to tell me about it?"

"There's not much to tell." She sat down in a corner of the sofa, leaning back against the cushions. "We rode in the park, did the circuit three times, I think. I never saw the bodyguard."

"You wouldn't. The man knows his job. Go on."

"We flirted." She shrugged again. "He didn't say anything of interest. In fact he barely mentioned Spain or his countrymen. If I brought the subject up, he deflected it, turned it back on me."

Greville nodded. "It's only to be expected. Vasquez is a master."

She grimaced. "I can believe that. His surface is smooth as silk, and as slippery as oiled leather, but every now and again there's a hint of steel, of menace. I don't think I'm imagining it."

"No, I'm sure you aren't." He pushed himself away from the desk and walked to the window that overlooked a narrow alley running at the back of the houses on South Audley Street. He moved the curtain aside and looked out into the darkness. The alley was deserted for the moment, but it occurred to him that this window would provide an intruder with easy and secluded access to the house. It would have to be secured. He should have thought of that sooner. It annoyed him to think that his vigilance was slipping.

"He wants me to ride with him in Richmond Park," Aurelia said.

Greville turned back to the room, letting the curtain fall shut behind him. "Most definitely not," he declared with finality.

Aurelia looked surprised. "Why ever not? I thought I was supposed to be cultivating him. Turning down invitations isn't going to get me very far."

"There are some invitations you won't accept. Richmond is too far and too secluded, and I can't guarantee my man will be able to follow you undetected. You'll see Vasquez only in town, and only in public places, Aurelia."

"I have a part to play, and I'll play it as I see fit," she said as flatly as he, her irritation at his tone flashing in her eyes.

"You seem to be forgetting that you work for me." His voice was suddenly rather soft. "I call the tunes here, and you play them."

"I thought we were partners," she said tightly.

"So we are, but it's a partnership in which one of us is more equal than the other."

She looked at him in frowning silence for a moment before asking, "What exactly are you afraid of, Greville? Is there something about Don Antonio that you're not telling me?"

"You know all you need to know." If he told her everything he knew about the Spaniard, she might inadvertently alert Don Antonio to that knowledge. Greville's best chance of defeating Don Antonio at his own game lay in the other man's assumption that the *asp* had no inkling of his real identity and thought they were playing a different game.

But he also had to be absolutely certain that Aurelia would not put herself at risk by acting unilaterally.

"I don't want you to get overconfident," he said carefully. "As we agreed, Don Antonio is a very dangerous man, and I don't believe you're ready to take him on alone. Even with a bodyguard. It's easy to make mistakes. Just because you've had some small success at the very straightforward tasks I've set you doesn't mean you can run before you can walk."

"Do you have any idea how insulting that is?" Aurelia demanded, getting to her feet.

He sighed and tried to pick his way through the quicksand. "I don't mean to insult you, Aurelia, but there are facts, and the most important one is that I call the tune. I'm not prepared to put you at risk. Do as I tell you, and you will be quite safe. For the moment all I need you to do is cultivate him while I try to find out what he's up to. It's as simple as that."

He came over to her, taking her hands in his. "Surely you can see my point."

"Yes, I can see it," she said, leaving her hands in his. "But it's still insulting to accuse me of overconfidence. Maybe for you these *straightforward* tasks that I'm so pleased at performing successfully are insignificant trivia, but they're not insignificant to me."

"Oh, dear," he murmured. "I didn't realize how offensive that must have sounded. I didn't mean to demean your contributions. I was just trying to make a point as forcefully as I could."

"Well, you certainly did that," she said, not willing to kiss and make up just yet. "Tell me, if it was Frederick engaged in this mission with you, would you have forbidden *him* to go on an excursion to Richmond with our quarry?"

He looked at her with a half smile of reproof. "No. Of course not. And you know why."

"But you still called the tune with Frederick?"

"Yes."

"And he never questioned your decisions?"

"Of course he did sometimes. And you're free to question them, too. But you have to accept that the final decision will be mine." He drew her against him, releasing one hand to push up her chin, his thumb stroking over her mouth, his eyes grave as he regarded her. "Your safety is my first concern, Aurelia . . . always."

It would be churlish to hold that against him, she thought, as his lips followed the path of his thumb over her mouth. She allowed herself to relax, her taut body softening into his embrace, wondering why she had so perversely objected to a decision that came only as a relief. She had absolutely no desire to be alone with Don Antonio under the trees of Richmond.

Chapter Twenty-two

LADY FALCONER RECEIVED Don Antonio in the salon the next morning. He came into the room, dressed as was his habit, in a black coat, lightened on this occasion with a gray-and-black-striped waistcoat, and gray pantaloons. The white folds of his starched neckcloth rose high beneath his chin, his tasseled Hessians gleamed mirror-bright, and he carried his hat and a slender cane.

He was without doubt an elegant and arresting figure, she thought, setting aside her tambour frame and rising from her chair to greet him. But all the elegance of costume in the world couldn't disguise the cruel line of his mouth, or the flatness of his black eyes.

"My lady." He swept a flourishing bow. "May I say how charmingly you look this morning?"

"You may, Don Antonio." She smiled as she extended her hand. "And I shall accuse you of shameless flattery, but be complimented nevertheless."

He kissed her hand, holding on to to it for a fraction of a second longer than necessary before releasing it. "It would be impossible to flatter you, Lady Falconer."

She merely smiled at that and gestured to a chair. "May I offer you refreshment? Coffee, perhaps, or would you prefer sherry?"

"I would be delighted to join you in whatever pleases you, my dear ma'am." He set his hat and cane down on a console table against the wall and sat down as gracefully as a cat, crossing his booted ankles.

Aurelia inclined her head in acknowledgment and rang the bell. Jemmy answered it instantly. "Coffee, Jemmy, please."

"Yes, mum." He bobbed his head and backed out.

"So, ma'am, have you given any more thought to our ride in Richmond Park?" Don Antonio inquired, flicking an imaginary speck of fluff from his immaculate sleeve.

Aurelia managed to produce a rather sorrowful air. "Unfortunately, Don Antonio, there is a difficulty. You see—" Jemmy arrived with the coffee and she waited until he had set it on the low table in front of her. "Thank you, Jemmy, that will be all."

"Right y'are, mum," Jemmy responded cheerfully, and scurried away.

Aurelia poured coffee into the shallow Sevres cups. "My husband has forbidden such an excursion."

A strange look crossed her companion's harsh countenance, then it was gone so quickly she could almost have imagined she'd seen it. "What a shame," he said, his tone without expression, his eyes black stones.

Aurelia looked rueful. "He is somewhat old-fashioned, I'm afraid, and, as I explained yesterday, rather overprotective. He does not consider me to be a sufficiently accomplished horsewoman to ride in Richmond without him beside me." Her smile was self-deprecating. "The rides in Richmond are rather wilder than the tan in Hyde Park, I understand."

"So I believe," he responded, then sipped his coffee. "I own I am disappointed, ma'am, but I respect your husband's position. He doesn't know me well enough to be certain I can protect his wife from hazards."

There was the menace again, a quick slide of a knife edge. It chilled her anew. She reached for the coffeepot again, hoping her hands wouldn't shake as she refilled her cup. The action provided momentary respite, enough for her to regain her composure.

"We may not have Richmond, sir, but my husband has no objections to excursions closer to home." She gave him a smile as she offered to refill his cup. "I promised to show you some of London's famous sights. We could take a carriage ride to see the lions at the Exchange, if you wish. Or stroll in Green Park."

"Is it true they graze a herd of cows in Green Park?" he inquired, watching her carefully. "It seems most eccentric in a city park."

"English law has its eccentricities, sir," she responded

with a light laugh. "Public grazing rights are jealously guarded. For centuries Londoners have had the right to graze their cattle in Green Park. And if you wish, the milkmaids will sell you a cup of new-drawn milk."

"A pleasure I fear I must decline," he said, placing his coffee cup on the table. "But the pleasure of your company, ma'am, is another matter altogether." The vigorous banging of the doorknocker resounded from the hall, and for a second a look of annoyance crossed his face.

Aurelia jumped to her feet as she heard the voices in the hall. "Oh, pray excuse me, Don Antonio." She flew to the drawing room door. "Liv . . . Liv, oh, how wonderful to see you. When did you get to London? And you've brought the baby." She embraced her friend before turning to the nursemaid holding a wrapped bundle. "Oh, do give him to me." She took the blanketed bundle and peered into the tiny, wrinkled face.

"Isn't he beautiful?" Livia asked, beaming with maternal pride. She moved aside a fold of blanket so that Aurelia could see him properly. "Prince Alexander, meet your godmama," she instructed.

Aurelia suddenly remembered Don Antonio, abandoned in the salon, and said, "I have a visitor, Liv. Come into the drawing room." Still carrying the babe, Aurelia led the way into the salon. "Forgive me, Don Antonio, for running out like that. One of my oldest friends has just returned to London with her new son. Livia, may I introduce Don Antonio Vasquez. Don Antonio, Princess Prokov."

Don Antonio bowed over the princess's hand. He was about to take his leave when Cornelia burst into the salon. "Here you are, Liv. I thought this was where I'd find you. Oh, do let me see him." She took the baby from Aurelia. "Isn't he adorable . . . but he's not in the least like your miniature, I have to tell you, Liv."

"No," Livia agreed, laughing. "I'm not much of an artist, I'm afraid."

Don Antonio coughed. "I must take my leave, Lady Falconer. I am de trop, I fear."

"Oh, forgive me, I was forgetting my manners in all this excitement," Aurelia apologized. "Nell, I don't believe you're acquainted with Don Antonio Vasquez. Don Antonio, Lady Bonham."

Cornelia regarded the Spaniard with frank curiosity. "Are you new to town, sir?"

"I've been here just a few weeks, ma'am."

"How strange that we haven't met before. In general, when one of my friends makes a new acquaintance, I usually make them, too." Cornelia cast a quick glance at Aurelia, who said nothing.

"I met Lady Falconer at Lady Lessingham's soiree," Don Antonio explained smoothly. "The countess provides Spanish émigrés with a place to gather and discuss our country's affairs."

"I see." Cornelia glanced again at Aurelia. "I didn't realize you were on such terms with Lady Lessingham, Ellie."

"I partnered her at cards at Lady Buxton's afternoon

party some weeks ago," Aurelia said casually. "And you know how interested I am in Spanish culture."

Cornelia most certainly did not know this, but she merely inclined her head in acknowledgment and said to Don Antonio, "I must send you an invitation to my ball, Don Antonio. It's to be next Saturday . . . rather short notice, I fear, but I do so hope you'll do me the honor of accepting."

"The honor will be mine, Lady Bonham." He bowed with a click of his heels and took a visiting card from his pocket, handing it to Cornelia, before turning back to Aurelia. "And now, Lady Falconer, I really must leave you with your friends. We shall talk about our little excursion another time." With another bow that encompassed all three ladies, he left.

"A suave gentleman," Cornelia observed, sitting down, cradling the baby in the crook of her arm. "I wonder how I've missed him on the social circuit."

She glanced quickly at Aurelia, who shrugged easily and said with perfect truth, "Greville knows him from somewhere."

"Oh, I see," Cornelia said, shooting a significant look in Livia's direction. "You seem to be on very comfortable terms with him."

Aurelia didn't miss the look but let that and Cornelia's statement pass. It was easier than attempting to untangle the situation for her friends. They both knew that Greville, like their own husbands, was involved in the underworld. Aurelia couldn't explain her own part

in that world without getting dangerously close to secrets that were not hers to share.

"I'll ring for some more coffee," she said, reaching for
the bell.

"Not for me," Cornelia said carelessly. "I don't seem
to care for it . . . or it doesn't seem to care for me at the
moment."

After an instant's silence, Aurelia said almost as carelessly, "I find it's tea I can't stomach."

Livia burst out laughing. "Oh, how perfect. Both
of you."

Cornelia looked at Aurelia. "Really?"

"Mm . . . hmm." Aurelia nodded. "You, too?"

"I'm fairly certain. But it's early days."

"Me, too. Very early. In fact . . ." Aurelia laughed a
little self-consciously. "It was only this morning that I
properly realized it." She'd had so much on her mind she
hadn't noticed the passing of the weeks, and the fatigue
and the faint queasiness she'd put down to her anxiety
over her meetings with Don Antonio.

"Have you told Greville?"

Aurelia shook her head. "Not yet." In fact she didn't
know when or even whether to tell him. Their partnership would come to an end soon, once this business
with Don Antonio reached a conclusion that satisfied
Greville. How would he react to leaving a child of his
own behind, to grow up without a father? Probably, she
thought bleakly, he wouldn't consider it particularly important. He would make provision for the child, of that

she was certain, but he had grown up without a father, to all intents and purposes without a mother either. So he probably wouldn't consider the parenting an issue. Perhaps she would just keep it from him. It would make his life easier. And she could manage alone. She'd done so once, after all. And she had her friends and would have a stable income once this was over. But she knew that this time around it would be so much harder than the first.

"Does Harry know?" Livia asked Cornelia.

"Not yet. I'll tell him in a couple of weeks. It's taken awhile, and he's never said anything, although I know he's wanted it so much. I have to be absolutely certain before I get him excited."

"I think it's perfect," Livia repeated, taking her son from Cornelia, gazing with adoration into his sleeping countenance. "They'll all be so close in age, like members of the same family, just like Stevie, Susannah, and Franny."

Cornelia was watching Aurelia's face, a slightly troubled look in her eyes. "When will you tell Greville, Ellie?"

"In a week or two."

Aurelia still couldn't understand how it had happened and was certain Greville wouldn't. There had been only one occasion when he had failed to take his customary precaution against conception, but that had only been a few days ago, far too soon to result in her present pregnancy. But such things happened, she knew, even in the best-regulated relationships.

"Then for now it's our secret," Livia stated. "My lips are sealed." Intuitively she changed the subject. "So, Nell, I have a most dramatic gown for the ball. Alex chose it. It's silver gauze over a black silk undergown, with a train edged in scarlet braid. And I have a scarlet ostrich plume for my coiffure."

Aurelia chuckled. "We'll complement each other beautifully, love. Mine is black spider gauze over white silk, and Nell is all in scarlet edged with black and silver lace."

"What a dramatic trio," Livia said.

"When have we ever been anything else?" Cornelia asked, shooting Aurelia another of her searching glances. "No one could say that the ladies of Cavendish Square, starting with Sophia Lacey, have followed convention. Don't you agree, Ellie?"

Aurelia smiled. "Oh, yes, Nell. Most definitely."

Don Antonio left South Audley Street and walked back to his lodgings. His initial anger at the frustration of his perfect plan was well under control, and his mind worked swiftly now to come up with an alternative. For a moment he had thought he would complete this job within the week. He was known for his meticulous work, but also for the speed with which he accomplished his missions. This time he had hoped to exceed anyone's expectations. But personal vanity had now to be put aside. He couldn't rush this job. But unless he was much mistaken, an alternative had been handed to him on the proverbial silver platter. The lady wouldn't ride with him in Richmond Park, but she *would* dance with him.

His invitation to Lord and Lady Bonham's ball was delivered to his door that evening, and he penned an instant reply. The following morning, he called upon Lady Falconer to request her hand for the quadrille.

Aurelia was somewhat distracted when her visitor was announced. Franny had a cold and was lying wanly on the sofa in her mother's sitting room, snuffling and complaining that she was bored and wanted to go to the schoolroom in Mount Street.

"That foreign gentleman is 'ere, m'lady. I showed him into the drawin' room," Jemmy said.

Aurelia bit back a denial. She had guaranteed to Greville that she would not allow maternal concerns to interfere with her other task. "Tell him I'll be down in a minute, Jemmy. Take the sherry decanter in," she said, reaching over to lay a hand on her daughter's forehead.

To her relief, Franny felt quite cool. "I'll be back in a short while, sweetie. Lie quietly and Daisy will bring you a cup of Miss Ada's chicken broth."

"I don't like broth." Franny sniffed vigorously. "I want gingerbread and honey milk."

Ordinarily Aurelia would have denied the treat outright, knowing well that the child was making the most of an ailment that would not be cured by sugar. But Aurelia was fatigued and queasy, and the thought of Don Antonio awaiting her in his black elegance downstairs did nothing for her state of mind.

"I'll ask Daisy to bring you some." She kissed the child's forehead. "But this is the last time, Franny. When I come back, you must have some broth and go back to bed for a nap."

Franny wisely decided to defer that battle and concentrate on her victory. "All right," she said, and coughed vigorously.

Aurelia couldn't help smiling as she left the room. The child was so transparent, and yet she had a certain skill when it came to arranging matters to her satisfaction. *Rather like her father,* Aurelia thought. Frederick had certainly arranged his life. Her hand brushed lightly over her flat belly. *What of this one?* The child of a man even more capable of manipulating the world to suit his own needs.

Oh, it was all too vexing and complex to think about. For the moment, she had to concentrate on Don Antonio Vasquez.

She walked into the salon, all smiles, hand outstretched. "I'm so sorry our time together was curtailed yesterday, Don Antonio, but Princess Prokov's visit was a surprise, and she is a particular friend of mine."

"Oh, I quite understand, ma'am." He kissed her hand. "And I find myself the beneficiary. I have received an invitation to Lady Bonham's ball, and I'm here in the hopes that I may claim your hand for the quadrille."

Nick Petersham had already claimed that dance. But he would accept an alternative with his usual easy grace. "I should be delighted, Don Antonio. It's one of my favorite dances."

"One of mine also." His black eyes met her brown ones, but, as always, there was nothing behind the gaze. It was as blank as Franny's virgin schoolroom slate. "I was also hoping to persuade you to accompany me on a drive to the Botanical Gardens at Kew. They are quite lovely at this time of year, I'm told."

"I'm afraid I cannot this morning, Don Antonio. My daughter is unwell and she frets herself into a fever if I leave the house. But as soon as she's better, I should look forward to such an excursion."

If he was put out by her refusal, he gave no sign of it. He bowed and said with a flickering smile, "Of course, your daughter's well-being must take precedence over my selfish desires. I do trust it's nothing serious. Have you summoned the physician?"

He managed to make his concern sound almost sincere, Aurelia thought, as she responded lightly, "No, I don't think that's necessary. It's no more than a slight head cold. But thank you for your concern, sir."

"One cannot be too careful with children." That slide of the knife's edge was there again.

Aurelia fought down a surge of nausea. She was just imagining the hint of menace. It was hardly surprising in her present heightened anxiety.

"I'll take my leave, ma'am." He bowed over her hand and continued to hold it in a warm, dry clasp. His voice oozed sympathy. "I won't keep you from your daughter any longer. But you should take the air yourself for a few minutes every day, you know. You must not catch the infection. Maybe tomorrow you will agree to walk with me, no further than the square garden, if you wish."

"You are very considerate, Don Antonio," she managed with what she hoped was a sincere smile. "A brief stroll tomorrow afternoon would be delightful."

"Then I shall call for you at two o'clock." He raised her hand to his lips again, then left her.

Greville was just entering the hall as Don Antonio emerged from the drawing room. "Good morning, Don Antonio." Greville tossed his high-crowned beaver hat onto the hall table and placed his slender cane beside it, before drawing off his gloves. "You've been visiting my wife, I take it."

The Spaniard's black eyes narrowed a little as he said, "I trust you have no objections, sir?"

"Not a one," Greville said airily. "My wife is free to choose her friends as she pleases."

"But not to ride in Richmond Park with them, I understand."

"No. Lady Falconer is a nervous horsewoman and I would trust no one's hand but my own on her bridle."

"Very commendable, Sir Greville." Don Antonio's lips moved in the semblance of a smile. "I trust you'll have no objections to my dancing with her at Lady Bonham's ball on Saturday."

"Oh, not in the least. My wife is as free to choose her dance partners as she is her friends." Greville moved back to open the front door for his departing guest. "I look forward to seeing you there, Don Antonio."

The Spaniard bowed his agreement and left. Greville closed the door behind him and stood frowning for a moment, then strolled into the drawing room.

"I didn't realize Don Antonio was acquainted with the Bonhams," he said, going to the decanters on the sideboard. "Wine?"

Aurelia barely repressed a shudder. "No . . . no, thank you. He was here yesterday when Nell and Liv paid a call. Nell invited him to the ball on the spot. She seemed to think that as he was a friend of mine, she should do so." Aurelia shrugged. "I didn't see the need myself, but it can't do any harm."

"Quite the opposite," Greville said, pouring claret into a glass. "How's Franny?"

"Miserable, snuffling, and making the most of it," Aurelia said with a light laugh. "I should go back to her."

She moved to the door, then paused as Greville laid a hand on her arm. "Maybe I'm imagining things, Aurelia, but I think something's not quite right with you." He looked closely into her eyes.

"Of course there's nothing the matter," she denied,

but felt her eyes slipping away from his. "I'm perfectly well." She shrugged a little. "I don't deny I find this business with Don Antonio exhausting. When I'm with him, I can't relax for a second, and it makes my body ache." She tried to laugh it off, but knew she hadn't succeeded. His dark eyes seemed to penetrate her skull.

"Maybe you need a tonic. Your appetite was never much to speak of, but it seems nonexistent these days. And I don't like those black shadows under your eyes."

"Then bring this business to a speedy close, Greville," she said, much more sharply than she'd intended. "I must go to Franny." She moved away from his hand and headed for the door.

Greville swore softly. He hadn't really considered the toll this mission would take on her. In many ways it was harder to play a part in a setting that was utterly familiar than it was to tackle a straightforward mission, however dangerous it might be. What Aurelia was doing was not in and of itself dangerous, but the strain of maintaining a charade every minute she was in company was not to be taken lightly.

It was not for much longer, though. Vasquez would soon make a move. Once he did, he would find his quarry ready and waiting for him. The biter bit. Greville could end it all quickly with a preemptive strike. A simple assassination. But he prided himself on his finesse. He was fairly certain El Demonio had more than one string to his bow on this visit to London; other people would be involved in setting up an intelligence network. For a while at least Greville would let the line pay out and see what else it caught. But once it was over, he would take Aurelia away for a few weeks. Somewhere in the country, where she could recover the bloom on her cheeks and the glow in her eyes.

Until the next mission that would bring it all to an end.

Chapter Twenty-three

"How's Franny this evening?" Greville, in his shirtsleeves, stood in the doorway between his bed-chamber and his wife's, inserting a diamond pin into the snowy folds of his cravat on Saturday evening.

Aurelia was sitting at the dresser, a light peignoir protecting the white silk underdress as Hester dressed her hair. The black spider gauze overgown was draped carefully over the arm of the daybed.

Aurelia turned slightly from the mirror to look at him. "She's quite better," she said with a laugh, "but she's still milking it. Even although she's been fit as a fiddle for the last three days, she's convinced that a carefully executed cough, and now and again a strategic sneeze, will persuade Daisy to bring her anything she asks for." Aurelia cocked her head slightly. "You do look very handsome, sir."

"I have many qualities, my dear, but handsome is not one of them. Is this pin straight?"

She got up from the dresser and went over to him,

saying severely, "False modesty is *not* an attractive quality." Her fingers deftly adjusted the pin.

He caught her wrist as she moved away from him, turning it up to kiss the soft, white, blue-veined underside. "Are you sure you're quite well, Aurelia?"

"Of course. Never better. Why wouldn't I be?"

"I don't know," he said, still holding her wrist. "But I do know when I'm not hearing the truth." He pulled her in towards him, placing his hands on her shoulders, feeling the warmth of her skin beneath the thin silk. "You're looking sadly fagged, my dear. After tonight, I'm resolved to send you and Franny into the country, to Mary Masham, for a couple of weeks. You both need some country air."

"Greville, you cannot *send* me anywhere. I am very well able to decide for myself what I need and when I need it. And I am certainly the only person qualified to make such decisions for Franny."

Greville ran his thumb over her eyelids, thinking that sending her away was the last thing he wanted to do. They had all too little time left. "Will you go if I promise to come down now and again?"

She smiled a little. "That might make a difference, certainly. You realize you haven't solicited a single dance with me this evening?"

He looked startled. "I didn't realize it was necessary."

She laughed. "My dance card is quite full, but I anticipated your forgetfulness and saved a country dance."

"Only one?" He raised his eyebrows.

"I rather thought you'd find one more than sufficient. Besides, I need to leave enough opportunity for Don Antonio."

"Yes, I suppose you do." A shadow crossed his eyes.

"We are always working, as you once said," she reminded him softly.

"Yes, and sometimes it's a damnable nuisance." He turned back to his own room.

Aurelia sat down at the dresser mirror again while Hester worked her usual miracles with the curling iron. Aurelia had never once heard Greville refer to his work in such terms. He lived for his work, breathed it in with every breath he took. But just then he'd really sounded as if he wished it to the devil.

"Are you ready for the gown, m'lady?" Hester lifted the black gauzy cloud reverently. "If I drop it over your head, it won't disturb your coiffure."

Aurelia put aside the puzzle for the moment. She shrugged off the peignoir and lifted her arms so that the gown seemed to float over her head and arms to settle smoothly against the close-fitting white silk sheath beneath.

"Lawks a mercy, m'lady, don't you look a treat," Hester breathed.

"She does, indeed, Hester," Greville said from the doorway. He was dressed himself now in a black tailcoat and pantaloons strapped over black slippers. "Quite stunning." He crossed the carpet towards Aurelia and brought his hands out from behind his back. "Will you wear this in your hair tonight?"

Aurelia gazed at the half circle of diamonds embedded in a stiffened band of black velvet. It was simple, elegant, and utterly beautiful. "Oh, yes," she said softly, raising her eyes to his. "How perfect it is."

She saw in his eyes something she had never been certain she had seen before. Sometimes a hint, but never this absolute, naked emotion. Greville loved her. He might not be ready to acknowledge it yet himself, but she knew, and the knowledge warmed her soul, filled her with a deep elation. Her hand brushed fleetingly over her belly as she sat down at the mirror again.

"Let me fasten it, m'lady," Hester urged, taking the adornment from Greville. "Just a pin here . . . and another here . . . and it'll sit tight for hours." She suited action to words, then stepped back to admire her handiwork.

Greville had indeed chosen perfectly. The black velvet against her pale hair, the diamonds sparkling against the black, the half-moon shape that was not quite a tiara and not quite a simple headband, suited Aurelia's understated style as nothing else could.

"Thank you," she said, raising her face for his kiss. He leaned over and brushed her lips with his before kissing her bare shoulder.

"Nothing has ever given me more pleasure," he murmured.

Aurelia touched his face lightly with her fingertips,

then rose. "I promised to visit Franny before we left. She wants to see my gown."

"Then let us present ourselves, my lady." He offered his arm with a ceremonial bow.

Franny was sitting up in bed when they entered the nursery. Her eyes widened. "You look like a princess, Mama. Is that diamonds in your hair?"

"Yes, they were a present," Aurelia said, bending to kiss her daughter.

Franny looked at Greville with wide eyes. "From you?"

"Yes, from me." Greville smiled.

"Mama looks like a princess and you look like a prince," Franny said, magnanimously expanding the compliment.

"Well, thank you, Franny," he said solemnly. "I fear I will never outshine your mother, but I hope to provide an escort of which she needn't be ashamed."

The little girl frowned at him. "Why would she be 'shamed?"

"Oh, he was only teasing, darling," her mother said swiftly. "We're going to Aunt Nell's for dinner and—"

"An' then to the ball," Franny interrupted. "I know. I wish I could go."

"My darling, you will be going to balls sooner than I want to imagine," Aurelia said with a soft smile. "Ten years goes very quickly."

Franny's expression implied only disbelief. "Ten years is a . . . a eternity."

Aurelia laughed and kissed her again. "Good night,

love, sleep tight, don't let the bedbugs bite." She tucked up the child as Franny snuggled under the covers.

"Have a nice time," Franny murmured sleepily as they left the nursery. "Wish I could go."

"An indomitable child," Greville said as they trod softly down the nursery stairs. "Some innocent youngster out there is going to fall in love with her in ten years' time, and God help him."

Aurelia chuckled. "She's not without compassion. And I have ten years in which to nurture the seeds."

Don Antonio Vasquez examined his reflection in the long mirror in his bedchamber. His shirt and waistcoat were a brilliant white. His coat and knee britches of black velvet. A square ruby nestled in the folds of his cravat, and another glowed on his signet finger. His spade beard was trimmed and combed, his hair curled and lustrous with pomade. He slipped a hand back beneath his coat and felt the slim, cool hilt of the dagger in its leather sheath nestled against the small of his back. Easy to reach, impossible to detect. Everything as it should be.

He went to the dresser and opened a drawer. He slid the small, pearl-handled pistol it contained into the pocket of his coat, feeling its light shape against his thigh. He didn't like firearms, knives were his weapons of choice, but a pistol was a useful persuader in certain circumstances, and he was taking no chances tonight.

He left the bedchamber and went into the sitting room where Miguel and Carlos both awaited him, standing rather awkwardly in front of the empty fireplace. "The carriage is waiting below, sir," Carlos said. He was dressed like a hired coachman in leather britches and jerkin, a muffler twisted around his neck. He wore jackboots, each of which concealed a knife.

"Good. Miguel, you know what you have to do?"

Miguel nodded. "Of course, Don Antonio." He wore the plain dark coat and britches of an upper manservant, top boots and a bicorn hat. He took out a small case from the pocket of his coat and flipped it open, revealing four delicate tools. "These will take care of part of the business, sir." He dropped the case back into his pocket, then, with a grim smile, flicked back one wide sleeve of his coat and with a deft twitch of his fingers extracted a slender dagger taped to his wrist. "And this the rest. I am ready, sir."

"So I see," his master said drily. "I trust there will be no need for your armory, but one must be prepared." He picked up his silver-mounted cane from the table by the door and pressed a little catch. The cane became a wickedly sharp blade, its edge glinting in the candlelight. He pressed the catch again and returned the blade to its concealment.

The clock struck ten and the three of them waited out the chimes before moving together to the door. Don Antonio swung a black silk evening cloak around his shoulders as he went lightly down the stairs to the street, where a young boy stood at the heads of a pair of horses in the traces of a plain hired coach.

"You've put them through their paces?" Antonio asked.

"*Sí*, Don Antonio. They're fleet. On a clear road they'll give us all the speed we need." Carlos tossed the boy a coin and climbed onto the box, taking the reins.

Miguel held the door for Don Antonio and followed him into the carriage, pulling the door closed behind them. He sat silently in a corner, knowing that when his master was preparing to work, he would brook no distractions. The carriage covered the short distance to Mount Street in ten minutes, and the horses drew up outside the Bonhams' house, blazing with light. Link-boys stood on the carpeted flagway ready to direct the carriages and light the guests up the steps and into the house.

Don Antonio stepped down to the street, his cloak swirling about him. He glanced back once at the carriage but said nothing. Miguel had his orders. Don Antonio strode up the steps and into the music-filled, brilliantly lit interior.

Cornelia stood beside her husband at the head of the stairs. The double doors to the ballroom stood open behind them, and the strains of the orchestra rose above the buzz of conversation. Jugs of scarlet tulips interspersed with black stood on every surface, and the candelabra were ablaze with silver candles. The guests were a whirl of black, silver, and scarlet, the gentlemen to a man in black and white, their ladies a complementary bouquet of scarlet and silver, with the occasional touch of black.

"It worked," Cornelia said in a breathless whisper, her cheeks flushed with success, her blue eyes bright as gemstones. "Isn't it magnificent, Harry?"

"A triumph, my love," he said with an affectionate chuckle. "I would never have believed when I first met you that you would garner so much pleasure from creating a society success."

"It was enormous fun to plan," she murmured half-defensively. "And it doesn't hurt once in a while to indulge in pure frivolity."

"Indeed it doesn't," he agreed, moving forward to greet the grande dame billowing up the staircase with a trailing swirl of damask train and cashmere shawls, an elderly lady puffing in her wake as she struggled to contain the spilling folds of material.

"Your grace." Harry bowed over his great-aunt's hand and kissed it, before easing her gently up beside him. He turned with a warm smile to greet the duchess's companion. "Miss Cox . . . Eliza. Thank you for bringing her grace."

Eliza Cox blushed and fluttered and disclaimed any part in her employer's presence. The Duchess of Gracechurch for her part stated, "Stuff and nonsense, Eliza had nothing to do with it. I wanted to see this flummery for myself." She raised her lorgnette and surveyed her hostess. "Very dramatic, Cornelia." She didn't sound as if it was a compliment.

Cornelia was far too accustomed to the duchess's manner to be in the least put out. She laughed and took her grace's hand. "Thank you for coming, ma'am. It would not have been the same without you. And I know how you don't care to go out much in the evening."

The duchess snorted and looked around her. "Well, I shan't stay long. Come, Eliza, let us see who else is indulging in this foolery." The duchess swept away, her companion, with an apologetic glance at her hosts, hastily following her.

"Well, that crowns your success, Nell," Harry said. "I really didn't think she would make the effort."

"Nell . . ." Aurelia emerged from the ballroom, laughing. "The duchess is actually wearing black and white . . . what a compliment. How on earth did you persuade her?"

"I didn't," Cornelia said, glancing at her husband. "But I suspect Harry had a hand in it. You know he can get his great-aunt to do anything if he puts his mind to it."

"Not so." Harry threw up his hands in disclaimer. "No one, but no one, can move that woman if she's unwilling."

Cornelia shook her head with a smile and turned back to the stairs, where a new arrival had made his appearance. "Don Antonio . . . thank you so much for coming."

The Spaniard bowed over her hand with a courtly flourish. "I was honored to receive your invitation, Lady Bonham . . . Lord Bonham." He bowed to his host and looked around. "The colors . . . what a charming concept, Lady Bonham. And black tulips . . . such a rarity."

"Yes, indeed, sir," Cornelia said. "I am fortunate in having a friend who seems to be able to conjure such rarities out of thin air."

Don Antonio gave a faint smile and turned slightly to where Aurelia still stood just behind Harry. "My dear Lady Falconer. How charming you look. Such a magnificent contrast."

"Thank you, Don Antonio." She responded to the compliment with a smile that was suddenly effortful. "Have you come to claim your dance?"

"I trust I may have more than one," he said, moving away with her into the ballroom.

"Alas, sir, my card is full," she said, gesturing to the dance card that was fastened to her wrist with a piece of gold silk. "But I have saved you the quadrille, as promised."

"Then I must be satisfied."

"Aurelia, this dance is mine, I believe." Nick Petersham appeared in front of her, hand extended. "Ah, evening, Vasquez." He nodded at her companion. "You're not trying to steal my dance, I trust?"

"Hardly," Don Antonio said with a thin smile. "I'll claim mine later." He bowed and moved off.

"Do you know Don Antonio, Nick?" Aurelia inquired as he led her to the set.

"I've met him once or twice in the clubs. Odd bird." Nick took his place opposite her and they offered the ritual courtesies as the music started.

Aurelia wasn't sure that was quite the description she would have used, it was rather too benign for a man who was beginning to make her flesh creep every time she saw him.

She was aware of Greville's eyes on her as she moved down the dance. He was standing against the wall, a glass in hand, apparently talking idly to a gray-haired, tired-looking man who looked as if he had had to drag himself bodily to the ball. She didn't know him, in fact was certain she had never seen him before, but she knew immediately that he and Greville were not having a casual conversation. No one else would see it, but she had been observing her husband for months now, and she knew when he was working. And he was working now. His lips moved lazily, his posture was relaxed, everything about him indicated he was having an inconsequential chat with his companion, but whatever they were talking about, it wasn't inconsequential. Although his eyes were following her, she didn't think she was the subject of their conversation.

"We're thinking maybe he's going to use the Marquess de Los Perez to set up the intelligence network . . . once he's taken care of you, of course," Simon Grant murmured into his glass of champagne, his weary eyes flickering over Don Antonio, who had just entered the ballroom. "The marquess has connections to King Carlos, but there are strong suspicions that he's a turncoat. He could assemble a court in exile here in London and use it as the perfect cover to send intelligence to Fouche."

Greville sipped his own champagne, his gaze still on Aurelia. "I'll instruct Aurelia to ask a few innocently probing questions."

Simon nodded. "Don't keep him on a string too long, Greville. You're his main target, and the most important task you have is getting rid of him before he gets his hands on you."

"I know. Believe me, Simon, I know. But I have some leeway I think. And if we can deflect another plot at the same time, then all to the good. Wouldn't you say?"

"I leave it you, Greville. Just don't take any unnecessary risks."

Greville gave a short laugh and pushed himself off the wall. "I won't. Now if you'll excuse me, Simon, I must retrieve my wife for the next dance."

Simon nodded and turned to find Harry Bonham beside him. "Excellent ball, Harry."

Harry smiled his disbelief. "What . . . or rather who . . . brings you here, Simon? Wild horses wouldn't drag you to a ball if you didn't have a good reason."

Harry's chief shrugged in acknowledgment. "Someone I wanted to get a look at. And now I've done so, I'm sure you and your lady will excuse me."

"Of course." Harry stood aside and watched his chief thread his way to the door. *Just whom had Simon Grant come to get a look at?*

"I know you don't really wish to dance," Aurelia said as she and Greville walked off the dance floor a minute before the orchestra struck up for the country dance. "So you don't mind going to the supper room instead, do you?"

"Not in the least," he agreed with some amusement. "It's just rather unusual for you to demand food as a priority."

"I didn't eat much at dinner," she offered in excuse. It was impossible to explain at this point the nausea that only food would assuage. "I'm just hungry, Greville."

"Fortunately, that's easily remedied." He guided her with a hand under her elbow in the direction of the supper room. "Besides, I wanted a quick word before your dance with Vasquez."

Her stomach clenched and she forced herself to relax. "Oh, yes?" she said with an assumption of ease, taking a seat at one of the small tables scattered around the room.

"What may I fetch you?" He stood with a hand on the back of the chair facing her, and his gaze was suddenly uncomfortably sharp.

"A little turtle soup," she said promptly. "With bread."

"As you command, ma'am." He turned, then glanced back at her. "Wine?"

"No, just lemonade, please."

Aurelia sat back and breathed deeply as her husband eased his way through the growing throng towards the supper tables set against the far wall. Even tonight, she must work. But for some reason the zest had gone from it. *Not for* some *reason,* she told herself. *She knew the reason perfectly well. Pregnant ladies did not make good spies.*

Greville came back to the table with a steaming, fragrant bowl and a basket of warm rolls. He set both before her, then fetched her a glass of lemonade and sat down beside her with his own glass of wine.

"So what do you need to talk about?" she asked, dipping her spoon in the bowl.

Greville spoke softly in the whisper that only she could hear. "Ask Vasquez about the Marquess de Los Perez . . . float the name, see if you get any reaction. Watch for the usual signs, a flicker of an eyelid, a twitch of a shoulder . . . you know what to look for."

"I do. Is this man in London?"

"Yes . . . arrived relatively recently. It's possible he could become the center for a Spanish intelligence network. We'd like to know if Vasquez has any interest in him."

Aurelia nodded and finished her soup. "That seems straightforward enough." She glanced at her dance card. "I should return to the ballroom, the quadrille is the next dance." She managed a smile as he offered his hand to help her rise. "Into the breach once more."

Chapter Twenty-four

MIGUEL STOOD IN THE DARK, deserted alley running behind South Audley Street and cursed softly as he attempted to lift a window, which when last he'd looked had been unsecured. It would have been the matter of a moment to flip the original catch, but in the meantime someone had strengthened the lock. Breaking it was not beyond his skill or his tools, but it would take time, and time was more than precious.

He worked as quickly as he could, making a small hole in the glass with the fine diamond point of one of the tools. The hole gave him access to the inside lock, and he worked with painstaking patience until finally the lock eased apart. He inched the window up just enough to allow him to roll sideways through the aperture.

The library was in darkness and the house was silent around him. He knew that only a few servants slept in the house, mostly maids. Only the night watchman could give him any trouble. He moved silently to the library door and opened it a crack, peering into the hall, which was dimly lit by a light in a sconce by the staircase. The watchman was slumped dozing on a chair by the front door, his head on his chest, low snores bubbling from his half-open mouth.

The man could count himself lucky the *asp* couldn't see him asleep at his post, Miguel reflected as he sidled into the hall, approaching the man in his chair from behind. A quick rabbit punch to the back of the neck and the snores ceased; the man fell forward and slowly crumpled from the chair to the floor.

Miguel trod soundlessly up the stairs. He paused at the top, listening. All was quiet. The nursery stairs would be at the end of the hallway in front of him. He was halfway down the corridor when he heard it. A low, throaty growl that made the hairs on his nape stand up.

Then the dog came at him. Massive forepaws on his shoulders knocked him to the ground and the hound stood over him, her meaty breath hot on his face. He closed his eyes against the sight of bared teeth and the fierce glare of tawny eyes and waited to feel the teeth ripping his throat.

Don Antonio moved gracefully through the stately steps of the quadrille. His eyes were on the time, but his partner wouldn't guess his preoccupation from the ease with which he performed the lengthy and complicated figures of the dance. She needed all her attention on her part. The dance was relatively new to London society, and Aurelia, like most of her friends, had danced it only a few times before. For all her instinctive dislike of her partner, she was grateful for his skill, which covered up her own occasional missteps.

As the last lively strains of the finale faded away, she allowed him to lead her off the floor towards the welcome breath of cool air coming from the hall. "That was pleasant exercise, sir," she said, flicking open her fan to cool her heated face. "You're more familiar with the dance than I am."

"I danced it in Paris many years ago," he said, his hand beneath her elbow as he guided her around the square landing towards a pair of open windows on the far side. "Let us take some air."

Aurelia went willingly enough, but instead of continuing to the open windows, he stepped behind a worked screen in front of a narrow door. His hand on her elbow tightened and an unformed panic gripped her. She looked up at him, her eyes wide with suspicion, then he had propelled her through the door onto a narrow, dark servants' staircase.

"Don't make a sound," he instructed softly. "Your daughter's safety depends upon it."

"My daughter . . . Franny . . . what do you mean?" She barely managed to get the words out through the fear that clogged her throat.

"She's safe enough. It's up to you whether she stays that way." He led her down the stairs, and slowly Aurelia regained her composure.

She stopped on the stairs, taking a firm hold of the iron banister. "Where is she?" she demanded in a voice as cold as it was calm. "I'll not take another step unless you tell me."

"I have her and I will take you to her. But if we don't make the rendezvous by a certain time, you will never see her again. I suggest you hurry." He jerked her elbow.

Could she believe him? Could she afford not to? Greville had drilled into her the mantra: trust no one. But this was different. She couldn't take the risk that he was lying about the danger to Franny. She continued her descent to the narrow hall at the bottom of the stairs. There she stopped. "I'm not going with you without proof that you have my daughter." A guttering candle in a sconce provided very little light, but she could still clearly see the hard set of his mouth and the blank coldness of his black eyes that told her nothing.

"Outside you shall have your proof," he said, unbolting the door at his back. Miguel would be back at the carriage now, with all the proof that the woman could need. She would go quietly, and the rest would slip into place.

Aurelia thought rapidly. Once she'd left this house, she would be dependent on her own resources. For as long as she stayed under this roof, she knew that Greville was close by, even though she could at present see no way of letting him know what was happening to her.

"If we miss the rendezvous, you will never see your daughter again," Don Antonio repeated, his voice hard and cold as obsidian. He opened the door, which she saw now led onto a narrow passage that ran along the side of the house.

Greville would notice her absence soon enough, and he would draw the right conclusion, once he realized the Spaniard was not there either. But she needed to leave a trail, something. She had no idea how often this staircase was used, but she had to take the chance, the only one she had.

Don Antonio was peering out into the passage, and swiftly she let her hand fall to her side, dropping her fan on the step above her as softly as she could. Maybe it was a forlorn hope that someone would find it quickly, but it was all she had. Greville would at least know where she'd left from, and the significance of the fan, their means of communication, would not be lost upon him. It screamed the Spaniard's involvement.

With the deepest reluctance, the sense that she was now abandoning all her defenses, Aurelia stepped past Don Antonio into the passage. She heard the door click shut with a dreadful finality. He put his hand beneath her elbow and propelled her towards the end of the passage, where it opened into the alley that ran behind the houses. The alley was deserted except for a single, unmarked carriage. From the open windows of the house drifted the sounds of music, voices, laughter. Such ordinary sounds of merriment. Aurelia felt as if she was living in some parallel universe.

The evening was growing cool and she shivered in her thin gown, goose bumps lifting on her bare shoulders and arms. "It might have been chivalrous to have provided a wrap," she snapped at her escort. The complaint cheered her. She had not sounded frightened or even disconcerted by her abduction, just as annoyed about the situation as anyone would be in the most normal of circumstances. The look he gave her, with just a hint of surprise, heartened her even more.

The carriage door swung open from within as they approached it. Aurelia stopped close to the back of the house. "I'll not get in without proof that you have Franny."

Don Antonio did not loose his grip on her elbow, but he called softly towards the open door, "Miguel?"

The man who jumped down was not Miguel but Carlos. "He's not back, sir."

Don Antonio's grip once more tightened on his captive. Then she felt the unmistakable muzzle of a pistol pressing into the small of her back. *"Get in,"* he demanded against her ear. "If you wish to see your daughter alive . . . get in the carriage *now.*"

Something had gone wrong, she knew immediately. But how to exploit it? Would he use the pistol? If he needed her alive, what good was she to him dead? She pulled back against his hold. "Where's the proof?"

"You'll have it soon enough. And your husband will

have your ear for his own proof." His voice was as low and deadly as the cold steel against her ear.

Now came the sharp pain of a cut, and a trickle of blood, sticky on her neck. Terror flooded her. Guns were one things, knives quite another. They had always made her shudder from earliest childhood.

She stumbled a little as he pushed her to the open door, and as she did so, she dashed a hand against the hot trickle on her neck, flicking her fingertips out to the ground. If Greville saw the drops, it would add to his knowledge, however sketchily. The man standing beside the carriage door gave her a shove upwards and she fell rather than climbed into the dark interior, but once again the months of Greville's training came to the fore. She still had her ear, even though the cut still bled, and now she had to think—with more clarity than she had ever mustered before. She heard Don Antonio's last words once again.

Your husband will have your ear for his own proof.

It was Greville they wanted, not her. She was merely their means to him. Knowing that brought an even deeper calm, and with it the certainty that something had gone wrong with the Spaniard's plan. He and the other man were talking in low, fierce Spanish just outside the carriage door. She couldn't hear clearly, but her Spanish was so rudimentary at the best of times it wouldn't help her. But Antonio's fury required no language to make it manifest, and the name *Miguel* kept coming up.

Vasquez climbed in, slamming the door behind him.

The other man jumped upon the box and the carriage moved off, out of the alleyway and into the main street. Don Antonio sat opposite Aurelia, tapping the gleaming blade of his knife into the gloved palm of his other hand. He watched her from narrowed eyes as light from the street threw occasional illumination into the interior. Aurelia kept her expression impassive, her body still and apparently relaxed in a corner. She wanted to touch the still stinging cut behind her ear, assess the damage, but forced herself to ignore it. She would not give him the satisfaction. And she would show him no fear.

She was feeding her composure on the faint possibility that he did not have Franny after all. This Miguel character had not shown up. She guessed he was to have brought the proof. If there was no sign of him, then it was not too much of an optimistic stretch to think that he had failed in getting hold of Franny. And if this lay only between her and Vasquez, then he would find her more of a challenge than he had bargained for. She turned her head to look out the window, trying to make a mental note of the route they were taking.

Don Antonio leaned over and flipped down the leather curtains, blocking out the light. Deliberately Aurelia leaned back into her corner and closed her eyes.

The Spaniard watched her, his mouth a thin, grim line. *What had happened to Miguel?* If the woman wasn't afraid for her child, she would be all the more difficult to break. Without Miguel it would be messy. He could do it himself, but he did not have Miguel's techniques, the tricks of the Inquisition. The job had to be completed tonight. The boat would be waiting for him at Blackfriars to take him down the Thames and out of the city. On horseback and alone at this time of day, it would take him less than an hour to get to the rendezvous. The tide would be full at eight o'clock, and he had to be on board by then, his business here accomplished. He could not afford the time to find out what had happened to his assistant. He had to break the woman quickly.

Greville became aware of Aurelia's absence only slowly, far too slowly he would later castigate himself. He had watched them during the quadrille, reluctantly admiring the Spaniard's skill at the complicated dance figures that would have defeated him on the first steps. It was a long dance, four or five different movements, and after a while he moved away in search of congenial company. He found Prince Prokov surveying the supper table with an air of mild curiosity.

"Ah, Falconer, perhaps you can enlighten me. What are those little things on the ice trays that people are extricating with those tiny pins?"

"Periwinkles. Cockles and whelks, too. Quite delicious, but I tend to think the effort barely worth the instant of taste."

"They are sea creatures?" Alex took a tiny shell from the platter and examined it closely.

"Yes, they cling to rocks. They're very common along

our coastlines and considered a delicacy among all sections of society. You'll find costermongers selling them all over the country close to the sea. A sprinkle of vinegar is said to improve them enormously."

Alex took one of the pins provided and prised loose the minute scrap of seafood. He tasted it, then shrugged as he swallowed. "I don't appear to see the point. But then Livia doesn't really appreciate the appeal of pickled herring, and that I do find hard to understand."

Greville laughed. He looked around. "I don't see your wife."

"No, she's closeted in some corner with her friends discussing the joys of maternity. Or that was what they were discussing when I left them, but it's possible," Alex added in musing tone, "that the subject was designed to send me away, and they are now deeply engaged in some other much more engaging topic that is not for the ears of men."

He looked at Greville with a smile, as if expecting agreement, then, seeing his companion's slight frown, said, "Aurelia was not with them."

"No, she was dancing with Don Antonio Vasquez," Greville said, his voice suddenly sharp. "Excuse me, Prokov." He spun on his heel and left the supper room. Alex, after an instant, followed.

There was no sign of Aurelia in the ballroom, no sign of her in the card rooms. Greville strode around the galleried landing where groups of guests were taking the fresh air from the windows after the exertions of the dance floor. Aurelia was not among them. And neither was Don Antonio.

"Who saw her last?"

Greville turned at Alex's quiet question. "Damn it to hell, I don't know. But we need to find out."

Alex nodded. "I'll go to the right, you question the left."

Greville strolled casually from group to group, inquiring with matching carelessness if anyone had seen his wife recently. Many remembered her dancing the quadrille, and a few remembered her leaving the dance floor with her partner at the finale, but that was such an ordinary occurrence no one had thought to see where she went next.

Until a maidservant appeared from behind a screen carrying something. She was making her way purposefully towards Hector, the Bonhams' butler, who stood at the top of the grand staircase, keeping a watchful eye on all and sundry. Greville moved quickly after her.

He saw her curtsy apologetically to the austere butler and extend her offering. Greville, with a polite word, took the object from her. It was Aurelia's fan. "Where did you find this?"

The girl look flustered, as if she was being accused of something. Greville said swiftly to the butler, "It's my wife's fan. I don't mean to frighten the girl, but it's important I know where she found it."

Hector had not managed Viscount Bonham's household for the last fifteen years without knowing when to respond without thought or question. He said to the maid, "Just tell Sir Greville where you found it, Millie."

"At bottom o' the back stairs, sir," the girl said, addressing Hector. "Lying on the second step up from the bottom. I don't know 'ow a lady's fan could 'ave got there, sir, indeed I don't." She sounded as distressed as if she'd been accused of stealing it herself.

"No, I'm sure you don't, Millie. I'm sure there's a simple explanation. Thank you for bringing it back so quickly." Greville smiled at the flustered maid, nodded to Hector, and walked away with the fan. His step appeared leisured, but he covered the distance between the gallery and the place where he had last seen Harry Bonham in the time it would have taken him to run it.

Harry was about to take the floor with his wife when he saw Greville. Something about the man's progress alerted him, and with a murmured excuse to Cornelia he stepped out of the set. Alex was there to take his place so speedily Cornelia wasn't sure how the transfer had happened.

"What's going on?" she asked Alex, as they offered the customary bows and curtsies before the dance began.

Alex merely smiled and shrugged, extending his hand to draw her into a figure. "Not sure, but we'll know in good time."

Cornelia nodded and followed her partner through the motions, although neither of then were concentrating on the dance.

Harry reached Greville, who said only, "Fetch Franny."

Harry gave a short nod of acknowledgment. "I'll send Lester. It'll draw less attention."

"You know best. He'll need the key to the back door and the words for Lyra . . . to get her to stand down."

Harry listened, took the key, nodded again, and left the ballroom with a step similar to Greville's in speed.

Greville went back to the gallery. He stepped behind the screen and went down the narrow staircase. There was no sign of a struggle. Aurelia had left her sign on the second step from the bottom. The door was still unlatched. He stepped out into the darkened alley and raised his face and silently howled at the moon for the idiot he had been. Criminal fool.

He had thought she would be safe in a crowded ballroom. He had barely taken his eyes off her for a moment. But it wasn't Aurelia they wanted, or rather, she was merely a means to an end.

They wanted him. They would communicate with him soon. Until then he could only pray he was not too late to take Franny well out of danger, and that they would keep Aurelia alive, at least until they had him.

He walked the alleyway slowly. A pile of dung marked where horses had stood for a while, close to the side door. It was still warm. He frowned down at it. Half an hour since it had been dropped. Maybe a little more. He bent to scrutinize the cobbles. Three rusty spots just behind the dung heap. His heart jumped against his ribs. It was drying but not solidified.

Aurelia was hurt, but not badly. And maybe she had

left the sign for him, as she had left the fan. She was still in control then. He followed the ruts of the carriage wheels out to the open street, but there was no way of telling which way they had gone from there. Too much traffic obliterated any small indication.

"Anything?" Harry, Alex at his side, appeared seemingly from nowhere.

"A few drops of blood in the alley. I think Aurelia wanted me to see them."

"She's hurt?" Alex sounded outraged.

"Not badly, I believe," Greville stated dispassionately. "It's me they want." He gave a short, mirthless laugh. "Anyway, they'll contact me soon enough if Aurelia's their hostage. They'll know I won't surrender without seeing her whole, so for the moment she's safe, and believe me, gentlemen, she has her wits about her."

"And how will you escape the trap?" Harry inquired, sounding almost as nonchalant as Greville.

"That, my friend, depends on the trap," Greville said. "Different snares, different teeth, different exits."

"Whatever you need from us."

Greville acknowledged Alex's statement of support with a brief smile. "Once you have Franny safe, I'll return to South Audley Street and wait for them to contact me."

"Let's go back inside. Cornelia and Livia need to know what's happening, I'm afraid. They'll hold the fort and maintain the illusion of normality for a while, but . . ." Harry shrugged.

"It can do no harm," Greville said, still reluctant to involve anyone in his own business, but realizing this was no longer only his business. By taking Aurelia as his partner, he had thrown open his whole operation to the possibility that others, admittedly those in his own shadow world, would claim a part if they thought it necessary. And if Aurelia was in danger, then they thought it necessary. He had no choice now.

They returned to the ball and the orchestra played on; the guests danced, supped, and played cards; and their hosts, and two of their hosts' guests, smiled bravely and kept watch for Lester.

Lester slipped his key into the kitchen door. It turned on beautifully oiled locks and he nodded his approval. The kitchen was lit by the low embers in the range, but nothing else. It threw enough light, however, for him to step to the door leading into the front part of the house. He knew about Lyra, and he knew a night watchman was on duty at the front door. But if an intruder had entered, then the watchman was in trouble.

He walked on cat's paws, through the door into the hall. He saw the watchman slumped upon the floor. But he had no time to check his well-being. Someone had entered the house, and that someone had been intent on taking the child. *Was he too late?*

Lester stepped silently up the stairs to the first landing. He stopped, listened, then heard the growl, soft yet even more menacing for that. He moved towards the sound, then stopped at what he saw. He spoke the words he'd been told to the dog, and the hound, without raising her head from her captive's throat, looked him straight in the eye.

Lester spoke further words as he walked softly towards the hound and the supine man. Lyra obeyed and raised her head, giving Lester room to put his own hand around the throat of the captive, pinning him to the floor. Lyra sat back on her haunches, beside her captive, watching while Lester ordered the terrified Miguel onto his belly and secured his wrists behind him.

"What a magnificent creature you are," Lester said, reaching a tentative hand to touch Lyra's head. The dog lowered her great head and allowed him to stroke her as if accepting praise for a job well done.

Lester yanked Miguel to his feet and kicked a door open onto a bedchamber. He shoved the man facedown on the bed and fastened his feet as securely as his hands, then wrapped a rope around his waist, fastening him securely to the bedposts at the foot of the bed.

"That should keep you until I come back for you, my friend," Lester said cheerfully. "But just in case, we'll have Lyra standing guard." He spoke to the dog, who had followed him and sat watching the proceedings, head cocked in apparent interest.

Now for the child. The dog wouldn't let him take her without the necessary words, but fortunately he had those. Whether he could get the volatile Franny down the stairs and out of the house without a great fuss was another matter. Lester squatted, took the dog's chin, and spoke the few words he'd been given, looking her directly in the eyes. Lyra listened, then gave a breathy sigh and lay down beside the bed, where their captive lay trussed.

Lester, relieved, rose to his feet and went, less quietly than before, up to the nursery. Daisy was asleep in her own bedchamber that adjoined Franny's, but he was astonished to see the child sitting up in bed, gazing wide-eyed, but utterly fearlessly, at the door as he slipped in. A small night-light burned on the table beside the bed.

"Lester?" Franny whispered. "Have you to come to take me to the ball?"

"Exactly that, princess," he said, scooping up blankets around her.

Chapter Twenty-five

THE CARRIAGE RIDE SEEMED to Aurelia to have gone on forever by the time the horses came to a stop. But it only seemed to. Greville had taught her how to keep a rough track of time even in the gloom imposed by the curtained windows of the carriage, and she guessed, by counting up to a hundred over and over at a regular speed, that they had been traveling for a little more than half an hour. The method was rough and ready, but it focused her mind and kept panic at bay.

She remained in her corner, eyes half-closed, her eyes on her abductor as the door was opened from the outside.

"Get out," Vasquez instructed.

She shrugged with apparent nonchalance and stepped out into an unlit yard. She looked quickly up at the night sky. The Big Dipper hung low and bright. Her eyes followed an imaginary line upwards from its bowl to the vivid brightness of Polaris. The driver stepped back a little from the door, and Don Antonio jumped down, taking

Aurelia's arm. She saw the silver glint of the knife in his other hand and controlled her shudder. But she said nothing, offered no resistance as he pushed her towards a low building looming at the far side of the yard.

The reek of horseflesh was strong in the air, and there was straw on the cobbles beneath her feet. It was a stable block, she realized, as she was thrust into a musty interior where the smell of horse was even stronger, mingling with the aromas of oiled leather and manure. The driver came in behind them, holding a lantern high, throwing shadows on the slatted walls and the stall partitions.

Vasquez unbolted a door to one of the stalls and gestured with a curt nod of his head that Aurelia should enter. She hesitated for only an instant, but it was enough for him to bring the knife up, laying its blade flat against her cheek.

"All right, all right," she said testily, stepping back into the stall. "You've made yourself quite clear."

"For your sake, I hope so." He closed the bottom half of the door and bolted it. He leaned his elbows on top. "You will notice the metal rings in the wall at the rear of the stall. I will utilize them if you oblige me to. But I'm sure you'll prefer not to be restrained, so I suggest you keep quiet." He stepped back and slammed shut the top half of the door, shooting the bolt with a definitive snap, leaving her in semidarkness.

Aurelia waited until her eyes had grown accustomed to the gloom that was relieved by the glow from the lantern shining in golden bars through the ill-fitting slats of the partition. The iron rings were all too obvious; presumably they were used to hold the halter of an unruly horse.

The comparison was not pleasant, she reflected wryly, sitting down on a bale of hay, leaning her back against the partition wall, and methodically sorting through what she knew and what she thought she knew.

First of all, Greville was Don Antonio's target. But had something gone amiss with the Spaniard's plans? It seemed that a man called Miguel was missing or had failed to keep a rendezvous. It seemed highly likely that he was to have had something to do with Franny. They intended to use Franny as a means to coerce her. Coerce her to go along quietly with her abduction . . . that seemed likely. Of course the blade of a knife and the willingness to use it had done just as well, she reflected grimly. But it was a clumsy means of abduction, and she had the sense that Don Antonio Vasquez did not care for clumsiness.

But why did they abduct her? Presumably to use her to trap Greville. But if that was so, they didn't know their target at all. Greville wouldn't walk into a trap, and he would certainly do nothing to jeopardize his own mission.

Not even to save her? She pondered the question as coolly as she could. Greville would not abandon her, unless he had absolutely no choice. That she knew. But if he had no choice . . . or if the choice lay between Aurelia and the completion of his mission. . . ? That she didn't know.

It was a bleak recognition, but not a surprising one. Greville had never been less than honest with her.

So either she saved herself or found a way to ensure that Greville could save her without jeopardizing himself or his mission.

Very simple . . . and from her position on a hay bale locked in a stable in the middle of God only knew where, well nigh impossible.

Lester carried Franny into the house through the kitchen. The kitchen was crowded with servants still catering to the guests in the supper room. A few distracted glances were sent in his direction, but no one had time to wonder what he carried or where he'd been.

"Robbie," he called sharply to a footman who was carrying a tray of glasses towards the servants' stairs. "Leave those, and tell Lord Bonham I'm in the kitchen. *Now.*"

No one in this house questioned Lester, any more than they would question Lord or Lady Bonham. The man set down his burden immediately and hurried up the stairs. Lester settled Franny in her blankets into a chair close by the range.

"I thought I was going to the ball," she objected. "But I can't in my nightgown."

"No, indeed, you can't, lassie. But I daresay a little marzipan won't come amiss." Lester took two of the sweetmeats off a silver platter, ignoring the cook's indignant splutter at his disturbance of the elegant arrangement.

Greville was first into the kitchen, and as soon as he saw the child, a wave of intense relief washed through him. Now he could give all his attention to Aurelia. He crossed to Franny and squatted on his haunches in front of her. "I'm sorry to have woken you, Franny. But your mother wants you to stay the night with Stevie and Susannah in the nursery here."

"Where is Mama?" Franny demanded through a mouthful of marzipan.

"She's dancing, sweetheart," Cornelia said from behind Greville. She exchanged a quick look with him as she came up to the child. "Let's go up to Linton, she's waiting for you." Cornelia scooped up Franny, ignoring incipient protests, and carried her away.

"There's a chap trussed up and waitin' on you, Sir Greville," Lester said in his laconic fashion. "That hound of yours is worth her weight in gold, I'd say. Had him by the throat, just waiting for me to scoop him up."

Harry, who had just entered the kitchen with Alex, let out a low whistle. "So they *were* after Franny, too?"

"So it would seem," Greville said grimly, making for the outside door. "But I'll find out soon enough."

"I'll come with you," Harry said.

Greville raised a hand. "No, I need no help for this. I prefer to do my own dirty work, and there's no knowing how difficult he'll be to break."

Harry shrugged. "As you wish. What *can* we do?" He glanced at Alex. "You're with us, Prokov?"

"Of course."

"Take a look around Vasquez's lodgings," Greville said, giving them the address. "There may be a clue, something . . . . although I doubt it. The man's a consummate professional."

"He still managed to leave one of his men behind," Harry pointed out.

Greville gave a short, hard laugh. "So he did . . . so he did." He strode from the kitchen and out into the cool night air. They wouldn't hurt Aurelia any more than they had already done, they would have no reason to, he told himself as he ran through the streets to his own house. They wanted him, only him. But it was false comfort, he knew. Vasquez would have no need of Aurelia once he'd got Greville, and he couldn't afford to let her go as a living witness to who and what he was. But he would keep her alive until he had accomplished his mission.

Greville let himself into his house and stopped for a brief moment by the fallen body of the night watchman. The man was dead. Another score to settle with Vasquez's henchman. He took the stairs two at a time, and heard Lyra's low growl as he reached the hallway at the head. The dog was standing in a bedroom doorway halfway along the corridor.

"So that's where you have him," Greville observed, coming up to the hound, laying a calm hand on her massive head. The dog pushed her head into his hand, then backed into the bedroom. She stood at the side of the bed, head cocked, as if offering him some newly caught prey.

"Well, well, what have we here?" Greville murmured at the prone figure. Miguel turned his head out of the quilt with difficulty and glared at Greville. Defiance was in the glare, but also fear. Miguel knew what to expect at the hands of the *asp*.

Greville shrugged out of his coat, laying it carefully over the back of a chair. He stood by the bed, rolling up his sleeves with exaggerated care. "Where is she?" he asked almost conversationally.

Miguel gazed up into those merciless dark gray eyes and a shudder went through him. Then he turned his face into the quilt in a gesture of rejection. Greville sighed.

❦

It was growing cold in the stable and Aurelia's gauze-and-satin ball gown offered little protection. She crossed her bare arms over her breasts and tried to control her shivers. Finally she stood up and banged on the door. "Don Antonio, I'm cold." It seemed almost better at this point to invite violence than to continue in this freezing uncertainty.

The top half of the door opened. "I told you to be quiet."

"Yes, but perhaps you didn't realize how cold it is. And as you can see, I'm scarcely dressed for it." Aurelia was astounded at herself. She sounded irritated and impatient, as if she had a positive right to demand creature comforts. To her immense gratification, she saw that her manner disconcerted her captor.

"Surely there's a horse blanket or something around here," she said, trying to peer around him into the rest of the building. He slapped her face with the flat of his hand and she jerked her head back. The door slammed shut.

Aurelia retreated to her hay bale again. The slap had stung, but no worse than that. It was more a warning than an intent to hurt. After a few minutes, the top half of the door opened again and something landed at her feet. She picked it up and shook out the rough homespun folds of a stale-smelling horse blanket.

She wrapped herself up gratefully, then remembered another of Greville's maxims. *Sleep when there is nothing else you can do.* Not that she thought Greville had expected her to need many of his maxims, those, at least, that applied to the riskier aspects of his work. But still, that one seemed to make sense in the present circumstances.

She pulled apart the hay bale and made a nest of sorts, then curled herself into it, snug in the blanket. She didn't expect to sleep, but somehow she did.

She awoke with a start at the sound of the door opening. Lamplight flooded the stall, and she blinked from deep in her nest. Don Antonio stood above her.

"I apologize for disturbing your beauty sleep, ma'am,"

he said with heavy sarcasm. "But perhaps I could trouble you for your attention."

Aurelia sat up, then stood up, keeping the blanket tight around her. Now she wished she hadn't slept. Somehow the calm resolution of earlier had deserted her, and all she could see was the cruel line of his mouth and the bottomless black depths of his impassive gaze. Now, she thought, now, he would hurt her.

Greville regarded Miguel with dispassion and said in fluent Spanish, "So if you didn't come here to take the child, why did you come?"

Miguel's bloodshot, pain-filled eyes gazed up at him. "A lock of her hair," he croaked. "Something to prove I had been close to her." He began to babble as he saw his tormentor reach again for Miguel's own little box of diamond-tipped tools. "He didn't want the child . . . too much trouble . . . just something to get her mother to cooperate . . . to be afraid for the child."

Greville nodded as if in complete understanding and agreement and inquired pleasantly, "So, where is Vasquez holding my wife?"

Miguel groaned. "I don't know."

"Oh, come now, my friend, you can't believe I'm such a fool. You were to take him the token . . . so where were you to take it?"

"I was to meet him outside the house . . . back of the house, when Don Antonio brought the woman out to the carriage. But that damned dog . . ." Miguel coughed, turning his head into the coverlet.

"But you know where they are now." Greville reached down and twisted the man's head so that he faced him and Miguel stared into the inexorable dark eyes. "Tell me," Greville murmured gently, before saying something softly to Lyra.

Miguel shrieked as the hound leaped astride him.

Aurelia looked at the parchment on the rickety wooden table in front of her. "This is a begging letter. My husband will know immediately that these pathetic words are not my own."

"It makes no difference," Vasquez stated. "It will bring him. Sign it."

"It won't bring him," she said quietly. "It won't convince him that I am alive. Only my own words can do that. He won't step into your trap unless he believes that my life is at stake." *And maybe not even then.*

"Oh, make no mistake, my lady, it most certainly is," Vasquez said barely above a whisper. The knife was in his hand once more and he saw her quick shudder. He had hoped that while he waited on the off chance that Miguel would finally appear, apprehension would soften her for him, but she'd given him no signs of it. But the knife frightened her. "And the *asp* will know that by now."

The *asp*? But then Aurelia lost all interest in such a

name as Vasquez ordered Carlos to hold her hand flat on the table.

"You will sign in your blood," Vasquez stated, laying the tip of the knife against the nail bed of her forefinger. "We shall see how long it takes to slice the skin from this pretty finger . . . about ten minutes, I should think. Ten very slow minutes." The knife point slid beneath the skin at the base of the nail and the world spun around her.

"Wait," she gasped. "I'll sign, but not this. If you want him to believe it's worth trying to save me, you will let *me* ask him to come." She flicked the parchment with her free hand. "He will think you forced me to sign a blank piece of paper and then wrote your own words above my signature. He will assume I am already dead."

Don Antonio regarded her in frowning silence. Then he dipped the quill in the inkpot on the rickety table in the stable and scribbled through his own lines. He turned the paper over. "Very well, write your own appeal. And I suggest you make it heartfelt." He dipped the quill again and handed it to her.

Carlos still held her left hand flat to the table, blood seeping from the tiny nick where a fold of skin was loosened. Aurelia's free hand shook as she wrote a few lines, signed the letter, and looked up at Vasquez. He took it, scrutinized it, still frowning. Nothing was amiss that he could see, and it had a satisfactory ring of desperation to it.

"One more thing. Press her finger against it, Carlos."

Carlos lifted her hurt hand and bent the finger,

pressing the cut against the parchment below her signature. Vasquez nodded his satisfaction, folded the bloodstained sheet over another one that he took from his pocket, and gave the package to Carlos with low-voiced instructions. The coachman left the stable, and Don Antonio gave Aurelia a push back into the stall. The door locked behind her.

Greville left the bedchamber, Lyra on his heels. There was no need for her to guard the man on the bed any longer. Greville was hurrying down the stairs when the door-knocker sounded loudly. He opened it to let in Alex.

"Any luck?" Alex asked, his gaze skimming over the body in the hall. "Is that him?"

"No, one of his victims," Greville said shortly. "But he gave me all he knows."

"This was on your doorstep." Alex held out a small package. "Harry's gone after the man who brought it, but I doubt he'll catch him, he was turning the corner into the square as we came up. We found nothing at the lodging either."

Greville scarcely seemed to hear as he opened the package and took in the contents on both sheets. His eyes hardened and his mouth grew grim as he saw the bloodstain. But he ignored it, concentrating on the words she had written. They were in her own hand, so she was still alive, even if she was hurt. But the hurt had not prevented her from thinking.

"About half an hour due north from here," he murmured with a low whistle of appreciation. "Clever girl."

"I lost him." Harry entered the house somewhat breathlessly. He glanced at the body. "Anything to be done here?"

"No," Greville said. "It's a little late in the day. Our friend upstairs . . ."

"Ah." Harry nodded his comprehension, then gestured to the package. "What is it?"

"Instructions from Vasquez and a note from Aurelia." Greville passed one of the papers to him. "Written under duress, but she's managed to pass on some information that fits quite well with what I got out of that piece of vermin upstairs."

Harry and Alex poured over the parchment. "I don't understand," Harry said as he finished reading. "She says she's frightened, she's exhausted, afraid they mean harm to Franny, and afraid for her own life. She begs you to follow their instructions or they will kill her. Where's the information?"

Greville half smiled. "She also says she's being held about half an hour due north from here."

"How is she telling you that?" Harry, the master of code, frowned at the letter. Then his face cleared. "Of course, each n is faintly underlined. Hence 'north.' But where's the half hour?"

"Look at her signature . . . the o."

Harry chuckled. The letter was neatly bisected. "Clever. She could draw a straight line at any point through the o without it looking like anything more than an idiosyncratic touch to her signature."

"May I?" Alex took the letter and nodded. "Of course. Even a quarter, or three-quarters could be done. Was this a trick of yours, Falconer?"

Greville shrugged. "One of several I taught her. I have to admit I didn't think she'd need most of them." His expression was dark.

"So, how does this information fit with what you learned from our friend upstairs?" Harry asked.

"An abandoned stable block outside a hamlet is as concrete as it got," Greville said. "He hasn't been there himself, and he wasn't expecting to have to find it for himself, since his instructions were to meet Vasquez at Mount Street with some proof that he had access to Franny. He was to travel in the carriage with Vasquez and Aurelia. But it has to be on a main highway, or just off one, for them to get anywhere outside the city in only half an hour."

Greville tapped the second sheet of parchment against the palm of his hand. "Vasquez's instructions are for me to meet him alone before dawn at the crossroads in the village of Islington. Aurelia's life for mine."

Greville's nostrils flared. "Of course he has no intention of letting either of us live. But before he gives me the coup de grâce, he'll use Aurelia to get information from me. Even though he's lost his Inquisition assistant, he'll still know how to do the job, just rather more crudely." A shudder ran up Greville's spine. They wouldn't touch

Aurelia . . . *his* Aurelia. And Vasquez would pay by inches for the hurt he had already caused her.

"They won't risk losing her until they have what they want from you," Alex said. "If we can find her first, and presumably this stable block must be close by, then we can get her out while you deal with your friend."

Greville nodded. "As long as she's conscious, she'll be able to help herself." He spoke with a dispassion that concealed his fear for her. She still had her wits about her, or she would not have managed to write her own letter. That was all he had to keep in mind to keep a clear and objective focus. Aurelia's safety first, the death of Vasquez second.

"Horseback to Islington," he said. "We'll find the stable building somewhere around the crossroads. Vasquez doesn't have time for a lengthy journey from where he has Aurelia to the rendezvous with me."

"What about upstairs?" Harry asked with a rather delicate gesture in the direction of the staircase. "Should I send Lester to clean up?"

"I'd be grateful," Greville said. "I don't have time myself. When he comes around, I'm sure they'll be interested in him at the ministry. He'll be a mine of information under the right questioning." Greville's mouth twisted in a grim smile. "We'll see how well the Inquisition stands up to having its own techniques used upon itself. I'll change and meet you in Grosvenor Square in thirty minutes. We'll take the North Road. We have two hours until dawn."

Harry and Alex left. "I'll leave Livia with Cornelia," Alex said as they walked swiftly to Mount Street. "I'd rather she wasn't alone."

"You might find she has her own opinions on the matter," Harry said drily. He surveyed the scene on the street outside his house. Linkboys and footmen were running up and down calling for carriages as the guests swarmed out of his house at the end of the evening. "We'll go in through the back," Harry decided. "I can't afford to get caught up in bidding farewell to our guests."

With Livia as an able aide-de-camp, Cornelia was holding the fort, glossing over her husband's absence and murmuring all the obligatory pleasantries. Harry made no attempt to distract her, and he and Alex had left the house again, Alex in borrowed riding britches, before the last guest had departed. Lester had gone to pick up a couple of good men to aid in the cleanup on South Audley Street.

"Where did they go?" Cornelia asked rhetorically as the last guest drifted down the stairs to the open door.

"Where's Ellie?" Livia countered.

"Harry might have left a message." Cornelia turned away from the stairs, suddenly aware of her bone-deep fatigue and aching feet. "Lord, I'm tired." She made her way into her own sitting room and fell into a corner of the sofa.

A discreet knock announced a footman with a folded sheet of paper on a silver tray. Cornelia recognized her husband's writing and snatched at it eagerly. "Thank you." She waved a hand in dismissal.

"Is there anything else I can get you, my lady?"

"No . . . no, I don't think so. Thank you." She opened the sheet while Livia waited intently. The footman departed and Cornelia said, "They've gone to get Aurelia back. That's all he says . . . isn't that just so *typical*, Liv, and so infuriating. Nothing about what's happened, or where she is, or why any of this . . ." Cornelia tossed the sheet onto the low table in front of her.

Livia leaned forward and picked up the note to read it for herself. "You forgot to mention that Alex suggests that I stay here until they return. Has he forgotten that his son is in Cavendish Square? I can't possibly stay here all night while little Alexander is half a city away."

"Send someone for him," Cornelia said. "You have your own carriage outside. Send them to bring the baby and his nurse. We might as well be all together in this, don't you think? We have Franny in the nursery already."

Livia required no persuasion. The carriage was sent to Cavendish Square, and the two women sat in the parlor as the bustle of the house quieted around them and the clock ticked, and the first faint gray of the false dawn appeared on the horizon.

Chapter Twenty-six

"That must be it." Greville spoke barely above a whisper as the three men sat their horses on the outskirts of a tiny hamlet just outside the village of Islington. In front of them stood a tumbledown building, its thatch wearing thin, the stone gateposts to the yard crumbling. Faint lamplight showed through the slatted walls.

"And we passed the crossroads a half mile back," Harry murmured.

Greville glanced up at the sky. Polaris was fading but still as due north as ever. "I'm getting into position."

His companions merely raised hands in acknowledgment, and Greville backed his horse onto the lane, before picking his way through the trees alongside the cart track that led from the crossroads to the building. At the crossroads, he took up his position to the side, behind a gigantic oak tree. He wanted to catch Vasquez off guard for a vital moment before they brought out Aurelia.

He sat quietly, waiting. Clearing his mind of everything, everyone. And most particularly of all thoughts of Aurelia. She had the power to distract him, to muddle his purpose with emotion. He knew what had to be done once Vasquez appeared, and it was never fruitful to revisit a plan.

When the stable door opened, Alex and Harry were standing beside their mounts, keeping calming hands on bridles and necks. They were well hidden, but the slightest movement could alert the man who stood now in the yard, his eyes on the reddening sky, his body alert, poised, listening. A rapier's silver sheath glistened in the light from the open door behind him. Then he spoke softly over his shoulder, and another man led out a broad-shouldered gelding.

Vasquez mounted, settled his rapier at his side. The telltale bulge of a pistol showed in his coat pocket as he twisted forward to adjust his stirrup. He spoke again to the man at his bridle, then rode out of the yard and onto the cart track leading to the crossroads.

Harry and Alex were a good twenty feet from the track, and downwind, but even so both held their breath as the man rode past. The horse did not catch the scent of his fellows however, and horse and rider went on past along the track.

"He's Falconer's now," Harry murmured. "Now we wait."

"I'd rather just go in and get her out of there," Alex muttered.

"We can't afford any sound that will alert Vasquez."

"I know that," Alex whispered.

"For what it's worth, I don't like waiting either."

Alex nodded. They had to stick to their plan. The henchman would bring Aurelia out soon. When he did so, then Alex and Harry would make their move. Silently.

Aurelia was still locked in the stall when she heard her captors moving around, talking in whispers, the sound of a stall being opened and the unmistakable creak of leather and the heavy clop of iron-shod hooves. So some part of the building was put to its proper use, she reflected, creeping to the partition, trying to peer out through the narrow strips between the slats.

It was impossible to see anything, however, but she could hear well enough. The whispers were in Spanish, so not much help, but she could at least tell Vasquez and his henchman apart by their voices. She heard the sounds of the outside door opening, then the horse moving away.

There had only been one horse. So was Vasquez going for his murderous rendezvous with Greville? Or had Carlos left? And what would happen if Greville failed to keep the appointment . . . failed to walk into whatever trap they had laid for him?

She couldn't think like that. If she did, the fear would paralyze her. She knew they would kill her, knew that if

Greville didn't come to her rescue, she would die in the next few hours. Never see Franny again, never smell May blossom or new-cut grass, never see the life that she carried enter the world. Panic swamped her. She leaned her forehead against the rough wooden planking of the stall and pressed hard, feeling the pain as the wood abraded her skin. The pain took her out of her panic, cleared her mind, brought focus.

She stepped back, ran a hand lightly over her belly in a symbolic gesture of reassurance to the life within, and banged vigorously on the door to her stall. A rough voice murmured a string of what sounded even in a foreign tongue like obscenities. But she had the answer to one question. She was alone with Carlos.

She backed away from the door and looked around the dimly lit enclosure for something . . . anything. Greville had said it was rare to find nothing of use in a confined space if one looked with trained eyes. All she could see here were straw, a length of twine that she had untied from around the bale of straw that she had used to make a nest, and the wooden sides that enclosed her. The iron rings were no use, they wouldn't budge. Only to be expected if they were intended to hold a rampaging horse. But what of the rough slats of the partition walls?

Aurelia moved slowly down the length, unsure what she looking for until she found it. A large splinter of wood. She pried it loose gingerly. It was long and thin, and sharp.

She picked up the length of twine and examined her armory with a critical eye. Not bad for a woman in a silk-and-spider-gauze ball gown. In different circumstances she would have laughed at the reflection, but now it merely served to help her focus, to find deep within herself the training she had had from Greville.

She positioned herself behind the half door to the stall, and in the angle, so that when the top half was opened she would momentarily be hidden from view. Then she started yelling at the top of her voice as she banged with her fists on the door.

Carlos cursed her again, then flung open the top half of the door, still hurling whispered abuse. When he couldn't see her, he stuck his head farther into the stall. Aurelia drove the sharp point of the splinter into his neck, just below his ear. He yelped, fighting to pull it free, spinning around with his back to the door. As he turned, Aurelia flipped the length of twine around his neck and pulled it tight with all her strength, using the door he leaned against as leverage. She didn't have the power to strangle him, she knew, but she could bring him down to his knees, render him helpless long enough for her to unbolt the bottom half of the door.

He slid forward, grabbing at the makeshift garrote, struggling for breath, the splinter still sticking out from behind his ear. As he fell to his knees, she lost her hold on the twine, but it was a matter of a second to draw the bolt. She thrust the door forward with all the power in her shoulder, and it knocked her jailor from his knees onto his face in the straw.

She jumped on him foursquare for good measure on her way to the door and heard him groaning behind her. But she didn't care how much damage she had done. The man would have hurt her child without a second thought given half a chance, and he deserved everything she could give him.

Aurelia burst out into the abandoned stable yard just as Alex and Harry came racing through the trees.

"Dear God in heaven, Aurelia," Harry gasped, leaning a hand down to her as he drew rein beside her. "We thought he had your feet to the fire."

She stared at them in disbelief. "How . . . What . . . What are *you* doing here? Where's Greville?"

"Dealing with your abductor," Harry said briefly. "And you shouldn't need to ask what we're doing here, Aurelia."

"No, I suppose not," she said with a faint smile. "Of course you'd be here, it's all in a day's work for you." She took the hand he held down to her and let him haul her up onto the saddle in front of him, asking again, "Where *is* Greville?"

"Meeting with Vasquez . . . only you were making such a racket that our best-laid plans have probably gone awry." Alex came up beside them. "How many did you murder?"

"None. But you need to secure one. I left him on his

face, but I doubt I did him enough harm to keep him there."

"I'll do that," Alex said, dismounting, a pistol already in his hand. "Harry, you'd better take Aurelia and see what's going on at the crossroads."

Don Antonio heard the faint sounds of shouting just as he reached the crossroads. It was a woman's voice. He rode on. Carlos could handle the woman with one hand tied behind his back. And it wouldn't hurt Falconer to hear his wife's cries. It would prepare him for what was to come.

The crossroads was deserted, the four tracks forming the cross stretching away as faint gray lines in the beginning dawn light.

He rode into the middle and drew rein. He didn't reach for a weapon. The *asp* would not kill him from a hiding place. Not unless he had the woman safe. Don Antonio felt his blood surge. He had waited for this day for too long. Oh, certainly he was on his country's work and would never lose sight of that, but he could satisfy his own niggling dissatisfaction with a past mistake at the same time.

"So, Vasquez, where is my wife? I can hear her well enough, but I must see her before we can discuss an exchange."

Don Antonio turned his head towards the small stand

of trees dominated by a giant oak on the right of the crossroads. He couldn't see the *asp,* but he didn't need to for this conversation. "She'll be here in a moment. Show yourself."

"Show me my wife."

Antonio took a whistle from his pocket, looked back over his shoulder, and blew one shrill note. "She'll be here in just a few moments," he said as if they were discussing the appearance of a horse for sale at Tattersalls.

"I wonder how I missed you at Lisbon," the voice mused from behind the oak tree. "I thought I knew everyone of interest who was there at the time. You slipped past my spies."

"And you foiled *me.* I don't make mistakes, *asp.*"

"No, I'm sure you don't . . . in general," Greville added with soft deliberation. He wanted Vasquez to be annoyed, a little off center. All the while he was listening for the sound that would herald Aurelia's arrival on the scene with whoever held her. As far as the Spaniards were concerned, it would be one against two then, with Aurelia in the middle. But in fact it was three against two. *Still with Aurelia in the middle.*

But Aurelia was not without her own resources, he told himself. She'd proved it already.

He heard footsteps coming from the track to the abandoned stable and judged it time to move out. He rode into the crossroads, his hand on his rapier, and with a nod saluted his opponent, who offered the same courtesy.

"Bring her here, Carlos," Don Antonio instructed.

"I can bring myself, Don Antonio." Aurelia stepped forward. She held a pistol.

Ye Gods and little fishes. Greville wanted to throw back his head and laugh. *His* Aurelia, all his. How she'd done it, he couldn't begin to guess. But he was fairly certain Harry and Alex had had little real part in it. The only sounds he had heard had been from Aurelia.

She leveled the pistol at Don Antonio. "Should I shoot him, Greville?"

"Well, that depends on how much of a grievance you bear him," Greville said, sliding his rapier from its sheath. "If you wouldn't mind too much, I would like to conclude the business in my own way . . . but I will defer to you."

·"I don't really care for shooting people," Aurelia said. "You should know, Don Antonio, that Carlos is being taken care of by Prince Prokov. Lord Bonham is just behind me."

Don Antonio seemed to ignore her. He looked at Greville as the first bloodred touch of the sun appeared on the eastern horizon. "Is that how you wish to conclude this, Falconer?" The Spaniard, too, drew his rapier from its sheath.

"No," Greville said, dismounting. "I, too, like a challenge, Vasquez. Aurelia, take my horse."

She went swiftly to take the reins, but she couldn't understand why he was doing this . . . accepting a challenge that he *might* not win, when all he had to do was shoot and walk away. But she knew, too, deep in her core, that

Greville had his own code of justice. He wanted this last battle to be personal.

He was a strange man, to put it mildly. He was capable of quite frightening emotional detachment. He didn't know *how* to love, but she knew that he loved her nevertheless. And she loved him. She loved him for his humor, for his all-embracing competency, for his devotion to his work, for the sadness and loneliness of his past life, for the selfless skill of his lovemaking. But mostly she loved him just for himself. She'd known that for a long time, and she *did* know how to love. And knowing how to do that meant she had to step away now and let him conclude this in his own way.

Her hand brushed her belly in the now habitual gesture. Once this was over, Greville Falconer had another love to acknowledge.

Aurelia moved back with Greville's horse to stand close to the oak tree. Harry had dismounted and was already standing there. He had heard the exchange and accepted as she had his colleague's decision. But with a swift move he took the pistol from Aurelia. It was his own, after all. Don Antonio Vasquez was not leaving here alive.

The two men stood facing each other, bright blades in their hands. By mutual consent they tossed their firearms to the ground, away from where they stood. Their blades saluted, touched. Greville danced back, the rapier in his right hand, but his left hand moved swiftly, and a dagger flew, catching his opponent in the muscle of his sword arm. Don Antonio's arm dropped, useless, to his side.

Harry knew, as Aurelia did not, that the wound was crippling. Shattered bones could sometimes heal, but ripped muscles were another matter.

Don Antonio stood there, his rapier at his feet, his good hand pressed to the bleeding wound. "Finish it."

Greville shook his head. He kicked the fallen rapier aside. "Oh, no, Vasquez. You threatened and hurt those whom I love this night, and for that I will not give you an honorable death. You will live to enjoy my country's hospitality."

Harry stepped forward. "Quite a haul for the ministry," he observed conversationally. "Come, my friend, we will utilize your carriage, since riding is probably beyond both you and your assistant." He twisted Don Antonio's wrists behind him, ignoring the man's shriek as the shredded muscle caused him to scream in pain.

Harry glanced back at Greville with a quizzically raised eyebrow. "I assume you and Aurelia can manage?"

"You may make such an assumption," Greville said, drawing her against him. "One horse will be sufficient. Tie yours to the back of the carriage."

Harry nodded and pushed his prisoner ahead of him back to the abandoned stable yard.

Greville held Aurelia tightly for a very long time as the sun began to rise. He needed the supple feel of her body, the warmth of her skin, the wonderful, familiar scent of her. He could feel in his own body her bone-deep fatigue as her body yielded to the relief from the dreadful strain of the last hours. When at last he kissed her, it was part benediction, part gratitude, but mostly just the glorious knowledge that he held in his arms his partner, his love, the woman who completed him in every aspect of his existence.

Aurelia rested in his embrace, too tired to be anything but the recipient of his kiss. But she understood and accepted everything it meant. When he raised his head and looked into her exhausted but still steady gaze and said, "I love you, my own," she raised a hand and traced the curve of his mouth and said, "I know, my own."

He lifted her then onto his horse and swung up behind her. She leaned back against him, letting her head fall against his shoulder, confident that if she fell asleep, he would hold her.

"I cannot leave you," he said, his breath whispering across her forehead. "I had thought that I could, but I cannot. You have taught me what it means to love, and what terror there is in the prospect of loss. You are all and everything to me, my love. And I will not lose you."

She raised her hand and stroked his face. "If that's a proper proposal, Colonel," she murmured sleepily, "then I accept."

He drew her tightly against him, filled with so much happiness he didn't think he could endure it. "Another elopement seems in order," he murmured.

Aurelia wriggled up a little on the saddle and turned her

head against his shoulder. "Have you enough resilience for one more piece of information tonight, my love?"

His dark eyes were clearly visible in the early-morning light. The black shadows deeply etched beneath them merely accentuated the sharpened expression. "After what you did tonight, sweetheart, nothing you could do or say would surprise me."

"Well, in about seven months from now you'll be a proud papa." She smiled at him. She thought she knew how he would respond now, but still she had just a flicker of fear that it wouldn't be right.

Greville drew rein, bringing his horse to a stop beside the road, ignoring the blast of a coach horn as the early-morning vehicle thundered past. "Oh, my love, I do so hope I will be good at it," he said, his eyes misted. "I promise you, I will do everything in my power to be the best father to Franny and to our child. And I will listen to you when I make mistakes. And I *will* make mistakes."

"We all do," Aurelia said, wiping his incipient tears with her fingertip. "Just as long as it pleases you."

"Oh, yes," he murmured. "It pleases me."

Epilogue

JANUARY 1, 1810

THE SONOROUS CHIMES OF the long case clock faded away, and the small group seated around the table in the dining room of the house on Cavendish Square rose as one to embrace each other at the start of a new year.

Cornelia touched her glass to her husband's, and he kissed the corner of her mouth. "That won't do," she whispered, circling an arm around his neck, kissing him full on the mouth.

"No," he answered as softly. "No, it certainly won't. I love you, Nell."

"And I you." She parted her lips for the kiss she had demanded.

Alex linked the arm that held his glass around Livia's elbow, drawing her up tight towards him, their glasses touching.

"To the New Year, my dearest love," he murmured, drinking from his glass as she drank from hers. He tossed his glass behind him in a gesture that Livia had by now learned was a purely Russian flamboyant manifestation of celebration, although expensive when it involved fine crystal, not that Alex gave such considerations any thought. With a careless shrug she sent her own glass to the same fate and raised her face for his kiss, tasting the champagne on his lips.

"I love you, my prince."

Greville held Aurelia close against him, reveling in her small-boned delicacy, the orange-water fragrance of her hair. He took her face in his hands, gazing down into the velvet depths of her eyes, and wondered if he would ever grow accustomed to the wondrous love he saw there, and to the depths of his love for her that seemed to grow by the moment, filling him with a happiness he would never have believed possible.

"Our New Year," he murmured, kissing her eyelids. "I have no words for how much I love you, Aurelia."

"We don't need them," she responded, kissing his mouth. "It's not always necessary to state the obvious."

He laughed softly as he kissed her. "You are adorable, my pragmatic wife."

There was a hush in the room for a few moments, and then by unspoken mutual consent the couples drew apart and turned outwards to their friends. The women embraced, half laughing, half weeping at the sheer pleasure of friendship; their menfolk, rather more restrained, shook hands, but there was no denying the warmth of their connection.

"This has to become an annual tradition," Livia announced. "We spend Christmas and New Year in Cavendish Square together with all our children. It is, after all, the place where we all found our lives and our loves."

"You're such a romantic, Liv," Cornelia said with a chuckle, hugging her.

"It may be a romantic notion," Aurelia said, "but it's the truth nevertheless." She touched her bosom lightly. "But on a totally unromantic note, something is telling me that Zoe needs feeding."

"I'm sure the Honorable William Bonham is getting that way, too," Cornelia said. "Shall we go up to the nursery, ladies, and leave the gentlemen to their port? Romance must wait upon hungry infants." She grinned at Harry, who inclined his head in acknowledgment.

"I know my place in the scheme of things," he said lightly. "But I *will* be waiting for you."

"Not too long," Cornelia promised.

"I'll bring Zoe down when I've fed her," Aurelia said to her husband. "So you can say good night."

Greville nodded, and his smile was so deliciously smug that Aurelia could barely conceal her amusement. Who would have thought that Colonel, Sir Greville Falconer would be such a besotted father. He could spend hours simply holding his daughter, gazing into her sleeping countenance. An enchanting rosebud of a countenance, Aurelia had to admit, but such patient, almost obsessive devotion to a basically unresponsive bundle of shawls was an aspect of her husband's character that she would not have expected.

Franny benefited, too, though. While Greville had always been patient with the child, he had never, in the early days of their partnership, tried to get to know her properly or to involve himself in her activities. Not so now. He was as interested in the intricacies of his stepdaughter's daily life as he was in his own. And Franny was repaying the interest with growing affection.

All in all, Aurelia thought as she followed her friends from the dining room, life was sweet.

❧

The door closed behind the three women, and Alex lifted the port decanter and filled his companions' glasses. They sat down again, gathered at the head of the table, and sipped in a reflective silence for a few moments.

"Remarkable, aren't they?" Greville said, gazing into the contents of his glass.

"Quite extraordinary," Harry agreed. "They've taken three, let's face it, very difficult men with an obsessional passion for the dirty work in the underworld and turned us into devoted patresfamilias, who are somehow learning how to accommodate two priorities."

"Simon Grant is learning how to accommodate all our priorities," Alex said.

"Are you happy working for the ministry?" Harry asked. "You haven't mentioned it since you approached Simon."

Alex nodded. "I see no conflict at the moment. It depends on the czar, but there's credible information that he's pulling away from the alliance with Napoléon." He raised his glass and drank deeply.

Alex reached for the decanter and recharged their glasses. He stood up, raising his eyes briefly to the risqué fresco on the ceiling above the table, then declared, "A toast, gentlemen. I give you the ladies of Cavendish Square." *All of them,* he added to himself.

His companions rose with him. "The ladies of Cavendish Square."